Praise for the Cat Star Chronicles

FUGITIVE

"A fabulous book with the galaxy's most enticing heroes... the Cat Star Chronicles is CATegorically the best exotic and sensuously erotic science fiction in the market. If you haven't read them, buy the whole series and give yourself a treat."

—*Star-Crossed Romance*

"Just the right blend of science fiction, romance, and erotica."

—*This Book for Free*

"Another stellar book in this phenomenal series that just gets better and better. Awe inspiring... It's sexy space travel at its finest."

—*Night Owl Romance*

"A steamy, action-filled ride. Ms. Brooks's world-building is impressive as well as creative."

—*Anna's Book Blog*

"Cat Star Chronicles has become one of my favorite futuristic series... There's plenty of kick butt action as well as laugh-out-loud moments."

—*Romance Junkies*

"The hottest one yet... Cheryl Brooks continues to delight with her alien races and sexy Zetithian men."

—*Moonlight to Twilight*

Other books in the
Cat Star Chronicles series:

THE CAT STAR CHRONICLES

VIRGIN

CHERYL BROOKS

sourcebooks
casablanca

Published by Sourcebooks Casablanca, an imprint of Sourcebooks, Inc.
P.O. Box 4410, Naperville, Illinois 60567-4410
(630) 961-3900
FAX: (630) 961-2168
www.sourcebooks.com

Printed and bound in the United States of America
QW 10 9 8 7 6 5 4 3 2 1

Dedicated to all of those readers who refused to allow the story of Zetith to end.

Chapter 1

He valued his freedom more than any woman,
until now…

———×———

THE REALIZATION HIT DAX LIKE A STUN BLAST TO THE
chest. He was staring at her. *For the third time*. Dax
never stared at women. Not even little blond waitresses,
no matter how cute they were. A moment before, Dax
would have said that his freedom mattered far more to
him than any woman. He wasn't so sure about that now.

These thoughts distracted him as he sat across the
table from his friend and mentor, Captain Jacinth
"Jack" Tshevnoe in a dark, dusty barroom on Luxaria
Twelve. Jack had, as usual, been fussing at him for
not settling down and starting a family like most of
the other Zetithian refugees, and though the repetitive-
ness of her speech might have caused his attention to
wander, it wasn't because he disagreed with her. With
his homeworld destroyed and his species facing extinction, he understood the need to reproduce. Growing up
aboard a starship filled with refugees, that need had been
drummed into him from the age of two, right up until his
present age of thirty-three, but while most men would
have given their left nut to be retired to stud, Dax had
other plans.

At least, he had in the past. Right now, however, reproducing was the only thing on his mind. He'd seen women who were far more beautiful—many of whom had thrown themselves willingly at his feet—so what was it that made this one so special? She was blond and perky, which was certainly appealing, but he'd never noticed that preference before. Yet, she was doing something to him, something extraordinary. Jack would have laughed out loud if she'd been able to read his thoughts. Fortunately, as a Terran, she lacked that talent.

His friends would have been laughing as well, for his virgin state was no secret, and though they'd done their best to interest him in various females, none had ever hit the mark. She wasn't near enough for him to catch a whiff of her scent—Zetithian males couldn't get it up without the aroma of feminine desire to stimulate them—but she had been close enough to him earlier when she'd served his Vrelka ale. He thought he'd detected something then, though it hadn't lingered long enough for him to get an erection.

Still, though his cock might have been uncooperative, his brain was working overtime. His mind was being bombarded with erotic images; what she would look like naked was first and foremost—her full breasts and softly rounded hips were easy to imagine, considering the low-cut red shirt and tight black slacks she wore. His breathing quickened at the idea of being close enough to inhale her scent, to feel the soft warmth of her skin pressing against his own, the touch of her hands on his body. No woman had ever touched him sexually, and though he tried hard to imagine her licking his stiff cock, sinking her teeth into his flesh while his own mouth tasted the sweet wetness between her thighs, the unfortunate truth was that he had absolutely no idea what to expect. And to plunge his shaft deep inside her… What would that *feel* like? He knew she'd be tight, hot, and slick around his dick—he couldn't help knowing that, just from the descriptions he'd heard others give—but he had always suspected that sexual union was one of those things you had to experience for yourself in order to fully appreciate. It was difficult to understand the sheer ecstasy of orgasm when you'd never had one.

Dax shifted uncomfortably in his chair. Normally a fairly laid-back, quiet sort of man, his fidgeting was bound to be noticed by Jack. His balls were tingling with wild anticipation, and he was salivating more than usual; he'd have been drooling if he hadn't kept swallowing, and the frequent sips of ale he was taking in order to mask this reaction did nothing to improve his self-control. He didn't just *want* to pounce on her and nip her with his fangs; it was fast becoming a necessity.

He raked a hand through his dark locks, wishing they didn't curl quite so tightly and that he hadn't braided them back from his face. A curtain of hair would have been useful to conceal the way his catlike eyes were glowing, which they undoubtedly were. At least he wasn't purring, something that Jack, being the wife of a Zetithian she called Cat, would have noticed.

The waitress's name was Ava, according to her name pin, and she appeared to be Terran, but not quite. Dax couldn't decide what the difference was, but at that point, he flat-out didn't care. Jack wouldn't be a bit happy if he were to choose a mate from an incompatible species, but Dax's choice of a partner was ultimately his own. And right now, he wanted Ava, wanted to taste every last bit of her. Wanted to delve into her succulent body and drown in her scent. Wanted to see the hunger and passion in her eyes as his cock penetrated her. Most of all, he wanted to give her joy.

But a man simply couldn't take a woman in the middle of a crowded barroom, could he? If nothing else, her employer was bound to object, even on Luxaria. Jack, on the other hand, would probably jump for joy. And her next words proved it.

"You really need to find a mate, Dax. It's important!"

"Don't worry, Jack," he said. "It'll happen someday."

"What? Me? Worry?" Jack said, laughing. "Never!"

But he knew she was worried. And Dax knew he was being stubborn, but perhaps that was about to change…

"Okay, lecture is over," Jack said, throwing her hands up in surrender. "Where've you been lately?"

"Timpala," he replied. "Waroun has family there."

"Why do you insist on hanging out with that disgusting Norludian? I mean, really, Dax! They give me the creeps."

"I may be a good pilot, but Waroun's one helluva navigator," Dax protested. "And he's a great guy. You just have to get to know him." Why Jack hated Norludians so much was anyone's guess, but Dax suspected she had been propositioned by one in the past, which might explain why the mere sight of them tended to make her gag. Waroun couldn't help being Norludian any more than he could help having the bulbous eyes, fishlike lips, and scrawny body of his kind, but Jack made no secret of her feelings on the subject. While she would allow that his flipperlike feet weren't too horrible, the way

Norludians tasted a female's sexual essence by attaching themselves with their sucker-tipped fingers grossed her out completely—added to the fact that Norludians never wore any clothing whatsoever.

"I think I'll pass," Jack said. "I'll buy you another drink if you'll tell me where you got that tattoo."

Dax grinned, displaying his fangs. "If I tell you, you'll throw that drink in my face."

"Oh, really? Try me."

Dax's grin widened. "Waroun's cousin did it."

A spasm of revulsion marred her features. "On Timpala, I presume? Holy shit, Dax! I'm sure having flames licking the side of your face and neck are the epitome of cool, but it's a wonder your whole head hasn't rotted off. I suppose he pierced your ear, too."

"Yeah," he said, flipping the gold hoop with his thumb. "Like it?"

"I'd like it a lot better if you'd had it done anywhere else."

"You worry too much, Jack. And now you owe me a drink." Twisting around in his chair, he waved at Ava, thrilled to have an excuse to talk to her again. This time, he was going to make sure he got a good whiff of her scent. "I'll have another Vrelka ale," he said as she approached. "And Jack's paying."

Dax was still smiling when he said it, his eyes drinking in the sight of her. Her small stature fascinated him, but exploring her scent would have to wait. Dax hadn't had a chance to draw another breath before he was rudely interrupted by a powerful-looking man with short, bristly blond hair who shouted at him from across the room.

"You quit looking at her like that! She's *my* woman!"

Dax stared back at the man, feeling his desires sink to his toes. He might have been a Zetithian, with a full measure of the attractiveness to women that most of his kind possessed, but this guy wasn't bad-looking either, and if Ava was already taken, there was no more to be said. Dax's home planet of Zetith had been blown to bits because of one jealous man; thinking that there were no others in the galaxy was shortsighted in the extreme. The fellow looked Terran, but given the size of him, there might have been something else thrown into the mix. "Don't want her, pal," Dax insisted, trying hard to keep his expression neutral. "She's all yours." Dax had the misfortune of seeing Ava wince as he said this and immediately wished he'd kept his mouth shut.

"Please, Lars!" she said. "He's a customer…"

"I've heard about you fuckin' Zetithians!" Lars shouted back, his speech slurred with liquor. "Damn cat-boys! All you have to do is purr, and the women come running. Wish the Nedwuts had killed the whole fuckin' lot of you!"

Dax knew he could handle the situation, but he also knew that it would be difficult to keep Jack from butting in. She'd been killing Nedwuts to protect her husband for so long that anytime a Zetithian was threatened, her hand automatically slid to the pulse pistol strapped to her thigh—which it was doing right now.

"I'm not purring," Dax said evenly. "And I'm not going to. Don't worry about it."

"You wanna fight, pretty boy?" Lars stood abruptly, his barstool hitting the floor with a loud clang. If anyone in the bar had been ignorant of the exchange, they certainly weren't now.

"Not particularly," Dax replied. Ava returned and set the bottle of ale on the table. It took every ounce of willpower Dax possessed to keep from grabbing her hand and making a run for it.

Jack paid for the drink without comment and watched as Ava went over to Lars, hopefully to talk some sense into him.

"You keep hanging out in places like this and shit like that will happen," Jack said quietly. "Trust me, I know. You're gonna get yourself killed if you keep this up."

"I doubt it," said Dax. "Guys like that are mostly hot air anyway."

"Maybe, but you got that poor little waitress in trouble, and all you did was order a drink. I'll bet that asshole beats the shit out of her as soon as she gets off work."

Dax threw up his hands. "What do you want me to do, Jack? Crawl in a hole and hide? I can't help being what I am."

"No, but—" Nodding toward the door, she added, "Look, they're leaving together."

"And I hope they'll be very happy," Dax said, surprised he didn't choke on the words. "But it's none of my business—or yours."

Jack gave him a wry smile. "Been hearing that all my life."

"Never stopped you, did it?"

"Nope. And it probably never will." Getting to her feet, she gave Dax a pat on the head. "Gotta get back to the ship now. Take care of yourself, big guy."

"I'll do that."

Jack threaded her way between the tables as numerous

eyes followed her. She might have been tough as nails, but she was still a good-looking woman. A Nedwut approached the open doorway, and, in an instant, Jack's pistol was in her hand. Not needing any further discouragement, the hairy beast took off running.

"Sorry," she said over her shoulder to no one in particular. "Force of habit." With a grin that wasn't the slightest bit apologetic, she holstered her weapon and left the bar.

Waroun must have been watching for Jack's departure, for he left his dark corner to take the seat she had just vacated.

"So, how's Jack?"

"Just fine," Dax replied, taking a sip of his ale.

"Still hate Norludians?"

Dax shrugged. "Yeah. Don't think she'll ever change her mind about that."

"She might change her mind if she'd ever actually have sex with one of us," Waroun said with a smirk. "You Zetithians may have fancy cocks, but it's not the meat, it's the motion, my friend."

Dax stifled a laugh. "I'm sure it is."

Waroun snorted. "Like you'd know. You've never been kissed, let alone fucked."

"Drop it, Waroun," Dax warned. "You know very well why I—"

"Tell every woman who wants you that she'll have to fuck me first? So you won't—what was it you said?—'ensnare unsuspecting women with your potent sexual prowess'?"

"I never said that!"

Waroun waved a dismissive hand. "Words to that effect. You *know* what I mean."

"Yeah, I know. Just give me a break. I get enough of that shit from Jack."

"Yes, but she means well."

Dax looked at his friend in surprise. "Since when do you go around defending Jack?"

"Maybe because she's right," Waroun replied. His bulbous eyes shone brightly in the dimly lit bar, making his appearance even more bizarre than usual. "Your bloodline is important. It wouldn't kill you to donate to a sperm bank, you know—and one of these days, someone else just might—kill you, I mean."

"Someone like Lars?" Dax suggested.

"Wouldn't be the first man to be jealous of you," Waroun said promptly. "And probably won't be the last. A little insurance might be a good thing."

"Oh, so now you're the voice of reason."

Waroun shrugged. "I know what I see, my friend, and you are a powerful woman magnet. The fact that I'm so repellent might not keep them away forever. That waitress was looking at you, you know. I was watching her."

"Waitresses *should* be attentive to their customers," Dax protested, not daring to hope that his interest was returned. "Can I help it if she's good at what she does?"

Waroun's lower lip protruded until it turned inside out. He obviously didn't believe a word Dax was saying. "Get over it, Dax. Women want you. You should be thanking your lucky stars for that."

Dax shook his head. "Can we talk about something else?"

Waroun laughed. "You mean like how that waitress asked me if we could take her to Aquerei?"

～～～

Ava had good reasons for wanting to leave Luxaria, and Lars wasn't the only one. First of all, as a planet, Luxaria basically sucked. It was one of those colonies that had been established with no rules whatsoever— just the law of the gun and the credit. The best Ava could say about it was that everyone seemed to have agreed to use the Standard Tongue—or Stantongue, as it was often called—as the primary language. Lars had been so sure he could make a fortune there, but he'd yet to amass any amount of wealth, and it didn't look like he was going to. Obviously, it took more smarts than Lars possessed for that.

Not that Ava cared for wealth, though it would have been nice to live on more than what her meager salary and tips could provide. Their living quarters were barely fit for animals, but she'd done her best. She couldn't help it if Lars was a slob and kept mucking up the place. A few more slugs with a frying pan might have straightened him up eventually, but it was becoming increasingly apparent that his head was a lot stronger than her right arm. Maybe if she used both hands...

Ava stole a glance at Lars as they set off down the street. He'd been pugnacious enough while he was in the bar, but right now, it was all he could do to stand up. Bashing him over the head might not be necessary this time. "You know, you really didn't have to try to pick a fight with that guy. He was just a customer."

"A fuckin' *Zetithian* customer," Lars grumbled. "I've heard about those guys. Women aren't safe around them."

Ava bit back a retort. Sometimes it was best not to

argue. "I've seen them before, Lars. It was no big deal then, and it's no big deal now." Trag, the one other Zetithian she'd seen, had been nice enough, but this one was more intimidating than anything. His clothes were unremarkable—a white T-shirt, gray cargo pants, and black boots. She'd seen plenty of guys with tattoos and earrings; even the dreadlocks weren't that unusual, but there was something about the hard glint in his eyes that made her shiver. He was incredibly handsome and had a wickedly sexy smile, but *still*…

"You were looking at him like you wanted to do him."

Ava counted to three as she gazed heavenward. *God grant me the serenity*… "Lars, if I'd wanted to 'do' him, I would have let him beat you to a pulp, and we wouldn't be having this conversation."

Lars staggered and nearly ran into a Scorillian family of three, which would probably have been the end of him. Grabbing his hand, she pulled him out of the way, all the while thinking she might have been saving herself a lot of trouble if she'd just let it happen. "You can't leave me," he mumbled. "It's not safe."

"That's a matter of opinion," Ava mocked. "I'm not what anyone would call 'safe' most of the time."

"I've done my best… kept my part of the bargain." Lars wiped his perpetually runny nose on his sleeve—one of his more endearing habits.

"There was never any bargain between us, Lars."

Lars seemed to ignore this, still mumbling on like he hadn't heard. "Made a deal."

"With who? The devil? If you did, he got the best end of it. I came here, expecting something good to come of it, but so far, nothing has. And I've had enough of waiting tables and living in a dump and having to deal with your jealousy and drunkenness all the time. You damn near lost me my job just now, and then where would we be?" Shaking her head sadly, she added, "I ought never to have left Russ."

"You know why you left him. He was boring."

"Boring is better than a drunk who beats me up whenever he takes a notion." She pointed sideways to a building even more dilapidated than the others on the street. "And you just passed up the flat." She couldn't bring herself to refer to it as a home or a house or anything of that nature. It was always referred to as "the" flat; there was no "our" about it.

"I said I was sorry for that."

"What? Which part? Beating me up or passing up the flat?"

"Hurting you," he replied. "Never meant to."

"Yeah, that's what they all say," she grumbled as she unlocked the door. "Get on in here and try to sleep it off. I have to go back to work."

Ava's disillusionment with Lars had begun almost immediately, but he had assured her that they would be rolling in dough soon and then they would move on to live in one of Luxaria's nicer regions. It hadn't taken long for Ava to realize that Luxton City *was* Luxaria's nicest region.

She sometimes suspected that Lars had been paid off by someone—a drug deal perhaps—because the trip to Luxaria had been expensive, and though they'd lived well enough in the beginning, their funds had quickly dwindled to the point that her waitressing job, which she'd taken purely for spending money at first, eventually became their primary source of income. For some strange reason, Lars seemed to think that getting an actual job was beneath his dignity, and since he tended to drink a lot and, she suspected, use a few illegal drugs, he didn't contribute much to the family finances. Whatever the source of his funds had been in the beginning, it had now dried up completely. Ava had been doing pretty well on tips lately, but she had kept the money hidden from Lars; otherwise, she wouldn't have been able to hang on to what little they had.

She'd about decided that she was stranded on Luxaria forever until the Norludian, Waroun, had struck up a conversation with her. He'd promised that the passage to Aquerei would be well within her means—though he hadn't named a figure—which got her to thinking that maybe things really *could* be different. Going to Aquerei wasn't something she'd ever considered before; the idea had just popped into her head as she talked with Waroun. Sure, her father had been a full-blooded Aquerei, but that was about all she knew about him. She'd never met him and hadn't the slightest notion of where to look for him. She wasn't even completely sure of his full name. The only thing she had left of him was the pendant he'd given to her mother before he disappeared. Ava had an idea that if Lars were to leave her, she wouldn't even have that much.

Therefore it was imperative that she leave him first.

Waroun had said if she wanted to go to Aquerei, she had to hurry. After throwing a blanket over Lars's snoring body, she checked the charge on her pulse pistol. It was getting low, so she set it in the charger and began stuffing what few belongings she possessed into a garbage bag. If Lars caught her at it, she could always say she was just taking out the trash—which wouldn't have been a lie, since most of her things qualified as such.

Except for one thing that Lars knew nothing about: the crystal pendant that had been given to her on her sixteenth birthday. Tears had shimmered in her mother's eyes as she handed Ava the box, whispering, "It belonged to your father. He wanted you to have it." Ava had known nothing about the stone prior to that moment and had hated her father for his absence from her life. But to her, this necklace was proof of many things—not only of her father's existence, but that he cared enough to leave her something beautiful.

She opened the hinged box, struck as always by the eternal beauty of the crystal. Shaped like an offset obelisk with a wide, faceted point at the base, its aquamarine color and perfect clarity sent flashes of blue-green fire dancing across the dingy walls of the flat. Ava wrapped her fingers around the hard, cool planes, marveling at how perfectly it fit in her hand, measuring the full width of her palm. Sometimes she thought she heard the crash of waves on a distant shore when she held it, could almost feel those same waves rocking her gently, reminding her of a homeworld she had never seen. Whether from the feel of the stone or the unspoken love it represented, she derived comfort from it, along with a measure of strength—both of which she needed rather badly at the moment.

She had tucked the box in her pocket and was about to head out the door when Lars came bursting into the kitchen. "You liar!" he roared. "You've packed your clothes!"

"That's what people normally do when they decide to call it quits."

Lars calmed down suddenly, and when he spoke, he sounded almost normal, but with a twinge of desperation in his voice. "You can't leave."

"Why not?" she demanded. "I don't owe you anything, Lars. I've had enough. I'm leaving, so you can just get over it."

"You can't leave," he repeated, seizing her by the arm. "It'll mean my death."

"I doubt that. You'll just have to find some other sucker to take care of you."

"You're not going anywhere!" he shouted, twisting her arm painfully.

"You're hurting me!" she screamed.

With that, he threw her against the wall. "I don't care," he snarled. "You've got to stay. I'll chain you up if I have to."

"You wouldn't dare!"

"Then don't make me do it."

"I'm not making you do anything," she said, panting. "Just let me go, Lars."

"No," he said flatly. "I can't do that."

Ava straightened up to her full height, which was about two-thirds of his. "Then make me want to stay."

Lars just stood there, an unreadable expression on his face.

Ava nodded. "I didn't think so."

"Where are you going?"

"To Aquerei to find my father."

All the color drained out of his face. "You can't go there. Besides, your father is dead."

She stared back at him in frank disbelief. "And just how would you know that?"

"I—I just know."

"A likely story." Ava shook her hair back defiantly and started to walk past him. If she could get to her pistol, she could stun him with it—maybe.

For one brief moment, it seemed as though her ploy might work, but as she approached, Lars made a grab for her. This time, however, Ava was ready for him. She made a dive for the stove and, hoisting the heavy skillet with both hands, she swung it in a sweeping arc, striking him in the head. Lars dropped like a rock—a really *big* rock.

Snatching up the trash bag that held everything she owned, she stuffed the charger into the bag and pocketed the pistol. "Good-bye, Lars." She heaved the bag onto her shoulder. "It's been grand, but now I'm outta here."

Chapter 2

IF DAX WAS SKEPTICAL, WHO COULD BLAME HIM? AFTER all, perky blond waitresses generally didn't book passage on his ship, especially not after talking to Waroun.

"I'm not making it up," Waroun insisted. "She wants to go there to find her father. Apparently life with Lars isn't all she'd hoped it would be."

"Well, then why the hell didn't she ask me?"

Waroun gazed pointedly at the ceiling while tapping his flippered foot. "I should have thought that was perfectly obvious."

He was right, of course. The fewer conversations Dax had with pretty women, the better—especially when they had boyfriends like Lars hanging around.

"Nobody ever suspects anyone to be arranging romantic liaisons with a Norludian," Waroun went on. "Isn't that why I'm your partner—so the women can feel safe? Not that we transport that many women, but—"

Since this was the least likely reason he would ever have gone into business with Waroun, Dax doubled over with laughter, drawing a few stares.

"Or did you do it just to piss off Jack?"

Dax wiped tears of laughter from his eyes. "No, I did it because you're an unscrupulous rascal who can navigate all the way to hell and back. The fact that it pisses off Jack is just an interesting side effect."

"Only interesting? Not satisfying or welcome?"

"Yeah, just interesting," Dax replied. "I like Jack a lot—I really do!—but she can be a bit overbearing at times."

"True. I just wish she'd let me—"

Dax held up a hand for silence. "Don't say it, Waroun. I really don't want to hear what it is you think she should do—and she wouldn't do it anyway. She's too much in love with Cat—and Cat would probably kill you if you tried it."

Waroun let out a deep sigh. "*Her* loss…"

"So, tell me more about this trip to Aquerei," Dax said, swiftly changing the subject. "Is she serious? Because, if so, she'll need to hurry."

"Already got your eye on her, do you?"

At this point, it seemed prudent to deny it, no matter how true it might be. Waroun would drive him completely crazy if he had any idea what had been going through Dax's mind. "No, so you can wipe that smug look off your face."

Waroun laughed. "You know where Aquerei is, don't you?"

"Not off the top of my head," Dax replied. "But I'm sure you're about to tell me."

"It's in the Norludian sector."

"Ah, so that's why she asked you instead of me."

"No, she asked me because I made a remark about the bruises on her arm, which led to the rest of our conversation."

Dax's stomach twisted into knots. "Jack said Lars would probably beat the shit out of her as soon as they left here. Damn, I should have creamed him while I had the chance."

"That certainly would have been interesting," Waroun commented. "He probably outweighs you by ten kilos."

"But I'm taller and quicker on my feet," Dax pointed out. "Longer reach. That's a plus."

"Better to just blast him," Waroun said. "You've got a good pistol. Even with your rotten aim, you probably could have hit him."

"Don't start that, Waroun. I miss a shot at one lousy Herpatronian and you have to rub it in forever."

"Perhaps I do tend to harp on it, but if he hadn't been coming after me, I might have been more forgiving."

"Dammit, Waroun, I said I was sorry!"

"Sorry doesn't cut it when something as big as a Herpatronian lands on you." Waroun wiggled his left arm pathetically. "I may never be the same."

Dax rolled his eyes. "That arm healed up just fine! The doctor said—"

"Forget that," Waroun whispered. "She's back."

Dax glanced up at the door, but all he saw were a couple of Drells creating a stir by shoving a pair of Cylopeans off their barstools. The hideous Cylopeans were retaliating by dragging the Drells off by their floor-length hair when Dax felt a tap on his shoulder.

"Can we go now?" Ava said urgently. She was breathing hard, as though she'd run all the way, and her light blond hair was swept back from her face and flipped up in the back, reminding him of a swan's folded wings. She still wore the clothes that were at least partially responsible for Dax's skyrocketing temperature, and her only luggage was a drawstring sack slung over her shoulder.

"This is Ava," Waroun said, introducing her as though

assuming Dax wouldn't have noticed her name—which ordinarily would have been true.

Dax gave her a brief nod in greeting, avoiding her eyes. "Where's Lars? Back home sleeping it off?" He inhaled as deeply as he could without being obvious and almost choked on his disappointment. Nope. No desire there at all. Dammit.

Ava's expression darkened. "More like he'll need stitches. I hit him over the head with an iron skillet."

"Should've done that before," Waroun remarked. "Would've saved you some bruises."

"I *have* done it before," Ava said. "It's the only way to get him to shut up. I was just a little more energetic this time." Pulling up a chair, she plopped down in it, setting her sack down beside her. "I hope you don't object, but I've changed my mind about where I want to go. I think Rutara would be best."

"Oh," said Dax. "And why is that?"

"That's where my mother is from—well, where she lives, anyway—and where I grew up. She's Terran, actually. I haven't seen her for a long time, and there are some things I need to discuss with her." Afraid that sounded a little weak, she added, "Besides, I have an old boyfriend there; maybe we can get back together."

"You seem to have really rotten taste in men," Waroun observed. "Are you sure your old boyfriend is any better than the one you've got?"

"Anyone's better than Lars," she said with a shudder.

Waroun's eyes lit up with lascivious delight. "If that's the case, I could—"

"Figure of speech," Ava said, waving him off before Waroun could go any further.

With her gesture, Dax noticed the thin web of skin between the base and first joint of each of her fingers. He tried to recall what he'd ever heard about Aquerei, but other than the fact that the surface was one big ocean with very little land and that, according to Waroun, the natives liked to mate underwater, he couldn't remember very much.

"What makes you think he'd be waiting for you?" Dax asked, sensing a ray of hope.

"He said he would," Ava replied. "Russ is a good man. I should have stuck with him—can't for the life of me remember why I left him for Lars. I must've been out of my mind."

Dax knew practically nothing about women, but he'd heard about the "bad boy" fixation so many seemed to have. He didn't understand it; leaving a good man for a bad one made no sense whatsoever, but then, he'd never been in love. "Do you really think he'd be that patient? I mean, how long have you been gone?"

"About…" Ava stopped for a moment, as though figuring up the time in her head. "Wow, it's been longer than I thought! Almost five years."

Dax was incredulous. "You mean you've stuck it out with Lars for that long, even knowing you had to knock him out to shut him up?"

Ava shrugged. "Well, it wasn't *all* bad."

"As big as he is, his dick must be humongous," Waroun said with a smirk. "But perhaps you'd like something slightly different." He ran his tongue over his lips and reached out toward Ava's hand with a sucker-tipped finger. He had just made contact when Dax spotted him.

"Knock it off, Waroun!"

"Only one little touch," Waroun protested. "Just a sample of her essence."

Glowering at Ava, Dax went on, "Don't ever let him touch you."

"Why not?"

"You don't want to know."

"Oh, really?" she said, squaring up to face him. "And what's so bad about letting him touch me?"

"Never spent much time around Norludians, have you?"

"Uh, no…" she replied. "I mean, I've seen them here in the bar before, but—"

"Well, unless you want to get fucked by one, don't let him touch you."

Waroun's bulbous eyes narrowed with suspicion as he crossed his arms. "You've never warned anyone else."

Dax winced as the Norludian began sticking his suckers onto his own skin and then pulling them off with a loud pop—something he tended to do when he was irritated.

"I never *needed* to warn anyone else," Dax pointed out. "And don't *do* that!" he added as Waroun popped off another fingertip. "It drives me nuts!"

Waroun stuck out his tongue in the Norludian equivalent of *"Fuck you."*

"Just take a look at him if you don't believe me," Dax said to Ava. "His tongue's already getting hard."

Ava's eyes widened. "You fuck with your tongue?"

Waroun grinned. "And I promise you would like it."

"I think I'll pass." Clearing her throat, she turned to Dax. "How much to take me to Rutara?"

"How much have you got?" Dax countered.

"Enough," she said evasively.

"Enough for what?" Dax shot back. "Enough to book passage or pay for dinner?"

Ava hitched in her seat and focused her eyes on the table. "Well, I don't know how much you'd want…"

"I will pay her way if she will fuck me," Waroun said promptly. His eyelids drooped as he stole another glance at her. "She excites me a great deal. Oh, and just so you know, Ava. You have to do me before you can do him."

Ava shuddered. "I don't want to 'do' *anybody*! I just want to go home!"

Dax felt his chances with her plummet yet again, that realization making his reply more brusque than he'd intended. "Well, now that we've established that, we can get on with the transaction. I repeat: How much have you got?"

"Not nearly enough," she mourned. "I just got to talking to Waroun, and then Lars was such a bastard and…"

She looked as though she was beginning to regret the whole thing, and if she really *wasn't* attracted to him, Dax would just as soon she didn't come anywhere near his ship, but business was business. "How much?" he said again. "And please, tell me the truth."

"About a hundred credits," she said with a world-weary sigh. "I know it's not much, but—"

"Okay," said Dax. "I'll take twenty-five."

"Really? You're kidding me, right?"

"No, I'm not. That's the price."

Waroun shook his head sadly. "He's such a sucker sometimes…"

"I always take a fourth, and you know it," Dax told Waroun. "Sometimes it's more, sometimes it's less." With those who were obviously down on their luck, Dax had made it a habit to take a fourth, though occasionally he took half if he thought the person he was dealing with was lying to him. He didn't think Ava was lying.

But Ava suspected that Dax was. "What's the catch?"

"No catch," said Dax. "But you won't be our only passenger, and we may not take the most direct route. Waroun's a helluva navigator, and he does his best, but we may take longer than some other transports."

"Ah, yes," she said wisely. "The scenic route. I should have known."

"So you're not in a big hurry to get there, right?" Dax reiterated. "We're clear on that?"

Ava nodded. "We just need to get out of here before Lars—"

"Where the hell are you, you fuckin' whore?" Lars staggered through the doorway, his head covered in blood.

"—wakes up."

"You must not live very far from here," Waroun commented.

"Not nearly far enough," Ava muttered. "Can we go now?"

"I presume there's a back door," Dax said, getting to his feet.

For a moment, Ava was stunned to silence by the sheer size of him. Dax had been intimidating enough while seated, but, along with everything else, he made Lars look short—which wasn't an easy thing to do. "Uh, yeah, sure. Follow me."

"Hold on a sec." Dax reached into one of his many pockets and pulled out a small sphere with a string attached to it. Yanking out the string, he tossed it at Lars. "Hey, Lars! Catch!"

Obviously taken by surprise, Lars caught it on the fly. The ball turned briefly into a mass of hissing snakes before enveloping the entire area with a cloud of thick, purple smoke.

"That'll slow him down a bit," Dax said.

"Probably just piss him off," Ava remarked.

"You already did that," Dax growled. "Now run!"

Ava led the way through the bar to the rear entrance, which opened out onto a dingy alley filled with assorted drunks and druggies from a dozen different worlds. Reaching for her pulse pistol was an automatic response.

"You came in this way?" Dax exclaimed. "You're braver than I thought."

"Living with Lars makes these guys seem tame," she shouted back at him. "And besides, I'm always armed." To demonstrate, she waved her pistol over her head. The drunks saw it and began backing off.

Now that they were outside the building, Dax sprinted on ahead, grabbing her other hand as he passed by. "Good. Just don't point it at me."

"Wouldn't dream of it." The strength of his grasp sent a shock wave through Ava, along with a sense of latent power and something else she couldn't identify. She had no choice but to run with him.

Dax was quick on his feet, but the Norludian was faster. "Follow me!" Waroun yelled as he ran past. Racing down the alley, he sped around the next corner and disappeared from sight.

Ava stared after him as she ran. "Hey, aren't we going to the spaceport? If so, he's going the wrong way."

"You can trust him." Dax tugged at her hand when she started to slow down. "His sense of direction is uncanny."

Ava snorted. "Maybe, but it's still wrong. The space-port is that way." She pointed back over her shoulder.

"Who said we were going to the spaceport?"

"Well then, how are we getting to Rutara?"

"Oh, we'll get there," Dax replied. "This is the scenic route, remember?"

"That's funny. I thought the scenery would be, you know, in space?"

Dax shook his head. "Not all of it."

Ava kept running. The entire alley was a blur of dilapidated buildings, trash, and stinking derelicts. As they ran, the caliber of their surroundings didn't improve. She was almost afraid to say it, but she blurted it out anyway. "We're heading toward the—"

"Worst part of town?" Dax finished for her. "Yeah. Gotta pick up a few more passengers. Three of them. Should be there by now."

A pulse blast ricocheted off the side of the tall sand-stone building in front of them, shattering a window across the alley.

"Guess Lars has his pistol too," Ava said grimly.

Dax reached into his pocket and pulled out another device, which he slapped on the wall as they rounded the corner.

Ava glanced back just in time to see a forest of trees sprout sideways from the spot, completely blocking the path behind them. "What are you, a magician?"

"No," Dax replied. "But I know someone who is."

The alley opened out onto the main street of what was essentially Luxton City's red-light district. Hookers of all shapes and sizes stood in every doorway, and the street was filled with the kind of men who would ordinarily have to pay big money to get laid—whether they were on their respective planets of origin or not. Ava was tough, but she'd made a point of avoiding this neighborhood. Not only because she had no need for the area's services; some of the customers had been known to take what they wanted from women—and men—who weren't selling it.

"They're over there." Waroun pointed to a cluster of beings standing next to a metallic blue speeder on the road ahead. He strode toward them at a brisk pace.

"You're meeting them *here*?" Ava gasped.

"Yeah, they all wanted to get laid before we left," Dax said with a shrug. "Guess they figured they wouldn't be getting any along the way."

"But we have you with us now," Waroun told Ava with undisguised glee. "This should be a fun voyage— for once."

"I told you I didn't want sex," Ava growled. "I just want to go home!"

"Better stick with him, then." Waroun cocked a thumb at Dax. "He doesn't want it either. In fact, he never has."

"Oh, shut up, Waroun," Dax snapped. "That's none of her damn business."

"A celibate Zetithian?" Ava asked with surprise. "I didn't think there *was* such a thing."

"I wouldn't say I was celibate. I'm just not a fuckin' horn dog like *some* people I know." The steely-eyed look that accompanied his statement was enough to make Ava believe it unequivocally. "And how did you—or Lars, for that matter—know I was Zetithian? We aren't what you'd call common."

"You aren't the first one I've seen," she replied. "A guy named Trag used to show up here once in a while. He was a pilot for an arms dealer—Lerotan Kanotay. Ever hear of them?"

"Yeah, I know Trag," Dax said. "Not well, but I've met him."

"He had this aversion to blue. Wouldn't tip a Davordian waitress because of her blue eyes. Weird."

"I wouldn't say he was weird," said Dax. "Just... opinionated."

"Whatever." Ava shrugged. "He always tipped me—not a lot, but he did tip me. I guess my eyes looked more green than blue to him—though they're actually a little of both."

"Let me see," said Waroun, turning around.

The Norludian stopped right in front of her, reaching out with both hands in a way that sent chills running down Ava's spine. "Don't touch me," she warned.

Waroun didn't lay a finger on her, but got right up in her face, which was just as disturbing. His huge eyes stared into her own, making her feel like a bug under a microscope.

"*That's* why you don't look Terran," Waroun said after subjecting her to careful scrutiny. "Your eyes are much bigger and rounder than a Terran's—and they're an odd color."

"How can you possibly tell in this light?" Ava protested.

"He can see pretty well in the dark," Dax said. "But my night vision is even better." Stopping, he pulled her around to face him.

If staring at Waroun's eyes was disconcerting, gazing up into Dax's feline orbs was even more so. She had taken them to be hazel in color, but instead of the haphazard mixture of shades the term usually represented, the iris was a brilliant green, highlighted by a dark brown outer rim. While this would have made them remarkable in any case, it was the soft golden glow from his catlike pupils that struck Ava the most. His eyebrows slanted upward in a way that should have been sinister, but only added to his appeal, as did his ears, which curved upward to culminate in a sharply pointed tip. An odd warmth suffused her entire body, and the longer his gaze remained fixed on her own, the more aware she became of her erogenous zones.

They were on fire, and she was melting. There was no other word for it. In another minute, she'd be nothing but a puddle at his feet. Dax leaned down for a closer look, his face barely a breath away from her own. She could hear a vibration in the way he was breathing; it sounded rough and loud, almost like he was purring…

"Hey, Dax!" someone shouted from up the street. "Come on, man! We're ready to go!"

Dax blinked hard and straightened up to his full height. He glanced down at Ava, looking like he'd just seen a ghost.

"Aquamarine," he whispered.

"Huh?" said Waroun.

"Her eyes. That's what color they are. They're aquamarine."

Chapter 3

DAX HAD NO IDEA WHY DISCOVERING THE COLOR OF HER eyes should have affected him so strongly, but he'd never purred for a woman in his life. He'd finally gotten a good whiff of her; she smelled so damn good, he'd reacted before he had time to think.

The sound of a scuffle behind him diverted his attention and, turning around, he saw Lars headed their way with scratches all over him and a branch clinging to the seat of his pants. Blood covered at least half of his face, but he was still waving his pistol at Dax.

"You Zetithian scum!" he roared as he approached. "She's mine!"

"Not anymore, pal," Dax said. "So back off!"

"You've been fucking her, haven't you?" Lars yelled. "I tell you I won't let—"

Dax didn't often lose his temper, but he'd had just about enough of Lars. "I haven't fucked *anybody*," he shot back. "She's leaving because she doesn't like getting beat up. So why don't you just shut up and go home!"

Lars ignored him and continued to advance. Realizing that talking wasn't getting him anywhere, Dax grabbed Ava's hand, flipped the setting on her pistol to heavy stun, and squeezed the trigger.

"Well, I'll be damned," Waroun said as Lars fell in a heap. "You actually hit him."

"Amazing, isn't it?" Dax said with a sardonic laugh. "Let's get going before he wakes up again."

"Which won't be long," Ava warned. "The frying pan does a better job."

"Anyone that hardheaded must have a little Herpatronian in his bloodline," Waroun mused, still staring at Lars's inert form. "Or a touch of Darconian—though I'm not sure that's possible."

"Have you ever considered that hitting him in the head might be making things worse?" Dax said. "I mean, shit like that is bound to scramble his brains eventually."

"I've been hoping it would give him a lobotomy," Ava said. "But it hasn't worked so far." She tipped her head to one side, adding thoughtfully, "Maybe I wasn't hitting him in the right spot."

"Remind me not to let her anywhere near the galley," Waroun muttered. "We might all be lobotomized before we get her to Rutara."

"Hey, it was your idea to bring her along," Dax pointed out. "If anyone gets conked over the head, it should be you."

"Aw, come on, you guys!" Ava said. "I won't need to hit either one of you—unless you hit me first."

"I don't plan on it," Dax snapped. Actually, hitting her was the farthest thing from his mind at that point. Another moment spent gazing into her eyes and he would have kissed her! Striding off in the direction of his speeder and his other passengers, Dax made an interesting discovery. She'd not only made him purr; she'd made his dick hard.

And, not only that, it was also slick with the orgasm-inducing fluid for which Zetithians were famous. Dax had been around lots of women, but very few of them had ever given him an erection—not that they hadn't tried—and none had made him want to purr. He hadn't done it intentionally this time; it had simply happened. It was all wrong, though—it was very clear that she wasn't interested in him. But if that was the case, then why had she smelled so good?

Anyway, it was supposed to be the other way around: When males saw a woman they were attracted to, first they purred and *then* they were aroused by her scent. At least, that's what he'd always been told. The fact that a woman's scent could be arousing whether he'd purred or not surprised him. Then it occurred to him that drowning in her eyes might have been the reason. After all, he'd had to get pretty close to her to do that.

Proximity, pure and simple. As tall as he was, looking right into a woman's face didn't happen very often. Most females only came up to his chest, and some only to his waist. Drells were somewhere around his knees—not that he'd ever been able to figure out which of them was female. One of his passengers was a Drell this time, so he'd have to make a point of asking. The other two passengers were Kitnocks, and though they were nearly as tall as he, Dax had long since decided that the only way you could tell the sexes apart was by the color of the body stockings they wore to cover their spindly limbs; females wore blue, and males wore red. Always.

As they approached, Dax spotted three scantily clad Davordian hookers waiting with his motley trio of passengers. Except for their luminous blue eyes, Davordians looked essentially human, but Kitnocks and Drells were humanoid only in the respect that they each had two legs, two arms, and a head. If those girls had provided the necessary services, they were either the toughest hookers ever born or the most desperate.

One of the Kitnocks, Teke, inclined his tall, cylindrical head as he waved a hand in greeting. "These ladies heard we were shipping out with a Zetithian and wanted to know if you'd be interested—"

"I'm not," Dax said, not bothering to wait for the rest of it.

"But they wanted to see if you had an aversion to blue eyes," Teke said. "Apparently they've come to believe that this is a trait among Zetithians."

"It's not," said Dax. "That's Trag's problem, not mine."

"No, his problem is that he doesn't like to fuck," Waroun said, aiming a sucker-tipped thumb toward Dax. "I, on the other hand, would be happy to partake of anything you ladies have to offer."

It might have been the light, but Dax could have sworn the hookers lost what little color they had in their fair-skinned faces.

"We have, um, other clients waiting," one of the Davordians said, averting her eyes.

"That's right," the others chorused.

"Works every time," Dax said under his breath as the hookers quickly withdrew.

<hr />

Still recovering from her reaction to Dax, Ava barely registered this exchange. No one, not Russ or Lars or anyone else, had *ever* made her melt. She made herself a promise not to get that close to him again, but she also knew that on a long space voyage this might prove difficult—especially if it was a small ship. With no more passengers than he took on—not to mention their apparent lack of class and, at least in her case, funds—the odds were against him being the captain of a luxury space cruiser.

"We'll make introductions later," Waroun said. "Now, if you'll all climb into the speeder, we'll be on our way."

Following Waroun's gesture, Ava climbed into the backseat of the sleek speeder to sit next to the Drell. They were rude little rats as a rule, but she knew how to handle them. All you had to do was swear at a Drell, and they backed down instantly. Kitnocks were another problem altogether. These two were obviously male, and though she'd waited on plenty of them, she didn't care for them at all. Their huge mouths made them look like caricatures drawn by children, and they had some very odd habits. Cracking their knuckles was the most annoying of these and was something they did constantly, unless they were holding something in their hands.

She'd heard that the knuckle cracking was a secret language among Kitnocks—and the fact that they mostly seemed to do this while among others of their kind made the rumor seem likely—but Ava had never been able to confirm this. Not that she cared. She'd always tried to avoid them in the past, but the best she could hope for in this instance was that their destination was nearby, because she was pretty sure that Rutara would be the last stop.

The Drell shifted over as Ava sat down—not away from her, but toward her, barely leaving her a place to sit, let alone allowing room for her sack. Obviously, the swearing would have to begin immediately. "Move the fuck over."

The Drell screeched like a scalded cat and scrambled to the far side of the seat. "I merely wanted to—"

"I don't give a damn." She was watching Dax climb into the driver's seat, noting that he looked as fabulous from the back as he did from the front. She briefly considered what he might have thought if their positions were reversed—though, given his aversion to "fucking," she doubted that the sentiment would be mutual. She sat up straighter and gazed pointedly in another direction. She didn't need to be getting the hots for a Zetithian. She'd heard about them. They were like highly addictive drugs; one hit and you were hooked. And besides, she'd had enough trouble with bad boys; there was no need to get hung up on another one.

And Lars had been a very bad boy. What *had* she been thinking? At the time, he'd seemed daring and handsome and dangerous and sexy. Now he was just ridiculous and mean. She should have known better, but if she didn't get it back then, she certainly did now. She wasn't going to hook up with another one. Maybe she *should* go back to Russ. He was a good man. Not terribly exciting, perhaps, but excitement was rapidly beginning to lose its appeal.

The last she'd heard from her mother—perhaps six months previously—led her to believe that Russ was still single. Hopefully he'd waited at least another six months, but even if he hadn't, Rutara was still a better place to live than Luxaria. Glancing around at the dusty, weedy, unkempt excuse for a spaceport, she concluded that almost any place would be an improvement.

All that aside, it was time to sit her mother down and have the talk they'd both always managed to avoid. Why did her father leave, and where had he gone? What did her mother know about him, about Aquerei? What Lars had said brought up even more questions. If her father was really dead, did her mother know, and, if so, why hadn't she told her?

Her attention drifted back to Dax. The Norludian sidekick was a definite drawback, but Dax was undeniably attractive, and at least he was clean. Not interested in romance, though, she reminded herself, and certainly not sex. As she gazed at his back, Ava was surprised to discover that what she had previously thought to be dreadlocks were actually very tight spiral curls, the front sections of which were pulled back into two long braids that hung down behind his ears. He drove the speeder with obvious expertise, but if he'd been concerned enough to spare her a glance over his shoulder, she hadn't noticed it. No. Not interested in her *or* in romance. If anything, he'd ignored her even more pointedly since the melting episode.

He'd been purring, though, and Ava was pretty sure that meant something in a Zetithian. She should have asked the hookers, but it was too late for that now.

The circuitous route they were taking made no sense to Ava, aside from the fact that they were avoiding a lot of traffic by going that way. She suspected that Dax and Waroun might be trying to throw off anyone tailing them; Dax took several quick turns that nearly threw her into the Drell's lap—a circumstance which was apparently as distasteful to the Drell as it was to Ava. This led her to believe that her fellow passengers might be even

shadier than they looked—either that, or Dax didn't
ever want to lay eyes on Lars again. Since this was also
Ava's intention, she didn't voice any complaints.

Arriving at the spaceport, Dax flew the speeder
over to one of the ships berthed there—a sleek Rutaran
Runabout called the *Valorcry*, which at least appeared
to be spaceworthy. There were larger vessels, but given
Luxaria's reputation, not many people were willing to
bring their big, expensive ships down to the surface, pre-
ferring to arrive in shuttles instead. Many of those that
had landed were so dilapidated, it was a wonder they'd
survived atmospheric reentry.

Dax hopped out of the speeder after bringing it to
a halt and paid off the two Davordian boys who had
apparently been hired to keep an eye on it for him. He
deposited ten credits in the meter box and then swiped
his identchip. The force field crackled briefly before
losing power.

*It costs ten credits to berth a ship, and yet he's only
charging me twenty-five to take me to Rutara? It doesn't
make sense!* Dax hadn't said, but Ava wondered if she
wasn't going to have to cough up more money before it
was all over. Perhaps part of her ticket was to be paid
by cleaning up after the other passengers, who were
undoubtedly paying more than she was. This prospect
didn't alter her determination to get back home, however; being on a ship with these guys couldn't possibly
be any worse than living with Lars.

Dax palmed open the lock on the hatch and, as the
gangplank lowered to the ground, motioned for his passengers to board.

As Ava climbed the steps, she was astonished by the

sight that met her eyes. The ship was not only service-
able, it was downright posh. Luxurious appointments
were everywhere, from ornately carved glowstone lamps
set on gleaming tables to soft leather seats strategically
placed about the main deck. There were paintings firmly
attached to the walls, and plush carpeting covered the
floors. Without thinking, Ava scraped her shoes on the
steps before entering.

"Nice place you've got here," she remarked as Dax
came aboard.

Dax shrugged. "It was like this when I got it—
belonged to a drug dealer."

"Oh, let me guess," Ava said dryly. "You won it in a
game of *kartoosk*, right?"

"Not exactly," Dax replied. "Since he was the one
responsible for destroying my world, his assets were divided up among the remaining Zetithians after his death.
This was his personal transport ship."

Ava's eyes swept the interior once again. "He
must've been worth a bundle."

"You could say that," Dax said with apparent disin-
terest. "Everyone have a seat here in the lounge. We'll
be taking off shortly."

Dax started to head toward the bridge but paused to
address the Kitnocks and the Drell. "Let me make one
thing perfectly clear: This lady is not to be harassed
while she's aboard my ship." The intimidating glare
that accompanied this directive had Ava's fellow passengers each nodding vigorously. The Drell scurried
over to one of the chairs, climbed up in it, and folded his
furry hands in his lap. The Kitnocks both cracked their
knuckles a few times but otherwise remained silent.

"The captain's pretty tough, huh?" Ava remarked as Dax and Waroun departed. Taking a seat near the hatch, she set her bag down beside her. "My name is Ava," she said by way of introduction.

"I am Teke," said one of the Kitnocks.

"And I am called Diokut," said the other.

At first, given that they were both wearing identical red body stockings, Ava couldn't tell them apart, but upon closer observance, she decided that Teke must be older than Diokut; the tiny tufts of hair sticking straight up from the top of his head were a salt and pepper mixture, whereas Diokut's hair was red—and not just auburn either. It was *really* red, like a candied apple. Their skin was a sickly-looking greenish brown, but she knew from experience that this was typical and not indicative of illness. She wasn't so sure about the Drell, who identified himself as Quinn.

Quinn was covered in coarse, unkempt gray hair that grew all the way down to his feet, and since the only thing you could see on him were his eyes and his mouth, he had no need of any clothing whatsoever. Even his hands and feet were hairy, and as smelly as he was, if it had been Ava's ship, she would have scanned him for parasites before allowing him to board. She was trying to decide how to casually request that he have a bath when the engines fired up. After only a brief warm-up, the ship lifted off from the docking bay.

Ava hadn't been on very many starships, but this one definitely had the smoothest ride of them all. The various ornaments didn't budge a bit.

They hadn't been airborne for long when a

dome-shaped droid with numerous arms hovered in with drinks. The Kitnocks each received a tall glass of a purple beverage, which Ava recognized as Morovian ale, but the thick orange stuff given to Quinn was a mystery. Approaching Ava, the droid held out a glass of water.

"Guess this means I'm definitely in economy class," she muttered. The surprising thing was that it didn't seem to be ordinary water. In addition to being significantly more refreshing, she could have sworn it made her hair grow a few centimeters—or something. Either way, it seemed to... move. She could feel it. The droid responded with a single satisfied beep.

After giving them all the opportunity to consume their drinks, the droid started in on Quinn with a brush and a vacuum cleaning attachment. When the Drell began to protest, Teke put out a hand to calm him. "Please, do us all a favor, Quinn, and just sit still."

"Are you saying I should submit to this?" Quinn demanded. "I am not in need of grooming!"

"Well, obviously the droid thinks you are, and we agree," Teke said, indicating himself and Diokut. "Don't you, Ava?"

Ava nodded in reply, afraid to say more. Drells could be very touchy, and this one was already ticked. Quinn almost went ballistic when the droid began spraying him with foam and then sucking it off with its vacuum cleaner "arm," but Waroun chose that moment to enter the lounge.

"Ah, very good, Kots," he said to the droid. "I was hoping you'd do that soon."

"Kots?" Ava echoed.

"Stands for Keeper of the Stars," Waroun said with a wry smile. "His former owner had a real superiority complex."

"No kidding," Ava said with a chuckle. "Couldn't you change the name?"

"Why bother?" said Waroun.

Ava shrugged. "I see your point."

Quinn chose that moment to file a formal protest. Jumping to his feet, he drew himself up to his full height, which was less than a meter, and stated angrily, "I do not wish to be groomed by a droid!"

"Then groom yourself and the droid won't have to," Teke suggested.

"You stupid, spindly, hairless freak!" Quinn began, rounding on Teke. "I don't care what—"

"You'll let Kots do it and like it," Dax said as he walked in—his tall, imposing presence startling Quinn and everyone else into silence. "I won't have my other passengers catching any vermin from you."

Quinn responded by holding out his arms for Kots to clean and didn't make another sound.

Oh, he's good. Keeping a Drell in line without using a single curse word was quite a feat. Teke and Diokut regarded him with increased respect. Ava wondered if she ought to go take a quick shower herself.

"Waroun will show you to your quarters," Dax told the Kitnocks. "Kots will take you to yours when you are clean," he said to Quinn. With a brief glance at Ava, he added, "You come with me."

"Aye, aye, Captain." Hopping to her feet so quickly that she saw spots before her eyes, Ava did manage to control her next inclination, which was to salute.

"Very funny," Dax said without the slightest trace of a smile.

Dax was torn between wanting to ignore her and wanting to stash her in his quarters for safekeeping. Not that she faced any danger, but there was something about Ava that aroused instincts in him of which he'd previously been unaware—and didn't want to be, particularly since she intended to return to her old boyfriend. Like every other woman who'd ever even begun to interest him, she was already taken. "Story of my life," he muttered to himself.

"What did you say?"

"Nothing," he replied. "Nothing important, anyway." *I should have sent her with Waroun. Why didn't I?* Ignoring his own question, he strode purposefully down the passageway toward his—or rather, *her*—quarters. The fact that they were next to one another was irrelevant. A wall stood between them, and there were two doors to be negotiated. No temptation whatsoever to visit…

He stopped in front of the door and opened it for her.

"Do I have to stay in here all the time?" she asked meekly.

"No, feel free to use any of the facilities aboard. There are entertainment systems and various other activities. Meals can be eaten in your quarters or in the dining hall, as you choose."

"Sounds like I'd have to dress for dinner if I do that."

"You may wear whatever you like." He glanced toward her bag. "Kots will take care of anything you might need."

"Um, when do I need to pay you for the trip?"

"When we arrive." Dax knew he sounded stiff, but the image of Ava dressed in something low-cut and clingy had assailed him the moment she'd mentioned dressing for dinner. He nearly started purring again.

"You're sure it will only cost twenty-five credits?"

He looked down at her with surprise. "Did you think I was lying?"

"No, it's just that… I don't know…" She mumbled something else he didn't catch.

"I won't cheat you, Ava," he said, surprised at how normal he sounded when he felt anything but. "I'm not Lars."

She nodded, seeming to accept this—at least for now. "Where do you sl—I mean, where are your quarters?"

He pointed to the door they'd just passed. "I'm not in there a lot. I usually stay in the ready room by the bridge, but if you ever need me…" Dax stopped there. It sounded like an offer he shouldn't be making. He stood ramrod straight, towering above her, when what he really wanted was to lean down and inhale her fragrance again. It was just a perfume of some kind, he told himself, trying to dismiss it. But the temptation was so strong…

She nodded, staring down at the floor as though reluctant to meet his gaze. Dax wanted to reach down and tilt her head back so he could see those eyes again—in a better light this time. They were the most mesmerizing he'd ever seen—almost childlike in their innocence, but with depths he couldn't begin to fathom.

Dangerous feminine depths. She wasn't trying to entice him, but she was doing it anyway. He'd been the recipient of some blatant come-ons in the past. This was different. She'd been tough enough earlier, but now she seemed reticent, almost shy.

Of course she felt shy! She was alone in the passageway with him, right in front of the open door to her room. As the only woman aboard, she was bound to be feeling isolated and vulnerable; he wouldn't be surprised if she thought that, despite his protests to the contrary, he would take advantage of the fact that her room was next to his. His only duty was to deliver her safely to her destination, not make love to her. He needed to remember that.

"Good night, then," he said. "Just call for Kots if you need anything… He'll wake you in time for breakfast."

Ava looked up at him and smiled. "What would you do without him?"

Dax felt his heart skip a few beats. "A whole lot more work, that's for sure. Or Waroun would. I don't envy Kots having to get Quinn cleaned up."

"Me either," she replied with a giggle. With that, she went inside her room and closed the door behind her.

As he headed back to the bridge, Dax had plenty to ponder. No, he didn't envy Kots, but he suspected he would have if he'd had to groom Ava instead of Quinn. He might actually fight him for *that* job.

Chapter 4

AVA HAD NEVER BEEN IN SUCH A LUXURIOUS ROOM IN HER life. She probably wouldn't have minded if she'd had to remain inside it the whole time—at least, not for the first week or so. The huge bed was covered with soft, downy blankets and a fur coverlet in a soothing shade of blue, and the matching carpet was even thicker than the one in the lounge. A small but elegant table and chairs sat beneath a porthole that offered a stunning view of the star-studded expanse of space. In addition to that, an ornate mirror doubled as the door to a spacious closet, and the richly appointed bathroom seemed larger than the apartment she'd shared with Lars. Light was provided by Darconian glowstones which, as Ava already knew, responded to thought. You had only to wish for more or less light and the stones would comply with that request. No one had the first clue as to how they worked, but one thing Ava did know for certain: they were ridiculously expensive.

Ava dropped her bag on the floor and sat down on the bed, only then realizing just how tired she was. It had been a *very* long day; what she needed was water. It was her element and never failed to energize her, washing the tension from her body. Stripping off her clothes, she stepped into the shower. The provided soap worked up into a rich, creamy lather and she felt soothed and pampered by the time she was finished. Wrapping herself in a thick towel that hung on a warming rack nearby, she dried her hair with a quick shake of her head. Ava had never completely understood this ability, but her hair seemed almost to repel water—a trait inherited from her Aquerei father.

Catching a glimpse of her round, nonhuman eyes in the mirror brought Ava up short. Whenever any alien characteristics had surfaced in her, her mother's wistful sighs and longing expression had served as a reminder that Ava's father hadn't been a casual fling, but was someone her mother had cared for very deeply. Ava herself had no memory of him. It wasn't until later that those sighs had driven Ava to seek solace in the form of her pendant. She thought it odd that a mere rock could have such a profound effect, but there was no denying the fact that when she looked into its depths, she could almost imagine herself swimming free in the oceans of Aquerei…

But Aquerei was only a story to her and might as well have been a myth. That wasn't good enough anymore. As soon as she got back to Rutara, she intended to get some answers to all those questions she'd never had the nerve to ask.

Shaking off the nostalgic feeling as best she could, Ava went on with her ablutions. After sampling the various lotions that were on tap, she found one that smelled like a spring meadow on Rutara. Closing her eyes, she could almost imagine she was already there, back home where she belonged, and in the arms of… Russ?

Why did that prospect seem less appealing now? Was it because of Dax—a man who probably had women melting into puddles at his feet all across the quadrant? She was merely one more conquest that he wouldn't give a damn about. She'd never met a man who was so indifferent to women—if she could believe him and Waroun—and there was no reason for either of them to lie about it. She wasn't on the hunt for a new man and certainly hadn't chosen Dax's ship just because he was the captain. It had been a spur-of-the-moment decision. It wasn't as though she'd planned her escape for months.

Or had she? She'd been socking away her tips for a good long while, which spoke volumes. She knew very well that the main reason women stayed in abusive or unhappy situations was because they couldn't afford to do anything else, and she was no different. Without her little nest egg, she wouldn't have even considered the idea of leaving when Waroun struck up a conversation with her.

Ava dumped the contents of her bag on the bed, surveying them with distaste. She had very little money, and her clothes were all old and worn; completely out of place in her current surroundings. As nest eggs went, hers was rather pathetic.

A short knock at her door was the only warning she had before Kots entered the room. He carried a tray of fruit in one of his many hands, a carafe of water in another, and had something shimmery and blue draped over one of his arms. Seeming to take no notice of the fact that Ava was completely naked, he set the tray and the carafe on the table and then held out a nightgown made from the most delicate fabric Ava had ever seen, let alone touched.

"For me?" she whispered. "I'm supposed to wear this to bed?"

Kots replied with a soft chirp.

Gathering it up, she dropped it over her head and sighed as the gown fell to her feet in soft waves, wrapping her in luxurious warmth. She felt like a fairy princess—a feeling she hadn't had since playing dress up in her grandmother's gowns as a child.

"Thank you, Kots. It's beautiful."

Kots replied with another chirp and left with no more ceremony than when he'd arrived.

Gazing at her reflection in the nearby mirror, she was amazed at how different she appeared than when she'd last seen herself. The lines of worry she'd thought permanently etched upon her face had vanished. Her eyes were wide with wonder, her hair gleamed like a golden sun, and her skin had taken on a glow that hadn't been there for a very long time.

"And all of this for a mere twenty-five credits?" she asked her stunned reflection. "There *has* to be a catch."

Dax sat at the desk in his ready room—a desk littered with landing permits, docking fee lists, and star charts. He had work to do, that much was certain, but he wasn't getting it done. He still saw her eyes—eyes that looked up at him the way they would if she'd been lying beneath him while they—

No, he warned himself. Don't go there. She doesn't want you. Dax had seldom imagined what a woman would look like lying naked in his arms, but he was doing it now. Her expression had been different in the corridor outside her room, but he was remembering the one he'd seen on the street in Luxton City. The one that made him purr…

It was Jack's fault, he decided. She'd been pushing him to take a mate for so long; it must've finally had some effect on him, making him do stupid shit like purring at one of his passengers—when they were running from that passenger's crazy, jealous boyfriend, no less.

He leaned back, resting his head in his hands. The tingle in his groin was only a memory now, but if he'd stood there with her a few moments longer, he could only guess at the consequences. He probably wouldn't have been making love with her at that very moment, but it would have been on his mind—which was wrong. That sort of thing was *never* on his mind—at least, not until he'd laid eyes on Ava. But that same mind wasn't behaving the way it normally did. It was leaping from one place to another like a Borellian grasshopper.

Tension knotted his gut as his thoughts jumped to Lars. That uncouth behemoth had been with Ava for five years and had undoubtedly had her many times. That realization sent a river of emotions racing through Dax: hatred, jealousy, envy, and, oddly enough, curiosity. Those big round aquamarine eyes haunted him, tormented him, and tempted him. This should not be happening, and yet it was.

His arms ached to hold her, and his lips longed to kiss her, to taste her… He wanted to know everything about her, from why she wanted to go back to Russ to why her hair flipped up in the back like it did. He'd seen a variety of hairstyles in his travels—many of them downright bizarre—but hers was uniquely appealing, though it might not have been unique among people with webbed fingers. Suddenly, the need to see if her feet were also webbed threatened to overwhelm him. He wanted to discover every intimate detail about her, from the way her hair grew to the way she would feel in his arms—and especially the way she would *smell*...

Dax didn't understand why her scent would have affected him if she wasn't interested, though her mixed blood might have been responsible. Perhaps all Aquerei/Terran women smelled like that. Dax had no way of knowing.

Dax knew he wouldn't sleep, but he wasn't getting any work done anyway, so he went to his quarters. He wasn't even through the door when he focused on the fact that Ava was right there on the other side of the wall—probably already asleep—lying beneath blankets that would bring out the blue in her eyes the moment she opened them. Dax didn't share Trag's aversion to blue. He liked blue very much. Aqua was even better.

As Dax lay down on his bed, his thoughts took another turn. With Ava, he might actually have the chance to be part of a family again. He'd lost his own so long ago, he could barely recall the day that Tarq had found him, alone and crying in the war-torn streets of their doomed homeworld. Tarq had never been able to explain how he'd managed to find Amelyana's ship, though Dax suspected that he'd been led by a vision—which was not uncommon among Zetithians. That the wife of their nemesis would try to save them was something Tarq hadn't known; he only knew that a safe haven awaited them at the end of their journey.

They'd grown up on a fugitive ship, doing all they could to keep their existence a secret in a galaxy where no one could be trusted. Tarq had been like an older brother to him, but while Dax had thrown himself into his studies, Tarq and the other boys had used every opportunity to practice the fine art of enticing Zetithian females. Too serious and abrupt, Dax had never been popular with his female shipmates, and with the boys outnumbering the girls four to one, the ladies could afford to be choosy.

As a boy, Dax had never understood why so few of the refugees were female, but Amelyana had known how picky Zetithian women could be and just how irresistible the men were to females of other species—her own human race being more susceptible than any other. Rescuing more males than females made sense in other ways, as well. Men could father thousands of offspring, but a female could only give birth to a limited number.

After the liberation, he and Tarq had gone their separate ways; Dax opting to roam the galaxy, while Tarq had chosen to remain in the Zetithian colony on Terra Minor, undecided as to his future.

The fact that very few women had ever aroused him caused Dax to doubt the possibility of his ever having a family altogether. But Ava had changed all that, allowing him a faint glimmer of hope. If only he could change her mind…

—∞—

Ava wasn't sleeping either. Her mind had drifted, taking her to a place where, submerged in deep blue water, her head broke through the surface to find Dax waiting for her in the shallows. Droplets of water sparkled on his bare skin, calling attention to every muscle and contour of his body. He was stunningly made, every part of him designed to entice a woman—whether she wanted to be enticed or not. As he waded toward her, his eyes began to glow with desire, and she could hear him purring. She swam into his arms, wrapping her body around his and drawing him inside her. With a low growl, he unleashed the fire of his passion, driving himself in deeper, plumbing the depths of her core in a way no other lover had ever done. Her head fell back as she cried out in rapture, her hands clutching his shoulders as she begged him for more.

And he gave it to her. His mouth came down on hers, devouring her lips, delving inside with his hot tongue while he purred deep within his chest. Breaking the kiss, he went for her throat, licking a fiery path up her neck and back to her lips, whispering words of love and nipping at her skin with his pearly fangs. Ava felt her orgasm building, reaching previous heights, and then going far beyond. His breaths shortened as his own pinnacle was attained, and then she felt a rush of heat and pleasure so exquisite, it brought tears to her eyes.

Stunned, Ava gazed out at the stars as they slid past her window. No fantasy had ever seemed so real. If it had been a dream, she might have understood, but though the aftershocks reverberated throughout her being, she knew that Dax wasn't with her—probably would never be—and her tears of rapture became droplets of sadness and regret.

Lars cast a cursory glance at the doorway as a trio of Aquerei men walked into the bar, immediately making him wish he'd stayed home. He'd never seen this bunch before, but even through the fumes of alcohol he could tell they were looking for him. Having dealt with their kind before, he didn't bother trying to run. One touch from the hairlike tentacles that sprouted from their heads could numb you, and with their iridescent greenish-gold skin and sinister, sloping cheekbones, the mere sight of them was nearly enough to turn a man to stone.

The leader of the group, a tall, elderly man with purple tentacles, approached and said without preamble, "Where is she?"

Lars didn't have to ask who the man was referring to. "Gone," he replied, avoiding the Aquerei's harsh round-eyed glare. "You're too late. A damned Zetithian seduced her right out of here several days ago."

His tentacles sparking with electricity, the man leaned closer to Lars. No doubt about it, the guy was pissed. "Perhaps you didn't understand what was at stake by letting her leave this world before we sent for her."

Lars rolled his eyes. "C'mon, man. I may not be very smart, but what part of 'it's worth more than your life' wouldn't I understand?" He took another swig of his beer. If these guys were intending to kill him, he might as well finish it. "That pretty cat-boy probably gave her a taste of his dick, and that was that. I don't care what drugs you use, nobody can beat out one of those guys when it comes to a woman. Nobody."

"And did you actually *use* the drugs?"

"Did 'til I ran out of them," Lars said with a sardonic laugh. "What the hell did you expect me to do when you creeps dumped me here and then conveniently forgot to pay me again? Did you think the money would last forever? Or did you think I could win her over with my potent male charm?"

"Never that," the Aquerei sneered. "Why Sliv hired you to begin with is beyond me."

"He was desperate, and I was available," Lars said bluntly. "And I didn't do such a bad job. He knew I wasn't her type, but Russ had had enough of the deal. I don't blame him for wanting to be rid of her. She's a real pain in the ass."

The orange-tentacled Aquerei snorted derisively. "The way I heard it, she was more of a headache."

Lars couldn't argue that point and let it drop. "So where is Sliv, anyway?"

"Dead—like you're going to be if you don't tell us where she is."

Though the man seemed anxious to make good on his threat, Lars chose to ignore it. "That's what I told Ava—didn't know for sure, but figured he must be, or I'd have heard from him before now." He paused and took a deep breath. "Look, if you're gonna kill me anyway, just shut the fuck up and do it. I'm sick of your shit."

"Tell us where she went, and we might let you live."

Lars began chuckling uncontrollably. "Guess I'm a dead man then—and as you know, dead men don't talk."

The elder Aquerei was hissing now. He was so close that Lars could almost feel the sting of his tentacles. "Where *is* she?"

"I don't know," Lars insisted. "She said she was going to Aquerei to find her father, but she could have been lying. Like I said, the guy was a Zetithian. Once he got hold of her, she probably forgot all about trying to find her old man. I chased them down to the whoring district, and then they stunned me. Where they went after that is anyone's guess."

"There aren't many Zetithians left, Eantle," their green-haired cohort murmured. "Shouldn't be too hard to narrow it down."

Eantle nodded. Focusing his attention on Lars once more, he went on. "Was he alone? Do you have a name—a description, perhaps?"

"Ask the bartender," Lars said with a shrug. "He might know him. I'd never seen him before. Tall guy—and I mean *really* tall—with black dreadlocks and a flame tattoo up the side of his face and neck. Had a Norludian with him—and he seemed to know Jack Tshevnoe pretty well."

Eantle's tentacles stopped crackling and fell into a smooth wave. Lars's next thought was that he might not die after all. "We'll find them."

Some particle of affection for Ava surfaced briefly. "Hey… when you do find her, what will you do with her?"

"Why, make her our queen, of course," Eantle said with a smile. "After all, we're the good guys—didn't you know?"

Lars sucked in a ragged breath as the trio turned and left as quickly as they'd come. "Sure couldn't prove it by me," he muttered to himself. He drained the last of his beer and waved at the waitress; he thought her name was Lrantee or something like that. "I'll have another."

Lrantee grinned and waved back at him. Her colorful dress swept the floor as she walked back to the tap. Lars liked the way she moved, and she wasn't bad-looking either—for a Twilanan. Plenty of people thought they were hideous, but Lars found something oddly appealing about the tusk on the end of her snout.

Chapter 5

HAVING SPENT THE PREVIOUS NIGHT FANTASIZING ABOUT Dax, Ava found it difficult to face her shipmates the next morning. She wanted to breakfast alone even less. Kots would have brought it to her in her room—she had only to ask—but when the summons came over the ship's comsystem, she obeyed. Of course, the fact that is was Dax's voice might have had something to do with it.

Probably a recorded message—not actually him speaking to her from out of nowhere—but she responded to it as though he had personally requested her presence; instinctively, automatically, and without any thought whatsoever.

"What *is* it about him?" she muttered as she reluctantly removed the lovely blue gown. Opening the closet, she let out a startled gasp.

There was only one outfit hanging there. It would probably fit her perfectly, but it wasn't hers. Every article of clothing she possessed had disappeared, as if by magic. She remembered what Dax had said about knowing a magician and wondered if that person just happened to be aboard the ship, hidden somewhere apart from the others, working his or her sorcery on the rest of them.

Whoever that magician was, they didn't know anything about her taste in clothes. The clingy, hip-length tunic was feminine and romantic, and its pastel aquamarine color a far cry from her usual grays and forest greens. The only colorful clothing she possessed was the red shirt her waitressing job required, and it, too, was gone. She suspected that Kots, rather than any magician, was responsible. He must have hovered in silently during the night and made the switch. But why? What did he care about her wardrobe?

Dax certainly wouldn't have ordered it. A man who wasn't interested in women wouldn't bother to tell the droid to give her something different to wear, would he?

The answer came without any further bidding: Waroun. It must be his doing, not Dax's. Dax wouldn't give a damn. Waroun was another story.

Chuckling softly, Ava shook her head and donned the tunic along with the black tights hanging next to it. Her shoes were also missing; in their stead sat a pair of satin slippers that matched the tunic. Also a perfect fit. After a quick glance in the mirror, she left the room and followed the discreetly flashing arrows along the corridor to the dining hall.

Upon her arrival, she began to suspect that the ship itself, and therefore the droid that served it, was responsible for her new look, rather than its crew. No ship as luxurious as the *Valorcry* would allow a sloppily dressed girl to breakfast in such a room. Soft music played while crystal chandeliers glittered overhead. The tables were draped with snowy cloths set with crystal, china, and utensils with the unmistakable gleam of pure silver.

Ava wasn't sure how it was possible, but even the two Kitnocks looked as if they belonged there, and Quinn was quite dazzling—for a Drell. His hair, which was now a few shades lighter, cascaded to his feet in shiny waves that drew the eye rather than repulsed it.

Waroun and Dax, on the other hand, looked pretty much the same.

Seeing that they were all seated at the same round table, Ava took the only available place, which just happened to be between Dax and Waroun. It was either sit there or be terribly rude and choose another table altogether.

"I see Kots has been working on you too," Waroun remarked. "It's always interesting to see what he thinks our guests should wear while they're aboard. I approve of his choice."

While this answered at least two of her questions, Ava wasn't sure she cared whether Waroun approved or not. Somehow having him *disapprove* might have been best.

Dax didn't voice any opinion whatsoever. "Don't worry, Kots will give your things back to you when you get to Rutara. He likes to make sure all of our passengers comply with his own version of the dress code. Everyone usually gets a kick out of it."

Ava wasn't sure "kick" was the right word. "It's okay," she said, staring down at her lap as she placed her napkin there. She was finding it difficult to sit next to him after the fantasy she'd had the night before. The fact that she could feel his body heat through the thin fabric of her tunic was bad enough. Gazing into his eyes was out of the question.

Still, she couldn't help but wonder how they would glow if she were to ever make love to him. Unfortunately, there was only one way to find out, and that would be extremely unlikely.

Kots brought breakfast in silver servers and set each of their plates before them, though Ava knew she had never placed an order.

"Fish for breakfast?" Waroun commented when Kots lifted the cover from her dish.

"Sure," she replied, relieved that she hadn't received anyone else's meal by mistake. The Kitnocks were eating porridge, but Quinn's plate was piled high with crackers, neither of which appealed to her in the slightest. Waroun had a bowl of berries that he was picking up one at a time by tapping them with a fingertip and popping them into his mouth. She wasn't sure about Dax's breakfast; it looked like ice cream, though it didn't appear to be melting.

Her fish was just the way she liked it: hot, buttery, and very fresh, the flakes practically melting in her mouth. Her goblet was filled with water again, but this time she watched as Kots poured it from what appeared to be a wine bottle.

"Aquerei water?" she read aloud from the label. "Really?"

Kots chirped in reply.

"Wonder where he got that?" Waroun said as he savored another berry.

"Who knows?" Dax replied. "There's quite a store of things in the hold. One of these days I'll have to figure out how to reprogram him with less expensive tastes."

Ava had been reaching for the glass but thought perhaps she'd better not. "Should I not drink it? I mean, if it costs that much…"

"Don't worry about it," Dax said. "Like I said, it's probably been in the hold for years. I'm sure Kots is tickled to death to have an Aquerei to serve it to."

"He's a very smart shopper," Waroun put in. "Nearly always gets a discount."

"My father was from Aquerei, but I've never had Aquerei water before." Ava took a sip. "I didn't even know there was such a thing, though it's probably out of my price range anyway."

"It seems to agree with you," Teke said from across the table. "You should see what it's doing to your hair."

"My hair?" she echoed in dismay. "Why? What's happening to it?"

"It's getting prettier," Dax said. "And it sort of ripples. Your skin looks brighter too."

Ava didn't know Dax very well, but his voice sounded odd to her—as though his throat was tight and he was having trouble getting his words out. Glancing sideways at him—and she promised herself it would only be a glance—their eyes met. He leaned back in his chair as he stared at her, but something in his expression held her captive, refusing to allow her to turn away. It didn't take much for her to imagine the man he'd been in her fantasy—a sexy, aroused beast who took her places she'd never been before. His gaze penetrated, his lips beckoned, and just the way he was sitting promised that he was everything she imagined he would be—and more.

———※———

Dax had no idea how long he'd sat there drinking in the sight of Ava's amazing eyes until Waroun spoke up. "Well, would you look at that," he said with a chuckle. "I think the Great Virgin is finally hooked."

With a little more provocation, Dax would have been sorely tempted to kill the Norludian as Ava, the spell now broken, spun around to face Waroun. "What?"

"Look at him! And listen… He's—oh my God, he's fuckin' purring!"

"I am not!" Dax insisted, but even he could hear the vibration in his voice.

"You are too!" Waroun shot back with a crow of laughter. "I can't believe it!"

Dax could believe it, because whether he wanted to admit it or not, his damned cock was getting hard again. He'd just gotten a whiff of her scent before Waroun had to go and ruin everything by distracting her.

Well, maybe he hadn't ruined *everything*. Perhaps it was for the best…

"Too bad he always wears those baggy trousers," Waroun went on. "With tighter pants, we could tell if his dick was hard."

Dax felt his face getting hot and noticed that Ava was blushing as well. "Shut up, Waroun," he growled.

Waroun held up a hand in protest. "I only speak the truth: When a Zetithian purrs, it usually means something sexual." In an aside to Ava, he added, "Just thought you should know that." At this point Dax was ready to throttle Waroun, but short of actual murder, there was no stopping him. "Now, if you smell right to him, his sex organ will get hard. I'd love to know if it's finally happened." Sampling another berry, he chewed it thoughtfully before adding, "Not sure it ever has."

Ava was stunned speechless, but Quinn came to everyone's rescue by choking on one of his crackers.

Teke got to his feet and thumped the Drell on the back, which sent the bit of cracker flying across the table to land on the edge of Ava's plate. "Perhaps this isn't the best topic for our first meal together," he said with a weak smile.

"Yes," Diokut agreed. "We should know each other better before discussing sexual matters at breakfast."

"Not sure we'll ever know each other *that* well." Ava flicked the cracker crumb from her plate. "But I suppose discussing the weather is out of the question."

Quinn was breathing easily again, so Teke sat back down and picked up his spoon. "On our world, such things are more *private*," he said with a remonstrative glance at Waroun.

"Not on my world," Waroun said gaily. "We talk about sex all the time… Matter-of-fact, it's just about the only thing we *do* talk about. The weather is always pretty much the same."

"Always raining or always dry?" Ava asked.

Waroun considered this for a moment. "Well, I guess it does change a little. But since it rains almost every day, it's pretty boring. The only thing to discuss is when it starts and stops, and you can tell that by looking out a window. Sex, on the other hand, is endlessly fascinating."

Something in the way he said it must have struck Ava as being hysterically funny, for she let out a peal of laughter that almost had Dax purring again. He was beginning to consider taking all of his meals in his ready room when, thankfully, Teke attempted to take control of the conversation.

"So, Ava," he began. "Is that your full name?"

"No." Her flippy blond hair swayed back and forth as she shook her head. "It's Avondia Karon."

"Lovely name," Teke said with a nod of approval. "Has a nice ring to it."

"The last name is French—at least, the pronunciation is French," she said, frowning. "Not sure about Avondia."

"Better than *his* name." Waroun snickered with a quick nod toward Dax. "Daxtronian Vandilorsk. Sounds like a fatal disease, doesn't it?"

"It's a perfectly good Zetithian name," Ava said. "I've heard a few others. They all sound like that."

"Yes, but would you be willing to tack it on to the end of *your* name?"

As suggestions went, it wasn't very subtle. Waroun was beginning to sound like Jack—goading Dax into liaisons with women he didn't want. Unfortunately, this was the one woman he really *did* want…

"Ava Vandilorsk," she said, trying it out. "It wouldn't be so bad."

"Too many Vs," Waroun said. "Lots of species can't make the V sound." With another snicker, he added, "You'd be Awa Wandilorsk half the time."

Dax was about to say it was a moot point, since Ava would never be faced with such a dilemma, but something told him he was better off keeping his mouth shut. Her next comment proved it.

"I could live with that," she said with a shrug. "I've heard a lot worse."

With that, she went back to eating her breakfast. Dax was already finished with his—partly because he hadn't needed to chew it, but also because the warm, creamy texture had kept him going, thinking that she would feel like that in his mouth if he ever—*oh, God*. He winced as he realized that not only was Waroun trying to fix him up with Ava, but Kots was doing his best as well: making her drink water that made her glow and giving her clothes that matched her eyes—not to mention giving him Sholerian cream for breakfast. It was a conspiracy against him. Or *for* him—he wasn't sure which—but he disliked being manipulated above all things.

"I wouldn't worry too much about it," Dax said. "I mean, you should be more concerned with how your name would sound with Russ's surname, shouldn't you?"

"Russ?" she echoed with a puzzled look. "Oh, yeah, right… Russ. His last name is Tucker."

"Ava Tucker," Teke said. "Sounds quite ordinary. I prefer the Zetithian's name."

"What's your full name, Teke?" Dax said, attempting to divert whatever was going on to something a little less sensitive.

"Just Teke," he replied. "We Kitnocks only have the one name."

"I see," said Dax. Not much conversation to be had from that.

Quinn nodded vigorously. "Drells, too."

"Must be hard to find each other in the phone book," Ava commented.

"Not really," said Quinn. "We don't have phones."

"Ah." Ava nodded and went back to eating her fish.

Dax just needed a break. As captain and pilot, he had plenty of excuses not to hang out with his passengers, though if truth be told, once Waroun set the course, the ship pretty much flew itself. The scanners looked ahead and altered the heading if there happened to be any debris in their path, otherwise, flying through empty space was pretty uneventful. It was trickier inside a solar system, where Dax's piloting skills were required.

Getting to his feet, Dax told Waroun to play the ship's

orientation video for the passengers before making a quick exit. Safe in the captain's ready room, he plopped down on his couch and tried to make sense of it all—his reaction to Ava in particular.

Dax had always avoided Jack's insistence that he mate and produce offspring for more reasons than he had given her. It wasn't the first time he'd had an erection, but it was uncommon. If it hadn't been for the others, Dax would have suspected there was something physically wrong with him. Ava had done it to him twice now. Obviously it had simply been a matter of finding the right woman—the right *available* woman.

But what did you do once you found her? Dax's basic sexual education had concentrated on Zetithian females, and there was a definite protocol for that—all sorts of carefully designed ways to get one to allow you to mate with her. Though he knew that human women weren't quite as particular, never having put that knowledge to use, Dax had forgotten much of what he'd been taught.

Maybe if he could get Ava alone and just talk to her, he might be able to figure it out—though after all the yapping Waroun had done at breakfast, she would probably avoid him from now on. Dax had been keeping women at arm's length for so long, getting her *into* his arms was going to be tough, especially if she wasn't interested—and might even be a little afraid of him. He'd seen the dismay on her face when she came into the dining hall and saw where she would have to sit.

Still, it would take a long time to get to Rutara—especially if they took on more passengers at one of the stops along the way. This would give Dax plenty of time to get to know her, perhaps even to entice her. One big problem with that: He had absolutely no idea how to do it.

Dax felt like his head was about to explode. He pulled the ball Jack had given him long ago out of one of his pockets. She'd called it a baseball and had once told him that he had an arm good enough to play for the Yankees—whatever *that* meant. He lay flat on his back, throwing the ball at the ceiling and catching it. Over and over and over again, until the monotony of it had reset his thoughts to a more manageable level.

He wasn't the first man to be clueless when it came to getting a woman. He wouldn't be the last. Sure, he'd probably make mistakes, but women were forgiving creatures, weren't they? After all, Ava had stayed with a guy who beat her up—and she'd had to hit him over the head too. She must have forgiven Lars for lots of things during their time together. Dax knew he was a better man than Lars, though that wasn't saying a whole helluva lot.

Russ was the one he had to worry about—the "good" man she was going back to—the man who claimed to love her and was willing to wait for her. The man Dax was beginning to wish was a cad, or a lying, inconsiderate sonofabitch who had only said that to make her suffer. She'd been wrong about Lars, so perhaps she was wrong about Russ. Unfortunately, the best he could hope for was that Russ had finally given up and found another woman.

If only he could be that lucky…

Chapter 6

AFTER VIEWING THE ORIENTATION VIDEO, AVA LINGERED at the breakfast table until everyone else finally drifted off to other parts of the ship—and there were certainly plenty of places to go. There was a game room, an exercise room, a full spa and beauty salon staffed by droids—she could get a makeover if she wanted—and the list of available movies and other interactive entertainments was lengthy. The *Valorcry* also boasted a small swimming pool and a live botanical garden on the lower deck, not to mention the numerous places of interest that were available for virtual tours. She and the other passengers had each been given a library module that claimed to have every book ever written imbedded in its memory, in addition to every piece of music ever recorded. Ava had never seen—or heard of—anything like it.

So far, everyone, with the possible exception of Waroun, had been very pleasant, but Ava had been sorry to see Dax leave her alone with the others. He was the closest thing to her own species, but it didn't look like he'd be hanging around much, especially after what Waroun had said. She'd seen him blush at the frank discussion of his sexuality—or lack thereof. He'd probably be too embarrassed to look her in the eye again.

She wondered how true Waroun's comments were. Ava couldn't imagine a man of Dax's age and physical attractiveness being as sexually naïve as Waroun suggested; somehow it didn't fit with the bad-boy image he seemed to be cultivating—though looking tough might have been an advantage, considering some of the shadier worlds he seemed to frequent, and his brusque manner might have been adopted to keep the unscrupulous from taking advantage of him.

Like she undoubtedly was. Twenty-five credits was a joke for passage to Rutara on a ship like the *Valorcry*. Hell, most ship owners would charge you that much for a tour of their vessel. She really needed to talk to him about that.

Kots hovered in to refill her water glass—again with Aquerei water—before she even registered the fact that she was getting thirsty.

"Maybe you should give me plain water from now on," she said to the droid. Aside from the fact that it didn't have the same effect on her, it was certain to be less expensive. "And you can give me back my own clothes. These are very nice, but—"

Kots cut her off with a loud buzz.

"That means no," Dax said as he entered the room. "You wanted to talk to me?"

Ava frowned. "Yes, I did, but how you could possibly know that is—"

"I got a message from Kots."

"He sends you messages?"

Dax nodded. "Through the ship's computer. Kots has a direct link."

"Yes, but I didn't tell him—or the computer—that I wanted to talk to you."

"Kots knows a lot of things he shouldn't know," Dax said. "Like what you want for breakfast. He's attuned to things the passengers want and does his best to provide them. Sometimes his methods are questionable, but usually quite interesting."

"So I've noticed," she said with a smile.

Dax didn't smile back. "You can tell him what you want to eat, but the dress code isn't negotiable. He considers this to be my uniform, or I'm sure he'd try to make me wear something else." He fixed a sharp gaze on her that wasn't the least bit shy and was quite intimidating, coming from someone of his stature. "Now, what was it you wanted?"

So much for being embarrassed. The breakfast table conversation might never have taken place—either that, or he was in no mood for personal questions and was making it clear by his tone.

"I, um, think maybe I'm not paying you enough," Ava began. Braving his scowl, she added, "Passage on a ship like this should cost a whole lot more than I've got. I can't help but think there's a catch—"

"This is the third time you've asked me that." His frown made his already slanted eyebrows appear almost vertical. "I've told you before there *is* no catch. I charge based on a passenger's ability to pay. For you, twenty-five credits is the price." His eyes narrowed. "I thought we were clear on that."

This wasn't going the way Ava expected. Wanting to pay him more shouldn't make him angry, but she half expected him to start snarling at her. "I know, but that was before I'd seen the ship and knew about all of the… amenities. I feel like I'm taking advantage of you."

"Well, you're not," he snapped. "Is there anything else?"

"N-no," she replied. "Sorry I bothered you."

"It's not your fault. Kots should learn to mind his own business." With that parting shot, he turned on his heel and left.

"Remind me not to ask *him* any more questions," Ava said under her breath.

Unfortunately, Kots heard her and beeped once.

"Stay out of it, Kots. Just stay the hell out of it."

The droid replied with a low mumble and floated out of the dining room. Ava headed off to the movie theater, having a sudden urge to watch a good murder mystery— preferably one in which the victim was a man.

So much for trying to entice her. Dax had been startled by the summons and then irritated that he'd been disturbed. On top of that, it turned out to be Ava who wanted to see him, and he'd been just as abrupt with her as he would have been with any woman. She hadn't helped matters by questioning his integrity, either. Was there a catch, she'd asked. Of course there wasn't a catch! He'd given her his price, and she'd agreed to it. Why did she have to keep harping on it? Suggesting that there might be more to the deal was insinuating that he would try to cheat her out of what little money she had—or take advantage of her position as the lone female aboard his ship.

Which he would not do.

She hadn't aroused him at all this time, and he'd been looking squarely into her pretty aquamarine eyes. It was a fluke, he decided. No point in carrying it any further. His earlier intention to entice her was a mistake.

He'd acted the same way he always did with women—especially the pretty ones—adopting an abrupt, no-nonsense manner with them before they got the wrong idea. He'd been told many times that he was rude. He didn't intend to be; it was just the best way to get them to leave him alone.

But, he reminded himself, he didn't want this one to leave him alone.

Asking Jack for advice was out of the question. He'd never be able to tolerate the "I told you so" attitude she was bound to take with him. Well, maybe she wouldn't, but he wouldn't give her the satisfaction. There was someone else he could ask, though. Threldigan. Yes, he would be perfect. He could talk a woman into giving him her firstborn male child and make her think it was her idea. Dax had never paid attention to the technique; he just knew that anytime the two men had been together, though a woman might notice Dax first, he was never the one she spent the night with.

That's because you never ask them.

Dax had never asked a woman out for lunch, let alone anything more intimate. Zetithian men were purported to be the hottest lovers in existence, and ever since the refugee ship had landed on Terra Minor, the word had spread like wildfire: *These guys are so hot that some asshole blew up their planet just because his wife took one as a lover.* The fact that it was true hadn't hurt the story any; Zetithian men *were* some of the best the galaxy had to offer—of the mammalian species, that is.

Except for Dax. Maybe if that reputation hadn't preceded him, he might have taken a chance, but with every woman he met expecting fireworks, he didn't bother to try.

When he'd been on the refugee ship with nothing but Zetithian women, he'd known they were difficult to entice and just figured he wasn't any good at it. He'd picked up the scent of their desire once or twice when the other guys purred and knew his body could respond, but he was never the one they were interested in. Since he'd gotten his own ship and traveled the galaxy, he'd met loads of women who thought he was the sexiest thing alive, but he'd yet to meet any non-Zetithian women who did it for him. Except Ava.

With a heavy sigh, he sent out a hail to Threldigan. He just hoped it wouldn't backfire on him.

~~~

Halfway through the movie she'd chosen, Ava was regretting her choice. The woman in the story was downright evil, and the man had been her unfortunate, if clueless, victim, which wasn't the scenario she'd had in mind at all. She scanned the archives and wound up watching a slapstick comedy that at least made her laugh. What to do next was a dilemma of sorts, but the makeover thing was sounding better all the time. If she was drop-dead gorgeous, Dax might at least be civil with her.

It doesn't matter whether he's nice to me or not. I'm going back to Russ. Remember Russ? The man who said he'd love you forever?

But he'd never made her melt, and he'd never purred, either…

The chime sounded, calling the passengers to lunch. When Ava arrived at the dining hall, the others were already seated and Dax was waiting just outside the door.

His pathetic attempt to smile at her was more a baring of his fangs than a genuine grin, and he rattled off, "I'm sorry if I was rude earlier. It won't happen again," all in one breath.

Ava couldn't help but laugh. "Feel better now?"

His openmouthed expression made her want to laugh even more, but this time she managed to suppress it.

"I—that was an apology." He sounded every bit as bewildered as he looked. "It was supposed to make *you* feel better."

"Is that what it was? I wasn't quite sure…"

Frowning, he gestured for her to precede him into the dining room.

"So, did everyone have a pleasant morning?" Waroun asked as Ava took her seat. They were at a larger table this time, which gave Ava the opportunity to sit between either Dax and Waroun or Dax and Quinn. She chose the former. Better the enemy you know…

Teke and Diokut were chattering away about the fabulous gardens. "I could spend hours in there, just breathing in the scent of the flowers," Diokut declared.

"I watched a movie," Ava said, carefully avoiding looking at Dax.

"We had no idea this was going to be such a luxurious ship," Teke said to Dax. "The price was so reasonable, we never expected…"

"There's no catch," Ava blurted out before Dax could respond. "Don't bother asking…" Her voice trailed off as she stared down at her lap. She seemed to be doing a lot of that.

Teke ignored Ava's remark. "As I understand it, this ship was given to you in a settlement?"

Dax nodded.

"What did you do before that?"

Dax shrugged. "Nothing."

"Nothing? But how could that be?"

"He was on a refugee ship from the time he was two years old," Waroun said. "Twenty-five years in space— give or take a few months—and never landed until a few years ago."

"I see," said Teke. "My, how… *confining* that sounds."

"It was," Dax said shortly, making it obvious that he'd rather not discuss his past.

"Like being in prison, I would think," Diokut put in.

Teke nodded in agreement. "But surely you had duties while aboard it. You were educated, I presume?"

"I learned everything they taught me," Dax replied. "Including how to fly the ship."

"Ah, then that explains it."

"Explains what?"

"How so young a man could have acquired such enormous wealth."

Dax appeared relieved, as though he'd expected Teke to say something different. Ava wondered why.

Then it hit her. This guy had been stuck on a ship full of refugees for most of his life. He might have been capable of piloting a starship and was probably very well-educated, but having lived a sheltered and regimented existence, he was bound to be socially backward. That brusque attitude of his was a cover for something… insecurity, perhaps?

"Were any of your own family aboard?" Ava asked gently.

"No," Dax replied. "I was the only one left."

Kots floated in with a tray, from which he distributed the plates. The aroma of vegetable soup wafted through the air as he served it to the Kitnocks. Waroun was given a bowl of peaches. Ava had a submarine sandwich and a big kosher dill pickle, and Quinn had crackers again. Dax took one look at the dish Kots set in front of him and put it back on the tray.

"That's not what I asked for," he told Kots.

Obviously prepared for this event, Kots made no sound, merely replacing the dish with a bowl of stew along with a small loaf of freshly baked bread.

"That's better," Dax said.

As Kots filled Ava's glass with root beer, curiosity got the better of her. "What was he trying to give you?"

"More Sholerian cream," he replied. "I had that for breakfast."

"Something you're craving, perhaps?" Waroun said with a smirk.

"Can I try it?" Ava asked. "It looks like a dessert we had on Rutara—a Terran dish called ice cream."

Dax opened his mouth as if to protest but snapped it shut as Kots set the bowl down next to Ava's sandwich. Kots beeped twice and left the room in the droid equivalent of a huff.

Ava scooped up a spoonful of what may have looked like vanilla ice cream but tasted like nothing like it. It was mildly sweet, but warm, rather than cold, and as the cream slid across her tongue, it set off a flavor explosion for which she was totally unprepared. It even made her nipples tingle.

"Can you understand why Kots thinks he needs that?" Waroun said wickedly.

"Obviously he wants him to feel good," Ava gasped. "I've never tasted anything like it!"

"It's a rare and expensive delicacy," Dax said shortly. "Not something I should be eating."

"Why not?" Ava asked.

"I'm not one of the passengers."

Ava didn't think this made any sense at all, but Dax's shuttered expression kept her from saying so. "A little of it would go a long way," she said. "But I'm not surprised you'd want something more substantial."

Waroun cackled but made no further comment.

Ava tackled her sandwich again, and nobody said much for a while.

"Where will we be stopping first?" Quinn asked, breaking the silence. "You never said."

"Not sure," Dax replied. "We'll probably pick up a few more passengers before we drop anyone off."

Dax's voice echoed through Ava's skull, sending out long feathers of warmth to tickle her erogenous zones. Swallowing with some difficulty, she glanced over at him, hoping to discover the reason.

Her mouth watered at the sight of him, and it was all she could do to keep from grabbing him by the hair and dragging him into her lap. The answer to her unspoken question came to her instantly. *No wonder that cream is so expensive! It's an aphrodisiac!* Doing her best to ignore the overwhelming urge to pounce on him, she ate a bite of her pickle instead, which helped some, but she still couldn't take her eyes off Dax.

"Hey, Dax," Waroun said from somewhere to her left. "These peaches smell really good. Here, take a whiff."

Dax turned to face Waroun and drew in a deep breath

to say something, but the words never came out as his gaze fastened on Ava. His eyes widened as he sucked in another lungful of air. For a moment, he looked like he was going to have a full-blown panic attack, but against all odds, he began purring instead.

If Ava had melted from looking into Dax's eyes once before, this time she was evaporating. She was vaguely aware of conversation between the others but had no idea what they were saying. His glowing, catlike eyes mesmerized her, and his purring drowned out every other sound.

Except for that incessant beeping. "What *is* that?" Ava said distractedly as Kots returned.

"It's a hail coming in," Waroun replied. "Priority message for you-know-who."

"I'll take it in my ready room," Dax told Kots, who was prodding him with a spoon.

Ava gazed longingly at Dax's back as he strode from the dining hall. *I had one bite of that stuff. Imagine what would happen if I ate a whole bowlful of it!* Someone should have warned her—Dax, if no one else—but none of them had said a word about the possible effect. Perhaps it was something that only affected Terrans or Aquereis, and the others didn't know it for what it was. It couldn't possibly have had the same effect on Dax; after all, he'd eaten a full serving and hadn't—

Then she remembered. He'd been staring at her like that at breakfast—purring, too. And then there was Waroun's comment about the Great Virgin being hooked. Maybe it *did* work on him, though surely not to the same extent, because if it did, Dax must have had the mental equivalent of a cast-iron chastity belt on his libido.

Now that Dax had found Ava and knew what she could do to him, it had taken every ounce of his willpower not to ravish her right there on the table. A woman had once teased him that when it finally happened, he was going to fall like a ton of bricks. By God, she was right. It had begun almost at first sight, and though the Sholerian cream probably helped a little, his cock was so hard it hurt, and his coronal fluid was already soaking into his pants. Her scent was beginning to fade, and his erection along with it, but if his mind hadn't been in such turmoil, he'd have done a little happy dance right there in the passageway.

She wanted him! He was sure of it now. Ava had to have felt some desire for him, or he wouldn't have smelled it on her—and the fact that she hadn't aroused him when she'd spoken with him earlier disproved the Terran/Aquerei mixed-blood theory. The Sholerian cream probably wasn't responsible either, because there hadn't been any aphrodisiacs involved when he'd gazed into her eyes out on the street in Luxton City. Yeah. She wanted him—wasn't acting like she did, but scents didn't lie.

Dax ran the rest of the way to the bridge, hoping the message was from Threldigan. He *really* needed some advice now.

Threldigan's handsome, dark-skinned face filled the viewscreen as he leaned forward to adjust the settings. "What's new, pussycat?"

"How many times do I have to tell you not to call me that?" Dax shot back.

"A few more," Threldigan said with a chuckle. "I don't hear from you in ages, and now, all of a sudden, I get this urgent hail. What's going on? You need more of my gadgets?"

"No, I've got plenty of those."

"Well, then," Threldigan said wisely, "you must be having woman trouble."

"Sort of," Dax began, not bothering to dissemble. "You see, I've finally found one I want, but I'm not sure what to do next."

"What are you worried about? Women practically fall at your feet!"

"Not this time, Threld. In fact, I'm not even sure she likes me—thinks I'm trying to cheat her or something."

"Imagine that," Threldigan said dryly. "Knowing how charming you can be…"

"Very funny," Dax grumbled. "I don't need sarcasm, I need pointers."

"On how to charm a woman?"

"Yeah, something like that."

"You've seen me do it a hundred times. Weren't you paying attention?"

"Well, no. I wasn't," Dax admitted. "To be honest, I never thought I'd need it."

"My God, this is funny!" Threldigan chortled. "They crawl all over you and you ignore them, and then the one you finally want ignores you!"

"I'm not sure she's *ignoring* me," Dax said after giving it some thought. "It's just that she's had some bad experiences with her last boyfriend, and she wants to go back to the man she left behind on Rutara. Says he was a good man and she shouldn't have left him."

"Which means she wouldn't want a reprobate like you?"

"I'm not a reprobate!" Dax exclaimed. "Why would you say that?"

Threldigan regarded him with a raised brow. "You're certainly trying to look the part—and you act it sometimes. I've seen you with women. You tell them all sorts of horror stories to get rid of them. It could be that your reputation has come back to haunt you, my friend."

"I've never told anyone any horror stories! I just tell them that if they want me, they have to do Waroun first."

"And if that's not a horror story, I've never heard one," Threldigan replied. "You make your bed and you lie in it…"

"So, what do I do now?"

"I think you'd better come and pick me up." Threldigan shook his head. "It's time I moved on anyway. I've always had a hankering to visit Rutara. Perhaps I should come along for the ride."

"Where are you?"

"Rhylos," Threldigan replied with a barely suppressed smile.

Dax winced. Rhylos had the virtue of being in a nearby star system, but that was about the only advantage to Threldigan being on that particular planet. "Think you could meet me at the spaceport?"

Threldigan threw back his head, laughing. "What's the matter? Afraid those two Davordian hookers still want your head on a platter—or, should I say, your dick?"

"As I recall, it was my balls they were after," Dax

said ruefully. "The only girls who ever took me up on the deal."

"Yeah, they fucked Waroun, and you still wouldn't do them."

"I never said I *would*, just that if I ever *was* to do it, they had to do Waroun first."

Threldigan grinned. "They were really pissed."

"Tell me about it." The two women had come after him with knives, swearing they'd castrate him if they ever caught up with him. Fortunately, Dax had been able to outrun them and had since made a point of never staying on Rhylos for very long, nor did he advertise his visits. "Waroun was pleased, though. He still talks about it."

"I'll bet he does. How soon can you get here?"

"In about… twenty-nine standard hours," Dax replied, consulting his charts. "We're not far from there, and it's on the way."

"How fortunate," Threldigan said pleasantly. "Should I spread the news?"

Dax gave him a sickly smile. "Not if you ever want to hitch a ride with me again."

"I won't say a word," Threldigan promised. "But you know how unscrupulous those spaceport officials can be."

"I'll wear body armor."

"You do that," Threldigan said. "I'll be waiting for your hail. In the meantime, don't do anything stupid to alienate this woman. You *know* how you are."

Dax sighed. "Yeah, I know. See you soon."

Dax terminated the link and leaned back in his chair. This could either be the best idea he'd ever had or one of the worst. Time would tell…

—◇◇◇—

"If she's on Rutara," Vandig reported, "no one has seen her. Her mother hasn't heard from her in six months, and Russ, well, he's very happy without her. Said she had a bit of a temper."

Eantle chuckled softly. Apparently Sliv's daughter was a lot like her dad. Easy enough to get along with most of the time, but *sometimes*… Eantle missed his old friend—had dreamed of watching the New Age begin at his side, but since that wasn't meant to be, it was up to him to see to it that Sliv's death hadn't been in vain.

"The port authority had him taking off with two Kitnocks and a Drell," Vandig went on, "but the ship hasn't landed on those worlds either."

"They haven't had much time," Eantle mused. "And he could easily have made a side trip to pick up someone else. It's probably worth checking out the surrounding systems, just in case."

"You make it sound like there are millions of us out there looking," Vandig said with a snort.

"True, but they apparently aren't trying to hide, either. That Dax Vandilorsk—the best I can tell, he might take you anywhere you want to go, no questions asked, but he's always followed the regulations and files a flight plan. He was going to the Kitnock and Drell homeworlds, and then on to Rutara. No mention of Aquerei."

"Which would've saved us a lot of trouble. She must've changed her mind."

Eantle thought for a moment before making a decision.

"Keep someone in the spaceport of all of those worlds. They've got to go somewhere."

"What about Rhylos? It's not far from Luxaria."

"Put someone there too. We'll find them."

Chapter 7

HAVING NO INTENTION OF LOSING HIS BALLS JUST WHEN HE might have found a use for them, Dax figured he'd send Waroun to meet Threldigan when the time came. He was on his way back to his quarters when he passed Waroun, who, not surprisingly, was thrilled at the prospect.

"I'll reset the course to Rhylos right away," Waroun said. Sighing, he licked his lips. "I can still taste those Davordian girls. Do you think you could—?"

"Absolutely not." Dax knew precisely what Waroun had in mind. "I'm not going anywhere near that brothel. If you want to look them up, you have my blessing, but something tells me they might go after your nuts too."

"If they can find them," Waroun said with a smirk.

The location of Waroun's gonads wasn't obvious to the casual observer, and though it wasn't information Dax had ever sought, he was well-versed in Norludian anatomy—an unfortunate hazard of spending time with one of the more garrulous members of the species. "They may find slitting your throat appealing," he warned. "I wouldn't risk it if I were you."

"Well, you aren't me, are you? The single most perfect moment of my life—until you had to go and blow it by getting nasty."

"I wasn't nasty," Dax protested. "I simply said I wasn't interested in any woman who'd just finished with someone else."

Waroun rolled his bulbous eyes. "Which is to say all hookers. You know what they say about a woman scorned. For the love of Leon, couldn't you have just lied and said your dick was broken?"

Dax could have used this excuse, though technically it wouldn't have been a lie. Davordians had never smelled right to him and therefore... "Just forget it, Waroun. We've been over this a million times. I'm sick of it."

"You always say that," Waroun grumbled. "So where does Threldy want to go?"

"Rutara," Dax replied.

"Well, now, isn't *that* convenient?"

"Sarcasm doesn't become you, Waroun."

"Nothing becomes a Norludian. Why do you think no one likes us?"

"Because you're weird little—"

"Don't get personal, now," Waroun said, cutting him off. "We can't help it if—oh, hel-*lo, Ava*." His voice was now soft as silk. "How *are* you this afternoon? Is there anything we can help you with?"

Dax spun around so quickly that Ava slammed right into him. He caught her in his arms and took a deep breath. Her intoxicating scent raced to his groin at the speed of light.

"Sorry," she gasped, backing away from his embrace. "I was just going to my quarters to..."

"Lie down for a while?" Waroun finished for her. "You *do* look tired. Busy day so far?"

"No, I just—"

"Didn't sleep well last night?" Waroun suggested.

"Uh, yeah, that's it," she said with a nod. "Too excited about the trip, I suppose."

"That'll do it," Waroun agreed. "You go right ahead and take a nice, long nap. I'll wake you in time for dinner."

Dax wasn't very good at reading women's faces, but if that quiver of her upper lip was any indication, Ava found this idea repugnant.

"Kots will do that," he said.

She looked relieved but only said, "Thank you," and slipped past him.

Waroun's eyes followed her. "You were headed that way too," he said as Ava's door closed behind her. "An assignation, perhaps?"

"A what?"

"An assignation," Waroun repeated. "You know… a lover's rendezvous?"

While this idea was appealing, Dax had actually been on his way to change his trousers. "Do you *ever* think about anything besides sex?"

"Rarely." Waroun stuck a thoughtful finger onto his chin. "There's nothing wrong with that. I only ask because I heard you purring and saw the look you were giving Ava at lunch. If the two of you had been alone and you hadn't received that hail, you would have nailed her right there on the table." Waroun's unblinking gaze cut right through him. "Wouldn't you?"

Dax didn't want to answer that—mainly because it was true.

"You might try talking to her first, or even kissing her," Waroun went on. "Just grabbing a woman and fucking the snot out of her isn't a good idea."

"I wouldn't do that."

"Ava is a very delicate creature," Waroun said. "She must be treated gently."

"Tell Lars that," Dax said with a snort. "Any woman who would hit a man over the head with a skillet—"

"—is a woman to be handled with care. Don't make the same mistake that Lars did."

"I would never hit a woman!"

"No, but rough sex can be just as damaging. You can hurt them if you aren't careful. You need to take it slowly."

"Like you ever take it slow!" Dax scoffed.

Waroun grinned. "True, but I'm not a Zetithian with a dick the size of yours."

Dax glared at him. "How the hell would you know how big my dick is?"

Waroun rolled his eyes. "It's no secret why Zetith was blown to bits—common knowledge, in fact. You need to learn how to—" Waroun halted abruptly, his eyes sharp with suspicion. "Wait a minute. That's why we're picking up Threldy, isn't it?"

"What?"

"You sent out a hail to him, didn't you? What's the matter—isn't my advice good enough?"

"Waroun, I never said—"

"Go on, be that way," Waroun grumbled. Waving Dax aside, he headed off toward the bridge. "See if I try to help you anymore," he said over his shoulder. "You'll bungle it, and then when Threldy gets here, he'll pick up the pieces and snatch Ava right out from under your nose. You *know* he will."

"No, he won't," Dax said. "He—he wouldn't do that."

Waroun stopped. Turning to face him, he demanded, "Have you *ever* seen a woman turn him down?"

"Well, no, but—"

"Or a woman he didn't consider a potential conquest?"

"No, but I—"

"It's a competition with him, my friend, and your score is a big, fat zero."

"Only because I never wanted any of the others," Dax shot back. "I can be just as charming as he is."

"Oh, please," Waroun groaned. "Don't make me laugh. You couldn't charm the skirt off a Davordian hooker if you weren't a Zetithian. Face it, Dax, when it comes to charm, you simply haven't got any." He continued on down the passageway, popping his fingertips off the top of his head.

"But I can purr," Dax called after him. "Threld can't do that, and—and women love it when we purr!"

"Maybe. But that doesn't necessarily mean they love *you*."

Once inside his quarters, Dax looked down and saw something he hoped Ava—and Waroun—hadn't noticed. Not only was there a wet spot in the front of his pants, but a huge bulge as well. *So much for being subtle or charming*. He knew Waroun was right, though it pained him to admit it, even to himself. Ava might have responded to him on a sexual level, but there was more to it than that.

Which was why he needed help. If Dax had only been interested in seduction, feeding Ava more Sholerian cream and purring might have done the trick—in fact, it nearly had—but the Zetithian in him wanted more. When there had been little or no hope of ever finding a compatible mate, it hadn't mattered. Things were different now.

Skimming off his wet garments, he glanced down again. His penis wasn't quite as hard as it had been a few moments ago, but it was still erect and didn't seem to belong to him. He wasn't used to seeing it in that state, but he knew exactly what he wanted to do with it. Waroun had been right: He wanted to grab Ava and not make love to her, but plunge in and fuck her until she screamed in ecstasy.

Just because she makes your cock hard doesn't mean she loves you—nor does it mean that you love her. It only means that sex is possible, and sex isn't love.

Dax blinked. Where had those words of wisdom come from? Was it something Jack had said or something he'd heard in school? He couldn't recall, but whatever the source, it was buried deep.

Tracing the edge of the serrated corona with a fingertip, Dax finally understood why the males of other species liked sex so much. It felt good to have an erection, but at the same time, it made you want more. The slick fluid had all but stopped flowing from the points of the scalloped head, but there was still enough that he could grasp his cock and slide his fist to the base. Yes, it felt *very* good. Somehow, he knew that a woman's hands would feel even better. A woman who would caress him and then let him inside her where it was warm and wet and felt like nothing else ever could.

He was losing it; his cock was shrinking in size, no matter how hard he tried to stop it. He fought to bring back the memory of her scent, but it was no use. There was only one way to get it back, but even though she was in the next room, she might as well have been a million star systems away for all the good it did him.

He understood now why men chased after women and broke down doors and, yes, withstood being hit over the head with skillets in order to get to the source of that need—and hold on to it forever.

Desire, lust, passion. A deep, aching want for something he couldn't have—at least, not yet. How could he possibly focus on being charming with this feeling inside him? If he was going to do it with words, he'd have to do it from across the room where he couldn't smell her or see her incredible eyes. Threldigan could help him with that, for, despite Waroun's warnings, he'd been a good friend in many ways. If Dax had ever truly wanted a woman, he was sure Threld would have helped.

Unfortunately, it would be a while before they reached Rhylos. What should he do in the meantime? Avoid her? Or see if his bumbling efforts would be adequate? If his previous attempts were any indication, they probably wouldn't be. He needed information, and he needed it now.

He changed into dry clothes and sat down at the desk, accessing the computer from there.

"I need mating behavior guidelines," he said aloud. "But for—humans, I guess." Muttering to himself, he scanned dozens of different topics from "How to find a mate" to "One hundred clues to sexual interest." The most promising was titled: *"She wants you. You want her. What now?"*

The list of dos and don'ts was endless. Make her laugh. Open doors for her. Smile. Brush your teeth. Take a shower. Don't buy her expensive gifts because she'll misinterpret your intentions. Don't be dominant—unless she wants you to be. Don't be rough—unless she's okay with it. Lean toward her, but don't invade her space. Take charge, but don't overdo it.

By the time Dax finally gave up and went to bed, his erection was a distant memory, and he'd concluded that his best bet was to tell Kots to keep Ava on a strict diet consisting of nothing but Sholerian cream and delete her wardrobe entirely. Then, and only then, would he stand a chance.

She might have only taken a taste of it, but what the Sholerian cream had done to Ava's libido was shocking. For one brief moment there in the passageway, she had been about to rip Dax's pants off, and if Waroun hadn't been there, she was afraid she would have.

For now, she knew the best course of action was to remain in her room until she felt normal again, but it certainly wasn't what she wanted to do. No, stripping Dax to his skin would have been her first choice, followed by engaging him in every sexual act she could think of. She wanted to suck his dick so badly she could almost taste it, and given that he was Zetithian, it was sure to be extra thick and juicy and delicious; she nearly had an orgasm just from thinking about it. Self-pleasuring was an option, though it wasn't sexual release she was craving, but sexual adventure—with one particular person. There was an ache deep inside her that she was sure only Dax could remedy. She'd never heard of an aphrodisiac that was quite so specific; even if Russ had been standing right there in front of her, she wouldn't have given him more than a passing thought.

It was frightening but simultaneously intriguing. She wanted the urges to pass, but at the same time, she was considering asking Kots for more of the stuff just so she'd maintain the single-minded courage to go through with it—*any* of it. Then she recalled, too late, that Kots was probably already on his way to her quarters with another dish of the stuff.

"No, Kots," she said aloud. "I didn't really mean that."

But she did. There was no arguing the point. Anything that would get her into Dax's arms was worth the effort.

No, she told herself, it's something I ate. When it wears off, I won't feel this way. Sure, he's a hunk, but he's not romantic or charming or any of those things I'd like in a man. I may never have to hit him over the head with a skillet, but he's still one of those bad boys I should avoid at all cost.

Russ. Good, safe, solid Russ. He was waiting for her. She would spend the rest of her life with him. Have his children. Grow old with him.

She closed her eyes and tried to picture him. His hair was… red. He had freckles and a nice smile. Yeah, that was him. She could see him now. His eyes were… what? Green? Blue? She couldn't remember.

Her eyes flew open as Dax's compelling hazel eyes seemed to gaze at her from the depths of her soul.

"No," she said through clenched teeth. "You won't get to me like that. I will *not* let you do it."

But she strongly suspected he already had.

———※———

Morning came and with it another day in the journey taking her back to Rutara, but Ava had no idea how far they'd come. That was the trouble with space travel; there were no landmarks along the way. One star looked very much like another, and the vast expanse of space didn't have road signs to tell you that Rutara was now fifty million light years away as opposed to sixty. In fact, aboard the *Valorcry*, there was almost no sensation of movement at all. For all Ava could tell, they might have been perfectly stationary.

She lay awake in her bed wondering whether Kots would come and get her if she didn't bother to get up. Would he come in and bodily dress her and push her out the door?

Doubtful. He was too much a servant to do that, but there was a bit of the autocrat in him just the same.

Sighing, she rolled out of bed. What did one wear when there was an incredibly hot hunk of a captain aboard and you really didn't want him to notice you, but you'd be pissed if he didn't? As she opened the wardrobe, it became apparent that she didn't have to spend a moment's thought on what to wear; Kots had already made that decision for her. All she found was a simple kaftan in a soft swirling pattern of yellow and aqua. Ava chuckled as she realized that though she'd never in her entire life dressed to match her eyes, she now had very little choice but to do so.

She hadn't thought a kaftan would be revealing— until she put it on and discovered that the fabric had a will of its own, molding itself to her shape so precisely that every curve and contour of her body was accentuated. The depth of the neckline made her wish Kots had given her a scarf to cover the vast expanse of exposed skin, but he obviously didn't think that was necessary.

However, she still had her pendant, which, given its size, would make her feel a little less naked and would look absolutely fabulous with this dress.

That was, if Kots hadn't taken it along with the rest of her wardrobe.

Thankfully, the box was still in the top drawer of the dresser where she had placed it for safekeeping. Ava had rarely worn the stone, mainly because it didn't go with any of her clothing, but also because she didn't want to advertise its existence to anyone on Luxaria—especially Lars. Unfortunately, the large crystal hung quite low on her chest, drawing the eye to the cleavage that the kaftan revealed. *So much for camouflage.* She was about to take it off when she heard the breakfast summons and responded to it as though Dax had been pleading with her to come dashing to his side.

Grumbling about what a pushover she was becoming—at least where Dax was concerned—she slipped on the matching shoes and hurried out.

Upon her arrival at the dining hall, however, she found herself alone. Kots wasn't even there. Had she been imagining the hail? Surely not. The chime had rung very clearly. Curious, she checked in the next room—which was even larger than the dining hall, and in another place and time could have been a ballroom. The soaring ceiling was adorned with frescoes, and carved molding framed what ought to have been windows but were, instead, visions of places Ava had never even imagined.

Landscapes with gently rolling hills were interspersed with those of softly glowing petals, shining leaves, the cool depths of jungles, and the distant glow of a sun rising over sand dunes. As she watched, the images melted to become entirely different: snowy mountaintops, fiery volcanoes, and the depths of an alien sea. The effect was stunning to the eye but soothing to the soul.

"This is the art gallery," Dax said from right behind her. "Beautiful, isn't it?"

Startled, Ava spun around to face him. "I—I must have missed this room on the tour."

"That's because it isn't on the tour—or the orientation video. I think the previous owner didn't want anyone in here and the ship knows it's supposed to keep it a secret. Most passengers can't even get the door to open." For once, his smile was warm rather than forced. "Kots must think you belong here."

Ava shrugged. "I just went looking when no one else was at breakfast. I didn't mean to trespass."

"You weren't trespassing," Dax assured her. "I don't mind if you come in here. Like I said, that was part of the ship's original programming."

Ava barely noted the door sliding discreetly shut behind him. They were alone together in a room filled with beauty and "the ship" seemed to want to keep them there. "Does Kots control everything?"

Dax shook his head. "The computer does that, but Kots is like an offshoot of the ship itself. It has a certain... presence, doesn't it?"

She nodded. "Has it ever trapped anyone in here?"

"Not that I can recall." Glancing over his shoulder at the closed door, Dax added, "But I can see why you might think that."

"Does the ship interpret thoughts—through Kots, perhaps?"

"Perhaps." Pulling a timepiece from his pocket, he added, "Breakfast isn't for another quarter of an hour."

"But I was called. I know I heard it!"

"And I was told there was something here that required my attention."

"Now, that *is* weird," she declared. "I—" Her thoughts were diverted as, suddenly, the pictures changed from dreamy landscapes to scenes of lovers entwined. One glance at the erotic images made Ava feel as though she'd been given another bowl of Sholerian cream. The lighting changed, becoming softer, more seductive. The room seemed to shrink in size as though closing in on them, forcing them together. She could have sworn that Dax never moved, but now, there was only a hand's breadth of distance between them. He was so close, she could smell him—woodsy and earthy, like tree bark, but as sweet and warm as cookies baking in the oven. His aroma drew her in like the scent of home at the end of a long journey. Comforting, soothing, but nonetheless compelling.

Ava wished she were taller, so she could have seen his eyes better, but they were so far away. Then she realized that she *was* growing in height and that their eyes were now on the same level. "How is this possible?" she whispered. "Is this whole room an illusion?"

Dax shook his head. "I don't know how it works. Interesting, though, isn't it?"

She reached out and touched his cheek. "I shouldn't be able to do this, but I can."

Dax leaned forward and inhaled deeply. Ava wondered if she smelled even half as good to him as he did to her. Would he taste as good as he smelled? The need to know the answer overwhelmed her. She could kiss him right now and doubted that he would resist. There was an openness in his expression she hadn't seen before. He was welcoming her into his arms, inviting her to taste his lips and feel the warmth of his body wrapped around hers.

Closing her eyes, she tasted her own lips as though they were his. She knew that sex with a Zetithian was addicting, but just being near him had almost the same effect. It stimulated her cravings, the need to feel his body as it covered her own and delved deeply inside her.

Her eyes were shutting out the visual, yet sound and scent came through loud and clear. She could hear him breathing, feel his warmth, and his scent surrounded her. Strains of soft music began to play, and when she opened her eyes, all she could see was Dax's face as he leaned closer. Their lips were almost touching—another whisper of movement, and they would be together.

Why am I resisting? Why am I not going that one last tiny little distance? It would be so simple to just let go and fall the rest of the way. He would catch her if she fell, and all she had to do was let him in…

Heaven was only a motion away—but was it heaven or temptation? Her conflicted emotions warred with one another. He was the kind of man she couldn't help but be drawn to, but this was how she'd gotten in trouble before—allowing emotions and desires to overrule her better judgment. Lars had lured her away from a good man. Dax had the same effect—stimulating her need for adventure, steering her away from the path she knew could bring lasting happiness and security.

There were too many selfish reasons for kissing him and too many righteous reasons to resist. It wasn't his choice, anyway. It was the ship and its minions that were controlling them. For some strange reason, they wanted them to be together, and what could a ship and its computer possibly know about love?

The chime rang out, calling the others to the dining room—the real chime, this time. Dax moved restlessly. She could tell he was tired of waiting, but he would have to go on waiting. She was not going to risk another mistake like the one she'd made before. Shaking her head, she asserted herself and her intentions. In an instant, the room returned to its original shape, and the door slid open. Dax was standing a good two meters away, towering over her as he had always done.

Without a word, he turned and walked out.

Chapter 8

DAX STALKED INTO THE DINING ROOM AND DIDN'T EVEN have to snarl at the Drell to get him to move aside. His ire was that obvious.

Waroun was right. He really *couldn't* charm the shirt, let alone the skirt, off a Davordian hooker. He was a disgrace to all of the men of Zetith whose renown as lovers was legendary. Should he have made the first move? Was that his mistake? She'd been about to kiss him—at least, he thought she had—but what had stopped her? He had no idea, but the scent of her desire had shut off like a faucet. Did he have bad breath or a disgusting body odor? Had the sight of him up close repulsed her? It hadn't bothered her before, but who knew what would offend or please a female from a different world—or more precisely, *two* worlds, since she was a hybrid.

Dax frowned as the thought occurred to him that hybrids didn't always breed true—and sometimes couldn't breed at all; they were often sterile or asexual. He shook his head. No, if Ava were asexual, she wouldn't have been with Lars, nor would she want to return to Russ. And she *had* responded to Dax before. He had absolutely no idea what the problem was, but he was pretty sure he'd been inspected and found lacking in some way.

Teke bade him a cheerful good morning, but Dax

merely grunted in reply. All of the encouraging thoughts he'd had the night before vanished with the morning, which did *not* make it a good one.

He sat down in the nearest chair, still mulling it over, when it occurred to him that it might not have had anything to do with Ava at all but was simply that odd room. He'd been telling the truth when he'd told her he didn't know how it worked. Perhaps they really *weren't* that close together, though the condition of his penis suggested that they had been. But why had her scent dissipated so quickly? Kots set a cup of coffee down in front of him. One whiff told him that it was mountain grown Letei coffee from Nraken. Definitely nothing wrong with his nose…

"Waroun was just telling us that we'll be making a stop at Rhylos," Teke said. "Would it be possible for us to remain there for a day or two? I've always wanted to visit that world. One hears so much about it."

Dax looked up in surprise, darting a glance at Waroun, who simply sat gazing back at him with a neutral expression.

Too neutral, in fact.

"If you're basing that on anything Waroun has to say, you'll be disappointed," said Dax.

"He *has* made it sound very exciting," Teke admitted, "but his is not the first description I've heard. Why, it's the playground of the galaxy!"

Dax gazed at the elder of the two Kitnocks, curious as to why he would be the one to voice an interest in seeing Rhylos rather than Diokut. "Aren't you a little old for that sort of thing?"

Diokut laughed out loud, but Teke ignored him. "Ah,

the snobbishness of youth," he said with a knowing smile. "It never occurs to you that your elders might like to have a little fun before they die."

"Didn't you have any fun on Luxaria?" Quinn inquired.

Without the benefit of any facial expression, it was difficult to tell whether the Drell was being sarcastic or sincere. However, having spent a little time on Luxaria, Dax opted for sarcasm. "I can't say I've had any fun on either of those worlds," Dax said before Teke could reply, "but if you'd like to stay there for a while, I'm sure no one else would object."

"Object to what?" Ava asked as she entered.

Dax stiffened. He was sitting with his back to the doorway, a circumstance for which he was extremely grateful. He wasn't sure he'd ever be able to look her in the eye again. A sudden stabbing pain to his forehead had him pinching the bridge of his nose as she swept past him to take a seat next to Waroun. His heart sank. She must really not like him if she'd prefer to sit next to the Norludian—and also the Drell, since Quinn was on her other side. Waroun's eyes were sparkling with thinly veiled lust as he took in the sight of Ava in that clingy thing she was wearing. Dax bit his lip, tasting blood.

"A little side trip to Rhylos," Waroun replied. "And may I say, my dear Ava, you would be among the loveliest women there. That dress looks positively stunning on you. The color brings out the depths of the ocean in your eyes."

Dax felt an instantaneous desire to throttle Waroun. Why hadn't he thought to compliment her dress? Or her eyes, or anything else, for that matter? He consoled himself with the fact that at least he hadn't spoken his mind and said he wanted to rip it off with his teeth. Wincing, he swallowed hard as she turned her gaze on him—a gaze that held no emotion other than curiosity.

"How long before we arrive?" She flipped out her napkin as though the interlude in the gallery had never happened.

"About another twenty hours or so," Dax replied. And during those hours, he considered never leaving the bridge. Threld would be able to help him—unless he screwed things up so badly that she wound up hating him forever. He didn't think he'd done it yet, and a moment's scrutiny confirmed it. She simply appeared to be indifferent, which was probably worse.

Mentally reviewing the list of things he was supposed to do to attract a woman, Dax couldn't recall having used a single one of them during their recent encounter—he hadn't even smiled—though perhaps he had leaned toward her just a bit. Obviously not enough to make a difference, but he *had* leaned. I should have kissed her, he decided. Then she would have understood how I felt about her.

But there was a problem with that. Dax had never kissed anyone in his life. Though several women had made the attempt, none had been tall enough to succeed. He'd had no practice whatsoever. What if he was a terrible kisser?

He stared at the plate Kots had just set in front of him and began eating it automatically, not even caring what it was. It looked vaguely familiar but tasted odd. Perhaps there was something wrong with his nose after all.

Then it hit him. "Kots," he growled. "Would you please bring me something that hasn't been laced with Sholerian cream?"

Kots beeped discreetly and removed the plate. Dax didn't dare risk a glance at Ava; Waroun's smug grin was quite enough. Hitching uncomfortably in his chair, he considered telling Kots to give it to Ava but decided he didn't want a woman who had to be drugged into finding him appealing.

Dax winced as Ava cleared her throat audibly. She had to know *exactly* what that stuff did to a person, but, thankfully, she didn't comment on it. "I don't mind going to Rhylos. But what's so special about it?"

"It's the hellhole of the galaxy," Dax replied.

Ava snorted. "I thought that was Luxaria's claim to fame."

"Rhylos is a very exciting world," Teke said eagerly. "They have entertainments that are not to be found anywhere else. It's a sparkling, delightful, beautiful place."

"And you can lose your shirt there," Dax muttered.

"Not to mention your balls," Waroun added with a smirk.

By this point, Dax was sure steam was coming out of his pointed ears. "Waroun, will you please not—"

"Very funny story about Rhylos," Waroun said with undisguised glee. "The world where the Great Virgin almost became the Great Eunuch."

"No wonder you don't like the place," Teke observed with a shudder. In the typical male reaction to such things—along with all the other men present—he crossed his legs as if to hide the family jewels from any would-be predators.

Ava began giggling. "You guys just kill me. The mere mention of castration has you sucking up your—"

"I am *not* sucking up my balls!" Dax snarled. "In fact, I'll—" He stopped short, suddenly realizing that the best response to that would have been none at all.

Waroun obviously didn't agree. "You'll what?" he cackled. "Show them to her?"

Dax was gritting his teeth so hard, he was afraid he'd snap off the tips of his fangs. Taking a deep breath, he said, "I'll show her anything she likes, but either way, it's none of your damn business, Waroun!"

His remark had a surprising effect on Ava. She let out a gasp and lurched forward, grasping the edge of the table.

Waroun's head snapped up as his bulbous eyes swept over Ava with frank fascination. "Was that an orgasm, dear?"

"N-no," she stammered, reaching for her glass of iced tea. "Just got a little choked."

"On what?" Waroun pursued. "You haven't eaten anything yet."

"Yeah, well, you don't always have to eat something to choke," she mumbled, taking a sip. Her hair immediately began rippling like a wind-tossed sea, and it was all Dax could do to keep from leaping up to delve into it with both hands. His mouth began to water, and it wasn't because he wanted food; the need to taste her was so overwhelming that his next breath came out as a loud purr.

"Kots has given you Aquerei water again, I see," said Quinn. "Wish it did that to *my* fur."

"He must be making the tea with it," Ava said. Blushing, she made an attempt to control her tossing locks. Dax's eyes followed her hand as it smoothed out her hair and then slid past her neck, drawing attention to her crystal pendant.

Swallowing hard, he blurted out, "Nice necklace."

"See now, that didn't hurt a bit, did it?" Waroun chuckled.

Dax gave his first mate a dirty look as Ava, ignoring Waroun, replied simply, "My father gave it to my mother before I was born, and she gave it to me when I turned sixteen."

"Aquerei stones are known for their quality," Quinn said.

"An heirloom, perhaps?" Teke inquired.

"I don't know if you'd call it an heirloom," Ava replied. "And I doubt that it's very valuable." Tilting her head back, she held the stone up to the light for closer inspection. The sparkle and color of it rivaled her eyes. "According to my mother, my father wasn't what you'd call rich."

"Still, it *is* very lovely," Quinn went on.

"I've hardly ever worn it," Ava said. "In fact, Lars didn't even know I had it—at least, I don't *think* he did—or I'm sure he would've tried to sell it."

Dax found this curious. "You were with him for five years and never wore it?"

Ava smiled, and Dax immediately felt another purr rising in his throat. That tiny taste of the cream was making control difficult.

"It wasn't Lars I didn't trust," she said. "Not at first, anyway. It was everyone else on Luxaria. Though now that I think of it, I can't recall *ever* wearing it before." Her slender fingertips grazed her sleeve. "I've tried it on, of course, but never had anything this nice to go with it."

As if he'd needed reminding about the frankly seductive dress she wore. Dax closed his eyes and counted to ten in an effort to control the impulse to pounce on her. He'd only made it to five when he had to open them again as Kots set another plate in front of him. Terran food, he noted. Eggs, bacon, toast... nothing that would hide Sholerian cream—unless the toast had been buttered with it.

"Well, we're very glad you have it now," said Waroun. "You are a vision."

Waroun was really laying it on thick. With a quelling look at his partner, Dax made another attempt. "It's like your eyes."

Ava glanced up as though startled by his comment. "What, the dress?"

"No," he replied. "I mean the stone."

Their eyes met across the table, but for Dax, she might as well have been sitting in his lap. He couldn't look away, couldn't blink, could barely breathe...

When she spoke at last, her voice was only a whisper. "Thank you." Those fabulous eyes held his for a moment before she looked down at her plate, blushing once again.

Dax couldn't take it anymore. He wolfed down his food and then, after making a brief apology to the group at large, mumbled something about having work to do and departed for the bridge. His only consolation was that he hadn't run from the room.

dangerous, alluring Zetithian. She couldn't see living with him, though. Ava was an earth and water girl; living perpetually aboard a ship wasn't the kind of life she aspired to, but then, Luxaria hadn't been the ideal world for her either. She couldn't remember the last time she'd gone swimming and often longed for the sea.

"What about Rhylos?" she said. "Do they have any beaches?"

Waroun smiled wickedly. "Lots of beautiful white sandy beaches." Smacking his lips, he added, "All nude beaches, too."

"You *have* to be nude?" Ava gasped.

"No, but nearly everyone is," Waroun replied with a snicker. "What happens on Rhylos stays on Rhylos."

Ava sat in stunned silence. For spontaneous swimming, the idea of shedding your clothing and jumping in had a decided appeal, but she wasn't sure she wanted other people watching. Then she thought about swimming with Dax, and every female organ she possessed did a backflip and her hair made a move she'd never felt before.

"Did you see that?" Diokut exclaimed. "Her hair curled!"

Waroun chuckled. "So it did." Cocking his head curiously, he said, "You see me naked all the time, so you must be thinking about feasting your eyes on the Great Virgin." Nudging her with his sharp elbow, he added, "You are, aren't you? That tall, sexy Zetithian with all of his goodies hanging loose and his tight buns right out there in plain sight?"

Ava's reaction was uncontrollable. She'd never known her hair to reflect her moods before, but there seemed to be no stopping it now. It felt as though it tied itself into tight knots before springing back to its original style. "Must be this water," she mumbled. "Thought I told Kots not to give it to me anymore."

"You did," Waroun said, "but he seems to have forgotten. Not that the rest of us are complaining."

"Is he always so… underhanded?"

"Kots always tries to give you what you want— whether you'll admit to it or not—and sometimes he confuses need with want."

"So you're saying I need it?"

Waroun shrugged. "Need… want… it makes no difference to Kots."

She studied the glass. It looked like ordinary iced tea, but the effect on her was anything but. "What happens when other species drink this stuff?"

"It's an intoxicant," Waroun replied. "Like wine."

"Ah," said Ava. "I wondered why it was bottled— and so expensive. We certainly didn't stock it in the bar where I worked."

"No hangover, either," said Waroun. "And not addicting or harmful, like some other substances."

"I'd like to try some," said Diokut. "Why doesn't Kots ever give it to me?"

"Therein lies a great mystery," Waroun replied.

"I guess you'd actually have to ask," Ava suggested.

Teke laughed. "Perhaps Kots deems you to be too young."

Diokut frowned. "But I am of age!"

"Perhaps not in his estimation."

With a resigned sigh, Diokut resumed eating his breakfast. Ava ate her fish and drank the tea without further comment, doing her best to ignore the havoc it wreaked on her hair. She wondered why Dax even bothered to fuss about the Sholerian cream. There was simply no arguing with Kots. He always managed to get the upper hand in the end.

Chapter 9

THERE WAS NO ARGUING WITH KOTS WHEN IT CAME TO her wardrobe either. This was something that Ava had already come to accept, but after taking a quick shower just prior to their landing on Rhylos, she opened her closet and nearly went ballistic. The only things in there were a pair of shoes and a skimpy aquamarine dress that looked like something a hooker would wear. Nothing else at all. Not even underwear or stockings. About the best she could say for it was that the shoes were comfortable enough for strolling around the town. Tossing the dress on the bed, she slammed the closet door and yelled for Kots.

Within a few minutes, the droid arrived and hummed into her room, even though the door had been closed and locked.

"I can't wear this, Kots. I need something else."

Kots let out a sharp buzz and began to leave as quickly as he came.

"No, really! I can't do it!" Dropping her robe, she slipped on the offensive dress and wrapped it around her. "I mean, look at it! It's only got these two dinky little snaps holding it together. I'll be lucky if it doesn't fall off before I leave the ship!"

Kots made a soft whirring sound that was undoubtedly intended to be comforting, but all it did was make her mad.

"Yes, I'm sure the color matches my eyes, Kots, but I look like a cheap slut in this getup!"

Kots buzzed again, obviously of the opinion that she did *not* look like a cheap slut, but Ava had different standards. She took a deep breath and counted to three.

"Look, I know you've been trying to get something going between Dax and me, but really, this is going too far. It's the most blatant 'come fuck me' garb I've ever seen. You can't seriously expect me to wear this. I won't do it!"

Kots crossed all ten of his arms in what was undoubtedly the droid equivalent of, "Oh, yes, you will."

"I might as well be naked!"

Kots didn't reply. It was apparent that it was either the robe or the dress, and she was not about to stroll along the streets of Rhylos in her bathrobe, even if it *was* a more modest garment. Doing the town in the nude was not an option.

Kots just hovered there, not budging a bit.

"Oh, all right! Might as well wear the damn pendant too. At least it will cover part of me. It better not be cold on this planet, or I'm gonna rip one of your arms off."

Kots beeped cheerfully and zoomed out before she had the chance to throw anything at him.

———

The other passengers were already gathered in the lounge when Ava arrived. All three of them looked up when she stormed in, but before anyone had a chance to comment, she snapped, "The dress is obviously Kots's idea of a joke. I don't want to hear one word about it."

Teke and Diokut began cracking their knuckles, but

Quinn gestured toward the viewport. "We were just watching the approach to Rhylos," he said. "Come here and have a look."

All thoughts of outrageous dresses evaporated as Ava caught her first glimpse of the playground of the galaxy. She had glanced through some of the data on Rhylos, but nothing could have prepared her for the real thing. Though only early afternoon aboard the ship, it was nighttime in Rhylos, and the city lights shone as brightly as the sun at high noon.

As they swooped in over the city, Dax seemed to be doing some pretty fancy flying. At first Ava thought he was showing off his piloting skills, but a couple of near misses made her realize that he was simply dodging the air traffic that swarmed above the city like bees around a hive.

"I had no idea it would be so breathtaking," Teke said in reverent tones.

Ava had seen cities before, but none could compare to this one. Playground of the galaxy was right—and this was only a small portion of it. Tall structures studded the surface like sparkling gems, some static while others were in motion. The entire city seemed to pulsate, as though it were a living being with a heart of its own. "Incredible," she whispered.

Quinn was bristling with excitement. Shoving Diokut aside, he announced, "I want to ride that," pointing to a revolving disk that tilted in every direction.

"How do you know it's a ride?" Ava inquired. "I mean, do you know what it does?"

"No," Quinn replied, "but it doesn't matter. I love a good spin."

Ava hated such things. They made her feel sick for hours. "Well, have fun. I just want to find out what *that* is." She pointed toward a mesmerizing circle of lights that expanded and contracted, changing color with each cycle.

"I believe that is the landing site," Diokut said. "We seem to be heading right toward it."

"Do you suppose we'll be meeting Threldigan there?" Quinn asked nervously.

"Perhaps," said Teke. "Does that prospect frighten you?"

Recalling what Waroun had said about the witch who could roast you alive, Ava considered this likely. She was a bit anxious herself.

Quinn nodded. "I hate magical things. They aren't natural."

"Not for you, perhaps," said Teke, "but for other species, magic is normal."

"There's nothing normal about magic," Quinn insisted. "If it were normal, it wouldn't be magic, would it?"

Teke voiced no further opinions, but this sounded perfectly logical to Ava. "Well, just try not to be rude and maybe Threldigan won't be tempted to use his powers on you."

Shuddering, Quinn turned back to the viewport as the lights on the landing pad changed from green to magenta. Considering the inherent rudeness of his kind, Ava thought it might be difficult for the Drell to follow this simple bit of advice. She made a mental note to speak to the magician as little as possible, since it had been her experience that most situations could be safely handled if all you did was nod and smile a lot. Quinn, on the other hand, seemed to be incapable of smiling.

Dax's voice sounded over the comsystem. "The *Valorcry* has landed. All passengers prepare to disembark."

To Ava's surprise, Quinn latched onto her hand and refused to let go. *Great! Here I am, about to arrive on the playground of the galaxy, and I look like I'm taking my pet Drell for a walk!* Her only consolation was that, thanks to Kots, Quinn not only looked more presentable, he actually smelled good.

Moments later, Dax entered the lounge. His clothes were the same as ever, but his grim countenance and commanding presence soon had Quinn cowering at her side. If he noticed her ridiculous dress, it didn't show.

Clearing his throat, he said sternly, "We will only be here for a few days. During that time, the ship will admit you whenever you wish, but do not attempt to bring anyone else aboard." Leveling a piercing gaze at Diokut, he continued. "Kots knows how to deal with intruders. If you have the credits to pay for a hotel, you may do so, but please report this to Kots. You can communicate with each other or with the ship using these combadges," he said as Waroun handed each of them a badge. "If you forget where we parked, the ship can help you navigate back to this location." He paused, letting out a weary sigh. "Carry only the amount of money you can afford to lose, and please, at least *try* to stay out of trouble."

Though Dax's tone suggested that he'd had to bail his passengers out of jail more than once in the past and had no desire to repeat the experience, Ava couldn't help but think how difficult it would be to get into trouble while dragging Quinn along wherever she went. However, since Dax was obviously in no mood to discuss the matter, she didn't mention it. Nod and smile, she told herself. Just nod and smile.

Dax palmed open the hatch, and the adventure began.

—⁓—

The first thing Ava noticed was the aroma of sizzling hot food wafting toward them on a gentle breeze. One moment before, she hadn't been the slightest bit hungry, but she now felt as though she'd been starving for months.

"Everything on this world is calculated to appeal to the senses," Dax warned them. "It may take some time for you to adjust, but until then, try not to overdo it."

Quinn was already following his nose, dragging Ava down the ramp like an eager puppy as he headed toward a vendor selling sausages. They looked ordinary enough, but the smell was irresistible.

Until he got a whiff of the pastries in the next booth and pulled her in that direction. "Are you sure you need me with you all the time?" Ava asked.

"What?" Quinn replied. "I, oh, perhaps I don't!" Releasing her hand, he reached for his money pouch and pulled out a credit chip. "They take these, don't they?"

"They accept any currency in the known galaxy," Dax replied, "but prefer standard credits. Cash only, and everything must be paid for in advance. They don't trust anyone's promises."

Waroun snorted. "Careful you don't spend it all in one place."

Before she left the ship, Ava had had no intention of spending any of her cash, but now she wasn't so sure. The need to acquire was increasing exponentially with each breath she took and every sight that met her eyes.

She knew what it was—subliminal messages were pouring into her mind, telling her to "Eat this!" "Do that!" "Buy this!" "Don't miss out!"—and though she did her best to ignore them, between them and Quinn, who now had a sausage in one hand and a gooey confection in the other, she was finding it hard to resist. She normally didn't even *like* sausages, but all of a sudden, biting into one was first and foremost in her mind, blanking out any thoughts of her dress or Dax and his dangly bits, whether he was naked or not.

One glance assured her that he was, indeed, still clothed. He was natural, unenhanced—but still gorgeous. "Is it the atmosphere, or what?" she mumbled, gazing up at the dark sky.

"No," Dax replied. "It's all done artificially. Most worlds don't allow this type of advertising, but anything goes on Rhylos, and more than one visitor has wound up destitute because of it. It's nearly impossible to save your money here. The push to spend is constant."

Thankful that she hadn't needed Dax's advice to leave most of her money on the ship, she ventured on, walking with great determination past the food vendors. It seemed to take every gram of willpower she possessed to do it—until she spotted the other shops. The first was operated by a Twilanan woman with a snout the size of a Drell's head and a curved horn protruding from the tip. The shop was lit with flashing lights and the lady's green and gold dress dazzled the eye.

"Come into my shop," she urged, reaching for Ava's arm. "Your man will be unable to resist you in one of my beautiful dresses."

Ava gasped at the swirl of patterns and colors in the

garment the woman waved before her. She was just about to take the plunge, regardless of the cost, when Dax bent down and said in her ear, "You don't need that, Ava. Tell yourself, *you don't need it*."

She turned to find his glowing hazel eyes boring into hers. "W-what?"

"Tell yourself you don't need it," he repeated. "Say it out loud."

"I—I don't need it," she stammered. She was almost convinced until another glance at it had her faltering. "But it's the most gorgeous dress I've ever seen." And was certainly better than the one she had on.

"Say it again." His tone was brusque, but authoritative.

"I don't need it."

"Good. Now say you don't want it."

"But I do!" Ava protested, knowing that without it, her life would be incomplete and barely worth living. Just having such a dress hanging in her closet would be the answer to her fondest wish, her most fervent prayer…

"Say it!"

With her gaze resting on his compelling catlike eyes, somehow it became easier. The dress was just a dress, after all—certainly not something to covet or to die for. "I don't want it," she said, and suddenly, as though a veil had been lifted, she saw that it was colorful but gaudy; the sort of thing she would never wear.

"That's all it takes?"

Dax nodded. "Most of the time. Sometimes it's more difficult—particularly when it involves something you would want anyway."

"Like you," she whispered. Realizing what she'd just said, she shook her head and attempted to correct her mistake. "I mean, like you would want food if you were really hungry or a new dress if you didn't already have enough of them."

He considered this for a moment, his head tipped curiously to one side. "Yes," he finally said. Gazing past her, he went on, "Looks like I'd better go coach the others. You can tell people about this for days in advance, but it doesn't do any good until you're actually here."

Ava nodded. This entire trip was turning out to be a lesson in self-control and denial—something she hadn't thought she needed to learn until now.

But perhaps she *did* need to learn it. Though she had never considered herself to be capricious, she was beginning to question that assessment. Her life with Russ had been comfortable enough—certainly no worse than living with Lars—and yet she had left that comfort for the unknown—but why? And why had Lars seemed so attractive at first? If excitement was what she craved, then going back to Russ, who was anything but exciting, didn't make sense. She only knew that she had been tempted and had succumbed, thus proving her own weakness. If it was all about temptation—and Dax was surely the greatest temptation of all—she feared she was losing the fight. Again.

Waroun had already fixed Quinn—though the fact that he couldn't hold another bite might have had something to do with it—and Dax was able to get Diokut on the right track with very little trouble. Teke was another matter entirely. The elder Kitnock seemed convinced that a starship was something he desperately needed, and the salesman stationed at the edge of the landing pad was more than willing to sell him a Kructan Flyer of his very own.

"No, you don't *need* a starship," Dax said as Diokut chimed in with his own admonitions that, one: Teke hadn't enough money to pay for it, and two: he couldn't fly it.

"But Dax could teach me," Teke insisted.

"There are lots of other things to buy here—nice things that would be much more useful than a starship."

"But what could possibly be more useful? Look at Dax. He has one, and he's able to earn a living with it. Goes anywhere he wants, sees places we can only imagine. I want that kind of life for myself."

"Believe me, it isn't all it's cracked up to be," said Dax. "It gets boring and lonely after a while. Just try this, please. Say 'I don't want it, and I don't need it.'"

He felt a hand touch his arm as Ava spoke up. "Excuse me? *You're* bored and lonely?"

Dax's jaw dropped. He hadn't realized she was standing right behind him—and in a dress like that, she would have affected him from across the street. He'd nearly choked to death when he'd walked into the lounge and only covered it up at the last second by clearing his throat and sounding like a dictator. He'd been trying not to stare, but it was nearly impossible. His eyes simply wouldn't cooperate. "I'm… just trying to make a point," he said. "This usually works…"

"Only if you do it right," came an amused voice. Threldigan was approaching, a long black cape swirling behind him, flashing his charming smile on the group.

After slapping Dax on the back in greeting, the dark-skinned Mordrial flung his cape around Ava and pulled her to his side. "And what have we here? A lovely Aquerei maiden? So far from water? We must remedy that. Everyone follow me!"

—w—

Ava had Threldigan pegged for precisely what he was the moment she laid eyes on him—a charming man who saw every woman, no matter how insignificant, as a prize to be won. Not that many would mind being his target. Lithe and handsome with a narrow mustache above a sensuous mouth, he had thick, curly black hair, intelligent eyes, and a killer smile—in short, the kind of man any woman would adore to have in pursuit of her.

Not that it mattered one iota what she thought of him. He was pleasantly charming, but falling in love with him was out of the question. *I am resisting such things and going back to Rutara to live a normal life, hopefully with Russ.* Maybe if she told herself that enough, she would believe it, like the "I don't need it and I don't want it" mantra for surviving Rhylos with her finances intact. Still, she hadn't missed the scowl on Dax's face when she suddenly became the center of Threldigan's attention. Perhaps a bit of competition would keep them busy enough that she wouldn't be tempted by either of them. Maybe.

Threldigan's cape seemed to shield Ava from the advertising bombardment, enabling her to view the city more objectively. The streets weren't paved with gold, but the sheer expense of it all was incalculable. With buildings that shone with excellent design and even better maintenance, Rhylos was as clean and perfect as Luxaria was rundown and filthy. Daylight might have altered that perception, but the city at night was nothing short of spectacular. Though Ava was certain that there were shadier neighborhoods somewhere—there *had* to be—this was not one of them.

———✦———

Dax couldn't believe his eyes. He'd been afraid to lay a hand on Ava for fear of offending her, and now there she was, snug in Threldigan's arms within moments of his arrival. And she was smiling at him too. It just wasn't fair!

"I told you so," Waroun said. "Once Threldy gets hold of them, you don't stand a chance, Captain." He walked on ahead, happily popping his fingertips off his bony little ass—an ass that Dax felt like kicking all the way to Rutara and back. "Hey, Threldy!" Waroun called out. "Know any hot, desperate Davordian girls?"

"A few," Threldigan said with a chuckle. "Want me to fix you up?"

"Immediately," Waroun replied.

Judging from his muffled speech, Waroun's tongue was already swelling at the thought. Dax's dick, on the other hand, was as soft as ever, but his temper was rising rapidly.

"Oh, Dax," Threldigan said, pausing for moment. "That reminds me. Did I tell you that some friends of yours are here on Rhylos?"

"Friends?" Dax echoed cautiously.

"Fellow refugees," Threldigan replied. "They've got a thriving business too."

Dax was almost afraid to ask what it was, but Ava did it for him.

Threldigan grinned at her. "What sort of business

do you *think* three healthy, unattached Zetithian men at the peak of their sexual prowess would have on a world such as this?"

"They're selling *themselves*?"

Threldigan nodded. "Damn straight they are. Got the coolest place you ever saw. You'll have to see it to believe it."

"Who—oh, let me guess," said Dax. "Onca and Jerden?"

"You got it. Tarq is with them too."

He was a little surprised to hear that Tarq was included, but all three were disgustingly handsome devils and avid womanizers. They'd made no secret of what they wanted to do when let loose on an unsuspecting galaxy filled with willing females.

"They can barely keep up with the demand for their services," Threldigan went on. "The ladies have to sign up a year in advance to spend a couple of hours with one of them."

Dax felt like throwing up. His only consolation was that if they were booked that far ahead, they wouldn't be able to fit Ava into their schedules. Not that she would want to—at least, not with Threldigan sweet talking her; he'd have her in his bed in no time, and Dax would be left out in the cold. He shook his head and walked on. He needed help, not competition. *What was I thinking?*

Threldigan was an excellent guide, pointing out the more prominent landmarks and attractions, and Ava drank it all in. Every species in the galaxy was represented, including a few who were undoubtedly purebred Aquerei. Their eyes were much larger and the webbing in their fingers more pronounced than Ava's, but that was nothing compared to their hair. The individual hair shafts were much thicker, came in a wide variety of colors, and waved and rippled like clusters of sea anemones. Ava thought it looked sort of creepy and was thankful that her Terran blood had been able to tone it down a bit.

There were many Twilanans, their brightly colored robes billowing out behind them as they walked, and several other species she couldn't identify. They passed a large group of Drells, but Quinn had already gone off on his own. Kitnocks were scarce, as were Norludians, but Davordians with their luminous blue eyes were everywhere. A few dinosaurlike Darconians lumbered past, followed by some six-fingered, flat-nosed humanoids who otherwise appeared Terran. The males wore pants that were open at the crotch, and each of them led a scantily clad, collared female by a leash attached to his wrist.

"Statzeelians," Threldigan reported. "The guys are real assholes. Without a woman to keep them in line, they cause all sorts of trouble." Ava's eyes widened as one woman began stroking her man's exposed penis when he threatened to slug a persistent salesman. "Works like a charm," Threldigan noted as the fellow immediately became more docile.

While this behavior was certainly very strange, it wasn't the most eye-opening, as Ava noticed that clothing—on any species—appeared to be optional. Ava wasn't bothered by it, but felt that some should have been more discreet, particularly when a woman with four sets of breasts walked by. Her outfit made Ava's dress seem saintly, and Diokut snickered as she passed them, while Teke began cracking his knuckles in earnest. Ava glanced over at Dax to see his reaction, but he was still wearing a scowl and wasn't even looking in that direction.

There appeared to be no law against the public drinking of alcohol—a popular intoxicant on nearly every world—but drinking yourself into a stupor wasn't tolerated. Ava saw more than one unfortunate soul being rolled onto a pallet by the clean-up droids and then floated away—presumably to a place where they could sleep it off.

"You can get as drunk as you like," Threldigan said in response to her query, "but you aren't allowed to clutter up the streets."

Speeders of all shapes and sizes zoomed past, but most people were on foot. The leisurely pace was best for seeing the sights and enabled customers to be drawn into the various shops with greater ease. Many services were free of charge—you could have your hair styled or your nails done for nothing—yet Ava could see that it was merely a ploy to sell you some product or other. If you were very careful, you could exist quite nicely on no money at all, Threldigan said, but the trick was in not being lured into buying something else.

"I once had my shoes remade for free and wound up buying a new coat to go with them," he said with a chuckle. "I did like the coat, but since it's never very cold here, I've yet to wear it."

"Then why do you wear the cape?" Ava asked.

Threldigan grinned. "To look more like a magician," he replied with a sweeping flourish, "but also to ward off evil."

So, there is *something special about the cape!* "There is evil here?"

"Oh, yes," Threldigan replied. "A great deal of it. One must exercise constant vigilance."

Ava chuckled. "Sounds more like Luxaria all the time."

"There are many similarities. It simply looks nicer and has a few more regulations."

"And the cape protects you?"

Threldigan nodded. "Watch."

With that, he removed his arm from her shoulder. "Walk on ahead of us as though you were alone."

Ava did as he instructed. Within moments, a smelly Cylopean fell in step beside her. "A lovely female all alone," he cackled. "You require an escort. Allow me to offer my services."

Ava shuddered and stepped sideways to avoid him, but he grabbed her arm, clinging like a leech. "Don't touch me," she ordered. Despite her words, the Cylopean persisted. She heard a growl nearby, which the Cylopean ignored.

"Ah, but your beauty calls to me. I cannot leave you alone. Unless, perhaps, for a price?" His dark, beady eyes narrowed as though assessing her inherent worth.

Ava knew she should have been frightened but only felt anger at the man's audacity. "Are you saying I have to *pay* you to leave me alone? I'd much rather take a swing at your big, ugly nose."

"That would not be advisable." The Cylopean reached for her pendant with a clawlike hand.

Threldigan was quick to react, but Dax was faster. With one punch, he had the Cylopean sprawling in the street. "Get lost," he snarled.

The Cylopean scrambled to his feet and scuttled away.

"My hero!" Waroun exclaimed in a worshipful falsetto.

"Shut up, Waroun," Dax snapped. Scowling at Threldigan, he added, "No more demonstrations." He grabbed Ava and pulled her against his hip. "You stay right there and hold on to me—and do *not* let go."

Threldigan was laughing, but Ava's heart was pounding. Being shrouded inside Threldigan's cape hadn't affected her in the slightest, but Dax... Oh, yes, *he* was the reason. He was too close. Too strong. Too tall. Too... *everything*. Her arm around his waist felt very natural, but his body heat lit a fire that raced from her fingertips all the way to her center and back again. She even felt a pulsation in her hair.

Gritting her teeth, Ava silently recited the prayer her mother had taught her so many years ago—with a few minor alterations: *Lead me not into temptation, but deliver me from evil...*

Evil? Dax wasn't evil. He was simply the temptation to turn her aside from the path she had chosen. The right path. The *only* path—

No, it was a really *stupid* path, she decided as she rested her head against his side. Never, never, *never* had she felt like this when walking with Russ—but temptation *should* feel good, shouldn't it? What would happen if she were to give in to it? Would a lightning bolt strike her from out of the blue? Would the earth open up and swallow her? Would she be deluged in a flood and drown? No, wait, she couldn't drown. That was one destiny that fate *couldn't* throw at her, but it was just about the only one.

But what if Dax was her destiny and the others

merely the mistakes to which everyone is entitled? The indecision was driving her crazy. Why couldn't there be a voice from on high to tell her that, yes, Ava, he is the one...

"There he is!" a woman's voice shouted. "He's the one!"

Ava was snatched from her reverie as Dax stiffened beside her. "Oh, *no*," he groaned. "Not now!"

Chapter 10

DAX'S PAST MAY HAVE COME BACK TO HAUNT HIM IN THE form of two irate hookers, but at least they didn't appear to be armed. They were still mad, though, and it didn't take a mind reader like Threldigan to figure that out.

The brunette looked as though she'd like to conjure a weapon out of thin air, while the blonde obviously intended to castrate Dax with her bare hands. Waroun was hopping up and down with glee, Threldigan was laughing his ass off, the two Kitnocks seemed puzzled, and Ava merely said, "Oh, let me guess… These are the ones who almost turned you into the Great Eunuch, right?"

Dax wanted to cry or scream or at least hit something. He'd just saved Ava from that scuzzy Cylopean—which had to count for *something* in the mating game—and now that she finally had her arm around him, he was about to lose his balls.

Not that he was giving them up without a fight. He'd never hit a woman in his life, but he would defend himself if necessary—or do what he'd done the last time and make a run for it.

"A deal's a deal," the blonde snarled. "We let that creepy Norludian do us both, so now you owe us each a fuck—or a nut."

"Yeah," the brunette agreed. "A fuck or a nut."

They were both planted squarely in front of him with hands on hips and fire in their deep blue Davordian eyes. While Dax cast about for a graceful way to escape the situation, he attempted to push Ava behind him and out of the path of danger. But Ava apparently had other ideas.

Ducking out from under his arm, she got right up in the brunette's face. "He's not fucking either of you! His balls belong to me, so back off, bitch!"

Dax was stunned. The very last thing he ever expected was to have Ava stand up and claim any part of him, let alone his balls. It was obvious that the Davordians hadn't either. Their eyes widened as the little Aquerei spitfire went after them, shoving the brunette in the gut and knocking her on her ass before drawing the blonde's blood with a quick jab to the nose.

"I said, back off!" Ava yelled. Her hair was standing on end and snapping with electricity. Dax had never seen a scarier-looking woman in his life. The two Davordians exchanged a quick but meaningful glance and beat a hasty retreat.

"Good thing she didn't have a frying pan," Waroun muttered.

"My, that was certainly entertaining," Threld commented mildly. "Does this mean you two are betrothed?"

Dax gaped at his friend. "I don't think she meant—"

"I figured I owed you one," Ava said quickly. "This makes us even, right?"

"Uh… yeah, sure… I guess." Dax was amazed that he could speak at all. He stared at her, fascinated, as her hair began to relax into its normal state. Then he realized that being "even" put him at a decided disadvantage.

"You didn't really mean that part about his balls belonging to you… did you?" Waroun asked cautiously.

"I dunno," said Teke. "She sounded pretty convincing to me."

"Not sure her hair would do that if she was faking it," Diokut agreed. "I think she just claimed you, Captain."

Obviously flustered, Ava looked more adorable than ever. "I—oh, *nuts*."

Threldigan chuckled. "Interesting choice of words." Dax watched with murderous jealousy as he gathered Ava up in his cape. "I think it would be best if I held onto you for a while. Let things settle down a bit." Turning, he set off with a purposeful stride.

Dax followed, but he certainly didn't want things to settle down. His cock was now wondrously hard, and Ava's scent was undoubtedly the reason. Perhaps she really *had* claimed him. There were stranger mating rituals—Dax had seen plenty of them—but the Aquerei were unknowns. For all he knew, the wild hair and ball-claiming ritual could be classic behavior.

Dax was ready to throw caution to the wind, carry her off somewhere, and end his virgin state with wild abandon before he lost his erection. But he knew quite well that his friend had never had to resort to such tactics.

But he's never kept a woman for very long, either. Dax continued to examine his options. If he really wanted to be with a woman—*any* woman—all he had to do was join his old shipmates in their brothel. They'd tried to get him laid more times than he cared to admit, and now they could actually make money off him. "So, where is this brothel of Tarq's?"

"Not far," Threldigan replied. "They'll be glad to see you." Grinning, he added, "They might give themselves a break and hire you out for the night."

"I don't need a pimp."

"*Sure* you don't," Threldigan said with a snicker. "You find hordes of women all on your own."

Dax shrugged. There was some truth in that. He found them all right. He just didn't want them. "So, how do they manage to…" Dax wasn't quite sure how to put it delicately, but considering Zetithian biology, he knew there might be problems.

"Get it up for any species that walks through the door? You'll see. It's quite ingenious, really."

"I'll just bet it is." Dax walked on, noting several appreciative glances from the women he passed. "We must be getting closer."

"We are," Threldigan said as two shapely Terrans sidled up to Dax. The younger woman was a dazzling redhead, while the other appeared to be old enough to be Dax's mother, though still quite attractive. Her eyes were a little glassy, as though she'd had too much tequila.

"Hey there, handsome," the redhead purred, snaking an arm around Dax's waist. "My name is Lura. Are you working tonight?" She stroked his chest with a seductive finger. "As big as you are, you're bound to have a cock like a *rolarten*."

"No, just like a typical Zetithian," Dax said as he attempted to extricate himself from her grasp.

"Which is big enough for any woman. Mom just got finished with Onca," Lura said proudly, pointing up the street to an enormous blinking sign that read, *"Once you go cat, you'll never go back!"* Smiling broadly, she added, "It's her sixtieth birthday. I wanted to give her something really special."

Ava stuck her head out from under Threldigan's cape. "And was it?"

The older woman blinked. "I—I'll have to let you know. I still haven't completely recovered." Turning to Lura, she asked, "What's my name again?"

"Treann," Lura replied. "Your name is Treann."

Treann nodded. "That's right. I remember now. And I'm from what planet?"

"Stralia. You remember… it's an Earth colony in the Aussie system."

"Okay, got it."

"It's a wonder she can walk," Waroun commented.

Lura patted her mother's hand. "I *told* you to stay longer. You could have spent the night if you wanted to. It was part of the package deal."

"I know," Treann murmured. "I just needed some air."

Ava was clearly intrigued. "Have you ever, um, done one of them?" she asked Lura.

"Several times. Mom's in the *laetralance* phase. It's what their semen, or *snard*, as they call it, does to you. It's like a drug. First the euphoria hits you, and then there's this amazing feeling of inner peace."

Treann let out a sigh. "And before that, the orgasms. Continuous, powerful, *amazing* orgasms…" Her voice trailed off, and her eyes took on a dreamy expression. "Never, in all my born days… Such joy… I may never be the same again." Swallowing hard, she licked her lower lip as though savoring something truly delicious.

"That big, ruffled cock… Ohmygod, it even *tasted* good." Treann directed her fuzzy gaze at Ava. "You're with the wrong man, dear. You need to get this one in your bed." She nodded toward Dax. "And don't ever let him go…" Giving Dax's hand a squeeze, she tottered off down the street.

"Hold on, Mom. You shouldn't be trying to walk by yourself." Hurrying forward, Lura took her mother's arm.

Dax watched as Treann leaned toward her daughter. "Promise me you won't tell your father, Lura, but that was the most incredible fuck of my life. It truly was joy—unlike any I have ever known."

"I know, Mom," Lura said, patting Treann's hand. "*Believe* me, I know."

Ava gazed after the two women, dimly aware of the tightening of her womb and the subsequent flood of moisture between her thighs. *Joy, unlike any I have ever known? Okay, Dax. I give up. Take me now. Get out your big, ruffled dick and let me have it. Right here in the middle of the street…*

But of course, she said no such thing. You had to have breath in your lungs in order to speak, and, unfortunately, Ava's respiratory system had ceased to function.

"Let's move on, shall we?" Teke said brightly. "We really need to check out that brothel! Perhaps there are others—featuring Kitnocks—in this district?" He looked questioningly at Threldigan, who nodded in reply.

They were standing on a corner, and Ava could see that beyond where they had first encountered Lura and Treann the street was lined with naked men lounging against the storefronts, accosting the various females who passed. In closer proximity, two handsome blond

Statzeelians were stroking each other's rather substantial equipment. It took Ava a moment to realize that they were identical. "Twins?"

"And we need your loving touch to keep us from killing each other," one of them said with a seductive smile. "Come now, lovely lady, admit it—you've always wanted to be with two men. Two identical men who will do anything to please you. Absolutely *anything*." Grinning broadly, he added, "We'll even do each other if you like." With a flick of his brow, he dropped to his knees and licked his brother's dick tantalizingly before sucking it into his mouth. The one left standing dug his fingers into his brother's blond curls and held him firmly as he drove his stiff cock in with quick, hard thrusts.

Ava had never witnessed anything like this—even on Luxaria—and had no idea she could be affected so profoundly. If she had been wet before, she was dripping now. The thought of having both of them was the most provocative, erotic notion that had ever been planted in her head. She could almost feel them inside her; she would straddle one brother, his big hard cock filling her pussy while the other one fucked her ass…

She hadn't realized she was walking toward them until Dax grabbed her from behind. "I don't need it, and I don't want it," he said in her ear.

"What? Of course you don't! But I want it! They're freakin' gorgeous, even if their noses *are* a little flat."

"Ava," Dax said firmly. "They will affect you the same way the other merchandise does on this world. Trust me, you *don't* need them, and you *don't* want them. Now, say it."

Ava winced and let out a long moan. "But I don't want to. I want them both, and I want them *now*."

"You'll be sorry," Dax warned. "You'll wish you hadn't done it."

"Never!" Ava declared. "I want sex so bad, I'd even…"

"Even what?"

"Fuck Waroun!" Ava screamed. "I'll even fuck Waroun!" And it was true. Waroun's big tongue would satisfy her craving very nicely. He could hold onto her with those sucker-tipped fingers and do her better than anyone ever had. But Dax was still holding her.

"She hasn't gotten laid in a long time, has she?" Threldigan commented.

"Probably not," Waroun agreed. "However, I'm perfectly willing to help her out."

"No you won't," Dax snarled. He spun Ava around to face him and, with his hands over her ears, he bent down until their noses were almost touching. *"You don't want it, and you don't need it."*

Ava tried to pull away. "No! I *do* want it. Right now!"

"It's not working, Threld," Dax said desperately. "Why isn't it working?"

Threldigan shook his head. "No clue—unless they've beefed up the pheromone level on this street recently. I've never been down here with a woman before—well, at least not a woman I was trying to discourage."

"Me either."

Dax had barely gotten the words out of his mouth before Ava lost all control and kissed him. It was a given that he was far better than anyone else on the street; sexier, better looking, and taller too. How could she possibly want anyone else?

Without warning, Dax gathered her up in his arms and stood straight up, pressing her breasts tightly against his chest. Her legs wrapped around his waist seemingly of their own accord but his lips… his fabulous, succulent lips… They tasted like everything she'd ever been told was bad for her, meaning that they were delicious and intoxicating—even better than Sholerian cream. Her hands lost themselves in his hair, grasping his tight curls to pull him closer as her tongue slipped into his mouth.

If his lips tasted better than Sholerian cream, then his tongue was a hot fudge sundae. With that in mind, Treann's words about Onca came back to her. She'd obviously been referring to his penis. Big and ruffled… never mind the taste; how would that *feel*?

If she'd been a magician, Ava would have waved her magic wand and made Dax as naked as every other man on the street. All he had on was a T-shirt, boots, and cargo pants. Even without magic, she could have him out of them in seconds, whether he cooperated or not. She wanted to taste him, to lick and suck him like that Statzeelian had done to his twin. Breaking off the kiss, she seized the front of his shirt and pulled.

The look on Dax's face was a mixture of emotions. Ava retained enough of her wits to see that, but even so, what he said shook her to the core.

"You can't have *them*, Ava," he whispered hoarsely, "but you can have *me*."

The Cylopean drew his hood closely around his face and leaned forward, avoiding the bright glare in the casino lounge—one of the few places the indigent could hang out and not be bothered. Plenty of millionaires pretended to be poor to keep from being preyed upon, and the needy used this to their advantage. "The stone," he whispered. "You should have seen it, Drak. The color of a sunlit sea and as big and long as your thumb. Oddly shaped, too."

His companion, a hunchbacked Vetla, scoffed. "Come on, Zirf. You're dreaming."

"No, I'm not. It was on a blond girl down in the commercial district—the main road from the spaceport. I'd have had it too, but she wasn't alone. I got pounced on by a big cat."

"A big cat? Oh really?" The Vetla leaned back in his chair and raised a furry eyebrow. "I think I've heard enough of your drivel."

The Cylopean looked pained. "I'm telling the truth. It was a man, but he moved like a cat."

"A Zetithian, perhaps?"

"Maybe so," said the Cylopean. "Never seen one of them."

"There are three down in the brothel district. Might have been one of them."

"Doesn't matter. All I know is I didn't stand a chance against him. He probably took the stone for himself."

"I doubt it. Very honest lot, those Zetithians."

The Cylopean snorted. "They run a fuckin' brothel, Drak. How honest is that? I mean, most men give it away."

"They aren't like most men," Drak said. "And if they were giving it away, they'd probably be drowning in women."

A thickset Aquerei man with sea green tentacles

sprouting from his head stepped closer. He had obviously been listening. "A Zetithian, you say? What did he look like?"

"Very tall, with black dreadlocks and a tattoo on the side of his face and neck," Zirf replied. "Tough guy, too. *Very* tough."

Drak snorted again. "You're just saying that because he was able to run you off. It wouldn't take much with a wuss like you."

Drak was always saying things like that to Zirf, so he was able to ignore this and addressed the Aquerei instead. "Do you know him?"

"No, but I know *of* him. His whereabouts are very important to some friends of mine."

Zirf's beady black eyes narrowed. "They willing to pay?"

"No, but I am," the Aquerei replied. "Five credits if you can tell me where he is right now."

"Right now?" Zirf exclaimed. "At this very moment? How the devil would I know that? I can tell you where he was and who he was with, but that's about all."

"That'll do," the Aquerei said shortly. "Three credits."

Zirf gave him the information, but as the credits were slapped on the table, he added, "Don't know that it'll do you much good. But he's here in the city somewhere. Good luck finding him."

"I'll find him," the Aquerei said. "He's got something we've been after for a very long time."

"The girl or the stone?"

The Aquerei smiled and shook his head. "That's something you don't need to know."

"You're probably right." Zirf picked up the credits.

The stone was worth a lot more, but this was better than nothing. Yawning, he stretched his arms out behind him, popping the joints in his shoulders. "Think I'll go lie down in the street and wait for the sweepers to pick me up. I'll at least have a decent place to sleep tonight."

The Aquerei was laughing as he left the lounge.

———

Wane eyed his cohort expectantly. "Have you found out who he is yet?" The two Aquerei occupied one of the many small private rooms available in the city's casino district for those who didn't wish their activities to be observed too closely.

Junosk nodded, his green tentacles snapping with excitement. "Dax Vandilorsk of the *Valorcry*. Thank God for the port authority records. He's got two Kitnocks, a Drell, and a Norludian with him, and guess who else?"

"A blond girl with a crystal pendant?"

"Oh, yeah."

"Too easy," Wane argued. Given what was at stake, this made no sense at all. "They should be hiding out, not advertising the damn stone."

"That's what I figured, but I've been giving this some thought, and I think maybe they don't know what it is."

"You've got to be kidding me. That stone has been hidden for centuries. Do you honestly think it would wind up with someone who would just parade it around like that?"

"Who knows? It could be that such objects have intentions of their own. But it could also be a fake," Junosk admitted.

"Or one helluva coincidence. Here we are, searching

every planet in the sector, and she just happens to land on Rhylos with the Aquina keystone dangling around her neck? What are the odds?"

"Well, we *have* been following the lead of the Unities. Surely Eantle has *some* idea."

"One would hope so. I'm beginning to wonder if we may have been too hasty in knocking off that Unity enclave. Who knows which, if any, of those left have the first clue?"

"They have to know something," Junosk insisted. "They wouldn't be doing what they're doing if they didn't."

"Okay, then," Wane said. "If they're following Vandilorsk, then we will too. God knows we haven't got anything else to go on. Maybe we could draw them in and trap them."

"How?"

"How the hell should I know? I'm making this up as I go along."

"Probably couldn't get to the girl directly," Junosk mused. "It would be hard to separate her from the group—don't forget that the Cylopean I heard all this from tried it and got pounced on by Vandilorsk, plus, somewhere along the line, they teamed up with Threldigan the Magician."

Wane rolled his big, round orange eyes. "This just gets worse and worse, doesn't it?"

"No shit."

"So, what, we nab one of the others and hope they'll come after him?"

"Works for me."

"Any idea which one?"

"Well, certainly not the magician. Messing with him would be more trouble than it was worth."

"Hmm, a Norludian, two Kitnocks, and a Drell, you say? Were they all there together?"

"The Cylopean didn't mention seeing a Drell. Now, that's not to say that he wasn't nearby, but if he tends to separate himself from the group…"

Wane was momentarily cheered, but his tentacles drooped when he realized the difficulties inherent in this plan. "One Drell looks very much like another, Jun. Finding the right one would be next to impossible."

Junosk grinned. "Not when you know his name."

Chapter 11

TO BE PERFECTLY CORRECT, DAX HAD NEVER BEEN ON THAT particular street with or without a woman. Naked men standing on the street corners didn't appeal to him in the slightest, though Waroun had always said that a few days spent working in a brothel would improve Dax's attitude toward women considerably.

But Ava had already done that. And when he'd snatched her up, she smelled like sex and flowers and sweet, delectable fruit. His cock had sprung to attention, and suddenly all thoughts of charm, slow seduction, and playing it cool went flying off into space. He hadn't said that simply to get her away from the twins. Right then and there, he offered himself to her, body and soul.

But would she still want him when they turned the corner to venture down a different street? What happened on Rhylos tended to stay on Rhylos, simply because the feelings you experienced there didn't follow you when you left. He'd seen it happen many times before; every purchase lost a portion of its luster as soon as you departed—which was enough to make anyone question their motives, as well as their heart.

Closing his eyes, he went on. "But it's just chemicals in the air that are doing this to you. If we head back the way we came, it'll go away."

Ava let go of him and slid to the ground. "Does that mean I can't really have you?"

Dax felt confused. "I—don't know, Ava. I just don't know. I felt something—still do—but if you don't then... well... whatever..."

"Oh, for pity's sake!" Threldigan yanked Ava out of Dax's arms and wrapped her in his cloak. "No wonder you're still a virgin."

"What?"

"I can't believe how bad you are at this, Dax! One minute you've got a woman in your arms, kissing you for all she's worth, and the next you're mumbling like a tongue-tied idiot."

"He's not an idiot," Ava said, her voice muffled by the cape.

"Be quiet and keep your head down," Threldigan told her. He glanced briefly at Dax before heading off down the street, announcing to the hookers: "This one isn't interested, boys, so you can just keep your dicks to yourselves."

"But she's so cute," a bronze sex god said from his doorway. He stepped into the light and leaned back against the wall to better display the sword tattooed across his chest. The hilt connected his nipples while the blade ran down his middle, the tip coinciding with the head of his penis. Dax didn't even want to think about how badly that must've hurt. The tattoo he had on his neck had been bad enough, but on his dick? No way! The bronze god grinned and began a slow, sinuous pelvic thrust. "I'd love to run her through with my sword."

Unable to think of a snappy retort, Dax followed in Threldigan's wake with the rest of the guys trailing behind him. "I hate Rhylos," he grumbled. "Really, truly hate it. That's why I never come here—and it's not just because of those damned hookers. This place makes me crazy."

"You didn't mean what you said?" Ava called out.

"Yes, I meant what I said, but you probably didn't hear it right." Dax had never been more disgusted with himself in his life. Ava had been in his arms—had even kissed him—but he wasn't sure what happened after that. Something had ruined the moment. Then he remembered. *He* was the one who'd ruined the moment. Why hadn't he just shut up and kissed her?

"We'll talk about this when we get to the Zetithian Palace," Threldigan said. "The pheromone effect is turned off in there."

"Oh, and why is that?" Teke asked.

Threldigan chuckled wickedly. "They don't need it."

Dax winced. Great. As soon as she saw what a Zetithian was *supposed* to be like, Ava would probably fall for one of them even without the pheromones in the air.

Tarq had always said he wasn't good for anything but sex. Onca was a player, no doubt about it. Dax didn't think Ava would be in danger of losing her heart to them. But Jerden? He was trouble. *Big* trouble.

The Zetithian Palace was easily the largest and most tasteful building on the street, the elegant entrance promising a much higher-class form of entertainment. No perfumes or pheromone-laced ventilators blew in the faces of passersby, nor was there a naked man standing by the door. Soft music played—music that Dax immediately recognized as Zetithian in origin.

The doorway led straight from the street into a jungle. Flowers bloomed everywhere. Leafy vines clung to the

walls, while rose-colored velvet daybeds lined the pe-
rimeter. A table laden with fresh fruit and dainty candies
sat in the middle of the room, its centerpiece a fountain
of sparkling red wine. Two women were lying on the
beds, one completely awake, but languid and smiling
as she sipped her wine, while the other looked to be in
even more of a stupor than Treann had been. Both were
unclothed but blanketed in deep red satin.

A tiny Zuteran female approached from behind her
desk. Her patterned red silk dress complemented her
startlingly pink skin, and her hair fell to her knees in
waves of purest white. She seemed surprised by the appearance of so many men, but smiled in recognition as
the gaze from her china blue eyes landed on Threldigan.

"What a pleasure it is to see you again, Threldigan."
Her voice was like liquid birdsong. "We've missed you."

"The pleasure is all mine, Roncas." Threldigan
bowed, planting a kiss on the hand she held out to him.
"I have brought a friend to visit the men."

"And others as well," she trilled. "So many males…
It is very rare that we see so many here, but you, my
dear," she said, turning to Ava. "You must first pass
through the medscanner. We cannot risk having any of
our men become ill."

Ava shook her head but didn't reply. Roncas seemed
to take this as an agreement that the men shouldn't be
servicing anyone who could make them sick, for she
continued on as though Ava was just another speechless client. "Should you wish to avoid conception, that
is your choice. However, the men do not practice any
form of birth control, and if you do become impreg-
nated, you must register the child with the Zetithian

Birth Registry." Roncas paused there, but then added apologetically, "Actually, I should say *children*, because there will be three of them!"

"Uh, no. I'm not here for anything like that. I—I'm with them."

Roncas grinned, revealing her silvery teeth. "Threldigan is a very charming fellow, isn't he?"

Ava stared at her blankly. "I suppose so. I mean, I just met him, but…" Dax felt oddly pleased by her lack of enthusiasm and watched with renewed interest.

"You are not his current paramour, then?"

"Well, no," Ava said, clearly puzzled. "I don't think I'm anyone's paramour."

Roncas laughed. "Give him time. He will have you in his power soon enough."

"Don't believe I'd care to be in anyone's power. It was bad enough being out in the street. How does anyone ever get past that first corner?"

"The twins are difficult to resist," Roncas admitted. "They have been in that location for some time. There have been complaints that they should rotate to give the others a fair chance."

"And what about the Zetithians?" Teke asked. "Do they not complain?"

Roncas cast him a look of disdain. "My Zetithians do not rely on foot traffic. They are seen by appointment only."

"Then why are they here on this street?"

Roncas shrugged. "The site was available, and the building suited their needs. Otherwise, it could have been anywhere in the city."

"I see," said Teke.

Dax caught his eye with a skeptical flick of his brow. Roncas followed the look, her teardrop-shaped eyes stopping on Dax. "Are you perhaps seeking a position here? We could certainly use you."

Waroun let out a guffaw. "The Great Virgin? *In a brothel?* Surely you jest!"

"Shut up, Waroun," Dax growled. "Unless you want to die right here and now."

"Ha! You talk tough, but I know—"

"Could we see the Zetithians?" Ava interjected. "We'd like to meet them."

"As it happens, they are on their break. This way, please." Roncas led them through an arched doorway clustered with fragrant blooms into an open space that nearly stopped Dax's heart.

It was Zetith in miniature. The entire building was open to the starlit sky above, and huge trees grew in profusion, while blooming vines wound their way up the trunks. Spectacular butterflies flitted about, and a bird swooped down, its metallic green wings almost brushing Dax's hair. A waterfall cascaded from the side of a cliff to form a stream that was channeled into a circular pattern by grassy banks. The center island was dotted with flowers, and orchids grew from niches in the trunk of a central tree. Tiny hovering lights lit the scene like fireflies on a summer night, while birdsong filled the air.

Roncas seemed pleased by their reactions. "These plants and birds are not native to Zetith, of course—all of those were lost when that world was destroyed—but the birds and butterflies of Barada Seven have settled in very nicely. Beautiful, aren't they?"

Ava's face was turned upward as she took in the view. "This is a *brothel*?"

"A Zetithian brothel," a male voice said from behind them.

Dax spun around to see his three old friends standing there, each of them wearing nothing but a broad grin.

Ava had been expecting more naked men, but none of those she'd seen on the street could even begin to compare with the trio she now faced. Dax was hugging each of them in turn, but Ava had gone weak in the knees, and it was all she could do to remain standing. Dax introduced them to the rest of the group, and Ava caught their names, but that was about all. No, there was no need to pipe clouds of sex hormones into the air around them. They exuded sexual heat without any adornment whatsoever.

The men were tall and muscular, with the same cat-like grace that Dax possessed. Onca had a thick mane of auburn curls and laughing green eyes, while Jerden was dark, almost brooding, and his ebony eyes smoldered with passion. Tarq was a blue-eyed blond with a square jaw and a sincere, thoughtful expression; he didn't look at all like the type to sell his cock to any woman willing to pay for it. None of them had hair that curled as tightly as Dax's did, and instead of being braided back, each of them had shining locks that hung past their waists. Ava couldn't help noticing that their substantial genitals were flaccid at the moment, but then Jerden came forward to take her hand and kissed her on the cheek, inhaling deeply as his warm lips caressed her skin.

Within moments, his penis blossomed from its

foreskin, and the ruffled head appeared, already dripping with the orgasmic lubricating fluid for which Zetithians were famous. "I am very pleased to meet you, Ava." Jerden's dark eyes roamed over her. "You are part Aquerei, are you not?"

Ava nodded. "My father was Aquerei—"

"And your mother must have been Terran. Very few species smell even half as good to us as Terrans do." He caressed her cheek with a deeply tanned finger. "But then, you have been out on the street, and the scents there have aroused you." Licking his lips as though preparing for a feast, he leaned closer, flicking her earlobe with the tip of his tongue. "If you wish, I could skip my break to accommodate your needs."

When he nipped her earlobe with a fang, Ava's mouth went completely dry. Her hair began to curl, while the ache between her thighs reached painful proportions.

"She doesn't need to hire us," Tarq said. "She's got Dax, doesn't she?" Jerden shot a meaningful look at his friend, who then mumbled, "Oh, yeah. That's right. The Great Virgin. How could I forget?"

Jerden touched the ruffled head of his cock then brushed her lips with his thumb, teasing them apart. "Please accept a free sample, then," he purred. "Guaranteed to give you joy."

As she tasted the slick saltiness on his skin, Ava was dimly aware that Dax had grabbed Jerden from behind, but it was too late. She staggered backward as her orgasm erupted with the force of an exploding volcano.

Dax caught her before she fell. As she gazed up at his glowing, feline eyes, she could see tiny lights twinkling in the branches above his head. He was purring.

"Holy moly!" she gasped. "I suppose you can do that too?"

"Yes, I can. Want some more?"

"Sure," she replied, blinking up at him. "Bring it on."

"Finally!" Threldigan exclaimed. "Hit it, Roncas!"

The floor beneath her feet began to vibrate, but several moments had passed before Ava realized that they were standing on a platform that was slowly rising up into the trees.

Chapter 12

They were alone at last, but Ava was standing perilously close to the edge. Dax pulled her toward the center of the platform.

"Don't worry," Onca called out. "You won't fall off—there's a force field. Just give a yell when you're ready to come back down."

Dax bit his lip pensively. Ava was still gazing up at him with that same expression on her lovely face, but—"Are you sure?"

"And don't you dare give her an out!" Threldigan shouted. "Just keep your mouth shut unless you're kissing her!"

Dax scowled down at his friends. "Thanks, guys. This makes me feel like such a—" He broke off there, unable to think of the right word to describe this situation. Idiot came to mind, but—

"Virgin!" Waroun cackled. "But not for long!"

"I'm sorry, Ava. I know they mean well, but—"

Ava put a finger to his lips. "You said I could have you, and I told you to bring it on. I meant what I said."

Dax still wasn't convinced. "It's not just because my crazy friends are teasing you with their joy juice or pheromones or whatever it is they have in the air here?"

"None of that." Reaching up, she pulled him down for a kiss. "Just you."

Onca yelled out, "Twist the rock if you need anything!"

Dax had no idea what that meant and didn't care. Ava's kisses had his mind fully occupied to the point that he didn't even realize he was purring.

Ava stroked his neck as though seeking the source of the vibrations. "How do you do that?"

"Don't know. It's innate among Zetithians."

"You're just a bunch of big, purring kittens, aren't you? I like that." Ava took his hand and pulled him down onto the grass, giggling. Rolling onto her back, she kicked off her shoes and lay with her arms stretched out on the turf. "This place is *so* cool!"

"It reminds me of the forests on Zetith," he said. "It's the closest thing to home I've seen since I left."

"Looks like paradise to me."

Dax glanced around at the twinkling lights and listened to the calls of the night birds while the real stars shone brightly above them. He was about to agree with her when he caught her gaze. She wasn't looking at the trees; she was looking at *him.*

A thousand different fears ran through his mind, not the least of which was that she might be disappointed. Jerden was probably a better choice. "Ava, I'm not—"

"Aw, Dax. Remember what Threldigan said? All you really have to do is shut up and kiss me."

Dax took a deep breath and stretched out beside her. "I can do that. But I'm pretty much clueless when it comes to pleasing women." He was really going to do it this time—if he didn't think it to death or talk himself out of it. *Keep your mouth shut unless you're kissing her, Dax. Don't talk, don't think, just feel. Just close your eyes and breathe…*

Which was possibly the best advice anyone could

have given him. Without thinking, he rolled over and covered her with his body. His lips found hers, and as he tasted her sweetness, her scent drove straight to his groin. Instincts long buried surfaced, and he licked her neck, savoring her warm skin.

She was touching him. Running her hands over his back, scratching him gently with her nails, slipping those same hands beneath his shirt—the shirt she'd very nearly ripped to shreds out there in the street. This time, she didn't try to rip it, but began steadily bunching it up in her hands until it was up around his neck. Then her hands were on his bare skin, sending sensuous tingles up and down his spine. The warmth of her palms stimulated him, soothed him, and aroused him. Dax was salivating like a starving man, his passion spiraling out of control. Suddenly, licking and kissing weren't enough. He raked her shoulder with his fangs, nipping her lightly.

"So you bite, huh? Should have known that. Let's see how you like it." Grasping his hair with both hands, she pulled him closer and bit him on the neck, right below the place where his tattoo flamed over his jaw to curl up his cheek.

Her sharp teeth ignited a fire in Dax. He needed more of her skin; needed to feel it warm and vibrant against his own. Growling, he yanked off his shirt and went for her clothes. He had to hand it to Kots; the little droid really knew how to dress a woman. The clingy fabric matched her eyes, but the way it crossed over in front had been driving him crazy ever since they landed. Dax soon discovered another nice feature; the dress was held in place by one little snap on each hip. Moving slowly, he unhooked the outer wrap and folded it back. Then he found the other snap, and the dress fell open.

It was all she'd had on aside from her shoes.

Dax's heart stopped beating for a moment as he drank her in.

She didn't seem shy, but when he stole a glance at her face, he was astonished to see surprise and uncertainty there, mingled with a trace of embarrassment.

He sat back on his heels. "What? I'm not supposed to look at you?"

She shook her head. "No, it's not that. It's the *way* you're looking at me. It's... different."

Dax tried to avert his eyes but couldn't. "I can't help it that you're beautiful, Ava. You're the most beautiful thing I've ever seen."

"I think there must still be a few pheromones affecting you. I'm not *that* pretty."

"I didn't say you were pretty. *Anyone* can be pretty. I said you were beautiful."

"I—I don't get it."

"Beauty is more than just being pleasing to the eye. Beauty is pleasing to the *soul*."

A long moment passed, and Dax was beginning to think he'd blown it again.

"You know something, Dax?" she said slowly. "For a guy who claims to be clueless, you're doing amazingly well."

He started to reply, but then he remembered: *Just shut up and kiss her.*

With a smile, he fell forward, and their lips met. He'd never felt so free, nor so privileged. He could touch her, kiss her, and mate with her. She might not be his forever, but right now, she was his to entice and enjoy. He would gladly give her everything he had.

Dax's skin tingled as Ava reached for his belt. Women had grabbed him before but had never made him feel like this. He craved her touch, anxious for her to explore every last bit of him. As she pulled down his zipper, he felt her lips smiling beneath his own.

"What's the matter?"

She laughed wickedly. "The commando thing."

"What?"

"No underwear."

Her laughter was infectious. "I've always felt like I needed the extra ball room."

"Oh, *my*…"

Smiling, he sat back on his heels as his gaze swept down her body to focus on her feet. "There's something I've been dying to know about you too…" Moving slowly, he lifted her foot and found the delicate membranes between her toes. "So it's true… your feet are webbed like your hands…"

He moved back up, and she reached for him, her warm hands sliding over his back to delve beneath the waistband. The feeling was soothing but also exciting. Arching his back, he slid forward over her soft skin, giving her better access. Slowly, she pushed his cargoes down past his hips.

Dax gulped in a breath as his cock skated across her stomach. Her hands on his ass had been fabulous, but this was incredible. He rose up to tease her belly with his cockhead's scalloped corona, letting his slick fluid puddle in her navel. Testing his control, he painted her skin with his cock, delighting in her soft moans.

Using only his lips, he made his way across her cheek, then down her neck to her unbelievably soft breasts. Dax loved the way she gasped when he licked her taut nipples, but her scent was drawing him downward to the source. Dipping his head between her legs, he tasted her—soft, wet, and delicious. Delirious from her scent and flavor, Dax teased her pussy lips apart with his tongue. Plunging into her core, he curled his tongue and took a sip.

The fire that ignited in his cock could only be quenched in the same place it began—a place where he would find both relief and joy. Dax got up on his knees, scooped up her legs, and pulled her onto him.

The feeling as he slid into Ava was unlike anything Dax had ever imagined. She fit him like a warm glove, and as her legs wrapped around his waist, Dax felt complete for the very first time. Closing his eyes, he held his breath, savoring the moment.

"Breathe, Dax," she whispered. "And look at me."

His lids flew open, and their eyes met. Hers were as round and beautiful as ever, but with an expression he'd never seen before—one he couldn't identify. Then he felt her orgasm squeezing his cock and realized what he'd seen. He waited until it passed, pleased that he was able to give her that kind of pleasure from the very beginning, but still not quite sure…

"Are you ready? I—I don't want to hurt you."

"You won't," she promised. "Bring it on."

And then he began to move, purring as he rocked into her. Slowly at first, feeling his way, but pretty soon he picked up the rhythm—a rhythm as old as time and as natural as breathing.

"You feel *so* good. I never knew how good it could

be, and I'm so *very* glad I waited for you—for lots of reasons…" His voice trailed off as he shifted to a different angle. The new position must have had some effect, because Ava made an odd sound. He wasn't sure if she was laughing or crying—though it might have been a little of both.

"You say the sweetest things. It's hard to believe I'm your first."

Dax shook his head. "I never said anything like that before." Leaning closer, he pressed a kiss to her cheek. "It's because of you, Ava. You bring out the lover in me."

Dax had never felt like much of a lover before. He was inexperienced with the act as much as the emotion. He'd been orphaned too young to remember how it felt to love his family, but it was coming back to him now. Ava aroused emotions that went far deeper than sex.

He'd been trying to take it slowly, but knowing that the best was yet to come—for both of them—had him increasing the speed and strength of his thrusts. Following his instincts, Dax did the one thing he remembered from all those sexual discussions he'd tried so hard to ignore. Thrusting in as far as he could, he let his dick do the work. Back and forth, around in circles and in every other pattern he could think of, he stroked her inner walls with his stiff cock while the orgasmic juice poured from the head. If he'd been trying to keep track of the number of her orgasms, he would have lost count then. It was impossible to tell where one broke off and another began.

Dax wished he could have kept it up for hours, if for no other reason than seeing his efforts reflected on her face. All too soon, his ejaculation began building, and

Dax knew he couldn't last much longer. Suddenly, his eyes squeezed shut and his mind went blank. He felt nothing but the force of his ecstasy, bursting through the dam to flood her core with his *snard*.

Opening his eyes, he watched it unfold. Within seconds, Ava's pupils had dilated completely, obliterating each iris until it was no more than a thin rim to the windows of her soul. Dax would never forget her expression until his dying day: It reflected sheer amazement, ultimate pleasure, and profound bliss. Knowing something about his own species, he'd expected that much, but her mixed Terran and Aquerei blood must have been responsible for what happened next. Her skin began to shimmer in the starlight, taking on an iridescent glow. While this was beautiful and wondrous to behold, it was nothing compared to what happened to her hair. As the effect of his semen took hold, her blond locks began tossing like waves on a stormy sea, swelling and cresting before crashing onto the shore.

A flash of light caught his eye. Glancing down, Dax saw that Ava's pendant was the source. Though it had slipped sideways to lie in the grass beneath her shoulder, the facets of the huge crystal had somehow captured the glow from her skin, sending out fiery sparkles rivaling those of a diamond. Then, as her skin lost its shine, the stone went dark.

Ava gazed up at Dax's glowing eyes and knew then that the rumors were true: Once you went cat, you *never* went back. Ava might have been a virgin herself, unsure

whether to lie back and let him do as he pleased or take
a more active role.

Stars twinkled behind him as his curly locks dangled
enticingly around his face. The tattooed flames licked
his neck and cheek the way Ava longed to do—and
would do—every chance she got. As her orgasm began
to subside, she felt the ruffled head of his cock stroking
her from within, prolonging the ecstasy. At last, her legs
lost their grip and she eased down onto the grass as his
penis slipped from her body.

"What was it Treann said?" she murmured. "Something about joy?"

Dax smiled. "It's the standard Zetithian pick-up
line—or a promise. I've never been sure which."

"Say it," she said. "I want to hear it from you."

"Come, mate with me, my love, and I will give you
joy unlike any you have ever known." He punctuated
it with a kiss that made it seem more like a promise
and less like a line. "That's the full version we were
taught as kids. I've never used it myself—never needed
to. Should I have said it at the beginning?"

Ava considered this briefly. "No, because then I
might have had some idea of what to expect. It was better this way." She let out a long contented sigh. "Is it the
same with all of you?"

"I'd like to think it isn't, but it probably is," Dax
admitted. "Might be better with some than with others.
I can only think of one woman who's ever been with
two of us, but she had already chosen one over the other.
I doubt if even she could give you an honest answer."

"It's a wonder she survived."

Dax laughed. "I don't think any woman has ever

died from having sex with one of us—at least, not that I know of."

"Maybe some of the repeat customers here could tell me." Grinning wickedly, she added, "Or I could take Jerden up on his offer and see for myself."

"Over my dead body."

Ava drew back in surprise. "That sounds rather possessive. Does this mean I belong to you now?"

Dax looked confused—but endearingly so. "Zetithians traditionally mate for life. I know it's different with other cultures—and my friends here obviously don't adhere to the custom—but I always thought it would be that way for me."

Ava didn't want to spoil the moment, but neither did she want to make promises she couldn't keep. "I wish I'd known that. Trag is the only other Zetithian I've ever met, and he was so popular with the hookers, I didn't realize he wasn't typical. If I had known how you felt, I'm not sure I would have gone through with this."

One glance at him was enough to remind her that reason didn't always prevail over desire. "Well, maybe I would have. You're the most tempting man I've ever met, but sex and love are two different things. You've never let yourself get close enough to any woman to understand the difference."

Dax nodded, but Ava wasn't sure he understood.

"What I mean is, I made a huge mistake with Lars. I don't want you to wake up someday and find that you've done the same thing."

His face was a wooden mask. "You weren't a mistake."

"Maybe not," she conceded. "But I'm not sure I could live the kind of life you lead. I'd need some time to think about it." Ava was a little surprised that she could think so rationally after making love with Dax. It was difficult to put him off, and above all, she didn't want to hurt him. Then she realized she already had. "I'm sorry I let myself get so carried away, Dax. I honestly didn't know."

"Don't be sorry. I just thought that because I wanted you, it meant something. Maybe it didn't."

"And maybe it did," she said quickly. "We don't know that yet. I can't promise to be your mate for life right now, but I will promise you one thing: I'll keep an open mind."

"So, we can… do this again sometime?"

Ava smiled. "Of course! What woman wouldn't want that kind of joy?"

"And we're… what? Dating?"

"Yeah, we're… dating. Just trying each other on for size. Is that okay with you?"

"Yes, but would you promise me something else?"

"Like what?"

Dax took a deep breath. "Don't let the others talk you into doing this with them."

Ava couldn't help but smile. "Ah, so we're dating exclusively, then."

"Is that a problem?"

"No. I'm sure they're all very good at what they do, but their lack of exclusiveness doesn't do much for me."

Dax grinned. "Yeah, I never wanted to do it with a hooker, either. It always seemed sort of… meaningless."

"Exactly."

"So, what do we do now?"

"How about twisting the rock? I'll admit I'm curious."

"Me too, but which one?" Since there were several

scattered about the platform, the choice wasn't immediately obvious.

"Try them all, I guess."

Dax stood up and Ava's good sense went flying off into space. It had been hard enough to keep from swearing her undying love and devotion when she was only looking him in the eye, but the whole package was impossible to resist. The other Zetithians were all remarkably handsome and well-built, but Dax came very close to her ideal—to *anyone's* ideal. He was flawless.

Propping herself up on one elbow, she watched as Dax went from rock to rock, testing each of them in turn. Barefoot and unclothed, his catlike grace wasn't camouflaged, making every movement a treat for the eye. If he'd been one to espouse nudity on a regular basis, Ava had little doubt that his virginity would have been stolen from him long ago.

Stealing it came very close to what she had done. His thoughts on what should happen next proved it. He wasn't a child; he was a grown man, and though he certainly knew how to handle himself, he was undeniably naïve when it came to matters of the heart. Had his heart ever been broken? And if so, by whom? Ava hoped she wouldn't be the one to do it, but wondering this made her realize just how little she knew about him.

She had been his passenger, not his confidant, and ships' captains rarely had the opportunity to spend enough time with anyone long enough to know them well. Certainly the physical attraction was there, but the mental attraction? Only time would tell.

"I found it," Dax announced. "It's a robotender. Want anything from the bar?"

"I don't suppose Aquerei water is on the menu."

"No, but they do have Zetithian ale. Wonder who's making that?"

Ava laughed. "What I'd like to know is where they got the recipe."

"From Amelyana," he replied. "She downloaded the entire Zetithian database into the ship's computer. She felt responsible for what happened there and did the best she could to save us and our culture."

"What *did* happen to Zetith, Dax? I never heard the whole story."

"We didn't fully understand it ourselves. We'd never been a warrior race. Our world was peaceful, but suddenly we were besieged and didn't know why. All we could do was fight back as best we could. Amelyana suspected that her husband, Rutger Grekkor, was responsible, but until he confessed and was killed, there wasn't a safe place for us anywhere in the galaxy. As it turned out, she *was* the reason we were almost exterminated—not the only one, perhaps—but it was her love for a Zetithian man that made Grekkor so insanely jealous that he set out to destroy us."

"Like Helen of Troy," Ava mused, though she doubted that Dax would understand the reference. "She must have felt very guilty about that."

"I think if she hadn't been able to save at least a few of us, it would have killed her. She dedicated her life to preserving our race. Too bad we didn't have a world of our own to return to. There are a lot of us on Terra Minor, but it isn't Zetith."

Dax took two bottles of ale from the robotender and handed one to Ava before sitting down beside her. He didn't seem the least bit shy about his nudity. For a man who'd never let anyone into his pants before, he seemed oddly comfortable without them.

Ava took a sip of the ale, finding it crisp and refreshing and only mildly intoxicating. "This is very good. With the right promotion and distribution, it would sell very well."

Dax laughed. "It's a wonder Jack isn't peddling it all over the quadrant." He studied the label. "Says here it was made on Terra Minor, which isn't too surprising. Like I said, that's where most of us are." He closed his eyes and took a long drink. "I've been to the Zetithian system a few times. Our beautiful world is nothing but a field of asteroids now. It's like visiting a cemetery or the ruins of a long-dead civilization."

"Describe it for me—the way you remember it."

"Just look around you. They did a great job on this place. The funny thing is, I'm still not sure if what I remember is the actual planet or the computer images we studied in history class. I was only two years old when Amelyana picked us up. Tarq was twelve, so he remembers it better. We had all been orphaned by the war, and Amelyana was the only 'mother' many of us ever had."

Ava sighed. "And I've never even *seen* my father. I guess we have more in common than I thought." She paused, weighing her words carefully before voicing them. "Let me ask you something, Dax. When was the last time you talked with someone like this?"

Dax smiled. "What, lying naked on a grassy bower up in the trees? Probably never."

"No, I mean it. The setting is irrelevant. It's the subject matter I'm concerned about."

His smile disappeared. "The answer is still the same."

She took his hand, giving it a gentle squeeze. "I'm deeply honored that you would share it with me. Thank you."

"Thank you for listening." A sheepish grin played across his lips. "And for the other things."

"You're not mad at me, then?"

"For what?"

"For not falling into your arms and declaring my undying love for you."

His grin widened, his fangs gleaming in the starlight. "Doesn't matter. I'm a patient fellow. I can wait."

Chapter 13

AVA HAD MEANT IT WHEN SHE SAID SHE WAS DEEPLY honored to be the woman Dax had finally opened himself to, yet she couldn't help feeling that she had succumbed to temptation, breaking yet another promise to herself. Her heart begged her to give him a chance, but she'd been wrong before. This time she wanted to be sure. If and when Ava finally said "I love you, Dax," she would mean it with all her heart.

"Are you in any hurry to go back down?" Dax asked, breaking into her reverie.

"Not really." Noting that Dax's erection seemed to have come back full force, she gave him a wicked grin. "Why? Do you want to go again?"

Dax shrugged and bit his lip. "Maybe."

Another pallet rose into the trees above them. "Break time must be over."

"Did you see that? Onca's actually got a Twilanan with him. Wonder how he manages to…"

"Get it up?"

"Yeah. I've never thought they smelled right."

"You may be the exception, Dax. As I understand it, I'm the first non-Zetithian who has ever affected you. The other guys might not be so choosy."

"Well, Threld did say they'd come up with a way, but I dunno… Not sure I could do that with anyone but—"

His blush finished his sentence for him, but Ava let

it drop. Zetithian ale might only have been mildly intoxicating, but the vision of Dax stretched out beside her with his stiff, ruffled cock pointing right at her was stimulus enough. She wanted to suck some Zetithian dick, and she wanted it now.

Setting the bottle aside, she crawled toward his groin. "If you'll just hold still, I'll help you with that."

Ava didn't give him time to react but went down on him with one swift motion. Biting him gently, she received a gush of his salty penile secretions for her delectation. The orgasms began almost immediately, and Ava struggled to keep sucking him. She wanted him to know what it felt like to come in a woman's mouth, and she wasn't letting go of him until he did. Gripping his rod at the root, she backed off, aiming it at her face to coat her cheeks with his slick sauce. She bathed her face with it and massaged her lips until he pushed against them. Opening her mouth, she sucked him in as she slid her hand downward. It was slick with their combined moisture, and he moaned as she spread it over his scrotum. The line beneath his testicles was so sensitive that when she touched it, Dax gasped, arching his back and lifting his butt up off the floor, allowing her free access to it. She dug her fingers into his firm muscles and moved him up and down, fucking her mouth with his meat.

Ava stole a glance at Dax; his eyes were wide open and his fangs bared as she sucked him, the wide, ruffled corona raking her tongue and spreading its magic potion over every surface. By this time, her orgasms were nearly constant and her body contracted uncontrollably as wave after wave of intense pleasure washed over her. Panting hard, she took a break from his cock and went for his nuts. Wrapping her fingers around the base, she squeezed until the skin pulled tightly over his big balls and, leaning down further, she gave them a tantalizing lick.

Dax let out a snarling purr and pulled her hips toward him. She'd been a little surprised that he would have licked her the first time, but she'd reckoned without any knowledge of Zetithian mating habits. Apparently taste was just as important as every other sensation. He lifted her onto his chest and settled her wet pussy on his face. His hot tongue found her clitoris just before he sucked it into his mouth.

Ava saw stars as he teased her with the tip of his tongue, and she tried to keep licking his balls but couldn't do it. She'd been intending to make him come in her mouth, but it seemed that Dax had other ideas.

"You've got to stop that," she gasped. "I want to get you off first."

Dax didn't say a word but let go of her clitoris and went at her from a different angle, drilling his tongue straight into her core and pumping her hips up and down before drifting back into a lazy circular pattern, proving that his tongue was every bit as talented as his cock.

"Dax," she groaned. "It's nearly impossible to give good oral sex while you're receiving it yourself."

"But you taste so good," he purred. "Hot… wet… creamy… I can't help myself…" His words trailed off as he took another swipe at her clit. "And I love the way you tighten up when I do that."

"It feels pretty good on my end too. But I really wanted to—"

"And something else," he added, "I know you aren't

like our women, and you might not appreciate this, but
I want to bite your ass so bad, I can hardly stand it."

"Yeah, well, trust me, the feeling is mutual."

Ava heard him growling, so she should have been
prepared, but even so, she yelped when Dax sank his
fangs into her butt.

Her hair was going wild; she could feel it snapping
like a thousand tiny whips above her head as she heard
Waroun shouting from below.

"Way to go, Dax!" he yelled. "Make her scream!"

Ava's hair went flat as she dissolved into helpless
giggles.

"I can't believe he's down there listening," Dax
groaned.

"Hey, it's probably the only entertainment he'll get
unless he goes after those Davordian girls."

"I know, but *still…*"

"Let's give him something to talk about then," Ava
said as she slid off Dax. "Sit up. I want you to watch."

Dax eyed her warily but did as she asked.

Ava lay on her stomach between his outstretched
legs. "Make all the noise you want, but don't try doing
anything to me unless you want to get your fingers in my
hair. Understood?"

Dax nodded. Heat radiated from his skin as though
it barely contained the fire within; his whole body
should have been glowing rather than just his eyes.
Never before had she seen anything to compare with
what was right there before her eyes. Long, thick, and
as strong as steel, his stiff organ quivered beneath her
fingertips as she covered it with his juice and traced
the network of vessels that nourished it. For a man who

had seldom used the required muscles, he had considerable strength and control; she watched in awe as the silk-covered steel rod rubbed against her hand like a cat seeking a caress.

Dax reached down and threaded his fingers through her hair, pulling her close enough to touch her cheek with the blunt head. He might have been following her instructions to the letter, but in spirit, he was taking significant liberties; his talented penis was teasing everything it could reach, and it was driving her wild. Ava glanced up, catching a brief glimpse of his glowing eyes and satisfied smile before her eyes drifted shut. He was doing it again—deriving his pleasure from her pleasure. As another orgasm racked her body, his cockhead paused at her lips as he whispered, "You *are* going to suck me again, aren't you?"

Ava parted her lips in reply, and he pushed his hot flesh into her mouth. The look of sheer ecstasy on his face told her how good it felt to him, but Ava was still convinced that she had the best end of the deal. The flavor was unlike any she'd ever tasted, but the effect was similar to eating dark chocolate laced with Sholerian cream. Savoring him for a moment, she concluded that even though such a flavor combination sounded fabulous, it was still nothing when compared with a freshly fucked Zetithian. Her flavor mingled with his was hot, sweet, and indescribably delicious.

She let go of his cock and smiled to herself as she licked his big, succulent balls. That was one flavor she could easily identify, for he tasted like fresh pecans. Cupping her hands beneath his cockhead, she said firmly, "Now, give me some juice."

Obediently, Dax flexed his pelvic muscles, sending rivulets of fluid running down into her palms. Lacing her fingers together, she wrapped her hands around his thick penis and slid them from the head to the base. The first stroke had him gasping for air, but when she sucked his nuts into her mouth, he screamed even more loudly than she had. Pumping her hands up and down relentlessly on his cock, she brought him to a quick, intense climax. Dax fell over onto his back, pulling his testicles out of her mouth as he came in her face with a roar, spraying her tongue and cheeks with his thick cream.

The resulting effect on Ava was tripled. She was in the middle of an orgasm from the joy juice that coated his scrotum, had another just from feeling his hot semen hitting her face, and then, right after that, came the euphoric effect from his *snard*.

———~~———

For several long moments, Ava would have been hard pressed to recall her own name, let alone the name of the star freighter that must have blindsided her. So this was how it felt to be *laetralant*... However, hearing an urgent, scuffling sound, she opened one eye and saw that Dax had rolled away from her and was in the act of hurriedly pulling on his pants. Snatching up her dress, he dropped it across her bare back.

"I think our time is up."

Ava was still only vaguely aware of her surroundings but noted that the platform seemed to be losing altitude. Sitting up much too quickly, her head began to swim and she nearly fell over again. The need for a stint in the recovery room after a trip up into the boughs with one of these guys was now perfectly understandable. A weeklong nap would have been even better.

Dax grabbed her hand and thrust it through the armhole in her dress. "Sorry, but unless you want Waroun to see you…"

Ava's head cleared immediately. "I, uh, get the picture." Wrapping the silky fabric across her chest, she fastened the last snap just as the platform landed.

"Oh, I am so disappointed," Waroun lamented. "I thought at the very least he'd be passed out in your arms."

"You thought *he'd* be passed out in *my* arms?" Ava echoed. "You've *got* to be kidding me."

Waroun stuck a contemplative finger on his chin as his eyes swept over her. "Tell me; was it good for you, dear?"

"I don't think I need to answer that," Ava replied.

"Sorry to bring you down so soon, but she's getting a little anxious," Tarq said with a nod toward a Terran lady waiting near the door. "Been booked for a year and a half."

The lady wasn't the only one to appear anxious. Tarq's penis was fully erect and had the most interesting sinuous shape, arching up from the root and taking a downward dip before rising up again at the head. Ava hated to stare, but it was the sort of thing that automatically drew the eye.

"That's certainly planning ahead," Teke remarked.

Tarq took the lady's hand and escorted her onto the floating bower Ava and Dax had vacated. As Ava watched it rise into the air, Waroun began cackling uncontrollably.

"What's so damn funny?" Dax demanded.

"For the love of Leon!" Waroun exclaimed. "The

Great Virgin has not only been deflowered, he's had his cock sucked!"

Dax glowered at his navigator. If looks could have killed, Waroun would have at least been rendered comatose. "How the hell would you know?"

Waroun reached out and lightly touched Ava's upturned cheek. "Still got a little *snard* on your face, don't you, Ava? Tell me, was it tasty?"

There was no point in denying the obvious. "Oh, yes. *Very* tasty."

"I'm getting a little kick of your essencenth, too," Waroun reported. "Ith's makin' mah tongue hart."

Dax was growling like a tiger about to pounce, but they were all distracted by the approach of Jerden with two women. One was a sultry Terran brunette who had already disrobed. The other had the luminous blue eyes of a Davordian, but her nose and ears were sharply pointed and her skin had a bluish tinge. Her bushy red hair was also unusual for a Davordian. Ava had never seen anything like her. "You do two at a time?"

Jerden's lips curled into a wicked smile as he took the brunette's hand and kissed it. "This is Audrey. She's our fluffer. If we have a client who doesn't smell right, she comes along for the ride."

"So *that's* how you do it," Dax remarked. "I wondered."

"Sounds like one helluva great job," Ava snickered. "Bet you have all kinds of applicants."

Jerden laughed. "We were having some difficulties, but after one scheduled visit, Audrey came up with the idea and volunteered for the position. We just have to feed her and let her sleep here—and fuck her at least twice a day. She doesn't need clothes."

Teke was clearly appalled. "You mean you don't even pay her? Why, that's little better than slave labor!"

Ava laughed out loud and patted the Kitnock's arm. "I wouldn't worry about her, Teke. I'm sure she's perfectly happy with the arrangement."

"I certainly am," Audrey said. Jerden pulled her close, inhaling deeply as she wound her arms around his waist. His cock responded instantly, becoming fully erect in a matter of seconds. She flicked her tongue over his nipple and grinned. "With me around, he can even fuck a Darconian."

"Tarq just needs a little of her pussy juice on his upper lip, and he can do pretty much anyone," Jerden said. "Me, I like the visual as well as the chemical stimulation. Onca can go either way."

"Doesn't that bother some of your clients?" Ava asked but immediately answered her own question. "No, it wouldn't—at least, not once you got started."

"Are there any females that are *not* affected by you?" Teke asked. "I cannot imagine that a Darconian would want—"

"You'd be surprised," Jerden said. "Most of them at least *say* they're affected. I think it's just a fad, myself."

Ava chuckled. "The 'I've been laid by a Zetithian' club?"

"Something like that," Jerden agreed. "The novelty may wear off eventually, but in the meantime, we're raking in the credits like you wouldn't believe."

Waroun's eyes were round with awe. "And you get all the sex you want. Can I get a job here too?"

Jerden shook his head. "No, but the Norludian brothel is just down the street. They're always hiring."

"And why is that?"

Jerden shrugged. "The Darconian women keep taking them to keep as sex toys—or so I've heard. Not sure how true that is."

"It doesn't surprise me a bit," Waroun said smugly. "We're really very sexy, you know."

Ava shuddered at the thought of a Norludian and a Darconian together. "Somehow I wouldn't think dinosaurs would be your type."

"I've always found Darconian women very attractive," said Waroun. "I love the way their scales differ in color, and the iridescence is quite lovely."

"You kill me, Waroun," Dax muttered. "You absolutely kill me."

Ava glanced around, mentally counting heads. "Where's Threldigan?"

"Onca's client decided she wanted more than one man," Audrey said. "Threldigan volunteered."

Waroun's eyes lit up. "Do you guys ever double-team anyone?"

"Yes, but it's double the fee," Jerden replied. "One lady paid for all three of us at once, but she couldn't take it." Shaking his head, he added, "Left here babbling on about Felix the Cat, whatever that means."

Ava giggled. "I bet a lot of your clients leave here babbling, but if she was expecting Felix the Cat, it's no wonder she couldn't take it." Dax seemed puzzled.

"Old Earth cartoon character," Ava explained. "*Very* old—about a thousand years, in fact—and nothing like Zetithians at all!"

"You know about cartoon characters from a thousand years ago?"

Ava shrugged. "Hey, everyone needs a hobby."

"I had no idea." Judging from the look on Dax's face, he still didn't get it.

"I know about all of them. Mickey Mouse, Donald Duck, and Felix the Cat, among others. My favorite is called Tigger, which is interesting when you consider…" Glancing up at Dax's feline features, she cleared her throat. "Well, maybe it makes more sense than I thought. What about you, Dax? Got any hobbies I should know about?"

"Hobbies?" His expression was completely blank.

"You know—stuff you do or learn about just because you like it and are interested in it, and not because you have to."

"I know what it means," said Dax. "And I've learned about a lot of stuff, I just can't think of any particular thing…"

Waroun rolled his eyes. "He's *so* boring. Whereas I, on the other hand, have an interest in many fascinating subjects—"

"Yes, and they all have something to do with sex, don't they?"

"But of course!"

"Speaking of sex, you must excuse us now," Jerden said. "My client is waiting." The lady in question stepped forward, taking Jerden's outstretched hand, her deep blue eyes aglow with anticipation. Though she was still clothed, her dress was so sheer it left very little to the imagination. Ava knew that Zetithians were aroused primarily by scent, but *still*…

"I'm surprised you'd need a fluffer for her," Ava remarked. "She looks like she'd be compatible with you guys."

"She *is* primarily Davordian," Jerden explained, "and we normally have no difficulties with them—"

"Yeah, all of you except for the Great Virgin," Waroun snickered. "No, wait. Can't call him that anymore." Tapping his chin he muttered, "Must think of something else…"

"—but she's also got a little Arconian and Edraitian in her bloodline," Jerden continued. "It throws off the scent."

"Though not the response." The woman's voice was deep and throaty. "I have been with Onca before. He's a delightful man, but I've heard that Jerden is better."

She raked Jerden's body with an assessing glance. He was smiling, but his smoldering eyes promised he would do everything in his power to substantiate that claim.

"Well, I guess we'll let you get back at it, then," Teke said. "Maybe we should be on our way… But should we leave without Threldigan? He *was* acting as our guide."

Waroun snorted. "If we wait for him, then Super Kitten will be ready to nail the Fish Lady again and we'll be hanging around here all night!"

"Super Kitten?" Dax echoed.

Waroun grinned. "Yeah! Just came up with that one. What do you think of it?"

"I think I liked being called the Great Virgin better."

Ava clapped her hand over her mouth, but the attempt was futile. Dax's chagrined expression sent her over the edge into near hysteria.

The others stared at her as if she'd suddenly grown horns.

Ava wiped her streaming eyes. "What? Didn't you think it was funny?"

"Well, yeah, but not enough to make our hair stand up in spikes," Diokut said. "Does it always do that when you laugh?"

"Never did before." Ava reached up and patted her hair. Diokut hadn't been kidding. "Must be that Aquerei water Kots has been giving me. Guess I'd better lay off that stuff, huh?"

"I dunno," said Dax. "I kinda like it that way."

Ava smoothed both palms over her head, but her hair refused to cooperate. "Well, that's good, because it doesn't seem to want to lay back down now."

"I don't think it's the water this time," Waroun said. "My money is on the joy juice."

Teke looked at him questioningly.

"Oh, you know… The Zetithian Secret Sauce?" Waroun snickered. "It's going to be fun seeing what else it does to her."

"You should have seen her when—" Dax stopped short. "Guess I shouldn't talk about that."

"Oh, do tell!" Waroun encouraged. "We want to hear all the intimate details."

Teke glanced at the others. "We do?"

Diokut nodded vigorously. "Yeah, we do. All of them."

Ava thought it best to change the subject. "Hey, um, I'm getting really hungry. What do you say we go have dinner somewhere?"

"Great idea," said Teke. "Perhaps Roncas can suggest a nice restaurant—one that serves a wide variety of cuisines. Do you think we should call Quinn?"

"He was pretty well stuffed back at the spaceport, so I doubt if he'd want dinner," Dax said. "But who knows what he's gotten into by now. Maybe we ought to check in with him." Activating his combadge with a sharp tap, he called out Quinn's name.

———∿∿∿———

Junosk might have known that he was looking for a Drell named Quinn, but that was about all. He'd been all over the city and into almost every casino, but as Wane had pointed out, one Drell looked very much like another, and none were particularly talkative—not to mention being nasty, rude little shits. They were hard to spot over the slot machines too. He had help, of course, and he'd paid out a number of bribes, but it wasn't happening fast enough.

Rapidly losing his patience and nearly exhausted, Junosk was about to resort to shooting any of the furry little beasts on sight when he stalked into the Yulanda. One of the classier casinos, every niche was filled with a lush, tropical garden or a spectacular work of art. Glittering dome lights cast a golden glow over players and dealers alike, and the slot machines were surprisingly quiet. For a brief rest, it was as good a place as any. His eyes still searching the room, he backed into a chair.

The high-pitched squeal that accompanied his descent told him that another of his quarry was there ahead of him. The Drell shoved him aside, his furry fingers flying over the control panel. "You idiot! Can't you see I'm about to win the jackpot?"

"Hadn't noticed. Sorry."

"Stupid quidnit," the Drell spat. "Look at my score. Ever seen one that high?"

Not being a gambler or a gamer, Junosk had no idea

what constituted a winning score but attempted to display a mild degree of astonished enthusiasm.

"So, Quinn," Junosk ventured. "Been in town long?"

"Just landed this evening," the Drell snapped. "Now shut up and leave me alone."

Junosk ignored the Drell's directives. "I've got the name right, haven't I? Quinn? And you're here with Dax Vandilorsk?"

"Yeah, yeah." Quinn kept his eyes on the game. The machine was going crazy, with enough blinking lights and crazy color patterns to trigger a seizure—which was probably the intention of the designer.

"I don't suppose you'd have any knowledge of a blond half-breed Aquerei girl, would you?"

Quinn gave him a quick glance. "You mean Ava? Nice girl. Very kind to me, but I think the captain has plans for her. I wouldn't bother with her if I were you."

Junosk kept his tone carefully neutral. "What kind of plans?"

"You're even stupider than you look," Quinn snarled. "Go away."

"This Ava," Junosk went on. "Does she have a crystal pendant?"

"So what if she does? I told you to go away."

In the next second, three things happened at once. Another voice called out Quinn's name, Quinn hit the jackpot, and Junosk pulled his pistol.

Chapter 14

"CAN'T TALK NOW," QUINN'S VOICE CAME BREATHLESSLY through the comlink. "I just—" His sentence was cut off abruptly by a blood-curdling screech. Then the link went dead.

Waroun broke the stunned silence. "Well, he's either getting laid, or he's just been murdered."

"Knowing Quinn, I'd say it was the latter," Teke commented. "Drells can be so rude."

"But he's been doing a lot better since he's had Dax keeping him in line," Ava pointed out. "Almost polite."

"Maybe," said Dax. "But I'm sure he reverted to his old ways as soon as we were out of sight—aside from all the other strange things this planet does to people." Dax tapped his badge. He called for Quinn several times but received no reply.

"He could be in a casino and just won the jackpot," Diokut suggested.

"Yes, but how likely is that?" Waroun argued. "Winning is *very* hard to do here. They don't just give stuff away, you know."

"Well, let's not stand around here wondering," Dax said decisively. "Those combadges have homing beacons in them. Passengers have wandered off before."

"And we've always found them," Waroun added. "Whether they wanted to be found or not!"

"Unless he or someone else has pitched his badge," Ava said.

Waroun snorted. "I dare anyone else to find it underneath all that hair. Besides, if he hadn't wanted to be found, he wouldn't have responded when Dax called him."

Ava was about to point out that having won a jackpot might have been enough to make Quinn reconsider that decision when Dax pulled yet another device out of his pocket. He checked the settings and pointed toward the door. "Looks like he's somewhere in that direction."

Waroun snickered. "How convenient."

"You might try calling him again," Teke said. "He might have tripped over his hairy feet and not been able to respond right away."

Dax did as Teke suggested, but there was still silence on the other end of the link. "Waroun and I can handle this while the rest of you have dinner. Roncas can give you directions, or if you want to wait for Threld, which might be the best idea, I'm sure he'd be happy to—"

"Do what?" Threldigan said, popping up behind Dax. Waroun let out a shriek, while Ava bit back a scream.

Dax gritted his teeth. "I really hate it when you do that."

"Keeps you on your toes," Threldigan said with a saucy grin.

Diokut stared at him, openmouthed. "How did you—"

"He won't tell you," Waroun said. "And trust me, we've asked him a million times. Won't say whether he teleports himself or can become invisible. *Most* annoying!"

Threldigan shrugged. "Magicians never reveal their secrets."

Ava, for one, had been looking right at Dax—how could she ever take her eyes off him again?—when Threldigan appeared behind him, seeming to materialize out of thin air. "But is it a trick or something you can actually *do*? As a Mordrial, I mean."

Threldigan swept forward to take Ava's hand. Bringing it to his lips, he bestowed a sensuous kiss on her fingertips. "Ah, but that would be telling, wouldn't it?"

"Come on, Ava." Dax snatched her hand away from Threldigan. "None of that, you old smoothie. She's mine now."

"Are you sure? Perhaps I should test her resolve. I wouldn't want my best friend falling for a woman who isn't steadfast in her affections."

Waroun glared at Threldigan to the point that his eyes protruded beyond the reach of their lids and his lower lip turned an interesting shade of green. "I'm not sure that's the sort of thing best friends are supposed to do. And besides, he's *my* best friend, not yours, and I think he and the Fish Lady were made for each other!"

Ava sensed an altercation in the making. "Um, aren't we supposed to be finding Quinn—or, barring that, someplace to eat?"

Dax bit his lip as his eyes darted back and forth between Threldigan, Waroun, and Ava. Apparently deciding that it wasn't safe to leave anyone behind, he turned and headed for the door. Dragging Ava behind him, he motioned for the others to follow.

The pheromone effect hit Ava like a quadruple dose of Sholerian cream with a little *snard* mixed in for good measure. Dax already had her hand in a firm grip but squeezed it gently. "Just hang on," he said. "We'll be away from here soon."

Ava nodded, but it was all she could do to keep walking. Moisture coated her inner thighs, and if Dax had suggested that he carry her while impaled on his dick, she would have jumped into his arms. Her mind made the short hop to sucking his cock and suddenly, she really *couldn't* walk.

"Dax," she gasped. "I *need* you."

Dax paused only briefly and the next thing Ava knew, she was riding him piggyback down the avenue. Ava had never fully appreciated the power in his body, but Dax carried her as easily as a child, his long legs striding onward while the others followed his lead. Wrapping her arms around his neck, she buried her face in his hair and inhaled his comforting scent. She tried not to think about the wet spot she made on his shirt.

As they moved further from the brothel district, the pheromone effect began to fade. Threldigan's words, which she had ignored at the time, revisited her. So, he thought she wasn't steadfast in her affections, did he? Anger surfaced briefly, only to be squashed beneath the weight of the truth. Having run out on two men now, there was no denying that her history couldn't support a claim to constancy.

Perhaps Dax *was* risking more than his virtue in hooking up with her. Part of her wanted to prove Threldigan wrong, but another part—the more realistic part—feared that he was perfectly justified.

Dax… He was a treasure beyond price. She knew that now, but would she be allowed to keep such a prize? She *wanted* to keep him, but was she worthy of him?

She felt his strength of purpose and dedication and wondered if Threldigan had ever possessed even a tenth of Dax's integrity. While the others were chattering on about what could have become of Quinn, Dax was actively engaged in trying to find him. He might have tried to act the part of a bad boy but it simply didn't ring true. Dax was a conscientious man at heart and took his responsibilities very seriously. Ava had seen that, and she'd seen the softer side of him as well. He hadn't fussed when confronted with her need. He'd acted in the best possible way, doing what he could to help her but not letting her deter him from his purpose.

Quiet competence was what Dax possessed. He wasn't flashy or flamboyant or cocky; he was simply in charge. There was no questioning his authority on his ship, and no one questioned it on Rhylos, either. They might have teased him about losing his virginity, but they respected him no less.

They certainly couldn't hold it against him now that he had become a man in every sense of the word. On the contrary, Ava thought he might have earned greater respect for having waited for… what? For her? She felt privileged to be the one to bring him into the light, but—

Without warning, Ava's thoughts took an abrupt turn. She felt like the luckiest woman who ever lived. Raising her head, she saw that they had entered a new district. Glittering casinos stretched into the distance like a strand of diamonds, and Ava knew she had only to pass through their portals to become the richest woman on the planet. Rock bands played on stages set in the middle of each block, and people danced in the street as though they hadn't a care in the world. Food vendors were interspersed between the casinos, their aromas as compelling as the need to try her luck. Shops of every kind waited impatiently to take money from anyone lucky enough to beat the odds and actually win something.

"I think you can put me down now," Ava said in Dax's ear.

"Not sure I want to." Dax didn't interfere as she slid off his back. Stopping to consult his tracking device, he pointed it at a throng of dancers. "He's around here somewhere."

Ava gaped at the crowd. "How will we ever find him here?"

"That's easy," Waroun said. "We just whistle and yell: Here, Quinn!"

"He's not a dog, Waroun. I don't think that will work."

Dax ignored this exchange and continued onward. Following the combadge signal like a bloodhound on the scent, he passed right through the hordes of music lovers. The band was one Ava had actually heard of, and she paused to watch the show.

There was a time when Ava had drooled over the lead guitar player, but having Dax around lessened his appeal considerably. He was still attractive, though, if only because of his long black hair—something Ava had always found irresistible. Why she had ever run off with Lars, who wore his hair short to the point of being nearly shaved, was a mystery. It was as if she'd been brainwashed or drugged into finding him hunky enough to want to live with him, but the effect had worn off as quickly as the pheromones upon leaving the brothel district.

This realization struck her with the force of a

Darconian's tail. *Had* she been drugged? The effects of Rhylosian advertising were very similar to what she'd felt back then, but why would Lars have felt the need to do such a thing? And if he had, why hadn't he kept it up?

She had no proof, but the notion took root in her mind and began to grow. If true, it would certainly explain a great deal—and make her seem far less capricious. Had she ever hit on this idea before, it would have seemed ridiculous, but now, having spent some time at the mercy of the no-holds-barred approach to commerce on Rhylos, she wasn't so sure.

The more she thought about it, the more plausible it seemed. She had met Lars while in town shopping for building supplies when she and Russ were remodeling the house they shared. Lars had offered to help load her speeder, and she'd been inexplicably smitten. Russ must have suspected she was under the influence of something, otherwise he wouldn't have said he'd wait for her when she told him she was leaving him and Rutara forever. Perhaps he guessed that it would wear off someday, and she'd come back to him.

Five years. If Lars had been drugging her the whole time, that would explain why she'd put up with him for so long. Whatever he'd used couldn't have been cheap, which would also explain why he'd quit giving it to her. After his money ran out, he simply didn't have the wherewithal to continue, unless he started stealing, and Lars wasn't smart enough to be a good criminal, which is to say, one who wouldn't get caught.

Ava thought furiously as they threaded their way through the crowd. Lars had been annoying as hell, but had always managed to talk her into staying. But had it all been talk, or was it something else? The day she finally left him, she'd asked him to make her want to stay, and he couldn't do it. The idea was far-fetched but made sense, except for one tiny little thing: motive. Ava had no money or important connections. In the long run, Lars had gained very little. He might have truly loved her, but it certainly didn't show.

Realizing she would probably never know the truth, she glanced about, looking for Dax. She spotted him just as he turned down the closest thing Rhylos had to a dark alley. Threldigan waved at her, and she jogged toward the men who were clustered near a dark niche. "Have you found Quinn?"

Dax shook his head as he stooped down to retrieve a small bundle. "Just taking a little side trip."

"I'm surprised the street sweepers haven't picked him up," Threldigan said. "Though that could be what happened to Quinn."

"What?" Ava said. "Picked who up?"

"Him." Dax glanced at the squirming ball of fur he held against his chest. A curly blond head emerged from beneath his arms and began licking his neck.

"A puppy!" Ava exclaimed.

"A very *hungry* puppy," Dax amended. "He's nothing but bones and a little fur."

"Are you sure it's a he?"

"Quite sure." Dax held the puppy up with its belly aimed toward her.

Ava nodded. "Yep, it's a boy."

Dax shifted the dog to the crook of his left arm and gestured with the tracking module. "Quinn is over that way," he said and started walking.

"You're keeping him?" Teke squeaked.

"Of course," said Dax. "Whoever he belongs to—if he belongs to anyone—obviously isn't taking very good care of him. I can't just leave him here."

Ava stood rooted to the spot, staring at Dax's retreating figure with openmouthed surprise. "Some bad boy *you* are."

She had been speaking to herself, but Waroun apparently heard her. "Told you it was all an act. He's got the softest heart of anyone I've ever met."

Ava nodded, still slightly flabbergasted by the sudden turn of events. A guy who picked up stray puppies couldn't be all bad—whether it was an act or not. Then she glanced around at his odd assortment of passengers and realized that in one way or another, they were *all* strays. She was the most lost and homeless of the bunch.

Quickening her pace, she caught up with Dax, who was speaking softly to the puppy.

He handed her the tracking device. "Here, hold this for a second."

Dax pulled a small piece of jerky from one of his pockets and fed it to the dog, who gobbled it down with gusto.

Ava shook her head in wonder. "You're the only guy I've ever known who would have tracking equipment and dog treats on him at all times. You must have been a Boy Scout."

Dax flashed her a boyish grin. "Got my Eagle when I was fifteen."

"I was only kidding," Ava said dryly. "Do you mean to say you really *were* a Boy Scout?"

"Yep. I can start a fire with two sticks and everything."

"You did that aboard a starship? No, wait. Scouting is an Earth custom—how did you—"

"Amelyana was Terran. She taught us her culture along with our own—and a few others. We're all multilingual—fluent in Zetithian, English, and Stantongue, and a smattering of other languages, as well." He shrugged. "Hey, we had to do *something* to keep ourselves busy during all those years, and I was a pretty good student. How to fly a starship wasn't the only thing I learned."

Ava was agog with curiosity. "Who was the first President of the United States?"

"George Washington."

"And the first human to set foot on Earth's moon?"

"Neil Armstrong. The first sentient was Luxon Detmar—a thousand years before Armstrong."

"Who organized the Earth colony on Rutara?"

"David and Shellenne Harper."

"What about math and science?"

Dax chuckled. "Well, I can add two and two and know the difference between male and female dogs."

"Which is all anyone really needs to know," Ava conceded.

"Hey, Dax," Diokut piped up. "What about—"

"Hush now," Waroun hissed at the young Kitnock. "Mustn't interrupt. Super Kitten and the Fish Lady are bonding."

Ava burst out laughing and slid her arm around Dax's waist. Holding him close while his puppy tried to lick her face felt very natural. It came as a bit of a shock to realize that she now had the right to do such things whenever she wished. No more holding back or hiding her feelings. Dax might not be her mate for life—not yet anyway—but he *was* her boyfriend, which gave her a seriously warm fuzzy feeling. *Big, sexy Dax and an adorable puppy… It just doesn't get any better than that.*

Diokut was clearly affronted. "I was only going to ask him if he knew the capital of Darconia."

"That would be Arconcia," Dax said. "I learned a lot of geography, too."

"Ever been there?" Teke asked.

"Yeah. That's where I met Trag's brother, Tychar."

Ava gasped. "You're kidding me, right?"

"Uh, no, why would I do that?"

"Tycharian Vladatonsk? The rock star?"

Dax rolled his eyes. "Aww, does my new girlfriend have a crush on him?"

"Well, no, but I *have* heard of him," Ava admitted. "He's very popular, you know."

"Yeah, I know. Just don't mention that to Trag. He's a little sensitive when it comes to having a famous brother."

"Can't say as I blame him for that."

"Yes, but Trag's the one who tracked down Rutger Grekkor and got him to confess to destroying Zetith," Waroun put in. "I'd say he has plenty of fame on his own."

Dax nodded in agreement. "Still, you know how it is. Everyone wants to be a rock star."

"What about you?" Ava asked Dax. "Do *you* want to be a rock star?"

Dax gazed down at her, his eyes dancing with mischief. "Well, no, but then, I'm not very musical."

"Couldn't carry a tune in a bucket?"

"Something like that."

Ava hugged him tighter as they continued the search for Quinn. It didn't matter that Dax couldn't sing a note. He was a big, purring kitten of a man who took in strays and rescued puppies off the street. She liked him very much, just the way he was.

Chapter 15

THEY FOUND QUINN IN A FANCY CASINO A LITTLE FARTHER up the street, out cold in front of a slot machine. Dax brought him around with a splash of water from a nearby fountain.

"I was winning," Quinn gasped. "The jackpot was mine, and then some quidnit shot me and stole my winnings."

"Quidnit?" Dax echoed. "What do you mean by that?"

"Oh, you know, the ones with tentacles on their heads. I've seen a few of them around here."

"You mean the Aquerei?" Dax glanced at Ava. "That's interesting."

Ava nodded. "Doesn't speak well of my father's homeworld, does it?"

"I wouldn't have thought *anyone* could get away with that sort of thing," Teke said. "Any casino I've ever been in had very strict security."

Threldigan shrugged. "Welcome to Rhylos. Some of these smaller places are a little lax."

"You call this small?" Teke exclaimed. "Why, getting lost in here is almost a certainty!"

Threldigan let out a sardonic laugh. "Getting lost is the whole idea. If you can't find your way out, you'll spend more money until you're flat broke. And then the place can get nasty."

"How do you mean?" asked Teke.

Threldigan gestured at Ava. "Have a seat at one of the slots."

Choosing a machine at random, Ava sank down into the richly upholstered chair that was provided. An alluring tune began to play, and a handsome man appeared on the viewscreen. He spoke to her in a seductive voice, urging her to deposit her credit voucher for an opportunity to win riches far beyond her wildest dreams.

"Now, tell that machine you don't have any money," Threldigan said. "Use any words or phrases you like. Believe me, these machines have heard it all."

Ava took a moment to recall the most obscure expression she'd ever heard to describe the bankrupt state. "Sorry, mate, but I've gone through the ready."

The man on the viewscreen instantly transformed into a hideous Nedwut. The music hit a discordant note, and the chair gave her a push, ejecting her from her seat. She stumbled, nearly running into Diokut, who caught her before she could fall.

Threldigan let out a world-weary sigh. "Any manipulative ploy you, or anyone else, can imagine is used on this world—as well as magic. It gets tiresome after a while."

Ava nodded her thanks to Diokut and smoothed out her dress. "Even with your cape?"

"Even with my cape. The idea of moving to Rutara is growing on me."

"Rutara *is* different," Ava said. "At least, it was where I lived, which was mostly rural. There are manufacturing regions too—Dax's ship was built there—but overall, the lifestyle is pretty plain. Nothing like any of this."

"Ah, yes," Threldigan said. "The simple life."

"I wouldn't have thought that was your style," said Dax. "Gonna stop using your magic?"

Threldigan smiled. "Never! I'll always have that, but whether I mention it to anyone or not is the question." Frowning, he turned to Ava. "They don't burn witches, do they?"

"Not that I've ever heard. Exactly what sort of magic can you do—I mean, aside from being able to disappear?"

Threldigan smiled but didn't say a word.

"Not going to tell me, are you?"

"Nope."

"Thought so."

"I can, however, help Quinn out just a bit." Passing a hand over the slot machine, Threldigan cocked his head to one side. "There, that should do it. Put in a voucher."

Quinn no longer had any in his possession, but Teke had stopped to change a few credits at the door. He fed in the voucher and tapped the screen. Ava watched as the random numbers sped by, stopping with a row of sevens. A loud bell rang, heralding the win.

Teke smiled at the Drell. "We'll split it."

"Done!" shouted Quinn.

Dax stared at his friend with surprise. "So, is this how you've managed to make a living on this world?"

Threldigan didn't bother to deny it. "Comes in handy if I'm a bit short when the rent is due."

"Okay, you can influence machines, make magical gadgets, and disappear and/or teleport yourself." Ava ticked the list off on her fingers. "Anything else?"

"My lady," he said with a sweeping bow. "I leave that to your imagination."

"Wait a second, I forgot the mind reading thing."

Ava crossed her arms and closed her eyes. "What am I thinking?"

"That you want to get dinner over with so you can get back to the ship and play snuggle bunnies with Super Kitten."

Ava burst out laughing. "Doesn't take a mind reader to figure *that* out."

Waroun pressed a fingertip onto his chin and then pulled it off with loud pop. "I'm wondering how you can play snuggle bunnies with a kitten—especially one with a new dog. Kots is gonna *love* cleaning up after a puppy."

"I'm sure he will," Dax said. "But this isn't the first dog he's had on board, and I doubt it will be the last."

"Knowing Kots, he's probably already got puppy pads spread out all over the carpet," Ava said. "Speaking of mind reading, how far away can he tell what you're craving?"

"I'd be willing to bet he's got Sholerian milkshakes waiting for both of us." Dax was smiling, but his eyes were like those of a hungry tiger.

Ava shivered with anticipation. "Sounds tasty, but I don't think we'll need them. *Zetithian* cream has the Sholerian variety beat all to hell and back."

"Come on, then," Threldigan said. "I know a good restaurant not far from here—if we can keep Quinn out of trouble long enough to get there."

"I'll be good," Quinn promised. "No more gambling and no more buying stuff I don't need."

"You bought something?" Ava glanced at the bare floor around his chair. "Did that get stolen too?"

Quinn shook his head, bristling with excitement. "I

bought this fabulous bridge in a place called Brooklyn. You should see it."

"I already have," Ava said dryly. "In pictures, anyway. How much did you pay for it?"

"Only fifty credits," Quinn replied. "It was a steal at that price."

"Oh, it was a steal, all right," Dax said. He held out a hand to help the Drell to his feet. "We aren't letting you wander off again, Quinn, so don't even think about trying."

"But what about my bridge?"

"A fool and his money are soon parted," Waroun muttered.

"Does that mean you think I'm a fool?" Quinn demanded.

"No, just someone who isn't used to the temptations of Rhylos." Dax patted the Drell on his furry head. "I thought your initial orientation would have been enough, but obviously it wasn't. I promise we'll take better care of you from now on. Are you hungry?"

"I'm *always* hungry," Quinn replied. "Do you suppose they have crackers at this place Threldigan mentioned?"

"I'm sure they do," Dax assured him. "Mounds of them."

"Great!" Quinn scratched his head, staring at the bundle of fur Dax held in his arms. "So, where'd the puppy come from?"

"Dax rescued him from the street." Ava was unable to keep what she was sure was a dopey-looking smile off her face. Something had changed in the way she felt about Dax. He wasn't simply a sexy starship captain now. Her feelings toward him were much more personal than that. She felt a sense of pride and kinship with him that was completely new to her—almost as though his good qualities reflected on her somehow.

"Can I hold him?" Quinn asked. "I like puppies."

Ava would have been hard-pressed to name anyone who didn't, but kindness to animals was nearly always a sign of good character in a person. She smiled to herself as she remembered one of her teachers who had been appalled at the lack of discretion one of Ava's fellow students had shown in choosing a boyfriend. "But what about his character?" the teacher had asked. "His honesty? His worthiness to be the father of your children?" To which the student had responded, "All I'm looking for right now is to have a good time." The teacher might have lost that round, but Ava was fairly certain she won the match, because she had been perfectly correct. You truly *did* need to evaluate a man based more on his potential as a provider and a reliable mate than his level of hotness or how much fun he was. It was a matter of establishing one's priorities and following through with them. Good boyfriends didn't always make good husbands.

Husbands? Where did that *come from?* Then she remembered Dax's assumption that a lifelong commitment would result from their physical union. The idea was naïve, but also very sweet. As if he'd read her thoughts, Dax took her hand, and they strolled down the street together, two lovers exploring the city at their leisure.

As his fingers laced together with hers, Ava felt another change. Street noises seemed to fade into the background, making her more aware of his presence, his movement, the warmth of his hand, the strength of his grasp. She wanted to believe this could be forever, although experience told her otherwise. Though she loved her mother dearly, there had been no happy married life to serve as an example. Only a father who had disappeared long before her birth.

Ava grasped her pendant as if to reassure herself it still existed and hadn't disappeared the way her father had. Simply holding it in her hand soothed and reassured her, reminding her of the love her parents had once shared. In giving the stone to Ava, her mother had passed that love on. Too bad she hadn't passed on a little more about her father.

Ava was well aware that not everyone had families like hers. Plenty of people remained together forever, though they weren't necessarily happy—at least, not all the time. No one had ever been blessed with a life of continuous bliss. This moment, however, stood out from the rest and would be worth remembering—long after her youth had faded and her children, if any, were grown and had children of their own.

Hovering lights lit the cobbled street, dimming the stars she knew shone overhead. Delicious scents filled her nostrils, while wandering musicians played romantic tunes. Cafés lined the street, interspersed with vendors selling fresh flowers of every hue and variety. When she stopped to inhale their fragrance, Dax bought her a bouquet, placing one large purple blossom in her hair. His fingertips grazed her cheek, sending unexpected tingles racing in all directions from that tiny point of contact. As a violinist approached, Ava felt a sudden desire to dance, to be swept up in Dax's arms and spun in circles until dizziness overcame her. Ava began to suspect that some pheromone or other subliminal suggestion might be responsible for her romantic mood, but she discounted this, firm in her belief that Dax, and Dax alone, was the reason.

"I don't suppose you know how to dance, do you?"

"Um, well, maybe," he replied. "But not out here in the street."

"Prefer a crowded dance floor?"

"I think so. It's less… conspicuous."

Ava sighed. "But not nearly as romantic."

"Is that what you want? Romance?"

"It's what we *all* want. Too bad men don't want the same thing."

"Am I doing that badly?"

She smiled at the violinist with regret. "No. You're doing just fine."

Dax disagreed. He didn't know *anything* about romance. If that was what Ava wanted from him, he was bound to fail. Giving her flowers was romantic—he'd have had to be born under a rock not to know that—but it wasn't enough.

Threldigan was still leading the way, or Dax would have been lost. When he'd been tracking Quinn, he had a purpose to occupy his mind. Now, Ava—the sight of her, his feelings toward her, but most of all, her scent—usurped his thoughts. Leaning down, he took her hand and kissed it, doing his best to convey his emotions.

Making love with Ava high up in the trees had been absolutely perfect. Dax would have gladly stayed there all night. As it was, all he could think about was getting her back to the ship—or anyplace he could be alone with her—because once was not enough. Not nearly enough. It would take a lifetime of loving before he could be sure she understood how he felt. Unfortunately, she still hadn't said anything about giving up on the plan to go to Rutara. Threldigan wanted to go there too, so *not* going there wasn't an option, no matter how much Dax might wish it. The fear that she might not stay with him almost made him physically ill. She *had* to stay with him now. She just had to.

Dax couldn't explain why he'd picked up that puppy, either. He'd never done anything of the kind, no matter what Waroun might say. Quinn seemed to be bonding with the dog already. Should he have given the puppy to Ava? Was a dog better than flowers? They were beautiful, but they wouldn't last nearly as long as a puppy would.

I should have danced with her. Kissing her hand again, he threaded his fingers between hers, amazed at how small they were in comparison to his. He was tall and gangly, while she was petite and delicate. There was nothing inconspicuous about him—whether he was on a crowded dance floor or not. Dancing with someone as small as Ava would have looked ridiculous.

But she would have been in my arms. Dancing was a great excuse for that…

The conversation went on around him, leaving Dax to his private thoughts. Somewhere along the line, he'd gotten the idea that once he made love with a woman, his worries would be over. Obviously, he'd been wrong.

When they arrived at the restaurant and were shown to their table, Dax spotted a man pulling a chair out for his female companion and decided to try it. He was a little awkward, but at least he didn't dump Ava on the floor. The smile she gave him after he scooted her up to the table did funny things to his heart. *Hmm. That works pretty well...* Then he tried handing her a napkin and wound up dropping her silverware on the floor.

"Ooo, nice move, Super Kitten," Waroun said. "Now you have an excuse to put your head in her lap while you reach under the table to pick up her fork."

"That was *not* my intention," Dax growled as he leaned over to retrieve it.

Waroun winked at him. "Maybe so, but it worked, didn't it?" He picked up his glass and took a sip. "Just don't spill wine on her dress. Things could get dicey pretty quick."

Dax was beginning to question the wisdom of dining together as a group. Separate tables would have been nice, or better yet, separate restaurants. Ava didn't seem to mind, but it was difficult to be romantic with Waroun around. Dax was even reluctant to hold her hand. Stealing a glance at Ava put most of his fears to rest, however, for the look she gave him was one of complete understanding. No, being romantic all the time wasn't necessary. There was, however, a dance floor and a live band playing. Perhaps after dinner he would ask her to dance. Not now when everyone was trying to decide what to order.

Their waiter was a Kitnock, even more willowy than Teke and Diokut. "We'll get very good service from him," Teke said after he took their order. "He's in the family."

Quinn nodded as he munched on a breadstick, but Ava seemed puzzled. "What, you mean you're actually related, or is it just because you're all Kitnocks?"

"No," Teke replied. "It's because he's gay."

"Oh, okay, gotcha. So, you are…?"

"Oh, yes!" Teke said eagerly. "Didn't you know?"

"Well, it isn't perfectly obvious," Ava said. "But then, I'm not all that familiar with your species." Her eyes darted back and forth between the two Kitnocks. "But you and Diokut aren't… *together*, are you? I mean, it doesn't seem that way to me…"

"Diokut is my nephew, actually," Teke said. "I'm just the gay uncle with a bit of money who takes him out to see the galaxy. We aren't a couple."

"I see," she said, though it was fairly obvious that Ava didn't, really. Even Dax wouldn't have guessed it. It was difficult enough guessing the sexual orientation of the more humanoid types, let alone the sticklike Kitnocks.

On impulse, Dax nudged Ava's leg with his knee, drawing a conspiratorial smile from her and instantly diverting her attention from the subject of gay Kitnocks. He felt a sense of kinship or camaraderie he'd never shared with a woman before. *It could be like this forever if I don't blow it.*

Suddenly, the fear that he *could* ruin everything hit him right between the eyes. A few thoughtless words or actions could make her hate him. That idea terrified him beyond belief. He'd have to make a point of asking her to cut him some slack. But what should he say to her? How could he make her understand how important this was to him? Could he ever find the nerve to say something like, *"Please, tell me if I screw up, Ava. Don't misunderstand me and just leave it at that. I know I'll make mistakes. If I say or do anything you don't like, just tell me. Give me a chance to fix it before you call it quits…"*

With a sigh of relief, Threldigan leaned back in his chair and removed his cape. "This area is one of the few that doesn't feel the need to bombard you with advertising. The proprietors would be offended if anyone suggested that anything other than the natural aroma of the food was bringing in customers. It's a welcome change."

"I can feel the difference too," said Teke. "It's much more relaxing here."

Quinn nodded vigorously and reached for another breadstick. "Good food."

The band was playing a slow, romantic song. Threldigan was doing his best to get Dax's attention, but Dax didn't need prompting. It was simply a matter of getting to his feet, holding out his hand, and saying, "Ava, would you like to dance?"

Chapter 16

AVA WAS A LITTLE SURPRISED THAT HE WOULD ASK HER SO soon, but it was a welcome diversion while waiting for their dinner—and also the best way to be alone with him in the relative seclusion of the dance floor. Unlike dinner companions, dancers generally paid very little attention to anyone but themselves.

As Dax captured her outstretched hand in his grasp, delight washed over her and she could feel her hair tossing in response. If he was astute at all—and Ava had no doubt that he was—Dax would soon learn to read her moods simply by looking at her hair. Unfortunately, she never knew what it was going to do next.

Ava had realized there might be a problem as soon as she mentioned dancing. To be truly good partners, a couple should be of a similar height, and she and Dax were nowhere close. When he took her in his arms, she was facing his upper abdomen. Gazing adoringly into his feline eyes was out of the question, unless she was looking for a major pain in the neck. Still, resting her head against any part of him was delightful, and she could hear exactly how hungry he was. "Are you sure you don't want to wait until after dinner?"

Dax shook his head. "I've been looking for an excuse to hold you ever since I put you down."

"I haven't thanked you for doing that yet. All of those pheromones on top of everything else were almost too much. I can understand why Treann was having so much trouble. It was like being drugged and drunk at the same time. It's much nicer here."

"So, you still like me without all the, um, encouragement?"

Ava smiled to herself. "Yes, Dax. I still like you."

"Good." He sighed with relief. "Though I think I'll have to be off this planet completely before I truly believe it."

"What's the matter? Don't trust your own sex appeal?"

"I don't trust anything that happens on Rhylos," he said bluntly. "There could be romance pheromones floating all around us, and we'd never know. They don't tell Threld everything."

"No? Well, perhaps not, but right now, I'm feeling nothing but what I should be feeling."

"Which is?"

"That I wish I were taller. I'd really like to be able to nibble on your ear while we're dancing."

Dax laughed. "That just gives me something to look forward to when we get back to the ship for the night." A tingle of anticipation was already spreading from where his fingertips were tracing circles on her back. The tingles intensified when his hand grazed her hip. "If we were alone, I'd solve the problem by picking you up. Then you could wrap your arms and legs around me and nibble all you like, and I could get my hands on all of you."

Ava's mouth went dry, and a quiver of desire shook her. "Sounds wonderful."

"It does, doesn't it? I probably shouldn't, but this *is* Rhylos."

She didn't immediately take his meaning, but a moment later it became perfectly clear when her feet left the floor. Her breasts pressed against his chest, and her mouth was within easy striking distance of his earlobe—the one from which a gold hoop dangled enticingly. He made sure her dress was pulled down far enough to cover her bottom discreetly, but his big hands would have served just as well.

Her imagination began to dally with the idea of dancing together, alone in her quarters—or his—to soft music with nothing between them, not even air. Dancing while they made love. His hot cock buried deep in her core, doing amazing things to her mind and body. Loving her while they danced… "Oh, Dax. You're making me crazy. No one's ever made me crazy before."

"And do you like being crazy?"

"Mmm, yes… It's *wonderful*." She flicked his earlobe with the tip of her tongue and felt him shudder in her arms.

"Yes, it is. More wonderful than I ever imagined." He took another breath as if to speak but hesitated a long moment as she mouthed his ear, running her tongue from the lobe to the pointed tip. When he finally spoke, his voice sounded unsteady and uncertain. "If—if it's ever *not* wonderful, promise you'll tell me. I'll do whatever it takes to fix it. *Anything*. Just don't give up on me or let it end too soon."

"I won't," she whispered. "I promise." It was an easy promise to make. Giving up on Dax was unthinkable. As for letting it end, forever was beginning to sound like too short a time to spend with him. One never knew what the future might hold in store.

Sucking his earlobe into her mouth, earring and all, she caressed it with her tongue, delighting in the salty flavor of his skin and the heady aroma that was uniquely his own. The pheromones in the brothel district might have been stronger, but the effect of his own brand of sexual attractants, though more subtle, went deeper to form a more lasting imprint on her psyche. Just breathing the air around him filled her with joy, desire, and love.

Dax was purring. The music was too loud for her to hear it, but Ava could feel the vibrations in her chest and the tingles in her nipples. He arched his neck, exposing it to her lips. Groaning, he begged her for more. "Bite me."

Ava bit him right on his tattoo and felt his knees buckle beneath him. "You have no idea what that does to me," he whispered. "No idea…" His voice trailed off to become the merest breath against her hair. When his mouth captured hers, his purr became a growl.

"This is what I want to do with you later." Sliding her down lower on his torso, he stopped when she felt the hard shaft of his erection pushing against the juncture of her thighs. She was already aching for him. If she had possessed the magical abilities of a Mordrial, she would have made the fabric that separated them disappear so that he could plunge his cock into her core, where it belonged.

"Hey, Captain," Waroun said from behind her. "Either drop your pants and do her or come and eat. We'd all love to watch, of course, but your dinner would get cold."

Ava felt her cheeks burning, and her hair swept forward as though trying to hide her embarrassment. "I take it that dinner is served?"

"Sure, but you don't have to eat it if you don't want to," Waroun replied. "You two are putting on such a great show, most people aren't eating anyway—or dancing, for that matter. They're watching *you*."

They had been in the midst of a crowd when they began, but with the exception of Waroun, they were now alone on the floor. Dax set her on her feet. "So much for being inconspicuous," she muttered.

"Let's eat, then." Dax sounded more cheerful than he looked, which led Ava to believe that Waroun's other suggestion would have been preferable.

Unlike other meals she had eaten with Dax at her side, this one didn't require any Sholerian cream to augment her desire. He did it all by himself. Just his large presence and the heat emanating from his body were enough to keep her passions at an all-time high. Every minute that passed brought her closer to fulfillment and, as far as she was concerned, the entire world could have gone to hell as long as the *Valorcry* was waiting to provide sanctuary for them.

Ava somehow managed to contribute to the dinner table conversation, though all she really wanted to do was make love with Dax again and, if his own lack of chit chat was any indication, Dax felt the same way. Quinn was still bemoaning the loss of the Brooklyn Bridge, and, given his dislike of magic, Threldigan's attempts to distract him with a few simple tricks were only moderately successful. Waroun was discussing the impossibility of homosexual Norludians with Teke.

"A Norludian male couldn't suck another guy's tongue without his own tongue getting hard," Waroun insisted. "They'd both choke to death!"

Diokut began flirting with their waiter out of sheer boredom when he wasn't passing breadsticks to the puppy under the table.

"You shouldn't lead him on like that," Teke admonished his nephew after they'd paid the bill.

"I can't help it if he's got the hots for me," Diokut protested. "I have no idea why, but—"

"Must be all that red hair," Ava suggested. "It's very sexy."

"You think so?" Diokut combed his fingers through his bushy mane. "Too bad the Kitnock *girls* don't like it."

"You could change the color, couldn't you?"

"Hmph," Teke said. "If hair coloring worked on us, do you honestly think I'd let mine be gray?"

"Gray hair isn't necessarily a bad thing," Ava said. "I mean, I'm sure Dax would be amazingly sexy, no matter what color his hair was."

"Possibly," Teke conceded. "But then, he has other things going for him."

"Yeah," Diokut said with a nod. "He's tall, dark, and handsome, plus he's the captain of his own starship. Chick magnet material for sure."

"And hung like a bull—"

Dax was in the process of sipping his wine and nearly choked.

"—moose," Waroun finished with an impish grin. "Knew I could sneak that in somewhere."

"Come on, Waroun," Ava chided. "When was the last time you saw a bull moose?"

"In holographic nature documentaries," Waroun said promptly. "I just love the parts about the mating season. They've got some seriously big—"

"Waroun!"

"—antlers."

"We have *got* to get him laid," Threldigan observed. "Tell you what, I'll take him down to the Norludian brothel and sign him up for the night."

"Wouldn't do a bit of good," said Dax. "He'd just have more to talk about."

Waroun gasped. "Could you do that? Really?"

"I'm sure they'd love to have you," Threldigan replied.

Waroun was already on his feet. "Can we go now?"

"I wouldn't mind going back to that area myself," Teke said. "I'm sure I could find someone who would interest me."

Even before Quinn and Diokut chimed in, Ava could see her plans for the night falling to pieces. "What about you?" Dax asked.

"I was thinking about going back to the ship," Ava replied, "but if everyone else is staying…"

"Don't worry, Dax," Threldigan said. "You two take the puppy and go on back to the ship. I'll keep these guys out of trouble."

Given what had already happened, Ava doubted that one man riding herd on those three would be enough, though she suspected that Threldigan's powers might give him an advantage. Dax obviously trusted him, because he didn't bother to argue but stood immediately and offered her his hand. "Ready?"

Laughing, she placed her hand in his. "Bring it on!"

~~~

Dax hadn't realized how much effort it took to field comments from his other passengers and listen to Waroun's snide remarks until he and Ava were alone again. The puppy, of course, didn't talk at all, and Ava seemed perfectly content to stroll along in a companionable silence through one of the more picturesque shopping districts, which was designed to resemble the ancient gardens of Nokrus. Huge, leathery-leafed plants curled up the lampposts, while their fluffy purple flowers bobbed at the end of coiled stems. The storefronts were fashioned from bundles of bamboo stacked in a variety of intricate patterns, and the main street was paved in the same manner. Dax gave these and the colorful mosaic sidewalks only a cursory glance. He only had eyes for Ava. There were undoubtedly a million questions buzzing around in her head, just as there were inside his, but she seemed willing to let the answers reveal themselves in their own time—until they happened upon a pet shop.

"We have to stop here," she said, pulling him inside. "You need puppy supplies."

"Supplies? Don't we just have to feed him?"

"Oh, no," Ava said firmly. "You need all sorts of things—brushes and collars and leashes and flea repellent—stuff like that."

"Really?"

"Yes, and he needs a name. You can't call him 'the puppy' forever."

"I suppose not. Any suggestions?"

"He's *your* puppy, Dax. You need to be the one to name him."

Dax had never named anything; he hadn't even changed the name of the *Valorcry* when he acquired it; hadn't seen the point. Holding the puppy up to his face, he studied the soft brown eyes and blond curls. "How about Jack?"

"He doesn't look a thing like Jack."

"How do you know Jack?"

"*Everyone* knows Jack," Ava said dryly. "And besides, she was with you in the bar when we first met. Remember?"

"Yeah, right. How could I forget? Okay, then, how about Cat?"

"No, and for the same reason."

Dax frowned. "You're making this very difficult. Have you ever had a dog?"

"Yeah, a couple of them. One was named Luke and the other was Chewie."

Dax knew that puppies chewed on things, but he didn't like the idea of encouraging a dog to do so by naming him that. "I like the name Luke." He studied the puppy's face again before holding him out to Ava. "See? He even looks like a Luke."

"He's the same color as my Luke. Is that what you want to call him?"

Dax shrugged. "Works for me, and it's easy to say."

"Okay, great. Luke it is, but Luke still needs a collar and a leash and puppy shampoo—"

"Kots can handle the shampoo part," Dax said. "And probably the flea repellent too. He's got everything."

"True, but it would be nice to have a leash so you could put him down to walk for a while. Now's as good a time as any to start training him. I'm pretty sure he's old enough."

In the end, Dax was persuaded to buy a plain brown collar and a leash and some treats. Luke devoured the treats, but was less enthusiastic about the rest of it. He finally fell in step with Dax while chewing on the leash, which, fortunately, seemed impervious to puppy teeth.

It hit Dax then that the only thing needed to complete this picture were a couple of kids trotting along with them. Better make that *three* kids, he reminded himself, which might have been one of the reasons he'd resisted fatherhood. The thought of having to deal with three babies at once—and there was no way he could expect his wife to handle them alone—was enough to make any man's dick shrivel away to nothing. He liked children well enough, but triplets? No one would really wish for that kind of responsibility—would they?

There were plenty of Zetithian men who wouldn't give it a second thought—after all, it was the woman who actually gave birth. But the idea of putting Ava through such an ordeal horrified Dax. She was so tiny, and he was so big. How would that work? Would she back down and refuse to be his mate just because of that? She was pretty tough, but everyone had their limits.

"What are you thinking about?" Ava asked suddenly. "How Luke is going to chew up all of your shoes?"

Caught by surprise, Dax blurted out his reply without taking time to consider. "No, I'm thinking about how hard it would be for you to have triplets."

"Well, that's certainly thinking ahead. But I wouldn't dwell on it if I were you. After all, it might never happen."

He stared at her, aghast. "You mean our species aren't compatible?" The idea that he might not be able to produce offspring with her hadn't occurred to him. Jack would kill him if he chose an incompatible mate.

"Well, that's always a possibility when you start mixing people from different worlds. Zetithians may be able to cross with Terrans, but the Aquerei mix might not work."

"I think the fact that your scent affects me is a good indicator," Dax said after a moment's consideration. He was pretty sure he'd heard that somewhere along the line. How true it was, he couldn't have said, but it was a comforting thought.

"You're probably right. I never really thought about having children. Russ and I weren't together that long, and the more time I spent with Lars, the less sex we had and the less I wanted to have anything to do with him, much less give birth to a child of his—aside from the fact that Luxaria is no place to raise children."

While this was good news in itself, never having broached this particular subject with any woman before, Dax wasn't quite sure how to put it delicately. "But you'd have mine?"

"Knowing that I'd have triplets wouldn't stop me, if that's what you mean."

Dax was somewhat mollified by this, but she hadn't answered his question. "Yes, but do you *want* to have my children?"

She paused to consider this. "It's a little early in our relationship to be worrying about that, but I can understand why it would be important to you. Do you want me to see a doctor before we go any further? I mean, if you're looking to rule me out as a possible mate, it might be best to find out sooner rather than later."

Dax's jaw dropped. "I—no. I mean, I thought you might not want me because of the triplet thing."

"Dax," she said gently. "I knew that was a possibility going into this."

"Maybe, but you hadn't had time to give it much thought."

"I'm okay with it. Really." She looked down as though trying to hide her smile. "But thank you for your concern."

"It's a lot to ask of a woman. I just wanted to be sure."

She squeezed his hand and brought it to her lips. Her kiss was quick, but Dax felt the tingle all the way to his toes. "I'm sure."

The tingle became a warm rush of emotion that momentarily robbed him of speech. She might as well have said she loved him.

Dax was oblivious to everything else that they passed by on their way to the spaceport. Desire had won out over fear—fear that she might desert him just when he fell in love with her. It was similar to the loss of his family and homeworld. No child of that age expects everything he knows and loves to be obliterated, and yet it had happened to him. He had survived, but at what cost? It hadn't affected all of them the same way. Most had gladly settled on Terra Minor and embraced the task of rebuilding their civilization. Dax knew he should have done the same, but the lack of a mate and the fear that he might never find one had weighed heavily in his decision. Better to spend his life roaming the galaxy, visiting all those worlds he had learned about, than growing cabbages on Terra Minor to feed the progeny of others.

But Ava had changed that. For the first time in his life, he felt as though he had a chance at happiness. Just the thought of her filled his heart with joy.

They were alone now. No Threld to tell him what to do, no Waroun to make suggestive comments—or unexpectedly support him—and no passengers to ride herd on. They would be together the entire night and possibly into the next day if the others didn't return. He could leave Luke on the ship if they decided to go back to the city. Kots could take care of him, and then he and Ava could do anything they liked.

Then there was the beach. Having grown up on a starship, Dax had never been immersed in water in his life. While the thought of Ava lying wet and naked in the sand made him purr, he had no intention of actually getting in the water himself. To him, the ocean was a bottomless pit filled with creatures waiting to suck him down into the depths. Anything could be lurking down there, ready to eat him alive. On top of that, he didn't know how to swim.

He'd seen other people out in the water, bobbing among the waves, and he understood the concept—at least in theory—but it was something he'd never learned and wasn't particularly interested in attempting. However, if Aquereis really did like to mate underwater as Waroun had reported, he might be called upon to try it. Dax didn't know if Ava shared this preference or not, and he was almost afraid to ask.

Realizing that, as tall as he was, he could be in fairly deep water and still touch the bottom cheered him considerably. He hated the idea of turning her down and probably would have agreed even if she'd asked him to do it while swinging from a lamppost.

Though the hour was late, the spaceport was humming with activity, and Dax and Ava passed through the checkpoint and then boarded the *Valorcry*.

Dax was now faced with yet another dilemma. Should he ask Ava what she wanted to do or just rip her clothes off as soon as the hatch was closed and take her right there on the floor? It might be more romantic to sweep her off her feet and carry her to his quarters—or should they go to her room?

In the end, Ava took the decision out of his hands. "I thought we'd never get here." After yelling for Kots, she unwrapped her dress, tossed it onto a nearby chair, and kicked off her shoes. "C'mon, big guy. Kots can take care of Luke. I want you naked. Right here, right now."

The timing of the Drell's win had been perfect for making the incident seem like a simple robbery. Junosk had only to wait in the shadows near the entrance for Vandilorsk and his companions to enter and find the unconscious Quinn.

Revealing himself to the Drell had been a necessary evil, though none of the group seemed to be worried that an assassin might be lurking around every corner. From that, he could only assume that the Drell didn't remember that Junosk had been looking for him, specifically. Or for the one called Ava.

The Cylopean's story led Junosk to believe that Ava truly didn't know what she wore around her neck. Anyone who understood the danger would have kept it concealed. She, however, was playing right into his hands.

As he shadowed her, he began to question the need for theft or murder. No one else knew of his discovery. Where was the harm in simply letting Ava keep the stone and go on with her life? The Great Alignment was imminent, and the flight plan for Vandilorsk's ship made no mention of Aquerei. Junosk need only ensure that she never set foot on that world until the time for the New Age had passed.

The New Age would bring profound change to Aquerei, something that Junosk was determined to prevent. However, though he could be as ruthless as the next man when dealing with those who understood the power of the Aquina, he balked at the murder of an innocent girl.

The odds were good that she would simply leave Rhylos and go on her way, taking the stone farther from Aquerei and the temple city of Rhashdelfi. The Great Alignment would come and go, and the stone would be rendered worthless.

The trick would be to hide it from those who understood its significance. Perhaps he could arrange another attempted theft, which would discourage her from putting it on display.

With these thoughts in mind, Junosk went in search of the Cylopean. Better to have Ava think that someone other than an Aquerei coveted the stone. He knew where Vandilorsk's ship was berthed and the schedule for its departure. He had time.

Chapter 17

AVA DIDN'T KNOW HOW SHE'D MANAGED TO KEEP FROM jumping Dax on the way back to the ship, and she hadn't been under the influence of any drugs, weird aphrodisiacs or pheromones, either. It was merely an overwhelming attraction to the hottest man she'd ever seen—pure and simple. She knew quite well why she hadn't gone after him sooner, but now that the ice had been broken, there was no reason to deny the way she felt. The deed was done, and it wasn't as if she could take it back. Not that she would have wanted to.

Kots gathered up the puppy and hovered away with him, presumably for a much-needed bath, and Ava pulled Dax's shirt off over his head. "You should never wear a shirt," she murmured. "You have the most incredible chest." His muscles were clearly defined without being bulky, and his broad chest narrowed to a waist that dipped into his cargoes—pants that she knew had nothing underneath them but a succulent man. She unzipped them and folded the fabric back to expose the treasure trail that led to his dark nest of pubic hair. His cock was pointing downward, out of sight, but the thick root was clearly visible. If he wasn't hard now, he never would be, because Ava felt her own slick moisture halfway to her knees. It had begun to flow just as soon as the others had left them but had turned into a flood when Dax started talking about babies.

She'd been so sure she and Russ could have the kind of family she'd never had herself, but she hadn't thought much about having kids ever since she'd run off with Lars. Somehow, he had never struck her as good father material. But despite his current lifestyle, Dax did, and the more she considered the matter, the more she became convinced that he would be the best father her children could ever have.

Sliding her hands down his back, she took his clothing with them, dropping his pants to his knees, exposing that luscious cock. Her mouth, which had nearly gone dry moments before, was now salivating like that of a starving beggar at a feast. Dropping to her knees, she took him in her mouth, sucking and licking the slick fluid from the head. He tasted like forbidden fruit, and his hot juice went straight to her core, setting off multiple explosive orgasms.

She could have sucked him all night, but his balls were dangling enticingly, giving her all sorts of erotic ideas. Ava sat back on her heels and pulled off his boots. When he kicked off his cargoes, the mere sight of him in all his naked glory triggered another orgasm. Pushing his legs apart to widen his stance, she gathered his balls in her hands for a gentle massage.

Dax moaned as she moved closer. Tilting her head back, she grasped his butt and pulled him down slightly, allowing his testicles to drop into her mouth. Guiding him with her hands, she pumped him up and down on her face, letting his nuts glide in and out past her lips. His erection hung just above her eyes, filling her visual field with nothing but hard, hot cock.

She could hear him growling as he reached down to grip his penis and slide his fist up and down the shaft.

Joy juice was pouring from the head, and his hand was awash with it, making soft sucking sounds as he pleasured himself. Ava wanted to tell him to stop—that his cock, along with his balls, belonged to her now—but she kept quiet, realizing that a thirtysomething virgin deserved all the sex he could get, and jacking off while someone sucked your nuts had to be one of the better ways to go. Digging her fingers into his ass, she urged him on.

It didn't take long. Dax may not have done it before, but he figured it out pretty quickly. She could tell from the purplish blush of his cockhead and his short breaths that he was very close. Arching her neck, she waited for him to come.

He didn't disappoint. His body stiffened, and his breath caught in his throat. A heartbeat later, he came in an arc that had to have landed halfway across the room. Three more spurts followed, and then the rest ran down over his fingers as he aimed it upward.

Ava let go of his balls and fell forward onto her hands and knees. Despite her stiff neck, she had no regrets; her own erotic satisfaction was worth every bit of the pain.

Within moments, Dax was on the floor beside her. Rolling her onto her back, he straddled her, resting his weight on knees and elbows. His hands tangled themselves in her hair, and she could feel it curling around his fingers. His lips covered her face with hot, wet kisses while his cock teased her belly. She couldn't believe the range he had with it. One minute he was tickling her navel and the next, the serrated head was gliding over her tight clitoris and labia. If she'd been a taller woman, she doubted that he could have done it.

She lay there beneath him, thanking heaven for their disparate heights.

Moving downward, he kissed, licked, and nipped his way from her neck to her breasts. Experience might not have taught him very much, but his instincts were impeccable; everything he did to her felt fabulous and new. His rough tongue on her nipples drove her to the edge of climax, but when he brushed them with the side of his fangs, she went over the top. Her body curled into a tight ball, and her hair went wild.

Dax pushed her legs apart, and she felt the tickle of his warm breath. The ache was becoming unbearable. First the visual of his big, thick cock dripping with desire before his climax, and now his smoldering feline eyes were locked with hers, his hot tongue waiting to taste her. His breath on her clit was driving her absolutely insane. A quick swipe of his tongue sent a pulse blast ripping through her body.

He turned, pivoting his body so that his cock and balls were dangling right in front of her face. "Look at what you're doing to me, Ava. Just breathing in your scent has me so hard... I used to think there might be something wrong with me. Women hardly ever affected me. But you, Ava..." His words sank into a deep sigh that deluged her pussy with warmth. "I'm so hard and it feels so good and you smell and taste like... I don't know what... but it's better than anything I've ever dreamed of."

He smelled good too. She pulled him down until his big balls were resting on her face, filling her nostrils with their scent. She licked them gently and then directed his cock to her mouth. Clear fluid dripped from the points of the head, coating her tongue with orgasmic essence. As he filled her with his hot, slick meat, her body became one giant orgasm, her clit straining to ejaculate the way his cock could. It shouldn't have been possible, but somehow something spewed forth anyway, hitting him in the open mouth.

His snarl would have made her think he found this objectionable if his cock hadn't suddenly erupted, spraying his seed on her face and breasts. Pressing his body to hers, he pinned his ejaculating cock it the valley between her breasts, sliding it back and forth in his own semen. Suddenly, it seemed that he couldn't take anymore; he was gone, and she felt chilled to the bone without him. But then he was back, pulling her legs up in the air and plunging his still-hard cock into her slit, pounding her with more power than a man ought to have left after an orgasm of that magnitude. Unable to resist his relentless thrusts, Ava lay flat on her back, her arms outstretched and limp, her heels resting on his shoulders. What her hair was doing, she couldn't have guessed and didn't care.

The soft, deep carpet cocooned her body in comfort while the vision of Dax's face suspended above hers took her to new heights. He was stretched out over her, his upper body supported by his hands. The muscles in his arms bulged with the effort while his hips undulated, driving his powerful cock deep inside her. The effect of his fluid seemed to be waning; her orgasms became less intense, then less frequent until they ceased altogether. She ought to have been disappointed, but she wasn't; just the feel of him moving inside her made her wish he could go on all night. She didn't care if she was stiff and sore for a week; on this night she could have no regrets.

Dax leaned down and captured her lips for a kiss, his tongue delving into the recesses of her mouth, tasting her, and purring like a big kitten. Then he lowered himself onto his forearms, kissing her neck and licking her ear, sending thrills racing down her spine. "I still can't believe this," he whispered. "I'm actually inside you… and I never want to leave."

"Take your time, Kitten," she said. "We've got all night."

"And then what? Does it end after tonight?"

"Shh," she whispered. "Don't think about that now. Just focus on this moment and this moment only."

Dax closed his eyes and arched his back. The flame tattoo licking the side of his neck drew her eye. She had bitten him there earlier, but there were no teeth marks on him to prove it. She didn't feel like biting him now; she wanted to kiss and caress every peak and hollow of his body. No pain, only pleasure. If it was, indeed, the only night they would ever spend alone together, she wanted nothing to mar its perfection.

"The inside of you feels as beautiful as you look… as beautiful as you *are*."

"Good for the soul?"

"*Very* good for the soul." He rolled onto his back, taking her with him. "Let's go to bed now—in your room. I want to see you lying on those blankets that match your eyes—although the view from this angle is pretty nice."

Smiling down at him, she said, "I could get used to hearing things like that. Tell me, has that room always been that color?"

Dax shook his head. "Kots redecorated it just a few months ago. I've never been sure why."

"It's almost as though he knew I'd be one of your passengers someday."

"Maybe he did. He knows a lot of things I can't explain, though most of it seems to come from people's thoughts—their needs, wishes, dreams—that sort of thing. If I had a dream or a vision of you, I certainly don't remember it."

Something in what he said jarred her memory. "Oh, that's right. I remember hearing something about Zetithians and their 'visions.' Too bad one of you didn't have a vision that would've saved your planet."

"No shit. The one time it would have really been useful, it failed us all."

"What about you? Have you ever had a vision?"

"Only one that I'm sure of," he said with a chuckle. "It was about Waroun."

Ava burst out laughing, a response that had an interesting effect on Dax.

"Couldn't help it," he gasped as he ejaculated. "Sorry!"

"Nothing to be sorry about," she sighed. "Ooo, this is gonna be a good one…"

Ava's head snapped back as something akin to a sonic shock wave hit her from within and an aura of warm contentment filled the small of her back and grew, reaching out to the periphery of her body. Her hair coiled like thousands of tiny springs and then whipped out straight with an audible pop.

"It does something different every time," he marveled, gazing at her hair. "But your skin is always the same. It… shimmers. It even makes your necklace sparkle."

"Really?" Ava held up the stone, studying it carefully. She saw nothing unusual; the facets flashed fire like any other crystal. "I'll have to watch for that next time. You do something different every time too—and some things I'm not sure about. I thought I felt it before… like there's something moving inside me."

"It's, um, the head of my dick," he said, blushing. "They—it—does that after I, um, you know…"

Ava rolled her eyes. "Not going to get shy and prudish on me all of a sudden, are you?"

"No," Dax grumbled. "I'm not, it's just, well, hop off and you can see for yourself."

"Not sure I want to do that," she said, but curiosity got the better of her.

Dismounting, she lay on her stomach between his outstretched thighs and took his cock in her hands. The serrated edge of the corona was indeed moving in a slow, undulating wave. "Now I *really* wish I hadn't gotten off." She let out a sob. "Can I get back on?"

"Wait a minute." Standing up, he held out his arms. "I wanted to do this all the way home."

"What—oh…" Ava let out a long sigh as Dax picked her up and settled her back on his cock. "I was thinking the same thing."

Dax grinned wickedly. "Now we can do it all the way to your quarters."

Curling her arms around his neck, she pulled him close and kissed him. He smelled like sex and candy and tasted even better. Then he started walking, and Ava couldn't have cared less whether the corona was doing its thing or not, because the bouncing thrusts as she followed his movements soon had her moaning with delight. "Are you *ever* gonna lose that erection?"

"Doesn't seem like it," he said with a chuckle. "And believe me, I have no problem with that. It feels great."

"Yes, but you know, most guys can't do that—and it can't be good for you. You've got to take a break sometime."

"Later. The way I feel right now, I never want a soft dick again as long as I live."

―⁓―

He wasn't joking, either. After spending a lifetime with a relatively useless penis, Dax was tickled to death that it was working so well. To get it to relax, he'd probably have to take a long, hot shower and then spend a couple of hours in a room where her scent couldn't follow him. He felt as though he'd been imprinted with her essence and knew he could have identified her by his sense of smell alone, even in a crowd of other women.

Dipping his head down, he kissed her, sucking her sensuous lower lip into his mouth. Ava meant everything to him. Dax already felt he belonged to her, body and soul, and prayed the feeling was reciprocated.

Just walking with his cock sheathed in her body drove him on. He was drunk on her scent, and every step brought more pleasure. Gazing into the depths of her eyes, he was amazed that his feet kept moving in the right direction.

He wanted to talk to her, to tell her how it felt, but did women like hearing such things? She didn't seem to mind—had been more forthright than he was—but would voicing his thoughts turn her off?

Ava took the decision out of his hands when she spoke. "Mmm, hot Zetithian cock. Feels so good, I can hardly stand it."

"I'm glad you like it." He hesitated. "Watching you

suck me is… incredible." His whole body quivered. "Do you really like doing that?"

"I suppose there are a lot of women who don't, and I'll admit, I wasn't always crazy about it, but it's different with you. *Everything* is different."

Dax was pleased to hear that. If Lars had been better—or even Russ—he wasn't sure he could have stood it. He leaned closer and kissed her, his tongue teasing its way into her mouth. Everything about her was different too. She was uniquely his, and every part of her was absolutely delicious.

As they approached Ava's quarters, Dax saw that the door was already open wide. The little droid had thought of everything, including the lighting. There was just enough light to see, but it was slightly aqua, matching the glowing color of Ava's eyes. "Kots must have been expecting this."

Ava turned in his arms to get a better view, giving new meaning to deep penetration. Laughing at his gasp of pleasure, she trailed her fingertips across his chest. "Liked that, did you?" She pulled him closer, threading her fingers through his hair as she traced the flames of his tattoo with her tongue. "What *is* it about you that makes me want to swing from the ceiling while we're joined at the hip?"

This sounded fascinating but difficult. "Can we do that?"

"Well, I'm sure if you think about it long enough, Kots will come up with a way."

"I'll think about it later. Right now, I want you on that bed so I can…" There it was again, that hesitation to say it out loud.

"Fuck me senseless?"

Dax gulped. "Um, yeah."

"Bring it on, Big Guy."

"Big Guy? What? You mean I'm not your kitten anymore?"

"You're anything you want to be. If you want to lie around and purr while I scratch behind your ears, then that's okay too. It's all good."

Dax grinned. "You can do that—right after I throw you down and fuck you senseless."

Ava screamed with laughter as Dax launched her onto the bed. "I would never have guessed that you could be this much fun. You were so stiff when we first met."

The vision of Ava sprawled naked on the sheets momentarily robbed him of speech. Purring like a tiger, he crawled up over her body, plunging into her core with a quick pelvic thrust. "I'm even stiffer now."

"So I've noticed."

Dax sighed with contentment. Lazily rotating his cock inside her, he felt something he hadn't noticed before. "You've got one place that feels different. Right… *there*."

Ava nodded. "It feels different to me too."

"Good?"

"Very good."

Dax brushed his cock back and forth over the hard ridge, delighting in Ava's moans of intense pleasure. Pressing upward with his cockhead, he pushed as hard as he could on that same spot until, finally, she lost all semblance of control. Screaming out his name, her body arched against him and her hair went wild.

Ava's gasps of ecstasy drove him on. Soon, her eyes were blissfully closed, and as she began to relax beneath him, a smile touched her lips. The taste of her was still on his tongue, and as Dax gazed at her lovely face, inhaling the intoxicating scent of her climax, he felt a joy too profound for mere words.

Ava's skin began to shimmer, imparting its light to the crystal that lay in the hollow of her neck. As the light from the stone grew, Dax opened his mouth to speak, but the sounds died in his throat. The glow from the stone ensnared him, drawing him in until solid matter seemed to vanish, sending him free falling through space.

As he fell, Dax realized that not everything had vanished. Ava was there with him; radiant, ethereal, and surrounded by an aura that seemed to have the pendant as its source. As he gazed upon her, the stone began to pulsate, sending forth blasts of blue-green light that nearly blinded him. Dax blinked to sharpen the vision, but it had no effect.

He was still moving inside her, but he felt as though he actually *was* inside her. Inside her body, inside her mind. No, it was more than that—deeper, more complete. He was inside her *soul*.

The moment he realized this, his climax exploded, and as it did, Ava's image expanded to exceed the full scope of his visual sense. He was aware that his eyes were wide open, but he saw nothing but the light shining forth from the crystal.

Ava felt the power of his orgasm and instinctively knew that something more than a mere sexual release had been attained. Through the haze of her own climax, she could see that his eyes were unfocused, the catlike pupils fully dilated as he gazed at the crystal. The stone captured the light from his eyes, reflecting it back, compounding the soft glow that normally emanated from his pupils.

"Dax?" she whispered urgently. "What is it? What happened?"

He shook his head, still staring at the stone. "The crystal... remember how I said it sparkled? This time was different, though. Stronger, like a... I don't know... a portal or a conduit to another... something." He spoke in hushed tones, as though fearful of being overheard and judged insane. "I was inside you, Ava. Really, truly inside you." His eyes became more focused, but his expression remained one of profound awe. "It was not only beautiful... it was... *spiritual*."

"What did you see?"

"I saw you, but... differently. It wasn't your body I saw—or even your face. It was something deeper; the pure essence of your being."

Ava had heard descriptions of orgasms before, but this matched none of them. She didn't know how to reply. "Are you seeing anything now?"

He blinked hard and sat back on his heels. "No... At least, nothing that I shouldn't be seeing, but... What do you think it means?"

"I have absolutely no idea," Ava said frankly.

"But it had to mean something," he insisted. "That sort of thing just doesn't happen every day."

"Not even to Zetithians?"

"What, you think it was a vision? I—no, I don't think so. At least, it wasn't like any vision I've ever heard about, or anything like the one I had. This was... different."

Ava took his hand and kissed it. "It certainly sounds that way. Are you sure you're all right?"

"Physically, yes, but… mentally? I don't know yet…"

The stone had always been a source of comfort for Ava, but a portal? To what? Another dimension? Ava couldn't deny that something significant had occurred, but a mind was quite capable of playing tricks on its owner. Exhaustion might have had more to do with this experience than anything. "Maybe we should try to get some sleep. You'll have a better perspective on it in the morning."

Dax still seemed perplexed. "Are you sure about that?"

"Well, no, not really, but sleep usually helps most things. Haven't you ever noticed that—or don't Zetithians have dreams?"

"Yes, we do, but I usually don't remember mine."

"Me either." Ava pulled him down beside her. "But they still help your brain sort things out. Not sure how it works, I only know that it does."

Dax nodded but then rose up suddenly. "I've never slept with anyone before."

Ava wasn't sure what to make of that. "You don't have to if you don't want to."

"No, that isn't what I meant. It's just new, that's all."

Ava threaded her fingers through his tight curls and pulled him down for a kiss. "It's been quite a day for you, hasn't it?"

"That's one way of putting it," he said with a chuckle. "I doubt that I'll ever have a better one as long as I live."

"You never know. I like to think that the best is yet to come."

"Don't know how I could ever top today. I lost my virginity, had a spiritual awakening of some kind, I'm about to spend the night with the one I…" Stopping there, he bit his lip as though trying to hold back his words.

"The one you what?"

Sighing, he kissed her again, deeply and thoroughly. "The one I love. And don't argue with me about it. Just because I've never been in love before doesn't mean it can't happen or that I wouldn't know it for what it is."

The look in his eyes conveyed the message clearly. If he wasn't in love, he might as well have been, because he believed it to be true. Perhaps that was all it took.

"I'm not arguing." Snuggling in beside him, Ava felt warm and contented—and loved. She couldn't think of a more perfect ending to the day… until Dax began purring.

Chapter 18

AVA HAD LOOKED FORWARD TO SPENDING A DAY AT THE beach with great anticipation. Despite her affinity with water, she'd never had the joy of swimming in an ocean—on any world. Unable to afford vacations to the shore on Rutara, she'd had to be content with public swimming pools, along with the occasional lake or pond. She hadn't been swimming at all on Luxaria. There were no large bodies of water near Luxton City, and the public pools were a hazard to the health of any species.

Strolling hand in hand with Dax to the nearest shore, Ava's first glimpse of the sea gave her a thrill unlike any she'd ever felt—except, perhaps, the vision of Dax without his clothes. Awestruck, she stood for a moment, taking it all in.

Sunlight danced on sparkling waves beyond rugged rock formations jutting from the sea out beyond the breakers. A pleasant breeze blew steadily over water as clear and blue as the sky, setting gigantic palm trees in motion. Flowering plants bordered the sand marking the boundary, their huge, brilliant blossoms forming a wall over thirty meters high. Waves lapped the shore, the occasional rogue crashing over those who waded in the shallows. The pure white sand felt silky and warm beneath her feet, and Ava loved the way it tickled her webbed toes.

On the beach, sun worshipers abounded, lying on gaily striped lounges or beach towels. Small tents dotted the sand above the high tide mark for those who wanted privacy, while beach umbrellas shaded the rest. And, as everywhere on Rhylos, there were shops and concession stands selling everything anyone might need or want on a day at the beach.

A quick glance at the other beachgoers proved Waroun correct. Clothing might have been optional, but if there was anyone there who wasn't nude, Ava hadn't spotted them yet. On top of that, fully a third were engaged in sexual activities of some kind. Fortunately, there didn't seem to be any children about. Ava was wishing a few of those present had opted against the nudity, but it served to eliminate Dax's inhibitions very nicely. He was easily the most gorgeous male on the beach and better looking than many of the women. His body was perfect, but as she'd noted before, it wasn't just the way he was put together. It was the way he moved—effortless, smooth, and fluid.

If Dax was still thinking about what had occurred the night before, he didn't mention it, leaving Ava to assume that he still wasn't quite sure what to make of it. She was of the opinion that it was more of a profound Zetithian sexual experience than anything to do with the stone, but she kept that to herself, focusing instead on the beauty of the day, and most of all, the ocean.

Stripping off her clothes, Ava sprinted across the sand and dove straight into the waves. The shock as she hit the cool salt water was orgasmic; a beached whale thrown back into the sea couldn't have felt more relief. Breathing the water as easily as air, she swam deeply, delighting in the steady pull against the webbing between her fingers and toes. Light from above penetrated the clear depths, and farther out, a coral reef lay before her, teeming with life. There were a few other divers about, but most required devices of some kind. Very few were as free as Ava.

She swam to the sea floor, graceful tendrils of seaweed brushing her arms and legs as she passed. The reef was almost entirely covered with plants, and their diversity challenged her imagination. Fish of every shape and color swam among the various corals—some fan-shaped while others looked more like flowers. Anemones waved their tentacles as she swam in for a closer look. Her fingers touched plants and animals she'd never seen, and whose names she would never know. Ava had studied aquatic life through books and such, but never having seen it firsthand, she now realized the vibrant colors and awesome perfection made names irrelevant. Terms like brain coral, sea urchin, nudibranch, and mollusk didn't begin to describe the stunning flora and fauna of the sea. They were all too beautiful for words.

Just like Dax.

Ava glanced up toward the surface. If only she could share this with him...

She swam upward, her hair waving like the tentacles of the anemones below. When she broke through the surface, she could see Dax standing at the water's edge as though afraid to get his feet wet. Luke was digging in the sand nearby.

"Oh, *wow*, Dax, just—wow! You've *got* to see this! There's a fabulous reef out here. It's like an enchanted forest! I've never seen anything like it!"

Dax bit his lip, frowning. "You were gone a long time."

He didn't seem angry, but if Dax was worried that she might drown, she knew the time she'd spent submerged would have seemed like an eternity. "Sorry about that. I've been dreaming of diving in a place like this all my life. It's absolutely incredible!"

Dax gave her a weak smile. "I'll take your word for it."

"Now, Dax, you've got to at least get wet." Wading through the surf, she took his hand. "Come on, now. You can do it. Just take a few little baby steps."

Dax seemed a bit leery of the water, but it wasn't long before Ava had coaxed him into water up to his knees— which would have been hip deep for just about anyone else.

She swam out into deeper water. "Come on out here. You can still touch the bottom."

"Yes, but it's not so much touching the bottom as it is that I can't see what's down there."

"Trust me, there's nothing dangerous here. Just some truly amazing sea creatures. But I'll check again if it makes you feel better." She dove beneath the waves and took a good look around. There wasn't much to see that close to the shore. A few small fish swam by, but certainly nothing with teeth. She surfaced, exhaling the water.

"How do you *do* that?" he said, shaking his head.

Ava shrugged. "It's the Aquerei in me. I used to freak people out when I went swimming as a kid, so I tried not to do it much."

"I'm sure it's nice to be able to breathe water, but I don't want my head underwater even for a second."

"What a wuss! Guess I forgot you were a cat."

"Doesn't seem to bother Luke any." The puppy frolicked along the shore, barking at the waves, obviously not minding a bit when they washed over him. "Too bad we Zetithians aren't more like dogs."

Ava shook her head. "I don't think that would be an

improvement at all. You're much better as a cat. Dogs don't purr."

Dax grinned. "Like that, do you?"

"Oh, yes," Ava said. "It makes me feel contented and sexy at the same time."

"Speaking of different species, Waroun once told me that Aquerei like to mate underwater. Is that true?"

"I wouldn't know," Ava replied. "Never been to Aquerei. It might be a common practice—I mean, it sounds great, and I'm sure I could do it, but I wouldn't want to drown you."

"Might drown the scent too. Can't fuck without it."

"I hadn't thought of that."

Dax burst out laughing.

Scowling, Ava splashed water at him. "It isn't funny."

"No, but the look on your face was priceless." Still chuckling, he added, "If it came to that, I could probably use some of the 'fluffer' techniques."

"Pussy juice on your upper lip?"

"Maybe, but you couldn't splash me like that again. You might wash it off."

Ava eyed his flaccid penis with disappointment. "Wish I'd thought of that before I got in the water. I probably don't have any left now. Bummer."

"Hey, there, Fish Lady," Waroun called out as he approached the shore with Teke, Diokut, and Quinn. Threldigan was nowhere to be seen. "Figured we'd find you two down here." He glanced sideways at Dax. "What's the matter, Super Kitten? Don't like the water?"

"Not particularly," Dax replied. "Ava wants me to learn how to swim, but I think I might do better in a swimming pool."

"Not being able to see the bottom is freaking him out a bit," Ava confided. "I checked and made sure it was safe, but he doesn't believe me."

"Oh, I believe you, all right," Dax said. "But I still don't like it."

Teke and Diokut were already removing their body stockings and, as Ava could have predicted, they had dicks that were just like the rest of them, which is to say, long and skinny, almost twiglike. In comparison, Dax looked like he had a tree trunk sprouting from his groin—or would have if it had been erect. She could easily change that by sitting on his face, but considering the stares he was getting from the other ladies on the beach, she thought it might be best to keep it down.

Threldigan sauntered up with a woman on each arm. Ava recognized the lady on his left as his partner with Onca from the night before, a lovely Mordassian with pale green skin and long tendrils curling from the nape of her neck. The other was one of Dax's infamous Davordian hookers—the brunette, to be precise. Ava swam closer to Dax. She was taking no chances that the Davordian might go after Dax's balls again—his wonderfully suckable balls…

Suddenly, sex on the beach was becoming a necessity rather than a fleeting desire. Reaching between her legs, Ava felt the slickness there despite the debriding effect of the salty seawater.

"Here." She passed her finger beneath his nose. "Take a whiff of this."

The effect was instantaneous. With his next breath, Dax's soft cock snapped to attention, ready for a rider.

Twining her arms around his neck, she backed away

from the shore, taking him with her. "Can't have that hooker spotting your hard-on," she whispered. "You remember her, don't you?"

Dax rolled his eyes. "How could I *possibly* forget? If she's here for a piece of me, well, she's not going to get it."

"Don't worry. I'll see to that. Your balls are mine, and I will guard them with my life."

Dax glanced over at Threldigan and his two ladies. All three of them were now lying on a blanket. Threldigan's cock looked like a Maypole with two maidens dancing around it. "Threld is keeping the ladies pretty busy, but you do whatever you feel is necessary. I kind of like the idea of you protecting them." He gestured toward her necklace. "Speaking of protection, should you be wearing that thing in the water? I'd hate for you to lose it."

Ava reached instinctively for her pendant. In her haste to explore the ocean, she'd forgotten she had it on. "The chain is really strong, and the attachment is secure. It's funny, but keeping it in a box in a drawer all these years seems so wrong now."

Dax smiled warmly. "If you'd left it in the box, I might not have had that spiritual event, or whatever it was, last night." His smile seemed to indicate that sleep had put the event into perspective as she'd suggested, at least to the point that he could deal with it.

Ava still had her doubts. "I'm still not sure the stone had anything to do with that. You Zetithians have visions anyway. Now, if *I* were to have a vision, I'd be more inclined to believe that the stone was responsible, my being half Aquerei and all."

"True, and maybe the stone just happened to be part

of what I saw, but it was still—" He stopped there, as though at a loss for words.

"Pretty cool?" Ava suggested.

"*Very* cool." Grinning, he added, "Of course, the *sexual* event was cool too."

"Ready for another one?"

"Absolutely."

Ava was keeping steady eye contact with him as she led him into deeper water. His penis was now fully submerged but remained erect. "You okay out here?"

Dax nodded. "As long as you're with me, I think I'd be okay just about anywhere."

"Sweet talker." She licked her lips. "Would it make you feel better if I sucked your dick?"

"Um, that would make *anything* better, but can you really do it in the ocean?"

"You bet I can!"

"Well, be that as it may, chest deep is as far as I'm going."

"Actually, chest deep would be perfect, because then I can suck you in complete privacy."

"Unless another one of your Aquerei friends swims by."

"There are several of them out here," Ava acknowledged. "Wonder if any of them is the one who robbed Quinn."

"He's probably keeping an eye out for him. Though I'm not sure what good it would do. If there were no witnesses, and it's his word against Quinn's..." Dax didn't have to finish that thought. Given their reputation for belligerence, no one would take the word of a Drell over an Aquerei.

Ava shuddered in revulsion. "We should probably

steer clear of all of them. I know I'm related to them, but honestly, Dax, they give me the creeps! Their hair looks more like a sea urchin than something that should be growing from a humanoid's head, and that iridescent skin is just plain fishy!" She swam up to Dax and climbed into his arms, peering over his shoulder. "Here comes one now," she whispered. "Where are Threldigan and his cape when you need them?"

The Aquerei man was almost as tall as Dax, with huge round eyes, high sloping cheekbones, and streamlined limbs. His reddish purple hair waved gaily in the sea breeze. Ava watched as he waded through the surf and then disappeared beneath the surface.

"See what I mean?" said Dax. "That's the second one I've seen do that."

"Where do you suppose they go?"

Dax shrugged. "Maybe they've all been invited to an underwater tea party—or an orgy."

"He'd probably be a lot of fun at an orgy." Ava giggled. "Did you see the dick on him?"

Dax rolled his eyes. "I wasn't looking at his dick."

"Really? How could you miss it? It was huge! No ruffle on it, though. Glad my guy is a Zetithian."

"Me too." Dax gave her a squeeze and a quick kiss.

Nuzzling his cheek, Ava made an interesting discovery—one she felt she should have made a long time before. "Now, I *know* you haven't had a chance to shave—don't Zetithians have beards?"

"Nope," Dax replied. "That's a human trait. Got a problem with that?"

"Not at all. I never liked the stubble thing anyway. It can be downright painful sometimes."

Waroun gave a shout of greeting and swam over to them. "So how was last night? Did you two decide to become mates for life?"

Dax and Ava exchanged a look. Ava was fairly certain that Dax was feeling that way, but she still had doubts—chief among them what a nice, virgin Zetithian boy could possibly see in a fickle half-breed Aquerei girl who barely had a credit to her name. Her next thought was one of Dax with another woman, and her hair immediately began to writhe. Perhaps she *had* mated for life.

Waroun waved his hands as though trying to erase his query. "Didn't mean to make you mad, Ava!"

"I'm not mad at you," Ava assured him. "I just… thought of something."

"Well, I'm glad it's not me you're mad at, but I'm tickled shitless that there aren't any frying pans around here."

"Never gonna let me forget that, are you?"

Waroun laughed wickedly. "Nope. Too good a story." He nodded out toward the open water. "Any idea what the Sea Urchin People are doing out there?"

"No," Ava replied. "And I don't think I want to."

"Great place to have a meeting if you don't want anyone else overhearing what you've got to say." Frowning, he added, "Aquerei can talk underwater, can't they?"

Ava thought for a moment. "I don't really know. It's not something I've ever tried. Maybe you have to be a full-blooded Aquerei."

"I'll buy that," said Waroun. "Glad you aren't—full-blooded, that is. Ugly sons of bitches, aren't they?"

Dax laughed. "I think Ava would agree with that."

"You know, you don't have to fuck way out here in the water," Waroun went on. "You can do it on the beach."

Ava glanced over at Threldigan. He was flat on his back, and the Davordian was riding him like a horse. "Can't you go watch them instead?"

Waroun waved a dismissive hand. "Boring. But you and Super Kitten... well, now, that would be a sight worth seeing."

Ava wasn't quite sure how to take that. "Did you spend the night in the Norludian brothel?"

Waroun wrinkled his nose in distaste. "You wouldn't *believe* the things you had to do to audition for that job! Awful, terrible things!"

"Such as?" Dax prompted.

"You had to do a Konklian!" Waroun said, as though everyone would understand the horror.

"Go on," said Dax. "Don't believe I know what they are."

"They're the meanest, nastiest women you ever—" Waroun broke off, shuddering. "Let's just say it was almost enough to make me give up sex forever!"

"And Threldigan said it was because the Darconians were taking all of them," Ava murmured.

"Guess he was wrong about that." Dax shifted his grip slightly, and Ava slid down on his stiff cock like a sheath over a sword.

"They said it was because I was tainted and had to be purified." Waroun apparently hadn't noticed what Dax had done, though Ava didn't know how he could have missed the way her eyes crossed when Dax's hard shaft penetrated her. "And that I'd been offworld too long, or some such garbage. Anyway, I just plain refused to do the Konklian and they threw me out."

The idea of Waroun being thrown out of even a *Norludian* brothel was too much for Ava. She began laughing uncontrollably, which had a considerable effect on Dax, who let out a yelp.

"What's the matter with you?" Waroun demanded. "She's not hurting you—oh, for the love of Leon! You really are fucking, aren't you?"

"Trying to," Dax gasped.

"You shouldn't fuck in the ocean," Waroun advised. "The pussy juice will get washed away. Causes too much friction. You should do it on the beach."

"Too much sand on the beach," Ava declared between giggles.

Dax smiled. Taking Ava's hips in his hands, he pulled her firmly against him and began sweeping his cock in circles. Ava bit back a groan but couldn't control her hair, which began tossing in time with the waves as they crashed onto the beach. "You've never done an Aquerei, have you, Waroun?"

"Your point?"

"Remember what you said about them liking to mate underwater? Well, I'm pretty sure it's true. They're *made* for underwater sex."

Waroun was clearly fascinated. "You mean the seawater isn't washing it away?"

"Nope," Dax replied. "It's making her slicker."

"But what about her scent? Don't you need to smell her to get it up?"

"You'd think it would be a problem, wouldn't you? But the water seems to be intensifying that too."

"Well, I'll be damned." Waroun shook his head in disbelief. "Who'd have thunk it?"

"Waroun…" Dax began.

"Go away?"

"Please."

"Oh, all right," Waroun said disgustedly. "Even Teke got laid last night, and Threldy's got *two* women! It's not fair, I tell you, it's just not fair!"

Ava pressed her face against Dax's chest in an effort to stifle her laughter, but Waroun heard it anyway.

"Go ahead and laugh," he grumbled. "Someday I'll get a chance to prove my sexual prowess, and then you'll be sorry."

The shout of laughter that accompanied this remark was compounded by an orgasm and came out as a strangled sound from deep in Ava's throat.

Waroun turned to swim to the shore, muttering under his breath. "Damned Zetithians. Don't even have to *try* to make a woman come. It happens automatically! What kind of skill is there in that?"

Ava would have disagreed if she could have spoken. Dax was doing something all right; it must have taken *some* degree of skill to stimulate every vaginal nerve ending she possessed. Sure, it might have been easier for a Zetithian, but it was still fabulous.

"I may not have much in the way of skill," Dax admitted. "But I'm a quick learner."

Ava couldn't have agreed more. Sighing, she captured his lips in a delicious, deeply satisfying kiss. What *was* it about Zetithians that made every part of them taste good? Granted, there were parts of him she was unlikely to ever put in her mouth, but still…

Ava's Aquerei nature began to assert itself, giving her ideas she'd never had before. Spreading her legs wide, she fanned her toes, feeling a pleasing pull as the water caught in the webbing between them. Breaking off the kiss, she rested her hands on his shoulders. Gazing at his face, she began an effortless swimming motion that carried her up and down on his rigid penis.

The sound of his purring augmented the crash of waves on the shore. Ava's entire essence seemed to center on the point of their connection as she floated in a steady rhythm. Dax's expression was one of sensuous delight, but she knew she could do even better. As she increased the force of her strokes, his head fell back and his barely audible "Ohhh" brought a smile to her lips and a throaty, seductive note to her voice.

"Feel good, Dax?"

He tried to nod but couldn't seem to raise his head. Ava didn't mind; she drank in the sight of his face, droplets of water sparkling like diamonds on the planes of his cheeks, the sharp gleam of his fangs beneath lips parted in ecstasy. His curls had relaxed in the water and were fanned out in a dark, swirling mass behind him—a mass that cried out for her touch.

Suddenly, it wasn't enough to have him inside her. Doing a backflip off his cock, she swam up between his legs, delighting in the feel of his genitals caressing her skin. His hair trailed over her backside as she surfaced behind him.

"Oh, Dax," she sighed. "You're a delight for all my senses. You look good, feel good, smell good, and I absolutely *love* the sounds you make, but the way you taste… Mmm, you're good enough to eat."

Dax sucked his lower lip into his mouth, his sharp fangs pressing into the fullness of his flesh. "So eat me."

Not needing any further encouragement, Ava dove down to suck his luscious meat into her mouth. She couldn't see his face very well, but was content with the feel of his eager thrusts and the sharp tang of their combined wetness. Dax hadn't been kidding when he'd said that the water made her slicker. Her cream seemed to adhere to his skin, mixing with his own orgasmic secretions to provide an unsurpassed degree of lubrication—one that enabled her to swallow him completely until softly curling pubic hair tickled her nose.

His balls bounced lightly against her chin as she used her arms and legs to propel herself through the silky water, his thick cock sliding in and out of her throat with each stroke. This was a surprisingly erotic feeling for her, but it was apparently downright orgasmic for Dax. Unable to hear his response, she felt the force of his ejaculation deep inside and her body reacted wildly as his snard was absorbed. The muscles of her womb flexed as a burst of radiant energy flooded through her, racing from her center to the far reaches of her extremities, culminating in tingling jolts that seemed to pulsate through each individual shaft of her hair.

She felt him begin to relax and reluctantly released him. Dax didn't hesitate a second, pulling her up out of the water and into his arms.

"That was incredible," he gasped. "And to think, I used to hate being in the water."

Ava giggled. "What in the world were you thinking?" Giving him a quick kiss, she added, "Of course, I've never actually done that to anyone before, but it seemed like the thing to do at the time."

"Glad I was your first. Believe me, it was an honor."

Ava considered that for a moment. "You know, for all practical purposes, you *were* my first—in all the ways that count, that is."

"Then I'm doubly honored."

Ava shook her head. "Believe me, the honor was all mine."

⸻⁓⸻

It took some doing, but eventually Ava got Dax to swim a few strokes. He managed a creditable breaststroke but still insisted on keeping his head above the water, which made it difficult for Ava, who didn't need to, to teach him. She was certain that his natural athleticism would overcome this obstacle in time, but after an hour or so of practice, they were both getting tired and decided to take a break.

Ava plopped down on a chair next to Waroun, who was sunning himself on a chaise lounge. He looked even more sallow than usual against the chaise's brilliant orange stripes. "How about some lunch? I'm starving!"

"Sex will do that to you," Waroun said smugly. Teke and Diokut both nodded in agreement from the comfort of their own chaises. Quinn, who was lying on a beach towel with a plate of sausages beside him, merely belched. Threldigan's two women, thankfully, were already gone, leaving Threldigan passed out on his blanket with Luke curled up beside him, neither of whom responded at all.

Dax collapsed gratefully on another blanket. "Swimming takes it out of you too. I need a nap!"

"Come on then, Waroun," Ava urged. "Let's go check out that concession stand and get some sandwiches."

"I'll come with you," Teke said. "Perhaps they've got some of those little shellfish I enjoyed so much last night."

"I'll eat anything you bring me," Dax mumbled. "Just as long as it isn't moving."

Ava was still having some difficulty adjusting to all the nudity on the beach, but Dax sprawled out face down on a blanket was enough to make her forget everything else. She just stood there, staring at his perfectly shaped buns.

Waroun hopped up and took her hand. "I see that look in your eyes, Ava, but trust me, he needs some rest!"

"I'd better come along too," Diokut said. "No telling what I'll get if I don't."

"Oh, just the usual squirming, fishy, wormy stuff!" Waroun said with fiendish glee.

The warning from deep in the blanket was quite clear. "None of that, Waroun!"

Waroun made a face. "Yes, Captain."

They had only gone a short distance before Ava realized that Waroun was still holding her hand, surreptitiously touching his sucker tips to her skin. "Tongue getting hard?"

"Yeth, and I won' be able ta eat anythin' ith I don' come."

"Nice try," she said, extricating herself from his hold.

Ava was feeling emptier than usual, but the line at the concession stand was mercifully short. With the approval of the others, she ordered the Interplanetary Lunch Special for six, which included drinks and a variety of tasty treats guaranteed to appeal to most palates. She had them toss in a few crackers in case Quinn wanted a break from the sausages.

They were on their way back when Ava was accosted by an Aquerei male whose pale greenish-yellow iridescent skin, filmy peach-colored robe, and lavender tentacles made him look more like a bizarre plant than an aquatic mammal. He said a few totally unintelligible words while gesturing excitedly at Ava's pendant and then reached toward her with his webbed fingers.

Waroun slapped the man's hand away. "What *is* it with everyone and that damned necklace?"

The Aquerei bowed and switched over to speaking Stantongue. "Forgive me, but I have never seen such a stone before my very eyes. It is surely the Aquina keystone!"

Ava stood gaping at him, not noticing that she was spilling one of the drinks until the icy brew landed on her foot. "Huh? Who are you anyway?"

The Aquerei made a sound like that of splashing water. "What?"

He repeated the sound, but then said, "Just call me Joss."

"Okay, Joss," Ava said briskly. "Would you mind explaining what in the world you're talking about?"

Joss spoke reverently, the gaze from his round, yellow eyes riveted on the crystal. "It is said that at the dawn of the New Age when the Aquina stones are gathered together in the temple at Rhashdelfi, the Oracle will speak, and the land and sea people of Aquerei will be united in their purpose at last."

"Holy shit! Hey, Dax," Waroun yelled. "Get over here! I think you need to hear this."

Ava raised a skeptical eyebrow. "That's funny. I thought the Age of Aquarius dawned a long time ago."

"That's not what he said," Teke pointed out.

"I know that," Ava said, rolling her eyes. "But it sounds about as preposterous as astrology."

"What?" Teke exclaimed. "You do not believe in the power that the stars have over us all?"

Ava let out a sardonic snicker. "Oh, please, spare me. I've read some of that crap, and trust me, that's all it is. The stars don't give a damn what we mere mortals are up to."

Teke and Diokut appeared slightly miffed. The Aquerei looked as though Ava had just spat on his grandmother's tomb.

"You were not raised as a believer in the Aquina?"

"Never even heard the word until now," Ava said. "But I'm sure you're about to enlighten me."

"What's going on?" Dax asked as he and Threldigan approached. "Is this guy bothering you?" Dax might have been naked and unarmed, but he still looked menacing.

"Not really," Ava replied. "This is Joss, and he thinks my pendant is going to bring about some sort of New Age on Aquerei."

Threldigan gasped. "Not the Aquina keystone?"

Dax stared at his friend. "You mean you've heard of it?"

"Yes, but it's always referred to as a myth," Threldigan replied. He glanced at Joss. "It is, isn't it?"

"Until now, I would have said that also," Joss replied. "But with the evidence right *there*…" He paused, staring at the stone as though expecting it to perform some miracle. Finally, he tore his eyes away, blinking several times before he could continue. "There were five Aquinas, each one a different color. Four are firmly set in the temple at Rhashdelfi, but the fifth, which I believe you now possess, was lost many years ago. It's possible that this could be a replica, but—"

Ava lifted the stone and studied it. It was the same elongated aquamarine crystal it had always been. Nothing about it seemed any different—or that unusual. "How can you tell?"

Joss peered closely at Ava. "Have you ever worn it before?"

"Not until recently," she replied. "To tell you the truth, it didn't seem appropriate."

"Has anything about you… changed since you began wearing it—or those around you?"

Ava threw a quick glance at Dax. She was still slightly skeptical about his "spiritual" experience, but when their eyes met, the look he gave her said *I told you so* as clearly as if he had spoken the words aloud. "Well, sort of," she began, "but nothing major. I mean, Dax had some sort of spiritual awakening, but I'm still not sure—"

"You should see her hair when she gets mad or laughs really hard," Waroun interjected. "It's calmed down a bit now, but it was in spikes yesterday."

Joss nodded. "It has begun."

"What has begun?" Ava demanded. "The New Age of Spiked Hair?"

"No," Joss replied. "The ancients predicted an era of peace, harmony, and understanding. A time when there would be equality and contentment for all."

"Yep," Ava muttered. "It's the Age of Aquarius all over again."

"Let me get this straight," Dax said. "We thought those were the effects of the Aquerei water she's been drinking since she became a passenger on my ship. Are you saying it's all because of the stone?"

"Yes," Joss replied. "Though it may have been compounded by drinking the water."

"What about the other stones?" Ava asked. "Is anyone wearing them?"

Joss shook his head. "Those stones are merely the completion of the set. This one is the key."

"You're saying that as though it's a certainty."

"I believe it is," Joss said firmly.

Ava remained unconvinced. "But you said it was lost. Was it truly lost, or was it stolen?"

"There are many legends associated with the stone," Joss replied. "Some believe it was taken by those in power to prevent the New Age from becoming a reality. Others contend that it is being hidden until the appropriate moment, at which time the stone will be brought forth and the Oracle will speak. Then there are those who say it was simply lost or stolen. No one really knows."

Diokut seemed puzzled, frowning at Joss. "But who would want to prevent the New Age? It sounds marvelous to me."

Joss smiled grimly. "Those who profit from war and strife would not wish for the profound changes that the stones would bring. It would not be the first time such an artifact was destroyed or hidden to preserve the status quo." He turned again to Ava. "Tell me, how did you come by the stone?"

"It belonged to my father," Ava replied. "He gave it to my mother before he left her, and then she gave it to me. I'm pretty sure it doesn't have any magical powers—at least, not according to my mother."

"It would have had no effect on her, as she must have been Terran," Joss said, scrutinizing Ava's features. "But to one such as you, the wearing of it would bring good fortune."

"Yeah, right," Ava scoffed. "Like I've been so *very* fortunate in my life." Then her gaze landed on Dax again. Her sarcasm vanished instantly. "Until recently. Wish I'd known I was supposed to wear it. Things might have gone a little better for me. To be honest, if I could say it had done anything, it brought me bad luck, rather than good."

Joss nodded. "It must be worn. Many centuries ago, it was passed from family to family. Those whose misfortunes were profound benefitted greatly from it."

Waroun snickered. "And those people gave it up willingly?"

"That was the greatest gift the stone had to give," said Joss. "It made the bearer wish for that same good fortune to befall everyone."

"If it has that effect, then how could it ever be lost or stolen?" Dax asked.

Joss shook his head, setting his tendrils in motion. "That is unknown. The temptation to wear it and enjoy its benefits would be strong for anyone who understood its value."

"And I had no idea…" Ava's voice might have gone silent, but her mind was a whirlwind of questions. She didn't even know where to begin. Had her father given her the pendant because he had hoped she would wear it and enjoy its benefits? Or had he known she would keep it safely in its box until the time for the New Age had passed? Ava was beginning to suspect that her father hadn't been in favor of the New Age. But if he'd wanted the stone to remain hidden on Rutara, his plan had backfired when she'd left Russ and gone to Luxaria with Lars.

Ava reminded herself that she had never even seen another Aquerei until her arrival on Rhylos. Had both Luxaria and Rutara been chosen for that very reason? Had it all been a plot? Had her father enlisted Russ, or even Lars, to keep her away from Aquerei—or had someone else discovered the secret?

Dax's question interrupted her thoughts. "So, when is all of this supposed to take place?"

"Very soon," Joss replied. "And it is said that if the stones are not conjoined at the time of the Great Alignment, it will be another thousand years before another opportunity arises."

"Talk about missing the fuckin' boat..." Waroun muttered.

"The planets of the Aquerei system are already nearing that phase," Joss went on. "After that, the alignment will begin to erode and the time will have passed."

"A planetary alignment gives us a pretty short window of opportunity," Dax observed. "We'll have to hurry."

Ava gasped. "You actually want to go to Aquerei?"

"Are you kidding?" said Teke. "I think I can speak for us all when I say we wouldn't miss it for all the goodies on Rhylos!"

"Even that starship you were coveting?"

"Even that," Teke said.

"This is far more exciting than sausages," Quinn said.

Ava had been so diverted, she hadn't even noticed his arrival. "Though they were awfully good."

"You wouldn't like them if you took them with you," Waroun pointed out. "If it was something you would normally like, Kots wouldn't have been serving you those crackers at every meal." With a firm nod, he added, "He knows everything, Kots does."

"Maybe he does," Ava said slowly. "He's been giving me Aquerei water to drink and clothes that matched the pendant—and were pretty enough that I'd be more inclined to wear it with them. I thought he was matching the fabrics to my eyes, but I could be wrong about that."

"That hasn't hurt anything," Dax said under his breath. "I really do like that color on you."

"So, what about it, Dax?" Teke said eagerly. "When do we leave for Rhashdelfi?"

Chapter 19

"Now," Dax replied. "We're several systems away from Aquerei, so we can't afford to waste any time." He was pleased to have the stone's powers confirmed—it meant that he wasn't losing his mind—but he still wasn't sure Ava believed it. He took her hand in his, giving it a gentle squeeze. "Your father left you something very important after all, didn't he?"

As he spoke, he traced the length of the stone with a fingertip, and instantly his mind was flooded with images—sights and sounds of turmoil and hatred mixed with fear. He saw a world awash with accusations—some demanding the return of the stone, others just as adamant to prevent the change. Children cowered in the shadows while their parents battled in the streets, and others cried laments for the fallen.

Civil war. Was there anything more horrific than neighbors and brothers fighting one another for supremacy? Angry debates between people who all claimed to want the same things, but couldn't agree on the methods. Stupid, bullheaded people...

"Dax?" He could hear the concern in Ava's voice and feel the touch of her hand, but his eyes couldn't see her. Instead, he saw ships firing on transparent strongholds—enormous cathedrals that seemed to be made of glass—their breathtaking structures dissolving into the boiling sea. He saw Ava and the stone shining brightly in the midst of battle while a disembodied voice spoke strange words he didn't understand. Screams of terror and outrage assaulted his ears, reaching a piercing, wailing note before diminishing into the sounds around him; the babble of conversation, the calls of sea birds, and the crash of waves on the nearby shore.

Dax blinked. Normal sunlight filtered past the vision to become the shapes of people and objects surrounding him. The heat of the sand beneath his feet, the feel of Ava's hand where it gripped his with calming warmth, and the sight of her lovely eyes all converged to bring him back to the present.

The transition ought to have been painful, but it wasn't. Dax simply took a deep breath, and the vision was gone, though the memory remained etched upon his mind in great detail. He turned to Joss. "I can see why you have chosen to leave your home, but are you willing to return to the chaos?"

Joss's hair reflected his change of expression, going from bewildered disorder to the serenity of comprehension in a heartbeat. He nodded sagely. "You have seen our world and know the dangers we face. Tell me, is there a future for us?"

Dax searched his memory, scrutinizing the events he'd witnessed. "I don't know. I saw the stone and the madness there, but the outcome…"

Joss smiled. "Seers don't always see what seekers wish to know."

Dax studied him carefully. "But are you truly a seeker?"

"I've never really been sure, though my presence here on Rhylos at such a time would suggest that I am not."

"Sometimes the greatest treasures are found by those who aren't looking for them." Dax glanced at Ava as the truth of his own words struck him. She was the greatest treasure he'd ever discovered in all his travels, but he certainly hadn't been looking for her.

Or had he? If asked, he'd have said that finding a woman to love had been the very last thing on his mind, but the aimlessness of his wanderings may have been deliberate. He had cast his net wide, visiting countless worlds but never finding anything of value until now—now that he might lose her to the horrors of war.

She was smiling at him. "Now, *that* must've been a real Zetithian vision! What else did you see?"

"War and destruction," he replied. "And you."

"Interesting combination," Waroun observed. "Was she wielding a skillet?"

"No. But I believe I heard the oracle speak."

Joss's tentacles stood on end. "What did it say?"

"I have absolutely no idea," Dax replied. "It was a language I don't understand." Turning to Ava, he hated what he knew he must say. "I don't want to take you there, Ava. I'm afraid of what might happen to you, but I believe we have no choice. Your destiny and mine—as well as that of Aquerei—are somehow connected. We have to go."

She studied him for a moment, her face an inscrutable mask of concentration. When she spoke at last, she said simply, "I know." Gazing steadily into his eyes, she continued, "I think I've always known. I should have stuck with my initial instincts. There was something about meeting you and Waroun…" She paused, shaking her head, as though trying to make sense of it all.

"Going to Aquerei was the first thought in my head. It was only after Lars told me my father was dead that I changed my mind. But something about that decision seemed wrong—and it wasn't just because it meant that I wouldn't be happy with Russ or would be happier with you. I see it now. The stone must have been trying to send me home."

Her words pierced Dax's heart like a dagger. He saw Ava living on Aquerei and their having a life together as being mutually exclusive. "You'll stay there." It wasn't a question; it was a statement of fact.

Ava was more cautious. "That remains to be seen. But you're right; I have to go to Aquerei. Everything that's happened since we met has been pushing me in that direction."

Dax nodded his agreement. If he hadn't felt the need for Threldigan's help in wooing her, they wouldn't have come to Rhylos. The chain of events continued, bringing them inexorably to this place and time, with this particular group of assorted beings. Ava had scoffed at the idea of the stone's significance at first, but he could see that her attitude had changed—seemingly because of the vision he'd had.

He thought it odd that she would put more stock in a Zetithian peculiarity than in what Joss had said, but perhaps this was the result of the deepening intimacy between them. Dax understood his purpose now. He was her means of transport and, whether she acknowledged it or not, she was his mate. He would give his life to protect her. Beyond that, he could only hope that their future lives would remain entwined—that is, if they *had* a future. He was enough of a student of history to know that the instigators of change didn't always live to enjoy the benefits of their struggles.

Waroun darted questioning glances at Dax and Ava. "So we're going to Aquerei now? Just like that?"

"Just like that," Dax replied.

"No need to go off half-cocked, though," Waroun counseled. "We should think about this. Plan our strategy and such."

"We can do that on the way." Dax didn't like the idea, but if they tarried, innocent lives might be lost. He didn't want that on his conscience, even if it meant that his time with Ava might be cut short. He looked at Joss. "How soon can you be ready to leave?"

Joss seemed hesitant. "I'm not sure I'm the best one to help you… Perhaps someone else—"

Ava cut him off. "Look, the more I think about this, the odder it seems. There are an awful lot of Aquerei here on Rhylos, and something tells me it's not a coincidence that Quinn was robbed by one and you just happened to meet us here. It's difficult to know who to trust, but as the old saying goes, 'Keep your friends close and your enemies closer.'"

"You believe I'm an enemy?"

"I'm saying it's a possibility," Ava replied. "You told us the story, but how do we know it's true? And if there are different factions, then how do we know which side you're on?"

"You don't," Joss conceded. "There are those on both land and sea who dream of the New Age and those who would fight to prevent it."

Waroun put up a hand. "Let me get this straight. You're saying there are *four* sides to this war?"

Joss nodded. "Centuries ago our species split. Some became primarily land dwellers, while the others remained in the sea. It is said that the division occurred because of political disagreements, which escalated into hatred over time. However, we remain the same species with nothing to distinguish one group from the other, aside from where we choose to reside."

Waroun rolled his eyes. "Oh, for the love of Leon! Couldn't you just *lie* and say it's the orange hairs against the purple?"

Joss shook his head sadly. "If only it could be that simple."

"It might be simpler than you know," Dax said. "My friend Threld can read minds." Threldigan began to protest, but Dax was adamant. "I know you won't admit to it, but all evidence suggests that you can—what can you tell us about Joss?"

"I'd really like to help you on this one, Dax," Threldigan said. "But I can only read women's minds, and not particularly well. I can influence some objects, but most of what you've seen me do involves magic tricks and illusions. And my gadgets are just gadgets. As Mordrials go, my powers are fairly weak."

"Well then, how do you get girls so easily?" Waroun demanded.

Threldigan shrugged, smiling sheepishly. "I'm also good at reading body language and other behavioral nuances. It's a gift—but, there again, I'm better with females."

"So you're no help here?"

Threldigan shook his head. "'Fraid not. I mean, I don't *think* he's lying, but I can't be positive."

Ava cocked her head to one side, peering thoughtfully

at Joss. "The reason you can't tell whether or not he's lying is because he hasn't ever said which side he's on."

Dax nodded. "Good point. We probably shouldn't take his word for any of this without corroborating evidence. I'd like to be able to say it was all true, but unfortunately Aquerei history isn't my strong suit." He glanced at Threldigan. "What about you? You'd at least heard of the stones."

"It matches what little I know, but the rest is easy enough to verify."

"True." Dax reached automatically for his pocket, only then remembering that he was naked. Motioning for the others to follow, he went back to where they'd left their things on the beach and rummaged through the pile of clothing. Pulling out the link to the *Valorcry,* he accessed the ship's computer. What he found supported Joss's story and his own vision, as well as the need for speed. "Looks like things are getting pretty bad there."

"Every faction suspects that the others have the keystone and are keeping it a secret," Joss said. "When the time of the alignment was in the future, we got along much better. Now that it is imminent…" He stopped there, throwing his hands up in a gesture of futility.

"The shit has hit the fan," Waroun finished for him.

Joss nodded, but Ava wasn't letting him off the hook yet. "You still haven't said which side you're on."

"I'd like to think I was neutral," Joss replied, "but I'm probably not. I *would* like to see an end to the fighting, however."

"You're slicker than your slimy tentacles, aren't you?" Waroun said. "You *still* haven't answered the question!"

Joss smiled, but was completely unapologetic. "Let's just say I'm keeping my options open."

"Does that mean you'll help us get the stone to the right place or not?" Ava snapped. Her own hair was starting to get a bit unruly, reflecting her growing exasperation with the man.

This was obviously the very last thing Joss wanted to do. "It was my intention to remain safely on Rhylos until the time of the alignment had passed."

"Then you should have kept your big, fat mouth shut, shouldn't you?" Waroun observed.

"But you do have a stake in the outcome," Dax said, "so you're coming with us."

Waroun chuckled wickedly. "You tell him, Captain!"

Joss's round eyes darted beseechingly from one determined face to another. "Surely you can find someone else."

"We probably could," Waroun agreed. "But I'm thinking that a big wuss like you would know all the best ways to keep out of the line of fire—oh, and don't call the captain Shirley. He prefers to be called Super Kitten."

Dax grinned. "I couldn't have put it better myself."

Lavender tentacles and shoulders drooping, Joss gave in at last. "I can tell I'm going to be very sorry I ever met up with you people, much less spotted that stone."

"Are you kidding?" Teke said. "We've had more adventures since we booked passage on Dax's ship than we've had in our entire lives put together!"

Joss winced. "That's what I'm afraid of."

"Cheer up," Waroun advised. "When this is all over, you can claim responsibility for ushering in the New Age. You'll be a superstar!"

Joss appeared to consider this for a moment, but if the idea cheered him any, it wasn't obvious.

—⁓—

Junosk stared blankly at the group assembled on the beach, still not quite believing what he'd just seen. Joss. How could he have forgotten Joss? But what were the odds that Joss would have gotten himself involved? He knew quite well that Joss didn't claim allegiance to any faction. He was simply biding his time until the storm on Aquerei blew over. Then he would return to pick up where he left off. But if that were true, why would he even talk to that girl?

Junosk was beginning to believe that the power of the stones was such that they would bring about the New Age no matter what any of them did. Getting the Cylopean to try stealing it again was pointless if Ava and her companions understood the stone's purpose. With Joss's contacts, short of blasting them all to oblivion, there would be no stopping them now. There was only one viable alternative left…

—⁓—

Joss's assurance that there were Aquerei factions searching everywhere for the Aquina keystone—people who wouldn't hesitate to kill for it—made them more cautious. Ava now kept the stone hidden from sight. Strolling through the streets as carefree tourists was no longer an option. Dax and Waroun kept their hands near their pistols, and Threldigan wrapped Ava in his cape as they hurried back to the ship as quickly and unobtrusively as possible.

Despite the fact that Dax didn't intend to charge him for the ride, Joss hadn't shown much enthusiasm until he boarded the *Valorcry*. "Very impressive," he commented, his estimation of Dax obviously rising a notch or two.

Ava marveled at the way Dax managed to get Joss to go quietly—though he did have a little help from Waroun. They were quite a pair. She wasn't at all certain that Joss could be trusted but didn't see that they had much choice. They could have accessed any number of maps to direct them to the temple but, as Waroun had so succinctly pointed out, finding it without anyone getting killed was the tough part.

Dax had been quick to initiate a plan of action, though he had the strength of his own vision to push him toward that decision. He'd seen her in that vision too. What part could she possibly have to play beyond handing the stone over to the high priestess? She wasn't the type to do anything remarkable or heroic. Granted, she was pretty handy with a pulse pistol, but she was a barmaid, not a commando.

Still, if she could survive the backstreets of Luxaria—which had few equals as a training ground for the streetwise—war-torn Aquerei should pose no significant challenges. Of course, on Luxaria, she'd done her best to avoid trouble. Now they were heading right toward it with Joss as their guide.

Ava didn't like Joss very much. His lack of honesty irked her, and as she saw it, he was nothing more than a rich man taking a vacation while his people were at war. He might have been concerned with the outcome, but he obviously intended to lay low until the shooting stopped. The fact that he'd spoken to her at all was surprising—he seemed surprised himself. He must have been shocked out of his mind to see the stone.

Her hand moved to touch her pendant in wonder. Whatever the future would bring, at this moment, she had a sense of the inevitable. She was going to Aquerei at last, and she was going there with Dax. Leaving Dax—or losing him—was becoming less of an option all the time.

―⁓―

But that night, lying in bed with Dax, Ava began to have doubts. "Are you sure you want to do this? We could give the stone to someone else…"

Dax cut right to the heart of the matter. "Do you know of anyone you could trust with such an important artifact?"

"I certainly wouldn't trust Joss—and like he said, it would be hard to tell which side anyone was on." Sighing, she snuggled closer, resting her head on his chest. "We don't have any choice, do we?"

"Not if you're in favor of bringing about the New Age. You are, aren't you?"

She raised her head to look him in the eye. "Of course I am. Why wouldn't I be?"

"Obviously some people think it's a bad idea, or they wouldn't be fighting."

"True." Ava rolled onto her back, staring up at the ceiling. "I'm still trying to figure out where my father came into all of this. Did he know it would turn out this way? And which side was he on? Did he leave the stone with me for safekeeping until the right time, or did he want it to disappear forever?"

"If he'd wanted that, he could have dropped it into the sea on any number of worlds, or cast it into an active volcano. Leaving it in your care indicates that he wanted it kept safe."

Ava nodded soberly. "And if he were killed, no one else would know where to look for it. Too bad he didn't leave any instructions with the stone. Makes you wonder if fate might have taken a hand in all of this. It's as if I was meant to have it, and then I was meant to…"

His fingertips grazed her cheek. "Find me?"

Ava nodded, leaning into his hand. It felt so warm, so strong… as though nothing bad could ever happen as long as they were together. In that instant, her doubts vanished without a trace, only to be replaced with a firm resolve. "Do you feel that?" she whispered. "That sense of belonging, of powerful, righteous purpose… I've never felt such a thing before."

"Like you know that what is happening was meant to be? The complete and utter rightness of it all?"

She nodded in reply. "Yeah. That." Gazing deeply into his eyes, she went on, "Thanks for letting me talk about this, Dax. I just needed to say it out loud—to convince myself that we're doing the right thing." Laughing lightly, she added, "You know what seems wrong now? My ever thinking about going back to Russ."

"It got you aboard my ship," Dax reminded her. "In that way, it was the perfect thing to do."

"It wasn't so much that it was a bad idea…" She paused, considering her words carefully. "I'm beginning to wonder… I mean, it wasn't Russ's fault that I left him. I think it was part of the 'plan' somehow, but—"

Dax shook his head. "I disagree. He doesn't deserve you—perhaps he never did."

Ava glanced up at him in surprise. "What makes you say that? Russ is a good man. He didn't leave me. I was the one who left him."

"Yes, but he let you go." Taking her hand, he kissed her palm. "I won't make that mistake."

Ava felt a glow of warmth curl through her body and out to the tips of her hair. She had needed this discussion to solidify her determination, but more than that, she'd needed to acknowledge the bond between them. Just the sound of his voice and his touch—his very presence—thrilled her, comforted her, and, above all, empowered her. With Dax at her side, she was capable of anything—even saving the world.

Chapter 20

DAX'S FIRST THOUGHT AS THEY APPROACHED AQUEREI was to wonder where on that vast, watery world he could possibly land his ship. There were no continents that he could see, merely a scattering of islands here and there. Granted, some of them were fairly large, but they were rocky and mountainous. Landing the *Valorcry* on any of them seemed foolhardy, if not impossible. The computer wasn't much help either; even a schematic of the planet didn't reveal where the spaceports, if any, were located. "Get Joss up here," Dax told Waroun. "I'm not ditching this ship in the ocean."

Entering a standard orbit, he gazed down at the surface as it rolled away beneath him. As a boy growing up on a ship where large quantities of water simply didn't exist, Dax had used water only for washing and drinking. His experience with Ava on the beach had taught him that it could also be recreational, but to live on a world that was almost entirely covered with water was beyond his air-breathing, land-dwelling comprehension.

The more he saw of Aquerei, the less he liked it. There were odd, shimmering spots dotting the seas, but the equatorial regions were covered with raging, continent-sized storms. Flying through one of them was not on his list of things to do for entertainment—especially not with passengers aboard.

Just about the time Dax was considering dropping

Joss and the stone on Rhashdelfi in an escape pod, Joss
entered the bridge. Dax had never transported an Aquerei
before, particularly one who was making the most of the
fact that he had been coerced into coming with them.
His assessment of Joss hadn't changed much during the
voyage; he was a hedonistic fop who was still whining
about having to return to his war-torn homeworld. Dax
had regretted the decision to bring him along from the
very beginning, particularly when he'd had the audacity
to tell Kots to modify the one small pool the *Valorcry*
had to meet his own personal specifications—which essentially meant turning it into a saltwater aquarium. Not
that there hadn't been a few aquariums in the botanical
gardens to supply the fish, but turning them loose in the
pool seemed ridiculous.

Dax knew that Kots could put everything back to normal once Joss was gone, but though Dax himself had
never put so much as a toe in that pool and wouldn't
have cared about the changes, Teke and Diokut had
complained. Apparently they didn't mind the salt water,
but the fish bothered them a great deal, particularly when
they began nibbling on the Kitnock's toes as they swam.

Mealtimes had been a nightmare. Joss ate seafood that
wasn't even dead, let alone cooked, and how Kots managed to provide it was a mystery. Threldigan, who was
fond of sushi, was the only one not totally repulsed by
it, but even he had turned a little green when the Aquerei
began crunching on the shells. The Kitnock knuckle-
cracking had reached annoying levels, and Quinn's
rude behavior had quadrupled. Ava hadn't said much,
but Dax suspected that Joss wasn't one of her favorite
people either, since he had managed to commandeer

every single bottle of Aquerei water aboard for his own personal consumption. About the only time they got any relief from his incessant demands was during the night, and even then, Kots tended to hide out with Dax and Ava to avoid him.

Any other time this wouldn't have been a problem, but Kots seemed to think that Dax needed advice on lovemaking and would occasionally buzz if he thought Dax was doing something incorrectly. Ava, bless her, had been quick to tell Kots to buzz off, particularly when he interrupted her concentration just prior to orgasm.

Consequently, when Joss finally showed up on the bridge, Dax was ready to strangle him with his own tentacles. "Where the hell are we supposed to land?"

Joss chuckled. "Why, at the Rhashdelfi spaceport, of course."

"May I remind you that this is supposed to be a covert operation?" Dax didn't bother to hide his sarcasm. Memories of his vision were quite clear. Danger, deception, and death awaited them all. To be careless was unthinkable.

"True," said Joss. "And I doubt they'd let us land so near the temple anyway. Too much hostile activity there."

Waroun began making popping noises with his fingertips. Obviously Dax wasn't the only one annoyed with Joss. "Well, then, would you mind telling us which is the closest port to the temple without being *too* close?"

"Hmm, let me think…" Joss tapped his chin with a webbed finger. "Mirolar, I believe. It's about fifty clicks from there to the temple, and we'd have to swim, but—"

"Haven't you been paying attention?" Dax thundered. "Swimming isn't an option!"

"Well, I suppose we could rent a boat. The tourist industry isn't what it used to be, but we may be able to find one to take you landers there."

"Oh, so we're *landers* now," said Waroun. "You don't have to make it sound like such a dirty word."

"I'm beginning to get a better feel for which side you're on, Joss."

"I meant no such thing!" Joss exclaimed. "It's just a way of referring to non-Aquerei!"

"Sure it is," Waroun mocked. "We always used the term offworlders on my planet. It sounds much less prejudiced."

Dax let out a long, exasperated breath. He'd never needed one before, but there was always the chance... "Kots! Do we have a boat?"

Kots's affirmative beep came over the comsystem instantly.

"Thanks be to Leon!" Waroun said gratefully. "That slimy-tentacled son of a drayl was about to drown us all!"

"Now who's sounding prejudiced?" Joss demanded. "Captain, I take serious offense!"

"Noted." Dax leaned forward over the pilot's console, pinching the bridge of his nose. If he made it through this alive, he was never going to let another Aquerei on his ship again—unless Ava had some relatives there. Otherwise, it was a no go.

———···———

"Why is it that the bad guys always get all the breaks?" Vandig lamented.

"No clue," Eantle replied, "but they usually do."

"How Ridan managed to miss them when they

landed…" Vandig's tentacles writhed with anger. "What an incompetent!"

"He was relying on the spaceport logs, and there are at least six ports on Rhylos," Eantle reminded him. "He couldn't possibly be in all of them at once."

Vandig shook his head. "The way we're spread out across half the sector, it's a miracle there are any of us left on Aquerei at all. I'll be so damn glad when this Great Alignment shit is over…"

"Now, now," Eantle said soothingly. "Don't get your tentacles in a knot. We'll find them."

"And then what? Tell them they've fallen in with a—"

Eantle cut him off. "Joss has never claimed allegiance to any faction. You know that."

"Just because we know it doesn't mean it's true," Vandig said. "And to think, that slippery bastard must have just walked right up to her and told her everything. It boggles the mind."

"Well, if any of us had been there, we could have done the same thing," Eantle said reasonably. "At least Ridan spotted Junosk and was smart enough to follow him; otherwise, we wouldn't have heard about any of this. It would have been better had he been close enough to catch up to Joss and the others before they boarded their ship, but this was *our* lucky break. We will make the best of it."

"That's what we get for playing it safe," Vandig grumbled. "We should have put a tail on Junosk from the beginning. It would have made things a lot easier."

"That's hindsight," Eantle said. "How were we to know they were so close?"

Vandig ignored this, giving voice to his most pressing

concern. "Tell me again that Joss isn't on their side, because if he is, we might as well give up right now."

Eantle was adamant. "He isn't a member of Opps and I won't give up. We owe it to Sliv to find his daughter and help her if we can."

Vandig snorted. "*If* we find her. What are the odds?"

"My dear Vandig, it is useless to play the odds in this matter. We must employ logic. Now, think: If you had the stone and were going to the temple, where would you land?"

"Mirolar," Vandig replied. "But I'm sure the Opps will be there too."

"Of course they will. They're everywhere, but so are we."

Vandig shook his head sadly. "I just wish we could be sure that Joss wasn't leading them into a trap."

"It might not be such a bad thing if he was." Eantle smiled as a plan began to form in his mind. "In fact, it might be the best thing that could happen."

Vandig's tentacles stopped moving altogether. "I'm getting confused."

Eantle laughed. "With any luck, so will the Opps."

———

Dax contacted the port authority at Mirolar, but the news was grim. "No starships are allowed to land on Aquerei until further notice."

"Anywhere?" said Joss.

"Anywhere," Dax snapped. "And I suppose you knew this?"

"Well, I've heard rumors, but—"

"They were obviously true. What are your planetary defenses like?"

Joss shrugged. "Minimal. It's not like we've ever been at war with anyone but ourselves."

"So it's unlikely that we'd get blown out of the sky; just arrested when we land. Is there any place we could land covertly?"

"Yeah, like there's so much *land* to choose from," Waroun snickered.

Joss seemed uneasy. "Well, I do have contacts on one of the bases, but—"

"Call them," Dax said, punching the comlink. "Now."

"Um, what do you mean by 'bases'?" Waroun asked.

Joss pointed at the viewscreen. "Do you see those flat spots on the sea? Those are the bases."

"And you can land a ship this size on them?"

Joss nodded. "It has been done in the past."

Dax rolled his eyes. "Oh, that makes me feel *so* much better…"

Ava stuck her head in the door. "What's going on?"

"You really don't want to know," Waroun replied.

"Try me."

"We've got to land the ship on some sort of floating glass thingy out in the middle of the ocean."

"They aren't actually made of glass," Joss put in. "They're made of water."

Dax's head began to pound. "This just gets better and better." He glared pointedly at Joss. "Explain that."

"It's pretty technical, but the bases are essentially made of water, held in place by a colloidal matrix." He smiled reassuringly. "They're quite strong—even the storms don't affect them, though they do rock a bit when one hits them."

"And we can set the ship down on one without squashing anyone or breaking anything?"

"Normally, no—they're populated with cities or industry—but I, well, I own one that is under construction near Mirolar. I've been out of touch for some time, but it may be complete enough to land on by now."

Dax had seen something similar in his vision. "But they can be destroyed, right?"

"I suppose so," Joss replied. "But it would take an enormously powerful disruptor to do it. I've never even heard of such a weapon."

"If my vision was correct, and I believe it was, then someone now has that ability. I saw 'glass' buildings being fired on by ships, and they sank into the sea."

Joss's tentacles wilted, and his skin lost some of its iridescent quality. "Ships? Why, there are millions of Aquerei living on those bases! I can't believe anyone would do such a thing!"

"War is hell," Waroun said grimly.

"What else haven't you told us, Joss?" Ava asked. "You won't say which side you're on, you won't—"

"I believe I just took a side," Joss said faintly. "The New Age must begin, and soon. With technology like that…" Clearly stunned, he turned bleak eyes on Dax. "There is no hope."

"Then tell your buddies we're setting down on that platform," Dax said. "And while you're at it, tell them to get the hell out of the way."

———

Ava knew that if anyone could pull this off, it would be Dax. She'd never been on the bridge while he was at the helm before, but simply watching him made her feel more confident. He handled the controls with the deft skill of a man who knew exactly what he was doing.

She only wished she could have felt more confident about their mission. All they had to do was take the stone to the temple and place it in its niche. The "oracle" would take it from there. Of course, first they had to land, and then they had to find the temple, making their way past who knew what kind of opposition. The stone had to be kept hidden too. One glimpse of it would set off a chain reaction among those for and against the coming of the New Age.

Having heard of the conditions on Aquerei, Ava longed to put an end to the conflict as quickly and easily as possible, and watching Dax intensified that longing. He was the embodiment of strength and vibrant life; for him to die on an alien world, fighting the battles of a foolish race of aquatics who couldn't get along with one another, was pointless and wasteful. If it weren't for Ava and her father—whichever side he was on—Dax wouldn't be here, about to risk his life for a people who would probably never hear of his courage, or his determination.

"I can't let you do this, Dax," she said, barely realizing she'd spoken.

"It's a little late for that now," Waroun said impatiently.

"No, it isn't," Ava said firmly. "We don't have to do this." With a glance at Joss, her expression hardened. "This is your fight, not his. I could give you the stone, and you could do this all on your own."

Joss blanched like a fish that had gone belly up. "You can't be serious."

"I'm perfectly serious. Dax, you don't have to do this."

Dax never took his eyes from his task. "Yes, I do. The vision… it's so strong in my mind… I can't ignore it."

She gritted her teeth in frustration. "Men," she said with disgust. "Always willing to die for a noble cause. Well, I'm not risking you! I'll go alone. No one will suspect me of having the stone. I could just walk right into the temple and—"

"Get yourself killed," Dax said, cutting her off. "Do you think I haven't thought about this? If there were an alternative, I'd grab it in an instant. But I have no choice, Ava. I may not be of this world, but something greater than all of us is at work here. I have to see it through."

Her tears began to flow. "I can't risk losing you, Dax."

"Do you think I want to risk losing *you*?"

"No," she replied. "I know you don't, but I'm not Zetithian; I'm replaceable. Think about how important you are, not only to me, but to the survival of your species."

"I can't let that affect how I live my life," Dax said evenly. "If I can't be free to choose my own path, then I might as well be dead."

"The Aquerei may be killing each other, but at least there are still plenty of them left." Ava was beginning to wish she'd never walked onto the bridge. Her voice trembled with emotion. "And you mean more to me than all of them."

"But think how you would feel, knowing that other lives were lost because we didn't act; didn't do what we were supposed to do. We may only be small parts of the cosmos, but we each have our own destiny. We were put here to do something… something important. Beyond that…" Dax paused, shaking his head. "I don't understand it, but my understanding doesn't matter.

I can see the absolute necessity that we do this, and we do it together." He glanced at her briefly before returning his attention to flying the ship. "We've had this discussion before."

Ava drew in a deep breath. "I know. It's just that now... well... you're much too precious to sacrifice."

"Then I'll just have to stay alive." He said this with such fierce intensity that Ava felt the impact of his words in the very core of her being. Her skin tingled as though a prophet had spoken, and her hair snapped with electricity.

"You'd better," she said quietly.

"I'll do my best," Dax promised. Smiling, he angled the *Valorcry* toward the atmosphere. "And for the record, you are *not* replaceable."

Her smile was automatic, but she didn't comment— at least, not aloud. *If only I could believe that...*

"So, Joss," Dax said. "Where is this base you were telling us about?"

Chapter 21

Ava was unprepared for the effect the oceans of Aquerei would have on her. Sunlight danced on seemingly limitless expanses, while currents visible even from the upper atmosphere seemed to carve the planet into sections. But it was more than a fascinating view; it called to her on a deep, primal level. If she had waited just a few moments before voicing her concerns, her own resistance would have dissolved like salt scattered across a wind-tossed sea. She could no more have abandoned this world than she could sprout wings and fly.

It was beautiful, awe-inspiring, but terrifying at the same time. The vast depths beckoned, and she longed to explore them all, to discover their secrets and learn their ways, despite the inherent dangers. This world was her birthright. Dax was correct in believing that she would not leave it. She wouldn't—at least, not willingly. Not until it was saved.

Following Joss's directions, the *Valorcry* skimmed the air just above the waves as the base shimmered in the distance. Seen from space, it looked like a shiny dot in the middle of the ocean. Close up, it was huge; the foundation for a great new city.

"So you own this thing, do you?" Waroun asked Joss.

"I do," said Joss, but he didn't seem very happy about it. "Unfortunately, the way things have been going, the city may never be built. Right now, all it's good for is a landing pad."

"And to think, we're giving you a ride home for free when we could've charged you a bundle," Waroun lamented.

"You're forgetting that I didn't particularly want to come here—at least, not right now." Joss peered at the viewscreen. "I don't see anyone out there at all—no sign of any work being done, either."

"Can you contact them?" Dax asked.

"I can try," Joss replied. "But from the look of it, I don't believe I'll get an answer."

"Well, at least there's no one in the way," Dax pointed out. "Where should we set down?"

"The northwestern corner," Joss replied.

"It could be a trap," Ava said. Gazing out across the deserted base, she felt as though an icy finger had touched her, sending shivers throughout her body. "It's certainly creepy enough."

"I've seen creepier places," Waroun said. "You know, the kind with dark corners for the bad guys to hide in? We'd be able to see anyone coming long before they could get to us."

"But if the opposition truly does have a disruptor capable of destroying the bases…" Joss stopped there, still visibly shaken at the very idea of such a weapon.

"I still don't get why there's a war at all," Ava said. "What does it matter whether someone chooses to live in the city or under the sea?"

"It's the same as any other civil war," Joss said wearily. "One side decides it hates the other for some trivial reason, and after the first death, things get ugly and then continue on until no one really knows why anymore. They hate because they've been taught to hate. Until everyone realizes that on the deepest level, they are all basically the same, it continues." He shook his head sadly, his tentacles flat and lifeless. "I wish for the New Age and the end of the hatred, but I'm afraid it is only a myth created by dreamers."

"Perhaps it isn't a myth," Dax said. "Perhaps it's only now, after much pain and suffering, that this form of enlightenment is possible."

"Going through hell to get to heaven?" Ava suggested.

Dax nodded. "Something like that."

Waroun blinked hard and stared at Dax, his big, bulbous eyes agog with incredulity. "Enlightenment? Since when did you go all spiritual on me?"

"I had an 'event' of some kind not long ago," Dax replied. "It… changed me somehow."

Waroun snickered. "That's what happens when you lose your virginity. You're never quite the same after that."

If Ava hadn't known the timing of it, she would have been inclined to agree with Waroun, but nothing before, or since, had been anything like it—unless Dax had kept it to himself.

Dax shook his head. "I don't think that was it, Waroun—at least, not entirely." He gestured toward Ava. "I think it had more to do with Ava and the stone than the sex."

For the first time, Joss appeared hopeful. "If that is so, then perhaps the stones are not myths after all. We may be sorry we did this, but go ahead, Dax. Set the ship down, and may the gods of Aquerei preserve and protect us."

Ava gazed curiously at Joss. "If you didn't believe in the power of the stones, why did you bother to tell me about them?"

"I honestly don't know," Joss said candidly. "Perhaps the stone called to me, or I was simply overcome by astonishment." He broke off there, his tentacles waving back and forth as if he had shaken his head. "To find the artifact that half of my world has been searching the galaxy for just dangling from the neck of a pretty girl on the beach was... miraculous."

"It could be that the stone itself is setting events in motion to ensure its safe delivery to the temple," Dax said. A moment later, the *Valorcry* settled gently onto the base, causing barely a ripple in the water that surrounded it. "But, either way, we're here."

"That's not a boat, Kots," Dax said as the droid opened the hatch to the hangar bay. "It's a hovercraft. I knew we had this thing—I asked you if we had a boat."

"Same difference," Waroun said. "If it can hover on land, it can do it on the water too."

Dax remained unconvinced. "But if it loses power, will it float?"

Kots beeped reassuringly and continued the extraction sequence. Pressing a control near the door, he sent the hovercraft, *Juleta*, floating gently to the surface. Dax couldn't think of it as "the ground," for the base he was standing on was so clear, he could see fish swimming beneath it, though they appeared to be several meters away. "Just how thick is this thing?" he asked Joss.

"The base was designed to carry the weight of an

entire city," the Aquerei replied with the closest thing
to a smile Dax had seen since they left Rhylos. "I don't
think you need to worry about it sinking."

Dax was actually more worried about the murky
depths beneath it than anything else, and the way it
rocked on the waves was making him feel slightly ill.
"I don't guess it ever holds still, does it?"

Waroun looked at him as though he'd gone insane.
"What do you mean? I can't feel a thing." He slapped
his flat foot on the surface. "Solid as a rock!"

"I must be more sensitive to its movement then,"
Dax said. "I can hardly *wait* to get in the boat."

"Actually, this thing is better than a boat on water,"
Threldigan said, gesturing toward the *Juleta*. "Waves
won't affect it much—unless they're really big ones."

Dax directed a baleful glare at his old friend but
saw no reason to back it up with a retort. Threldigan
had been very helpful in preparing for the invasion of
Aquerei, making lots of new "gadgets" during the voyage, only joining the others for meals, with the result
that he had amassed quite a large bag of tricks. As usual,
he was wearing his cape but seemed to have lost a bit of
his devil-may-care attitude. Dax suspected he'd never
been part of an invasion force before—and certainly
not one that was so hopeless. Though they'd all armed
themselves with every type of weapon the *Valorcry*
had to offer, they were still immeasurably outgunned
and outnumbered. This prospect had sobered all of
them—even the two Kitnocks had ceased their knuckle-
cracking conversations—except for Ava. She was grinning broadly as she gazed out across the open sea, fairly
shivering with excitement.

"What a beautiful ocean!" she exclaimed. "I can't wait to dive into it!"

Dax shuddered in revulsion. Standing chest deep near the shore on Rhylos had been one thing; diving head-first into the fathomless sea was quite another. "You *are* going to ride in the boat, aren't you?"

"What—oh, of course I will." She seemed slightly distracted. "It's probably too far to swim, anyway, isn't it, Joss?"

Joss shrugged. "Depends on how quickly you want to get there. We're about twenty-five clicks away from Mirolar to the south and Rhashdelfi to the north." With a smug grin, he added, "Can you see why putting a base here would be profitable?"

"I'm sure you'll make millions," Dax said dryly.

"Oh, much more than that," Joss assured him. His tentacles were tossing merrily in the ocean breeze, though Dax suspected that their happy dance had more to do with the prospect of monetary gain than the wind.

Ava was still gazing longingly at the sea, having ventured partway down the gentle slope that formed the shoreline of the base. Dax knew she could handle herself in the water, but, concerned for her safety, he moved in behind her anyway, ready to catch her if she slipped.

She smiled up at him as he approached and stepped back onto the level platform. "So, which way do we go and how far is a click?"

Dax pointed over her shoulder to the northwest. "That way, and a click is about two kilometers."

"Fifty kilometers, then." With a wistful sigh, she leaned back against him. "Farther than I want to swim, that's for sure."

Enfolding her in his arms, Dax leaned down to nuzzle her neck, noting that her scent reflected her disappointment. "Once the stones have done their thing, you can swim as much as you like."

"Sounds fabulous." She sighed. "I've never lived anywhere that I could swim as much as I liked."

Dax felt her quiver of anticipation and understood how she must be feeling—the way he would feel if, by some miracle, Zetith had been recreated and he had just landed there. "Does it feel like home?"

"It does—though I'm sure this is the last place you'd ever want to live—but just look at it, Dax! Can you see how clear and clean it is? These waters must be teeming with life." She gasped in awe as a large fish breached the surface. "What an absolutely perfect world…"

"It's not perfect yet," he reminded her. "It's up to us to make it that way."

Nodding, she raised his hand and pressed her lips to it, sending a thrill racing all the way to his toes. "You're right. Let's get this invasion started."

The others had already boarded the *Juleta*. Kots was hovering nearby, mumbling as he held Luke's leash. Dax and Ava both gave the puppy a hug, but he still whined his displeasure at being left behind.

"We'll be back as soon as we can," Dax told the little droid. "But if anyone tries to board, steal, or impound the ship, you know what to do."

Kots chirped and headed back aboard the *Valorcry* with Luke trotting behind him.

"What's he supposed to do?" Ava asked. "Self-destruct?"

"No," Dax replied. "He's supposed to lock the hatch and lift off."

"He can fly that thing all by himself?"

Dax nodded. "He can't do anything fancy, but he can get it off the ground."

"Maybe he ought to do that now," Ava suggested. "Might make it less obvious that we were ever here."

"True, but I don't think anyone tracked us here, and with a war going on, there's not much interstellar traffic around this planet. I didn't see any satellites in orbit, so they'd have to rely on line of sight. I don't know about you, but I can't see a damn thing."

The *Juleta* was a large, oval-shaped craft with high railings on the sides and a row of passenger seats in the middle. As the others climbed aboard, Dax took the helm, which was located on the port side nearer to the stern than the bow. He was familiar with the controls, but navigation at sea required a different technique than traveling on land. He would have to rely on the instruments. Firing up the engine, he steered the *Juleta* toward the edge of the base and then out over the open water.

"Are there actual cities beneath the surface?" Teke asked.

"Yes," Joss replied, "though there aren't any near this base. The Opps would have fought the construction if there had been—and they haven't been crazy about the bases as it is."

"You keep calling them 'Opps,'" Diokut said. "What does that mean?"

"The Opps are those who oppose unity, and the Unities are those who support it," Joss explained. "As I've said before, there are two factions on land and two factions in the sea. It's very confusing and nearly impossible to guess who you're dealing with. And they all want the stone."

"Do any of them actually work together?" Teke asked.

"You'd think they would, wouldn't you? But they never have—at least, not that I've ever heard."

"The funny thing is, out here, it looks so peaceful," Waroun observed. "You'd never know there was a civil war going on."

"You just *had* to say that, didn't you?" Dax growled as he glanced at the navigation console.

"What? Why?"

"Because there are three ships heading right for us. Big ones."

Ava looked worried. "Warships?"

"I can't imagine they'd be friendly," Joss said. "Someone must have seen us land after all."

"That's the trouble with the sea," Quinn said. "They could be all around us, and we'd never know until it was too late."

"It's already too late!" Dax yelled as a grappling hook sailed over the starboard side, attaching itself to the railing with sharp pitons that bit deeply into the metal. Two more hooks followed the first. This was *not* good. "Try to cut them or throw them off!"

Waroun was the first to reach the hooks, but though he tried desperately to dislodge them, they wouldn't budge. Teke had armed himself with a knife the size of a short sword and began using it to hack at the ropes, but whatever they were made of was tougher than the knife. Ava screamed as three Aquerei began to climb aboard. Dax knew she was tougher than that, and wasn't a bit surprised to see that she'd already drawn her pulse pistol. Taking aim, she stunned one of them before Joss intervened.

"Hold your fire!" he shouted. "These are my men from the base."

"How the hell can you tell?" Waroun snapped. "They all look the same to me."

"Trust me, I can tell," Joss yelled back.

"We saw you land," one of the men gasped as he slid onto the deck, "but couldn't reach you in time. We've been hiding in the depths for days. It's bad, Joss. Really bad."

Two more Aquerei swarmed over the side, dragging the one Ava had stunned along with them. Dax hoped there weren't any more of them, for the *Juleta* only had seating for twelve, aside from the pilot. Any more than that would put them over the weight limit, and sinking would become a definite possibility.

Dax swore as three more scrambled up the ropes. The controls spiked as the *Juleta* tipped dangerously to starboard. "Some of you get over here on this side," he bellowed. "We're going to flip over if you don't!"

The Kitnocks and the Drell were quick to follow orders. Ava pulled Waroun back from the side, and Joss and two of the men dragged the unconscious man to an open space behind the seats. The others clambered into seats, the water still sluicing from their streamlined bodies. Essentially nude except for their seaweed loincloths, they looked like the day's catch spilling onto the deck of a fishing boat.

"What can you tell me about those ships up ahead?"

"They're bound to be Opps," a green-tentacled man replied. "They ran us off the base." Turning to Joss, he went on, "They knew you were coming. They just weren't sure when."

"How the hell could they know that?" Waroun demanded. "And why would they think we would land here? We didn't know that until just a little while ago ourselves."

"But there were all those Aquerei on Rhylos," Ava said. "They must have been tailing us the whole time. They saw us with Joss and did the math."

"But why would they just follow us?" Waroun asked. "They could have stolen that rock from you anytime— or just killed us all."

"Could be that you guys are more intimidating than you realize—remember when the Cylopean tried it?" Ava shrugged. "Who knows? I mean, if we can't tell which side anyone is on, maybe they can't either."

If Joss's bleak expression was any indication, that was probably true. Dax was playing scenarios through his head. Surrender to the approaching ships, hand over the stone and go home, evade them and thus add even more distance to their journey, or pretend to be on their side—whichever side it was—or stand and fight a hopeless battle and probably all be killed. Then there was the other option: He hadn't brought along a magician for nothing.

"Hey, Threld, what have you got?"

"Decoy drones," Threldigan replied. "But—"

Waroun rolled his eyes. "What the devil is a decoy drone?"

"They make duplicate images of an original."

This sounded interesting. "Can they float?"

"Never tried using them on water," Threldigan replied.

"No time like the present," said Dax. "Toss one out."

Threldigan reached into his bag and pulled out a small shiny cube. "The only problem is that it won't keep up with us as we move forward."

"Then maybe we should stay put." Dax cut back the throttle, and the *Juleta* slowed to a crawl, the repulsors keeping them hovering just above the water. "Good thing the sea is calm today." The thought of huge waves swallowing them up didn't set well with him at all.

"So, Threldy," Waroun began. "Just how do these things work?"

Dax chuckled to himself, knowing that Threldigan would never tell, and Waroun should have known better than to ask.

Threldigan gave him a crooked smile. "Magic." With that, he threw the cube overboard.

Thankfully, it didn't sink, but bobbed lightly on the surface. As they watched, a mirror image of the *Juleta* and its passengers began to unfold from the cube.

"Ha!" Waroun shouted. "We'll look like an entire fleet! How many have you got?"

"Twelve," Threldigan replied. "But we might not need them all—just enough to confuse them." He tossed out four more and, suddenly, there were five *Juletas*.

"Now all we need is something that looks like a really big gun," Waroun said gleefully. "And we'll be all set!"

"Give me your pulse rifle," Threldigan said. "And don't worry, I'll give it back."

Waroun did as he asked, but Dax could tell he wasn't very happy about it; Waroun was quite fond of that rifle, having won it from a nasty Udwend in a game of *kartoosk*.

Threld set the rifle on the railing at the bow and put a

small round sticker on it. Instantly, the rifle grew to ten times its original size, as did those on the decoy drones. "Illusion dot," Threldigan said. "And no, I'm not going to tell you how it works."

"So, now we're a fleet of six with really big guns. I like this," said Joss. "At least we *look* intimidating."

Dax gazed ahead at the approaching ships and consulted his instruments. They were definitely slowing.

Everyone seemed more confident, until Joss threw in one more comment. "Of course, if they have any of those disruptor weapons that can destroy a base, we're doomed, but maybe they don't have them on every ship."

"What are you talking about?" the green-tentacled man gasped. "A weapon that can destroy a base? That's impossible!" The other Aquerei men all seconded his statement, their tentacles snapping with indignation.

"Nothing is impossible," Dax said grimly. "If we didn't think that, we wouldn't be here."

The three ships, which had previously been in a tight formation, now split up as though trying to surround their flotilla. They were even larger than Dax had initially thought—no way would even the big guns Threldigan had "installed" make a difference to them. Several new targets had just appeared on the navigation screen when Ava let out a yell.

"Holy moly!" she exclaimed. "There are five more ships behind us, coming up fast!"

"Yep, we're doomed," Waroun said, slumping to the deck. "Might as well just sit tight and go peacefully." He smiled weakly. "Been nice knowing you, Ava. Just wish I'd gotten a better sample of your essence before I died."

"We aren't doomed," Ava said fiercely. "And I'm not just going to hand the keystone over to these people."

Joss's men gaped at her in astonishment. *"You have the stone?"*

"Yes, and they're not going to get it!" Before anyone could stop her, Ava leaped onto the railing and dove into the sea.

Chapter 22

AVA'S ENTIRE BODY REJOICED AT HER DECISION. KICKING off her shoes, she swam deeply into the cool water, delighting in the silky feel of it on her skin. The Rhylosian Sea had been fabulous, but diving into this ocean was like coming home. As she descended, she was amazed at the brightness of the light filtering down to the sea floor. Visibility was much sharper than in the waters of Rhylos, and the sea was surprisingly shallow. She could swim to the bottom with no difficulty whatsoever and wondered if all Aquerei seas were as shallow.

Recalling that Joss's base was halfway between Mirolar and Rhashdelfi, she glanced up at the *Juleta* hovering above her, noting the direction of her bow. Her eyes then searched the ocean floor until she spotted a trail carved through the rocks in the same direction. Despite the convenience of this discovery, a frisson of fear swept through her. A trail meant that this was a frequently used route—a route that could be watched by anyone from any faction. Her keen eyes swept the vicinity, alert to any danger. She saw nothing more frightening than a few solitary fish. If any Aquerei lived in these waters, there was no evidence of it. This was simply the road between the two cities.

Ava drifted downward, pulling herself effortlessly through the water. The tug on the webbing between her fingers and toes thrilled her, and her ears quickly adjusted to the depth, enabling her to hear strange underwater sounds. Schools of gleaming fish swam past with no apparent fear, and she felt her own fears begin to subside. Knowing that her pulse pistol would function under water gave her added courage, though the knife thrust through her belt would have been more useful in an underwater fight. Even so, she hoped it wouldn't come to that. Shallow though it was, it was still a very big ocean, and she would be very difficult for anyone to find.

Bottom dwellers and crabs scuttled aside. Eels moved ribbonlike through the water, only to disappear into crevasses in the rocks below. As her eyes adjusted further, she could see the trail stretching on ahead. Rolling onto her back, she swam as effortlessly backward as she had going forward. The *Juleta* remained stationary, hovering just above the surface as she left it behind.

When she strayed from the path to discover where an eel made its home, Ava began to realize why she had moved so much more quickly along the trail. A strong current flowed at that depth, propelling her toward Rhashdelfi. Still, fifty kilometers was a long way, and though it was early in the day, she couldn't hope to arrive before nightfall. The thought of being trapped beneath the surface in the dark frightened her. Who knew what dangers lurked that her humanoid eyes couldn't see?

A shadow passed over her. For a moment, she feared a leviathan might be on her tail, but quickly realized the shadow had been cast by the Aquerei ships cruising toward the *Juleta*. She felt a moment's anxiety for the safety of Dax and the crew but doubted they would face any real danger as long as she held the keystone. Between Dax's competence as a commander and Threldigan's gadgets, they might even escape.

The Aquina hung safely around her neck, hidden beneath her shirt. Ava felt the stone's power flowing through her as she swam, and her confidence grew. She had seen a map of the island and knew where the temple was located. With any luck, she would be concealed in darkness when she made landfall. She might even be able to get to the temple unnoticed. After all, even the Aquerei had to sleep.

They had to eat, too. Hungry, she noticed a fish nibbling at a fleshy plant growing between the rocks. She had never tried to eat while submerged, but this seemed to come as naturally to her as breathing the water. The plant was sweet and tender, and she picked more of it, munching as she swam. After a bit, she grew tired and allowed her body to drift with the current, feeling a oneness with the sea and the pulse of the planet.

At last her Aquerei nature was being given free rein. She was the daughter of two different worlds; her Terran side was just that, "of the Earth," but her Aquerei side was of the water. The stone floated against her chest as she swam, reminding her that she was only present in that glorious ocean because of it. Sharing this experience with Dax would have been a joy, but it saddened her to realize that, even with diving equipment, he would never be a true creature of the sea.

Time seemed to have no meaning there in the depths, until it began to get dark. If there were underwater signposts showing the number of clicks remaining in her journey to Rhashdelfi, Ava couldn't read them. How many clicks could a girl swim in one day, even with a current to carry her onward? Joss's reply had been vague, which implied he'd never made the journey himself.

As darkness fell, Ava's fears were eased by the luminous quality of everything surrounding her. The fish she'd seen during the day were gone now, replaced by bioluminescent species that swam slowly while tiny points of light gleamed from their fins and raced over their bodies. Plants that had been dull and colorless in daylight were now aglow with brilliant colors. Pulsating with the flow, they marked the trail while the current carried her on.

Ava wondered if the current was natural or contrived, though its location, strength, and convenience made the latter more likely. There was a different sort of technology at work on this world. With the probable dearth of conventional building materials, water construction made sense. Ava could scarcely imagine the majesty of cities made entirely of water. The Temple of the Aquina would surely be among the most beautiful structures in the galaxy.

Just as her impatience to see these wonders reached its peak, she saw the lights.

~

Dax stared at the spot where Ava had jumped, still unable to grasp the enormity of what she had done. Part of him wanted to dive in after her, but, fortunately, his sensible side overruled that impulse.

Waroun's eyes bugged out of his head. "I can't believe she did that!"

"How very selfless of her." Teke spoke with such reverence that Dax half expected him to say a prayer. Quinn, on the other hand, was jumping up and down and screaming at Joss to do something.

"She'll be fine," Joss said. "However, it might be best if we were to lure these ships away from her." He looked pointedly at Dax. "Trust me, she will make it to Rhashdelfi."

Dax lost the tenuous hold on his temper. "In the middle of the ocean with nothing to show her the way? You must be out of your water-breathing mind!"

"I assure you, if I thought she was in any danger—"

"There's a road down there," one of Joss's men interjected. "We've been living along it for a several days and haven't seen a soul. We can only guess at what's happening in the cities, but there's been no one traveling between them."

"I can tell you what's happening there," Dax said fiercely. "Your people are killing each other in the streets."

The man paled visibly. "Are you—how can you be sure?"

"He had a vision, Rolst," Joss said.

Rolst snorted his skepticism. Dax was about to enlighten him when Waroun took a dive to the deck. "They're shooting at us!"

"Hopefully they'll go for the decoys first," Threldigan said. "I have one other gadget that might help…" Reaching into his bag, he pulled out a teardrop-shaped vial and sprinkled a drop or two on Waroun. He scattered the rest of the contents about the deck. Nothing happened.

Waroun stared at the droplets on his arm and snickered. "My, that was useful."

"Actually, it was," Dax said. "Take a look."

The men on board the nearest ship were running in all directions, screeching as though all the hounds of hell were snapping at their heels. The high prow of the ship swung around as the streamlined vessel began a hasty retreat.

Threldigan looked quite pleased with himself. "We now appear to be a gigantic version of Waroun. The effect will dissipate eventually, but until then, for all they know, we're basically a sea monster."

"Oh, thank you very much, Threldy," Waroun sneered as he jumped to his feet. "Just *had* to pick the one Norludian in the bunch, didn't you? Oh, no, couldn't *possibly* have used the Drell! He's much scarier than I am."

"That's very good, Waroun!" Threldigan said. "Keep waving your arms and wiggling your fingers. That's what they'll see. Stick your tongue out and look fierce!"

"What?"

The blank look on Waroun's face had Dax howling with laughter. "Way to go, Waroun! Scare the piss out of 'em!"

"You mean they're really seeing me right now, only huge?"

"That's right," Threldigan replied. "This is your big chance at stardom. Get it? *Big?*"

Waroun cackled with glee and did his best imitation of a terrifying monster—which wasn't much of a stretch for him—and soon, the three ships that had been coming from the direction of the temple began backing off. The five that approached from the south, however, didn't slow down one iota.

"I'm not sure that helped us very much," Teke observed.

"No, wait!" said Quinn. "They're changing direction!"

Everyone held their breath as the elegant vessels sailed past their little "flotilla" as though they didn't exist.

"I don't believe it!" Waroun exclaimed. "They're going after the other ships!"

"Can't say as I blame them," Threldigan said dryly. "I'd steer clear of a giant Norludian too."

"We should head straight for the temple now," Joss urged. "The port is on the north side of the island, but this vessel would have no difficulty landing on the shore at Rhashdelfi."

"And you think we'll find Ava there?"

"I'd bet my life on it," Joss replied. "Trust me. She can't miss it—she might even get there ahead of us."

Joss's men seconded this, and though Dax still had his doubts, it wasn't as if he had the ability to go after her. "What about you guys?" he said. "Couldn't you go down there and help her?"

"I doubt if she would trust us without some explanation," Rolst replied.

Joss nodded. "He's right. Ava doesn't understand our underwater language—"

"And if we don't have the stone, no one will have any reason to bother us, will they?" Waroun was still snarling and gesticulating madly at the departing ships. "We can just cruise on to Rhashdelfi."

Threldigan chuckled. "You can stop that now, Waroun. I don't think anyone is looking this way."

"I'm having fun, though." Waroun blew a big

raspberry at the ships and grinned. "It's not often you get to be a sea monster."

"True," Teke agreed. "But you're starting to look more silly than fearsome, and they're probably more afraid of being outnumbered than they are of you."

Dax waved at the departing ships. "So, Joss, would you mind telling us what that was all about? Do you think they know who we are or what?"

"No clue," said Joss, "but I think we should get going, regardless of who they were."

Dax suspected that Joss wasn't telling the truth, but if Ava was already on her way to the temple, he saw no reason to hang around waiting for anyone else to find them. Nodding, he aimed the *Juleta* toward Rhashdelfi and opened the throttle.

It was fully dark when Ava waded through the shallows onto the sand. There were lights in the city above, but the beach was dark and deserted. Dax and the others were nowhere to be seen. She had felt safe in the sea, but she now felt alone and vulnerable—a feeling compounded by the sound of pulse rifle fire from the city above. Though the route to the temple was ingrained upon her mind, something told her she wasn't meant to go it alone. Not so much that she couldn't have, but that she wasn't supposed to.

As she emerged from the sea, the weight of her land-based self dragged her down, sapping the remainder of her energy. Exhausted, she found a sheltered spot near a cluster of large palm trees and lay down to rest, but sleep was elusive. Her mind was awhirl with snippets of thought, chief among them the fact that she had never spent so much time submerged before—on any world. It had been exhilarating but further demonstrated the differences between Dax and herself. Waroun had jokingly called her the Fish Lady, but his jest held more than a grain of truth. Dax could no more have followed her through the water than he could have leaped from a cliff and sprouted wings. He had visions too—something else that set them apart. Never having had an experience even remotely similar, she couldn't begin to relate to it.

Despair and disillusionment crept into her psyche, tormenting her mind and ravaging her soul. As she sank into the depths—not of water, but of mind—she felt the sting of tears as she gazed at the night sky. Stars twinkled above her as though smiling at her fears and sorrows. They had no compassion, no feeling, and were certainly no help.

At the height of her despair, her eyes were drawn to five brilliant stars forming a straight line across the heavens. Instinctively, her hand crept to the stone around her neck, seeking comfort. As her fist closed around its solid form, she realized that these were planets, not stars. The Great Alignment had begun. The time for her to act was now—not tomorrow or next week, but this very moment. Still clutching the stone, her other hand reached up, as though attempting to touch the shining orbs. Their light sent her strength, enveloping her with a profound sense of inner peace, and all of her fears sank into nothingness.

"I will not fail you," she whispered as Dax's face swam into view. "I will not fail."

———*w*———

Dax couldn't believe he'd found her. Despite the coolness of the night, she was warm, beautiful, and incredibly alive. Dragging her into his embrace, he clutched her to his chest, kissing her as never before.

Joss had been so certain of this outcome, but the delays from evading ship after ship had altered their course, driving Dax to near insanity. Though they hadn't been attacked, Dax would have fought a thousand Aquerei ships to reach her. There could be no greater joy than holding her in his arms, no greater loss than to be denied a life spent at her side, and no greater love than the love they felt for each other.

"Promise me you'll never do that again," he whispered against her cheek.

"I can't," she replied. "It was *glorious*. Dax, you have no idea… you can't possibly imagine…"

Dax felt his heart sink to the depths of the ocean and beyond. "I knew it. Now that I've finally found you, I'm losing you to this world."

Her voice was steady and firm. "No. You'll never lose me. Don't even think it. The alignment has already begun. The planets are calling to me. I'm not just a forgotten grain of sand in the middle of a vast universe anymore. I'm part of it now, never to be alone again and never to be parted from you." Her voice sank to a whisper as she reached up to caress his cheek. Dax felt her fingertips, petal soft upon his skin, infusing every fiber of his being with her love. "What we do now, we do together."

"Then let's do it." Dax scooped her up in his arms and stood as Threldigan tucked his cape around her, shielding her from evil. Dax could hear the sounds of battle: the clash of weapons, the whine of pulse rifles, and the sizzling pop of laser fire. There was no time to waste. The city was under siege, and lives were being lost. Determination filled him, sending him onward into the night.

Armed to the teeth, the others formed a phalanx around him, Waroun taking point along with Rolst and the rest of the Aquerei men. Joss and Threldigan flanked him, while Quinn and the two Kitnocks brought up the rear.

"I can walk," Ava protested. "Put me down."

Dax was loath to let her out of his arms for any reason. "No, save your strength. You may need it later on." Speed was desirable, but stealth more important to their mission. He glanced at Joss. The Aquerei was clearly terrified but didn't falter. Perhaps he was tougher than he seemed. "We need a good story if someone stops us for questioning. It's your job to come up with one."

Joss nodded. "The temple is a place to take the sick for healing or the dying for cleansing of the spirit. We may not be the only supplicants trying to get through, but it will still be difficult." He gestured toward the rocky peak above them. "The temple is at the top of that cliff."

"It looks like a good place to die right now," Diokut said. Dax tended to agree.

Following the path, they rounded the base of the cliff where a horrific sight met their eyes. The street was wide, both sides lined with graceful statues. It should have been a place of beauty, but bodies of the dead and dying littered their path while others attempted to drag the wounded to safety. Further on, the front lines were engaged in a fierce battle for control.

"We'll never make it through that," Teke whispered.

"Yes, we will." Threldigan reached into his bag and tossed out a handful of decoys. Fearsome monsters sprouted from the seeds he'd sown, sending the combatants on both sides fleeing for cover. Dax and the others rushed forward through the gap created in the ranks as their Aquerei vanguard began firing, cutting through what remained of the resistance. Though Dax knew that each of their weapons was set to stun, watching men fall ahead of them was still tragic.

"Has the whole world gone mad?" Joss shouted. "At this rate, everyone will be dead by the time the alignment is over!"

"Which is why we need to hurry," Dax said, his long strides carrying him ahead of the others, despite his extra burden.

Opening the front lines had allowed others to follow them through the gap before the defenders could close ranks. Threldigan tossed out another of his gadgets, sending a wall of black smoke billowing up behind them to discourage any pursuit.

One of their Aquerei vanguards fell. Waroun sent several wide pulse blasts into the shadowy street beyond, clearing the road ahead. The street curved upward around the towering crag, providing little cover as they progressed. Dax hadn't been able to understand why there should be a fight when the stone was presumed lost, but then the horror of realization struck him: The Opps were attempting to destroy the temple.

Their only hope was that the Unities could hold out until they reached the summit, but they couldn't hold out indefinitely, and none of the defenders knew they were coming. At some point, hemmed in by the Opps, the Unities would either surrender or do something desperate.

As the stone pavement exploded in front of them, it became apparent that the moment of desperation had arrived.

Chapter 23

WAROUN WIPED THE DUST FROM HIS FACE. "HOLY SHIT! That was close!"

The bomb might have cleared their path of enemies, but the rubble it left behind was difficult to negotiate. Reluctantly, Dax put Ava down, and together they picked their way through the debris.

Teke stunned yet another of the Aquerei who were now swarming up the road. "How the hell do they know who they're fighting against? I *still* can't tell the difference!"

Threldigan tossed another handful of gadgets as they all turned and fired. "I can't either. Don't trust *anybody*!"

Masses of Aquerei fell as they sent more stun blasts into the hoard and Threldigan's illusions drove them back. This time, it appeared that a troop of fearsome Darconian warriors were advancing down the mountain.

"We've got to keep moving!" Dax yelled, pulling Ava onward. Protected as she was by Threldigan's cape, she was barely visible; if he let go of her hand, he knew he'd never find her again. As they rounded the next bend, another explosion ripped through the street, knocking them both to the ground.

Dax pulled her to her feet. "Are you okay?"

"Yes," she gasped. "But there isn't going to be anything left for us to save if they keep that up."

"I just wish they'd set those things off *behind* us

rather than in front of us," Waroun complained. "It's starting to get on my nerves."

"Too bad we can't tell *them* that," Joss said with a gesture toward the temple.

They could see it now, glowing high above them in the darkness, its graceful columns seeming to sprout from the rock, converging to form a vaulted roof. In structure, it reminded Dax of a temple from Earth's ancient Greece, but there the resemblance ended, for the Temple of the Aquina was made not of marble or sandstone, but of a clear, crystalline rock that had been carved from the very heart of the peak. The steps leading up to it were crowded with defenders. Dax could see sparks from the clash of blades as well as the explosive flashes of projectile weapons as they fired upon the Opps, who had already broken through to storm the sacred place.

Ava stared bleakly at the masses of defenders. "How will we ever get past them?"

"We have to reach them first," Dax said. "After that, it might be worth trying to talk our way in, but our best bet is to join the fight against the Opps and then work our way toward the temple."

"We could show them the stone," Ava suggested.

"Yes, but if we do that too soon and any of the Opps see it…" He stopped there, knowing that he didn't have to finish that statement. The stone would make them the target of the fiercest fighting yet.

Waroun threw a scathing glance at Joss. "Too bad we don't have any notorious freedom fighters among us. You know, someone the Unities would recognize immediately as being on their side?"

Joss winced, but this seemed to give Threldigan an idea. "What about it, Joss? Is there anything that would 'magically' get us through?"

Joss shook his head. "Not unless you could make Ava look like a sea goddess."

Threldigan grinned. "I believe that could be arranged."

"Or something so incredible that would distract everyone for a few minutes," Dax said. "Just long enough for us to get past them—and preferably get them all to look up at the sky."

"Got just the thing," Threldigan said.

In spite of the gravity of the situation, Dax laughed out loud. "Trust you to have the answer, Threld! Even in the middle of a battle!"

"With a magician around, our odds definitely improve," Teke said with a nod. "And I, for one, would love to have the odds on our side—for once."

"We've still got to get closer, though," Dax said. "As pissed as they all are, nothing will distract them for long."

Ava shook her head. "I still don't understand how any 'oracle' can stop this madness. I mean, what could it possibly say that would change anything?" She was looking at Joss, who merely shrugged.

"Well, it better be good or we're all in trouble," Waroun said roundly. "It was hard enough to get this far. I don't relish the idea of fighting our way back down this road."

Dax didn't say it aloud, but when Ava's eyes met his, he knew she was thinking the same thing. They might not live long enough to do it—any of them.

Ava was already moving on. Dax had to admire her

courage. Whether she felt an affinity for this world or not, she was still the bravest woman he'd ever known— even more than Jack.

Jack… Dax sighed as he marched onward. If he died without siring any offspring, Jack would be *so* put out with him. Ever since she'd found Cat, the survival of the Zetithian race had become the main thrust of Jack's life and should have been his. Dax understood her now. He wanted children—lots of them—and he wanted Ava to be their mother.

He took Ava's hand as they flitted from shadow to shadow along the roadside. The place was eerily beautiful by night; in the daytime, it would have been breathtaking. Huge monoliths carved with sea creatures lined the road as they neared the summit. Statue after statue reared up around them, each one chiseled from the living rock.

Another explosion split the night, illuminating the swarm of Opps attacking the line of defenders below. Somehow, the gap had been closed, cutting off their pursuit.

As they rounded the next turn, Dax could see that the Opps probably didn't need reinforcements to achieve victory. The defense was already weakening. They could now tell which side was which—the Opps were trying to reach the temple, while the Unities were pushing them back—but the fighting was intense. Whatever Threldigan had left in his bag of tricks had better be good.

Dax darted behind a statue of a mermaid, one of the last that formed a semicircle below the foundation of the temple. Her crown was crumbling and her trident had lost a prong, but she still looked regal. Motioning for the others to get behind him, he peered over the mermaid's upswept tail at the battle raging above.

The final approach was narrow and steep. The road curved slightly to the left of their position before taking a right turn, culminating in a flight of steps leading up to the entrance. The long side of the rectangular temple was directly above them, but it was cut off from their position by a steep boulder-covered slope that would have taken hours to climb through, if they could have done it at all.

Joss moved up to stand beside Dax. "For there to be so much carnage in such a sacred place…" He shook his head, shuddering. "I wish my eyes had never seen it."

Dax ignored this. "Is there another entrance?"

Joss shook his head. "The western portal is the only way in. The northern face is another rocky field such as this, and below the eastern end is a sheer drop to the sea. I suppose it could be scaled, but without the proper equipment, you'd be a fool to attempt it."

Dax let out a bark of laughter. "We're already a pack of fools. What's one more foolish blunder?"

"I could climb it," Waroun said.

Dax eyed his first mate with newfound respect. "With those sucker-fingers of yours, I bet you could."

"There is no need for that," said Quinn. "I brought this."

Everyone turned to stare at the little Drell. Reaching beneath his furry pelt, he unwrapped a long length of rope from around his torso, complete with a grappling hook. As he released the spring, the barbs of the hook deployed. He nodded toward Joss's men. "It's one of theirs. I thought it might be useful."

"I'll never fuss at you again, Quinn," Diokut chortled. "You can be as rude as you like."

"Actually, sending Quinn on ahead isn't a bad idea," Threldigan mused. "He could probably get past that bunch of idiots on audacity alone."

"Let's hope that isn't necessary," Dax said. "But we'll keep that as a backup plan, just in case." Coiling the rope, Dax was intrigued by the texture of it. Though undoubtedly strong enough to bear the weight of several men, as well as being resistant to knives, it seemed to be made of nothing but braided seaweed. "We should save the big guns for the last minute, Threld. Got any minor distractions?"

"A few," the magician replied. "Too bad I don't have any more of those Darconian poppers left. They were very effective."

Dax nodded, shouldering the coil of rope. "Waroun, Ava, and I will try to get into the temple from the rear while the rest of you stay here and work on the distractions. Stay out of sight as much as you can."

Threldigan held out his hand. Dax gripped it firmly. "Good luck."

"Thanks. We're gonna need it."

Moving eastward beyond the ring of statues, the way was rocky and uneven. Dax and Waroun had little difficulty, but Ava stumbled a time or two; being barefoot didn't help her very much. Dax tried not to think about her pain but kept on at a steady pace.

A stone wall had been built along the cliff's edge to keep the unwary from venturing too close, but this was easily climbed. Upon reaching the top, Dax could see that Joss hadn't been kidding. The entire eastern side of the island looked as though it had been cleaved from another land mass with a sharp knife. Dax peered over the precipice at the waves foaming against the dark cliff face below.

It was a very long way down.

———~~———

Ava hadn't realized just how vast the temple was when viewed from a distance, but now, it loomed above them like an enormous glittering spider. She still couldn't figure out how they were going to reach it without getting killed. The crag was like a pyramid that had been split in half from top to bottom. Viewed from the east, it would have looked like a huge triangle with the temple sitting on top of it. What Dax was proposing was to use the grappling hook to snag the eastern parapet, swing out from the side like a pendulum, and then scale the wall. Ava knew she couldn't have made it through the boulder-studded slope without breaking an ankle, but this looked downright suicidal.

Dax and Waroun worked on the rope, tying knots in it at regular intervals. "To give us time to rest," Dax explained.

Ava stared up at the temple and shook her head. It was only about ten meters above them, but it might as well have been fifty. "Are you *sure* about this?"

"Absolutely." His task now complete, Dax tapped his combadge. "Okay, Threld. Set off the first one."

Moments later, a sparkling rocket shot into the western sky and exploded in a shower of luminous orange sparks.

Waroun was incredulous. "Fireworks? That's all he's got left? Fuckin' fireworks?"

"Hey, it's better than nothing. I'm sure it got

someone's attention." Dax swung the rope, but the hook bounced off the parapet. The barbs hadn't deployed.

Reeling it in, Dax reset the hook and tried again as another rocket went off, but again, the hook hit and then plummeted toward the sea.

"My, this is encouraging," Waroun said. "Maybe I should just climb up and secure it."

"Good idea," said Dax. "Wrap it around one of the columns—but keep your head down. We can't risk anyone seeing you."

"Wait! You need to wear Threldigan's cape."

Ava began to take it off, but Waroun stopped her. "No capes. I'd just get tangled up in the damn thing and fall in the ocean."

Dax handed the hook to Waroun. "I'll hold onto this end of the rope."

"You know, I'm surprised none of the Opps are trying to get in this way," Ava said. "It seems the most logical approach."

"Maybe not for fish people," Waroun said. "Now, if they were Norludians, this would have been the tactic of choice."

"Maybe we should just let you take the stone," Ava suggested.

Waroun drew back in horror. "No fuckin' way! It'll probably kill a Norludian to even *touch* the damn thing. I'm not getting near it!"

"It didn't hurt me when I touched it," Dax said. "But it did do *something* to me… Well… maybe you're right. Maybe you *shouldn't* touch it."

"Not *gonna* touch it, so it's a moot point anyway." Crawling out to the edge, Waroun reached out with one hand and sucked his fingertips onto the rock face. "Not bad," he commented. "Yeah, I think I can get up there without any trouble."

Having said this, he then lost his grip and tumbled over the side. Ava bit back a scream as Dax braced himself for the tug on the rope. She held her breath as Waroun began cursing down below.

"I've got hold of the hook!" Waroun yelled. "Pull me up!"

"This is going *so* well." Dax hauled in the rope, grinning at Ava. "Having fun yet?"

Ava drew in a shaky breath. "Not really. Where is all of that bravery and determination when I need it?"

"Still there," he said. "It's just waiting until you *really* need it."

Waroun's head appeared at the edge of the cliff. "Thanks, Captain," he gasped. "I owe you one."

"Are you okay?"

"A little banged up, but not bad," Waroun replied. "I must be a real numb nuts fool, but I'm gonna try that again. No rock wall is gonna get the best of *me*!"

"That's the spirit," Dax said approvingly. "But this time, you might try crawling further up the rocks here before you try it."

"And get both hands on the wall before you step off the edge," Ava added.

Waroun waved and set off again, his sucker-tipped fingers gripping the tumble of boulders while his flipperlike feet seemed to mold themselves to the uneven surfaces. He looked like a bug crawling over gravel in the darkness as he periodically hopped from one slab of rock to the next. After a short distance, he stopped and spoke to Dax through his combadge. "I think I can make it the rest of the way on these rocks. I can still get to the temple and tie the rope."

Dax voiced his approval, and Waroun continued his climb.

Ava nestled against Dax as they watched Waroun's progress. "Think that rope is long enough?"

"I certainly hope so, or this isn't going to work at all." He checked the coils on the ground at his feet. "It's not as far as you think."

Ava could feel her heart pounding, and her hands were slippery with nervous sweat. "How are we going to do this? I'm pretty sure I'm not capable of scaling a wall."

"No problem. I'm an Eagle Scout, remember? Trust me, living aboard a ship for years the way we did had us literally climbing the walls. I can do it, Ava—you just have to hold onto me."

"Any other time that would sound appealing," Ava muttered.

It seemed to take hours, but Waroun finally reached the temple. Dax signaled Threldigan for another diversion.

The magician set off another round of fireworks, even more impressive than the first. Spinning wheels of fire sliced through the darkness, careening toward the combat zone at the foot of the temple steps. Defenders and attackers alike quailed, and Waroun scampered to the nearest column. Looping the rope around the base, he hooked it securely. With a quick wave, he slipped back over the side, disappearing into the rocks.

Ava stared doubtfully at the slender rope. "Do you really think that flimsy piece of seaweed will hold us both?"

Dax nodded. "Waroun gave it a pretty thorough test, don't you think?"

"I just hope he didn't weaken it."

"He didn't," Dax said. "We'll make it."

"How do you know?" Then it hit her. "Did you have another vision?"

"No," he replied. "In the first one, I saw you and the stone, and now that I'm here, I realize that you were actually inside the temple." He gazed down at her, his cat's eyes glowing in the darkness. "We can do this, Ava. I'm sure of it."

Ava drank in his gaze as though she would draw strength from it, and perhaps she did. Staring out across the scree-covered slope and then at the wall of the cliff she and Dax would presumably scale, she whispered, "I suppose it helps to know that, but what helps me the most is having you here with me."

Dax nodded. "We're stronger together."

Ava couldn't help but smile. "Heavier too. I don't envy you having to climb that wall with me weighing you down."

"That's not how I see it at all," he said. "You give me strength as well as wings."

She eyed the rope and the distance with less confidence. "I sure hope you're right."

Dax pulled on the rope, testing it against his weight. "Feels secure. Climb on, and I'll tie us together."

Ava giggled. "Now, *that* sounds wonderful." Realizing that she might never have another opportunity, her mood changed, becoming more sober. "Dax, if I haven't said this before, I'm saying it now. No matter what happens, I love you."

"I knew that."

"Cocky fellow." Though her words may have sounded careless, they were anything but. "Do you love me?"

"I believe I've already told you that, but I'll tell you again when we reach the temple."

"You'd better."

"Don't worry. I will." Giving her a quick kiss, he helped her onto his back and knotted the rope securely around her. Then he moved to the brink and leaned back, bracing his feet for the jump.

Ava wasn't completely successful at keeping the tremor out of her voice. "Ever done this before?"

"From this angle? No. But I saw it in a movie once."

"Oh, that makes me feel *so* much better…"

"Get ready to fly," he said.

And he stepped off the edge.

Chapter 24

THE FIRST SWOOP WAS FUN. BUT AFTER THEY HIT THE WALL and spun, crashing into it twice more before Dax managed to regain his footing, Ava was forced to reconsider that assessment. No, not fun at all, she decided, though she did manage to keep from screaming in his ear. He might not have heard her even if she had; the sounds of the battle raging at the temple were barely audible now, drowned out by the wind and the roar of the sea below.

Dax faltered only twice. Once when a bird swooped down to scrutinize the oddity of people climbing the cliff, and the other when a foothold crumbled beneath him. If he had been using any ordinary rope, his hands would have been bleeding, but this seaweed version seemed to offer a firm grip without being abrasive. Ava did the best she could not to interfere, not even looking up when she heard Waroun calling out encouragement; focusing instead on the steady, methodical movements in Dax's body. It was almost like riding a horse; as he moved, she moved with him, enabling his movements rather than hindering them. So intent was she on the climb that she was startled when Waroun reached out to take her hand.

"I just told Threldy to set off another one," Waroun said as he pulled her into a niche near the temple's foundation. Dax followed closely behind her, and

Ava heaved a sigh of relief when he was safely on the ground. Unfortunately, their location was still perilous, for though the defenders were valiantly holding their line, the mob had pushed even further into the temple.

Ava stood staring at them for a moment. "It's almost as if they knew we were coming."

"Well, let's not let them down."

Ava could see the four Aquina stones glimmering from a triangular altar in the center of the temple. There were no guards. Anyone who might have been protecting the crystals was now engaged in the struggle on the western portal.

Threldigan outdid himself this time, setting off a howling, hurricane-force wind that ripped through the temple from across the eastern parapet, pushing friends and foes alike down the steps.

On cue, Dax and Waroun climbed up the foundation, pulling Ava up after them. With the wind at their backs, they raced toward the altar. Three Aquerei saw them coming and battled against the wind to intercept. Dax, however, had the advantage and tackled two of them before rolling to his feet to stun the third with a pulse blast.

"I don't believe it!" Waroun screamed. "You got him!"

Dax ignored him. "Hurry, Ava!" he yelled. "The stone!"

Ava reached down and pulled it from beneath her shirt. The keystone was already emitting pulsations of intense blue-green light bright enough to illuminate the entire structure.

The wind dropped as suddenly as it had arisen, and a hush fell over the temple as the unruly mob ceased their struggles. The planets were aligned in the dome above the altar, bathing the stones with a brilliant aura. Ava ran to the altar. Ripping the chain from around her neck, she slammed the keystone into its niche.

For a long moment, nothing happened. Then, as if the keystone had set the others on fire, the stones emitted trails of multicolored light that raced across the floor to climb the columns. The light trails then converged, engulfing the entire temple in a dazzling array of light. A searing beam formed, shooting down at an angle from the center of the dome.

And struck Dax in the chest.

"No!" Ava screamed and ran to his aid but had no idea how to help him. Still standing, Dax struggled as his entire being became suffused with blinding light. When the light reached its peak, his arms sprang out from his sides as his head snapped backward, his eyes fixed on the dome. He could have whispered, and everyone present would have heard him, but a voice that was not his own came ringing forth from his lips, rocking the temple with the force of an earthquake.

"By the hand of a lost daughter of Aquerei shall the New Age begin."

The ray of light withdrew, retreating to the sky, and darkness engulfed the world once more, leaving nothing behind but the twinkling of the stars and the sound of Dax's body hitting the floor.

Ava dropped to her knees beside him, pulling him into her arms, searching desperately for a pulse or a breath—any sign of life at all. There was nothing.

A babble of voices began. "Was that the oracle speaking?" someone asked.

"It must have been," said another.

"But what does it mean?"

As more voiced their disbelief and bewilderment, their words became an annoying hum, pushing Ava to the breaking point.

"Who gives a damn what it meant if it killed him?" she screamed. "Do you people have so little regard for life? Don't you know it's the most precious thing we have—in fact, it's the *only* thing we have? He isn't even of this world, yet Dax gave his life for you. Stop your childish fighting and learn to live together in peace. This is a marvelous world; I've seen the ocean floor, and I've seen your temple. You must focus on what is good and beautiful and forget your hatred."

Magnified by the natural acoustics of the building, Ava's words reverberated throughout the temple, the echoes dying slowly in the stunned hush that followed.

"She has spoken!" someone shouted, breaking the silence. "The lost daughter of Aquerei has spoken, and we must listen!"

"What are you talking about?" Ava demanded. "All I want is for you people to go away and leave us alone." When no one moved, she shouted, "Didn't you hear me? Go home!" With that dismissal, she forgot them as her eyes were drawn to Dax's face, serenely beautiful even in death. Dissolving into tears, she buried her face in his hair, holding him tightly. She didn't care what happened to the Aquerei now. It was their problem, not hers. Dax had understood the risks but had been willing to take them anyway. While this was certainly heroic, cherishing the memory of a dead hero wasn't what she'd had in mind when she fell in love with Dax. Her heart twisted in anguish as the vision of their future together vanished.

Waroun knelt beside her, reaching out to touch Dax's neck with a rubbery fingertip. "I have to be sure. Zetithians can fool you sometimes."

"What do you mean?" Ava whispered.

"These damn cats seem to have nine lives," Waroun replied. "They heal faster than any species I've ever seen. Trauma that would kill anyone else just slows their pulse and respirations to the point that most people can't detect them, but I can." Waroun's sucker-tipped finger seemed to fuse with Dax's skin. He closed his eyes for a long moment, concentrating. When he finally opened them, a big, goofy grin split his face. "He's not dead."

Ava didn't dare believe it. "You're just saying that to make me stop crying. He's gone, Waroun. I don't like it one little bit, but I can accept it—or I will eventually."

Waroun pulled his fingertip free with a loud pop. "Well, just don't bury him at sea until you've given him plenty of time to wake up. You know how he hates the water."

Waroun was still smiling as their cohorts pushed their way through the crowd to join them in the temple.

"We heard what happened—and what you said afterward," Threldigan said. "Whether it was a magic show or not, those people believed every word of it."

Teke nodded. "The story will spread, and the fighting will stop. You wait and see."

Quinn was jumping up and down with excitement. "You did it, Ava! You brought an end to the war all by yourself."

"No, I didn't," she said. "None of this would have happened without your help, or Dax—" She choked on his name, still not quite believing that Waroun was telling the truth.

"Are you sure he's dead?" Threldigan asked. "Zetithians are really hard to kill, you know."

"No, I *didn't* know," Ava snapped. "But everyone else seems to."

"We've known Dax a long time," Waroun said. "You've just never been around when he got hurt before. Trust me, he's alive."

"They go into a state of hibernation until they heal," Threldigan added. "I'd be willing to bet he wakes up as good as new."

Ava was beginning to see a glimmer of hope. "How long before we know?"

Threldigan shrugged. "A day, maybe three—even up to a week if the injury is severe. You just have to give him time."

"He may have all the time he needs," a tall, elderly Aquerei man with purple tentacles said as he approached. "He is the Oracle of the Aquina, and we will care for him as befits his stature." The man smiled warmly at Ava. "You are so like your father—in so many ways. He would have said something equally blistering to the people had he lived—though it sounded much better coming from you."

"You knew my father?"

"Yes, I knew him. Sliv was a good man, if a trifle unorthodox in his methods. My name is Eantle, and your father and I worked together for years to keep the stone safe. Unfortunately, the Opps were doing their best to eliminate anyone who knew anything about the stone, and many were killed, your father and the select few who knew the secret of the stone's location among them. I have been offworld, searching for clues ever since his death, retracing his travels, trying desperately to discover where he might have hidden the keystone. Rutara was, unfortunately, one of our last stops."

Ava was astonished. "Are you saying that my mother knew about this?"

"She was never told about the significance of the stone, though your father would have done so eventually. When you came of age, its guardianship fell to you." His lips thinned with disgust. "Unfortunately, unlike the stone, you were entrusted to the care of some highly questionable guardians. When the Opps were closing in on our faction, Sliv apparently decided to move you to Luxaria. Aquerei seldom visit that world, so he must have believed that you and the stone would be safe there. Russ, your first caretaker, didn't want to leave Rutara, so Lars was recruited." Eantle shook his head sadly. "He was a very poor choice, I'm afraid— particularly after Sliv and his secret-keepers died, and the rest of us had no idea where you were. When Lars didn't receive regular payments, your relationship suffered greatly. We only located him some time after you had boarded the *Valorcry*."

Ava pulled Dax closer, stroking his cheek. "Then it would have been a mistake to return to Russ?"

Eantle's smile was apologetic. "He would not have welcomed you, Ava. He was hired to keep you safe and happy. He didn't love you."

"I'd believe that of Lars," she said brusquely. "But not Russ..." Though it did explain why Russ had been so willing to let her go.

"Russ too, Ava." Eantle's voice was gentle. "He didn't have to drug you as Lars did, which is why you ultimately left Lars to return to him. I only wish we had found you sooner."

"I'm not." As the truth began to sink in, many things became clear to Ava, not the least being that Russ and Lars had been *hired* to be her companions! No wonder she'd fallen in love with Dax, despite her determination to resist the temptation. "If you had, I wouldn't have met Dax, and I wouldn't have missed that for a whole shipload of Aquina stones." She paused for a moment. "Tell me, if it was such a closely guarded secret, how did the Opps find out about my father?"

"The Opps retraced the stone's path through history, ultimately discovering that your great-grandfather had been its guardian at one time. They then traced it to your father and discovered the identity of several of his most trusted associates. Other members of the group, myself included, knew only that the stone had been given to a daughter, but nothing concerning her identity or whereabouts. I knew he had spent some time on various worlds, but searching entire planets for Sliv's half-Aquerei daughter was difficult at best.

"However, once we located Russ, finding Lars was relatively easy. He admitted that he had been given a large sum of money initially but had frittered it away. When your father and his inner circle were killed by the opposition, Lars was left with no money and no one to contact for more. He then lacked the means to control you, thus enabling you to leave him when the opportunity presented itself. Lars apparently didn't know the whole story—which was fortunate—or he would have undoubtedly stolen the stone. He only knew that you needed to be kept on Luxaria until your father returned. Lars had been threatened with dire consequences if he failed in this mission, hence his determination in spite of the fact that he had not been contacted for some time."

Ava nodded. "He said something along those lines the day I left. I suppose he told the Opps about this too?"

Eantle shook his head. "No, they only got wind of you when you went to Rhylos. It seems that an Aquerei named Junosk, whom we captured after you landed here, overheard a report of the attempted theft of the stone, which gave them a head start. Our faction was keeping tabs on them, so we knew they were on to something. They bumbled the opportunity, of course, but *still*…"

"Which is where I came in," said Joss.

Eantle eyed Joss warily. "I never dreamed you would ever take a side—but you finally did. What changed your mind?"

"His vision," Joss replied with a gesture toward Dax. "Weapons that can destroy the bases…" He paused, shuddering. "I knew then that the New Age was our only hope."

"A weapon that can destroy the bases?" Eantle's tentacles stood up in spikes. "There is no such weapon." His tone was abrupt and final, leaving no room for argument.

Ava's eyes narrowed with suspicion. "Are you saying his vision was false?"

Eantle shrugged. "I only know that such technology does not exist at present—at least, nothing that could destroy the bases without wiping out the entire planet. Perhaps the vision he saw was of what might happen should the coming of the New Age be prevented."

"But if that was what it took to get Joss to take a

side," Threldigan pointed out, "it was obviously a necessary component."

"Trust the captain to get it right," Waroun said proudly. "He's not the type to have shabby visions."

Ava bowed her head, hiding her smile in Dax's hair. The longer she held him, the more attuned she became to his spirit and the life force still strong within him, and the more convinced she became that Dax truly would survive and return to her.

"We guessed that you would be landing on Joss's base," Eantle reported, "and the Opps obviously made the same assumption. After that, it was just a matter of letting the Opps attempt to intercept you, and then be ready with ships to run them off, thus allowing you to continue on to the temple." His expression was smug. "Quite simple, really."

"We were *allowed* to continue?" Threldigan scoffed. "It certainly didn't seem that way to me."

"And it wasn't simple at all," Diokut added. "We were nearly killed! Several times!"

Waroun stuck out his lip in indignation. "Are you saying that my sea monster routine wasn't the reason they retreated? I was terrifying!"

Eantle laughed. "You were, indeed, but they saw us coming, as well."

In Ava's opinion, everything would have been simpler if Eantle's cohorts had taken their role a step further. "But if your troops had escorted us to the temple—"

"The effect would not have been the same," Eantle said wisely. "Your struggle against adversity and your steadfast determination in the face of insurmountable odds proved your right to usher in the New Age, Ava. If it had been easy…" Eantle stopped there. Spreading his hands, he let them draw their own conclusions.

Ava nodded. The tale of their perilous journey would eventually become legend, solidifying belief in the New Age and making it manifest without further intervention from anyone. The war would end now, simply because Ava, identified by the oracle as the lost daughter of Aquerei, had told them to stop fighting and go home. "I see your point, but so much pain and suffering…" Shaking her head sadly, she gestured toward the fallen, many of whom had not lived to see the New Age begin.

Eantle knelt and took Ava's hand, placing a kiss on her palm. "If there had been no battle at the temple, only those who longed for the New Age would have been present when the stones were conjoined—a truly unforgettable event, as I'm sure you will agree—and your words would not have been heard by those who needed to hear them the most."

"True, but—"

"As you journey through life, Ava, you will find that there is good in all things, no matter how bad they may seem at the moment." Laying a hand on Dax's chest, he added, "What we have deemed lost is all the more cherished when it is regained. This New Age would mean nothing if the times before it had not been not troubled. Through strife, we grow as a people—an unfortunate truth, perhaps, but a truth, nonetheless."

Eantle rose, motioning for the former combatants, now reduced to the level of awed bystanders, to approach. "Carry the Oracle," he said. "And do not forget the honor he bestows upon you."

Ava watched as twelve Aquerei gathered and lifted

Dax, their interlocked arms providing a secure sling
for his tall body. As they moved forward, the throng
on the temple steps parted, allowing them to pass. Ava
came next, taking Threldigan's arm. The others fell in
behind them.

A faint glimmer of dawn lit the eastern sky as they
began their trek down the avenue from the temple. Their
descent differed greatly from the upward climb. Instead
of the deafening din of battle, people now lined the
street in reverent silence, many reaching out to touch
Dax or Ava as they passed. Ava's emotions were a
blur of anger, embarrassment, and astonishment; only
the knowledge that Dax was still alive kept her from
screaming at them. That they should feel this way now
was difficult for Ava to comprehend.

The crowd amassed at the lower levels was enormous, but Ava's attention was captured by the city
itself. The impressive buildings and lights of Rhylos
were eclipsed by those of Rhashdelfi, and she stood for
a moment, transfixed by the sight. Though not transparent, the structures had apparently been crafted from the
same colloidal matrix as the bases. As the first rays of
morning struck them, the entire city lit up like a star.

Shielding her eyes from the light, Ava walked on until
exhaustion began to overtake her. Without Threldigan
for support, she would have collapsed, but she only had
to stumble once for a dozen Aquerei to leap to her aid.
She fell into their waiting arms and into a deep, welcome slumber.

Chapter 25

DAX AWOKE TO DARKNESS SO COMPLETE, HE FEARED HE might have been blinded. Then, as his eyes slowly regained their focus, he realized that it was the darkness of night, rather than blindness. He had no clue to his whereabouts. The last thing he remembered was Ava placing the stone in its niche and the resulting explosion of light. What else had occurred, he could only guess at, but he knew one thing for certain: He was not sprawled on the stone floor of the temple. He was lying naked in a softly yielding bed covered in sheets so light, he barely felt them against his skin.

Nor was he dead. He could feel his heart beating, its rate steadily increasing to normal and his respirations doing the same. He had been in a regenerative state, as opposed to merely sleeping, but the reason for it was unclear. There was a fresh, sweet taste in his mouth, as though he had been given a cordial of some kind while he slept—perhaps an Aquerei remedy for whatever it was that had happened to him.

Inhaling deeply, he picked up Ava's scent and knew he was not alone. Reaching out, he found the soft, smooth warmth of her bare skin. The emotions connected with that action assailed him, mind and body. Love flooded his being; he felt her trust and her total connection to him. No matter what else happened in his life, he wanted her to be that close to him. Always.

As he gathered her into his arms, she sighed deeply, nestling against him. Without conscious thought, he began purring.

"So," she whispered softly, "you're awake. I was beginning to think it would never happen."

"How long was I out?"

"Three days," she replied. "Three miserable, horrible days. Everyone said you would recover, but—"

Dax hugged her tightly. "Now you know how I felt when you jumped off the boat. Joss was so sure you couldn't drown and would find your way to the temple, but I had some serious doubts."

"It seemed like the only solution at the time—and it was an experience I wouldn't have missed for all the Aquina stones in the world, whether they had magical powers or not."

"Magic?" he echoed. "Do you mean it worked?"

Ava gasped in surprise. "You mean you don't remember?"

"Not a thing."

"It was you, Dax." Her voice was hoarse with awe. "You were the Oracle."

"Impossible. You, I could understand, since you're half Aquerei. But me? How could an alien like me be a part of their prophesy?"

"I don't know," Ava replied, "but you were. Maybe you were just in the right place at the right time, but a beam of light hit you, and the Oracle spoke through you as if you were a portal to be used and discarded." Dax felt a quiver shake her body as she continued. "I thought you were dead. In fact, I was sure of it. But Waroun and Threldigan said you would survive. Thank heaven they were right."

Dax couldn't argue with that since "used and discarded" was pretty much the way he felt. "What did I say?"

"It didn't even sound like your voice. All you said was, 'By the hand of a lost daughter of Aquerei shall the New Age begin.'"

"Meaning you, I presume, but do you mean that's it? Nothing more profound than that?"

Ava giggled. "No, but I gave them all a piece of my mind and amazingly enough, they took it to heart." She paused before adding reflectively, "No one has ever paid that much attention to anything I've ever said before. Of course, it'll probably never happen again, but I guess this was the best time to be heard."

"And the fighting stopped just like that? Amazing."

"Yes, it was," she agreed. "I wish you could've seen it. I was too upset to watch my mouth, and, basically, I told them all to quit acting like a bunch of idiots and go home."

Dax laughed aloud—a wonderful, cathartic laugh that seemed to cleanse him of any lingering effect from the Oracle's "use" of him.

"There's just one problem," she went on. "Now that I have 'spoken,' I can't even stick my toe out the door without someone rushing up to polish the ground for me to walk on."

Dax laughed even harder. "You're kidding me, right?"

"I only wish I was," she said ruefully. "I can hardly *wait* to see what they do when you're up walking around. You'll probably have a bajillion virgin handmaidens at your beck and call and never have to lift a finger again as long as you live."

"That might be fun for a day or two, but I don't believe I'd care for a steady diet of it."

"Me either." Sighing, she added, "I wouldn't have minded living here for a while, but—"

"Do you mean we don't have to stay?"

"I think they'd like us to, but we aren't exactly immortal. What I mean is, we'll die eventually anyway, so I can't see that it matters a whole helluva lot in the long run. I think we've done our bit. The rest is up to them."

Dax felt himself relax with her reply. Aquerei was a nice place to visit, but the idea that there were people living at the bottom of the sea was sort of creepy. He really didn't want to live there—unless Ava did.

"I found out something else too. It seems that my father paid Russ and Lars to keep an eye on me. Neither of them ever loved me at all."

While Dax was pleased to hear this from his own perspective, her subdued tone was more than enough for him to understand her feelings. Taking her face in his hands, he kissed her gently. *"I* love you, Ava. And no one had to pay me to do it, either."

"I know that now. It's the reason I fell in love with you, despite my best intentions. I thought I was fickle and weak; turns out I was drugged—at least, I was until my father was killed and Lars ran out of money."

Dax had an idea she had more thoughts on the subject, not the least of which was that she had spent most of her adult life with men who had only been pretending to love her. If she'd wanted to go back and mop up the floor with them, he would have been happy to help her and was already wishing he'd caused Lars even more permanent damage than he had. "So what do you want to do now?"

"Spend the rest of my life loving you."

For one heart-stopping moment, Dax was unable to breathe, let alone speak. Even if he had been immortal with all of eternity stretched out before him, he would never hear any words that would affect him more deeply. Swallowing hard, he asked, "Are you sure you don't want to stay here and be the Goddess of Rhashdelfi?"

"Nope. I just want to be with you. Wherever you go, whatever you do."

Dax was overjoyed but thought that a woman like Ava would need more. "What about exploring all the oceans in the galaxy? I can take you anywhere you want to go. Free of charge."

"I'd like that, and your ship *could* use a hostess. Think Kots would take me on?"

"He would if I told him to," Dax replied. "But I'd still want to keep you as my own personal goddess." He nuzzled her neck, purring. "One I would worship religiously every day of my life."

"Oh? And just how would you go about worshipping me?"

"Like this." He flicked her earlobe with the tip of his tongue.

"That'll do for a start."

"I promise to make it my sacred duty to discover hundreds of new and exciting ways to please you."

Dax wasn't sure, but if the funny choking sound she made was any indication, Ava liked his idea. Kissing her again, he breathed in the scent of her desire and felt his cock begin to stir. At that moment, he realized that they'd both been virgins when they met; she who had never been with a man who loved her, and he who had never known a woman he could love.

And Dax did love her, He was glad he hadn't denied his feelings, because now he would spend the rest of his life with Ava in his arms. "Think you're ready for that?"

"Oh, yeah," she replied. "Bring it on—if you're feeling up to it, that is."

"If I was any more 'up,' I'd be floating."

"I—um… Mmm…"

Dax didn't have to ask if she liked what he was doing; he could smell her reaction as he kissed her deeply, his tongue plumbing the recesses of her mouth. She tasted sweet, as though she had also partaken of whatever cordial he'd been given. "What have you been drinking?"

"Aquerei water," she replied. "Makes my tongue kinda slippery, doesn't it?"

That was a gross understatement. "Got any of more of it?"

"Yeah. Want me to drink some and then suck your cock?"

So much for him worshipping *her* body. "You can suck any part of me you like."

"You'd better have some too. You're bound to be thirsty after three days. I tried to give you some earlier, but I was afraid you'd choke on it if I gave you very much."

He took the carafe she handed him and drank. The water was crisply sweet and very refreshing. "No wonder this stuff is so expensive."

"Would you believe it's actually derived from

seawater? I'm not sure how they get the salt out of it, but it's not bad."

"What makes it so sweet?"

"Sweet? Really? I don't get that at all."

"Maybe only Zetithians can taste it. It doesn't seem to have any intoxicating effect on me, either—or if it does, it's very mild."

"Mmm… Kiss me and tell me what I taste like."

Dax did as she asked, noting that the sweetness had doubled. "Very slippery and extra sweet, but then, you always are."

"Maybe it's a matter of my being Aquerei as much as the water itself," she suggested. "Of course, I *have* been drinking it off and on ever since I boarded your ship—didn't have any on Rhylos, though. Maybe I should lay off it for a while and see if there's any difference."

"I've got a better idea." Pushing her onto her back, he dribbled a small amount of water between her thighs and went after it. She was incredibly sweet and slick as he pleasured her engorged clitoris with his tongue. Ava's sighs drove him on, and he licked and sucked her with wild abandon, enjoying every moment of it until, with a sharp cry, she reached her climax.

As her body contracted, Dax's tongue slid deeply into her slit. His eyes nearly popped out of his head. Though he'd never had an orgasm without an ejaculation before, he was pretty sure he was having one now. The only difference was that it seemed to take place in his brain, rather than his genitals, though his cock was throbbing painfully with each beat of his heart.

"Holy moly, Dax! That was fabulous! It did something to you too, didn't it? Here, have some more."

Tipping the carafe, Ava poured more water over her sensitized flesh. Dax thought his head would explode from sheer ecstasy. As it was, he was seeing fireworks where there weren't any.

After a few moments, Ava experienced yet another orgasm, and Dax sat back on his heels, gasping for air. "I don't think I can take much more of that. I'm… I don't know… hallucinating or something. It's like, well, it's probably like what happens to you when you lick me—either that, or I'm actually tasting your orgasms."

"That is just too cool!" Giggling, she added, "I guess guys can't handle the multiple orgasm thing, whereas for women, the more the better."

Her laughter was infectious. "I'm sure I could get used to it eventually, but right now, I'd much rather do something else."

He might have been seeing fireworks, but there was still nothing wrong with his night vision. He watched with growing anticipation as Ava took a sip from the carafe and moved toward him. His cock was exuding rivulets of orgasmic syrup, but she ignored it completely, going straight for his balls. Dax spread his legs apart, giving her full access to anything she might want to suck. His lips formed an *O* as his wish came true when she sipped first one testicle and then the other into her mouth, coating his scrotum with the viscous combination of her saliva and the Aquerei water. Back and forth and in and out, she sucked his nuts while he rubbed his hard cock on her face. Trying desperately to hold back, he bit his lip until he tasted blood.

Dax saw stars as Ava let his balls pop out of her mouth. "You can come if you need to, Dax. I don't mind.

Trust me, I'm already having a great time." As if to prove it, Ava pulled his cock to her lips and went down on him, mixing his syrup with her own creamy wetness.

Dax couldn't control himself any longer. He came with such force that his semen would have shot across the room if she hadn't been holding him in her mouth.

As he savored his climax, Dax wondered if it was possible to taste what his *snard* was doing to her through a kiss. There was only one way to find out. Ava's hair was flying in all directions and her skin shone like a pearl as he held her by the shoulders and gently backed away. His mouth came down on hers in a deep, penetrating kiss.

At first, Dax felt nothing more than delight from the soft warmth of her lips. He was about to conclude that he should have taken a sip of the water first when something amazing happened.

Heat began to curl in the small of his back, growing in strength until it broke through at last, sending tendrils of warmth throughout his body. When it finally reached the tips of his fingers and toes, the heat surged into his head, filling him with exhilaration, which was soon replaced by a sense of deep inner peace. His mind drifted downward through space to land weightlessly on a cloud of perfect bliss. Dax had felt something similar to this in the aftermath of lovemaking, but Ava's pleasure was far more profound than his own—and he was getting it secondhand.

At last Dax understood why women couldn't get enough of the men of his race, why others couldn't compete, and why this great strength had ultimately been their downfall. He had been right to wait for a woman he truly loved, rather than, as Waroun had put it, risk ensnaring unsuspecting women with his potent sexual prowess.

Anyone experiencing this would want more and would have gone through hell to get it, putting up with virtually anything to maintain her supply. It wasn't something to be taken lightly. Sex was one thing, but this was perilous. His friends at the Zetithian Palace were being totally irresponsible, even criminal—in the moral sense, if not in the legal one. It was almost as bad as selling addictive drugs, though he knew it wasn't physically harmful.

Dax searched his memory, trying desperately to reassure himself that he hadn't enticed Ava with sex alone. It was important that she love him for himself, not merely the sensual pleasures he could provide. There had to be clues—proof that she'd been attracted to him, with or without the street pheromones, Sholerian cream, or the effect of his own body fluids—but what were they? It all seemed so long ago now, the time before she was his, both to enjoy and to pleasure.

Then he remembered. The Davordian hookers. Ava had fought them off like a tigress protecting her young. She'd said she'd done it because she owed him one, but Threldigan had suspected that it constituted a betrothal. Waroun had been skeptical, but the Kitnocks thought her claim on him was genuine. There were other things too. No, he hadn't ensnared her; he truly had fallen in love with her and she with him.

Breathing a sigh of relief, he covered her body with his own and joined with her. Ava had said that most guys couldn't keep an erection after they climaxed—and

Dax knew this to be true—but in this particular instance, he was doubly pleased to possess that ability. It was one thing to pleasure each other, but quite another to actually become one body, one being, one soul.

She was completely naked now, with no stone around her neck to adorn her body. She didn't need it, though, for she was perfect just as she was: his one and only love. He would keep her safe and whole and love her every day of his life. He didn't need a vision to tell him these things; he felt it in his heart and knew the joy of it. Zetithian men told their women that they would give them joy unlike any they had ever known, but the reverse was also true. There was joy in being mated for life, producing children and, in turn, teaching them how to live, but most of all, how to love. Dax had missed that as a child. His children would not. He would not donate sperm to be distributed among strangers. Only Ava would give birth to his children. They would grow up under his watchful eye, knowing the love that he had been denied.

When his seed left his body at last, there was no oracle to tell him that in giving it, he became a part of her, just as she became a part of him. Oracles were not needed to tell you what you already knew.

Ava's only regret in the coming days was that she was unable to share the wonders of Aquerei's oceans with Dax. To the south of Rhashdelfi, the Temple Sea was relatively shallow, but the northern shore was rocky, with craggy formations rising from the depths. A wide channel passed between the peaks, enabling the glassy ships to sail into port, their high, curved prows reminding Ava of sea horses as they bobbed at their moorings. Farther out to sea, there were more submerged mountains, many of which had been excavated to form cave-like dwellings. While these were no less beautiful than the structures of Rhashdelfi, theirs was a more natural beauty. Living corals studded the exteriors, interspersed with sea anemones whose shapes and colors left Ava speechless. Schools of silvery fish swam in the open waters between the peaks, while brightly colored varieties hovered near the rocks.

Ava tried to share what she'd seen with Dax, but no mere image could convey her feelings, nor could she find words to describe the stunning sights hidden beneath the surface. When she mentioned her frustration to Eantle, he smiled his understanding.

"Visitors to our world cannot fully experience Aquerei if they have to remain on the surface. To that end, we have developed a mask that enables others to explore our seas. I will see to it that Dax is provided with one."

Eantle was true to his word, but when Ava first saw the mask, though it was quite beautiful, she had serious doubts about its effectiveness. Crystal clear and shaped to completely cover the eyes, ears, and nose of the wearer, it didn't look as though it would help anyone breathe—quite the opposite, in fact. "I don't know if this will help or not. Dax doesn't even like to get his face wet, let alone go diving."

The Aquerei smiled. "There are many ways for air-breathers to survive in the sea, but this is the closest to actually being Aquerei."

Ava turned it over in her hands, shaking her head with doubt. "How does it work?"

"It is crafted with the same technology as the bases, but with a more porous matrix."

"Meaning?"

"It allows air-breathers to breathe the water and see as well as an Aquerei. Hearing is also enhanced."

Eantle gave her a few more instructions, but Ava remained doubtful. Though she trusted his word, she would have preferred to see it demonstrated on someone other than Dax. "One size fits all?"

"No, but this should fit him without any difficulty."

Ava laughed. "The 'difficulty' will be getting him to try it on."

Eantle bowed, a mischievous smile touching his lips. "I leave that task to you."

Dax knew how much Ava longed to show him the underwater wonders of Aquerei. He had been wrestling with the idea of using goggles and a snorkel when Ava handed him a delicate mask, insisting that he accompany her to the beach.

"And when we get there?"

"You'll see," she said mysteriously.

Dax chuckled. "That's what I'm afraid of."

Shedding their clothing by the shore, the mere sight of Ava lured Dax into the sea. She was like a dainty water sprite, laughing as she danced among the gentle waves. Dax would have followed her anywhere—even into the ocean.

When he was chest deep, Ava looked up at him

with an expression of understanding in her aquamarine eyes. "This will be hard for you, Dax, but I know you can do it."

Dax snorted his skepticism. "Yeah, right."

"No, really. All you have to do is take a deep breath and hold it. Then put the mask on. It will adjust to the shape of your head."

"And then what?"

"You put your head under the water and exhale slowly through your nose. With your next breath, you'll be able to breathe the water."

"Just like that?"

Ava nodded. "Just like that." When he hesitated, she raised his hand to her lips for a kiss. "I love you more than life itself, but I also love the sea. I need to share this with you."

This much, he understood. Dax wanted to share all the wonders of the galaxy with Ava, but for that, he needed his ship. All this took was a leap of faith.

And it was quite a leap. Dax figured that "next breath" he took would be impossible, given the apparent solidity of the mask. "Where did you get this thing? From Waroun?"

"No, Eantle gave it to me. And I'm sure he wouldn't risk letting the Oracle of the Aquina drown."

"Good point." Dax closed his eyes, thinking that a pleasant memory might help to calm his nerves. Smiling, he recalled making love with Ava in the surf on Rhylos. "Too bad I won't be able to pick up your scent underwater."

Ava giggled. "You'll never know 'til you try."

He opened one eye. "Trying to motivate me?"

"Something like that."

After reaching between her legs, Ava then slid her finger across his upper lip. Dax responded with an erection so intense, he would have taken a deep breath whether he'd intended to or not.

"Now, hold it, and put on the mask."

Dax followed her instructions as though commanded. Leaving him no time to protest, Ava pulled him down hard.

Exhaling in a flood of bubbles, Dax opened his eyes. Beyond the sloping sand near the shore, he could see a path stretching off to the south. Without thinking, he swam toward it, still holding Ava's hand. Upon hearing an odd sound, he turned toward her. She was laughing.

No longer a mere water sprite, Ava was now a true sea goddess. Her blond hair waved about her head like a crown, and her round aqua eyes sparkled with delight as she drifted beside him. Dax pulled her into his arms and kissed her, only then realizing that he was breathing quite naturally. The mask seemed to have become a part of him. Teasing his lips apart, she slipped her tongue into his mouth, and Dax felt the power of her kiss spiraling straight to his groin.

Laughing again, Ava swam up through his arms, the soft curls at the apex of her thighs tickling his chin as she passed. The seawater made an excellent carrier for her powerful scent, and he swam after her like a predator on the hunt.

Dax was amazed by how well he could match her strokes when he didn't have to worry about breathing. Despite the fact that he hadn't grown webbing between his fingers and toes, his longer arms enabled him to keep up with her with very little effort.

Ava led him further along the path, pointing out various fish and other sea creatures. From his own studies, as well as what she had taught him, Dax recognized corals and anemones and fish whose colors defied description—all with astonishing clarity. Tiny flowers snapped shut when his fingertips touched their petals. Anemones waved as he passed his hands over their tentacles. Among the fish, Dax had never seen such vivid blues, or yellows so intense. A purple fish swam past, its gossamer fins trailing behind it like a windblown scarf. Another anemone beckoned to him, its light brown tentacles tipped with greenish gold. Sea urchins bloomed with bristling spikes, sucking down into their tubes when he ventured too close. Everything was in motion—waving, dancing, floating—like the goddess who swam beside him.

A sly smile touched Ava's lips as she kissed her way from his mouth to his groin. When she reached his cock, her body contracted in orgasm. Her evocative scent mixed with the water he breathed, the effect so intense, Dax was sure it was being absorbed through his skin. Despite the coolness of the sea, his body was aflame with need. Ava's skin was already beginning to shimmer, taking on colors Dax had never seen until this first dive. When a blue-green fish pecked at her shoulder, he realized she was assuming the hue of whatever sea creature was closest to her. He tested this theory, taking her in his arms and propelling her toward a purple anemone. He was rewarded when she turned a delicate shade of lavender.

Dax felt the water swirling past his genitals but knew that Ava's heated core would surpass these sensations. When he thrust into her warmth, his body rejoiced. Ava's legs curled around his hips, and Dax rocked into her, his thrusts propelling them both through the crystalline water. He swam forward along the ocean trail, Ava clinging beneath him, his cock buried in her core. Her expression of sheer ecstasy drove him on, and Dax became more adventurous, his arms pulling them both toward the surface before diving back to the ocean floor.

Ava's hands touched his face, her fingers threading through his hair. With an impish grin, she surged closer, nipping him on the chest. Her sharp teeth electrified him, and Dax gripped her hips, pulling her tightly against his groin. Gazing into her eyes, he began a sinuous dance within her succulent core that rivaled the sway of the currents. He let the flowing sea carry them on as they mated, sweeping them first near the shore and then back toward the south. The trail formed a loop there; Dax could see how Ava managed to reach Rhashdelfi so easily, but if she hadn't swam on toward the beach, the bend in the current would have carried her back toward Mirolar.

On a whim, he swam away from the path. Without the current, they remained stationary, floating just above the reef. Dax rolled onto his back, gazing up at the amazing sea goddess astride him, drinking in the sight of her shimmering skin as it reflected the ever-changing colors of the reef dwellers below. A huge ray swam past, its triangular fins flapping like a pair of wings as it flew through the sea. Ava glanced at it and smiled. Mimicking the ray's movements, her graceful arms swept through the water, enabling her to rise and fall on his cock. Dax felt a vibration in his throat, and though he could hear no sound, he knew he was purring.

Stretching out beneath her, Dax let Ava direct their flight with little nudges of her knees. His steady strokes carried them onward, his body in complete harmony with the enchanting woman who rode him, enveloping him with her love. Dax couldn't imagine a more perfect moment.

Power began to build in his groin, and blood surged through his vessels as Ava took him to new heights of ecstasy. He marveled at the way this beautiful creature had drawn him into her world, somehow making him an integral part of it. Still soaring through the depths, he plunged upward, sending his love flowing into her body.

When her climactic cry came at last, Dax felt the pull as Ava's body sucked him in, fusing them together like never before. Iridescent hues flashed from her skin, and riotous waves rippled through her hair, but nothing could compare with the love he saw shining forth from her eyes. The symbiosis of their spirits was now complete, and together they formed an entirely new entity. She was his, and he was hers. Forever.

———

There was no wedding ceremony; their experience in the Temple of the Aquina was quite enough to prove that Dax and Ava were bound together forever. Though the adoration of the Aquerei was genuine, Ava knew they had to leave and let the people find their own way to peace and tranquility.

She and Dax met with Eantle and other leaders from the newly formed council, which consisted of representatives from both above and beneath the surface of the oceans. The ushering in of the New Age had been a dramatic catalyst for change, and with the keystone returned to its proper niche in the temple, its beneficial influence could now be felt by all.

Ava and Dax promised to return every year on the anniversary of the Great Alignment to remind the people of Aquerei of how close they had come to destroying their beautiful world with hatred and violence. Though the oceans of Aquerei would undoubtedly call to her on occasion, Ava decided that a short annual visit would be quite enough to feed her spirit and was also about as much time as she thought she could stand being treated like a goddess.

The *Valorcry's* passengers were assembled, waiting to board the *Juleta*, which would carry them across waters that were now peaceful and free of enemies. Ava was already looking forward to another voyage through space to return Quinn and the Kitnocks to their respective homeworlds, and then, after a side trip to Rutara to drop off Threldigan and see Ava's mother, it would be on to Terra Minor, Darconia, and Earth to visit the various Zetithian settlements. Ava was anxious not only to meet Dax's friends but also to explore the oceans, particularly those on Earth.

Joss and Eantle were both there to see them off, along with a crowd of fervent admirers—mostly female—several of whom apparently still held out hope that Dax might remain on their world just so they could get a look at him now and then. Waroun was openly sad to

be leaving Aquerei. In the aftermath, word that he had
been instrumental in helping Dax and Ava to reach the
temple had spread, and he'd finally gotten his wish.
With a wistful sigh, he gazed longingly at the crowd
of women, some of whom were waving at him, smiling coyly. "I'm really going to miss those Aquerei girls.
They're *wonderful*."

Hearing this comment, Joss laughed heartily, and a
beaming Eantle stepped forward to speak. "Our people
cannot thank you enough. You are all welcome on this
world at any time."

"Don't worry, Waroun," Ava reassured him. "Those
ladies will have a whole year to miss you—and you
know what they say about absence making the heart
grow fonder."

Waroun brightened considerably, waggling his
tongue at a lovely lass whose lavender tentacles curled
in reply.

Joss, who had achieved a certain level of stardom for
his role in the miracle of the New Age, then made a
long-winded speech that had Waroun muttering. "See,
I *told* you he would take all the credit!"

When all the farewells had been said at last, Dax
climbed aboard. His hazel eyes sparkled with joy, and his
oh-so-kissable mouth sported a roguish grin as he reached
out to take Ava's hand. "Ready to meet the family?"

While Ava knew that none of them were actually related to Dax, she couldn't imagine any clan not wanting
to claim him. He might have looked a bit like a pirate,
but he had to be the handsomest pirate who'd ever lived.
Smiling, she placed her hand in his. "Ready as I'll ever
be. What about you? Are you ready to meet my mother?"

"Absolutely." He pulled her onto the deck. "Looking forward to it."

"I'm sure she'll love you, but be warned," Ava said darkly. "She'll expect grandchildren."

"Hey!" Waroun said suddenly. "I just thought of something. If you two have babies…"

"Oh, here it comes," Teke groaned.

"They'll be—" Waroun dissolved into hysterical laughter, barely able to breathe, let alone speak.

"Go on, Waroun," Ava urged, bowing to the inevitable. "Just spit it out."

Waroun's eyes were nearly popping out of his head as he choked out the word. "Catfish!"

Threldigan chuckled while Diokut, who obviously didn't get the joke, seemed puzzled. Quinn made a sound Ava had never heard from him before. Teke merely shook his head.

Dax shouted with laughter as he hoisted Ava into his arms. "Got a problem with that?"

"None whatsoever," she replied. "Bring 'em on."

Acknowledgments

My heartfelt thanks go out to:

Whoever it was at Sourcebooks who said, "No, the series can't end at six! Cats have nine lives, so there must be nine books!"

My readers and staunch supporters on the Cheryl Brooks Erotic Blogspot, who have given me ideas and encouragement throughout the writing of this book.

To Benjamin Godfre for providing the visual inspiration for Dax. Sorry you didn't make the cover, Ben!

To my family and friends for their love, understanding, and unwavering support. I couldn't do this without you!

About the Author

Cheryl Brooks is a critical care nurse by night and a romance writer by day. Previously published works in her Cat Star Chronicles series include *Slave, Warrior, Rogue, Outcast, Fugitive,* and *Hero.* She is a member of the RWA and lives with her husband, two sons, two horses, five cats, and one dog in rural Indiana. You can visit her website at cherylbrooksonline.com or e-mail her at cheryl.brooks52@yahoo.com.

ESCAPE TO THE WORLD OF THE CAT STAR CHRONICLES
BY CHERYL BROOKS

READ ON FOR AN EXCERPT FROM

HERO

AVAILABLE NOW FROM SOURCEBOOKS CASABLANCA

Chapter 1

HIS SWIRLING CLOAK WAS WHAT CAUGHT HER EYE, BUT EVEN from across the crowded park, his aura of sadness and regret went straight to her heart. A little girl ran after him as he walked away, and when he stopped and knelt beside her, she held out her hand, offering him something. His long curling hair fell forward as he accepted it, revealing a streak of orange in the otherwise black locks. There was a brief exchange that Micayla couldn't hear, but whatever the girl had given him must have been quite a treat, for his smile after tasting it was a mixture of wistfulness and delight.

Micayla had never seen him before, but, being a newcomer to Orleon Station, this wasn't surprising. So far, Windura was the only one she saw on other than a co-worker basis, and that was mainly because their quarters were next door to one another.

"Hey, Micayla," Windura called out from the corridor behind her. "Let's meet for lunch, okay?"

"Yeah, sure," Micayla replied. Tearing her eyes away from the man, she turned to greet her Vessonian friend. "Lunch would be great."

"The main dining hall at eleven hundred?"

"Fine," Micayla replied, forcing herself to smile. Glancing over her shoulder, to her dismay she saw that the man had already gone. She strained her eyes to find him among the huge potted plants and benches of the space station's "park." "Did you see that guy—the one in the cloak with the long black hair?"

"A cloak?" Windura echoed. "Why would *anyone* be wearing a cloak? It's hot as hell in here!"

It wasn't the first time she'd heard Windura complain about the heat, but then catering to the preferences of a variety of different beings made the choice of ambient temperature difficult. "Maybe so," she said doubtfully. "But some people are just cold-natured…" She stared off in the direction he must have taken. "What's back that way?"

"Some of the more disreputable parts of the station," Windura replied, flipping her long blond hair over her shoulder. "You're better off not going down there."

Micayla nodded absently. "I'm sure you're right," she said, but something about him was so compelling that if Windura hadn't intervened, she'd have gone running after him in a heartbeat.

"We've got to get you better oriented to this place," Windura went on. "A girl like you needs to know the ropes."

Micayla frowned. "What makes you say that?"

Shaking her head, Windura replied, "If you don't know that by now, then I can't help you." With a quick grin, she added, "See you at eleven," and was gone.

Micayla stood gazing blankly at the throng of children, unable to recall why she had gone to the park in the first place. Ordinarily it would've been a cold day in hell, let alone Orleon Station, when a man distracted her *that* much, but then she remembered: *Tea. You're here to get tea.* Getting in line at Starbucks, she ordered a tall cup of hot, foaming chai and then headed off to work.

The communications center was a hive of bustling activity, and Micayla had to squeeze past several other officers to get to her station, nearly spilling her tea as she finally plunked down in her seat. The guy from the previous shift had left his candy wrappers scattered about, and she gathered them up, grumbling as one of them stuck to the console.

"Sorry about that," he said from behind her. Reaching over her shoulder, he retrieved the last of them, his chest pressing lightly against her back.

Micayla shifted away from him slightly. Scott was Terran and an attractive fellow with a terrific smile, but he was getting a little too... chummy. As a female of an unknown species, if there was one thing Micayla had learned, it was that Terrans and whatever she was weren't compatible—at least, none she'd met so far—and having grown up on Earth, she'd met quite a few.

"That's okay, Scott," she said. "I'm sure I leave tea stains for Xantric to wipe up when she comes on duty."

"Not sure she'd notice," Scott said with a shrug. "And if she did, you'd never know it. Twilanans never complain about anything." He turned to leave, but then paused, adding, "Not much traffic on the system for the past couple of hours, but I'm sure it'll pick up for you."

Micayla took a sip of her tea and nodded. "It always does," she agreed. "Get some sleep."

Scott sighed. "Too bad you and I work different shifts. Otherwise, we could spend a little more time together—instead of me just going back to my quarters and dreaming about you."

Micayla felt a pang near her heart and wished she could have felt something other than regret when a man said such things to her. Steeling herself against his inevitable reaction, she purposely avoided his eyes, focusing instead on resetting the instrument panel with her fingerprint on the log entry. "Dreams will have to suffice, big guy," she said. "I'm not looking for a boyfriend."

"You always say that," Scott grumbled. "Sure I can't talk you out of it?"

"You could try," she said, wishing it really *would* work, just once, "but it probably won't do you any good."

"Ice Queen," he muttered.

"I've been called that before," she said wearily.

"Treacherous Temptress?"

"Been called that too."

"You're kidding me, right?"

"You'd be surprised." Micayla sighed. "And believe me, it's nothing personal, Scott. I have no problem with being friends, but if you want more than that, I'm simply the wrong species."

Seeming to take this as an invitation, Scott turned and leaned against the partition that divided the workstations. "What are you, anyway?"

"No idea," she replied. "But I'm not human, that's for sure."

"No shit," Scott said. "You're better looking than any Terran I've ever seen. I love those cat-like eyes of yours. The elfin ears are nice too, and the *fangs*…" His voice trailed off there as though indulging in some erotic fantasy.

"The better to bite you with, my dear," Micayla quoted. When her stepmother had first read her that story, she probably never realized that Micayla identified much more with the wolf than with Little Red

Riding Hood—though, in truth, she looked more like a lion or a panther than a wolf.

If Scott's response was any indication, being savaged by a lioness was the answer to his wildest imaginings. "Would you?" he asked eagerly. "Please? Pretty please?"

"Absolutely not," Micayla said firmly as a hail came through the system. "Get going, now," she added, shooing him away. "I've got work to do."

Scott withdrew with obvious reluctance, mumbling imprecations under his breath as he went.

Micayla redirected the hail and wondered if it would be worth it to try to spend a little more time with Scott. He was a nice guy and it would take no encouragement whatsoever to—no, she decided. It wasn't worth the pain. Her lack of interest in the opposite sex wasn't her fault, but he would end up despising her for it and then she'd be right back where she started.

Her attitude wasn't precisely a lack of interest, however; it was more a lack of desire, and though she knew what desire was supposed to feel like—she had one fantasy that never failed to elicit that response—it never seemed to work with a flesh and blood man. The man she'd seen in the park might have been different, though; she'd at least felt something for him, if only compassion. Had the little girl been his daughter, telling him good-bye as he left on a journey through space? Was she a friend or a complete stranger? Micayla had no way of knowing, but the more she thought about it, the more she itched to find out.

She glanced up as Dana took her seat at the next station, apologizing to Roxanne for being late. "I had such a tough time getting Cara out of the park!" Dana was saying. "She started talking to someone and didn't want to leave. I'm surprised she didn't go running after him."

Micayla had never met Dana's daughter, but she knew the feeling. It had taken every bit of her strong work ethic to remind her that running after men in cloaks wasn't in her job description. "A stranger?"

"Yes, and you'd think I'd have taught her not to do that by now, wouldn't you?" said Dana. "But since I talked to him myself, I can't say I've been setting a very good example, can I?"

Micayla couldn't help but laugh. Dana was probably the friendliest person she had ever met. Talking to any-one—stranger or not—seemed to come very easily to her.

"And he looked so sad," Dana went on. "I think she cheered him up a little."

Micayla felt her pulse quicken. "Why? What did she do?"

"Climbed up in his lap and wiped away his tears," Dana replied. "She made him smile, too—she gave him a strawberry."

Her heart was pounding now. "What did he look like?"

Dana cocked her head to the side, gazing thought-fully at Micayla. "You know, he looked something like you," she replied. "I don't know why it didn't occur to me at the time, but he had the same kind of cat's eyes, and his eyebrows were upswept like yours. He even had fangs." Dana laughed softly. "And he could purr like a kitten."

"Did he say anything else—like who he was or where he was from?" Micayla asked breathlessly.

Dana's soft brown curls bounced as she shook her head. "No, he just got up and left."

"I—I think I saw him too," Micayla said. "He had long black hair and was wearing a cloak, right?"

Dana nodded. "Do you know him?"

"No, but I wish I did. There was something about him that got my attention."

"He probably gets plenty of that," Dana said with a giggle. "He was *very* handsome—especially when he smiled."

Micayla felt a surge of emotions. Regret for not having run after him, despair that she might never see him again, and envy that Dana had actually spoken with him—and all this because of a man she'd never even met. How very odd…

~~~

Trag went back the way he'd come with a heavy heart. Nothing in his entire life had prepared him for the way he'd felt that morning, and he'd spent twenty years of that life as a slave. The fact that he'd been a free man and the pilot of a starship for the past three years didn't matter—he still felt trapped.

"Inheriting" a fortune in jewels from his former master might have provided him with the means, but something was missing from his life and until that space was filled, he felt adrift. He'd opted to take the job as Lerotan Kanotay's pilot, mainly because he couldn't come up with a better plan. Living among Lerotan's rough, uncouth crew was nothing like he imagined freedom would be, though his years of slavery might have had something to do with why he felt that way. Lerotan had teased him more than once about having been the Darconian queen's pampered pet.

Unlike Trag, his brother, Tychar, had done something far more interesting with his life, but he had talent as a singer and a woman who loved him. Trag could have gone on tour with Ty's band, but playing the flunky younger brother to a rock star didn't appeal to him in the slightest. There would always be a place for him aboard Jack Tshevnoe's ship, but Trag thought it was a bad idea for so many of the few remaining Zetithians to be together on one vessel. If the Nedwuts attacked and blew the *Jolly Roger* to bits, it would wipe out half of the six that were left of his species.

At least the six that were known. There could have been others in hiding, but with the increased bounty being paid on Zetithians, the Nedwut bounty hunters were more determined than ever to capture the remaining few. This meant that Trag often had to fight to stay alive and though he hoped to find other survivors— perhaps even a female—the odds were slim. Just that morning at the breakfast table while their ship cruised toward Orleon Station, Lerotan had teased him that perhaps this was the day. Trag, however, had not been quite so optimistic.

"Maybe," he had said. "But knowing my luck, even if we *did* find a Zetithian woman, she'd probably already have a mate, or she'd be the wrong age for me."

"And she'd automatically want you if she *was* the right age and not taken?"

This comment hit Trag like a stun blast to the chest. "I hadn't thought of that."

Lerotan roared with laughter. "Let's say we *do* find one that's eligible, what's to say she'd be so desperate that she'd want you?"

"Well, I—if I'm the only one left that doesn't have a mate," Trag sputtered, "she'd *have* to take me!"

"Oh, yeah. I'm sure *I'd* want a woman who only took me because of a lack of options."

Trag scowled at Lerotan but knew he was right. "I didn't mean it that way," he said. "What I meant was that if she's Zetithian, she wouldn't want anyone *but* another Zetithian."

"Oh, so it's different with the women?" Lerotan said skeptically. "You can do the Terran female/Zetithian male thing but not the other way around?"

"That's right," Trag said, crossing his arms firmly. "Hell, they didn't want *us* half the time, and we're irresistible. What makes you think they'd want anyone else?"

"You cocky Zetithians," Lerotan said with a wag of his head. "Always think women will want you no matter what. Well, let me tell you something, Trag. The males of other species have cocks as big and fancy as yours— some even have more than one. You aren't *that* special."

"Well, someone must've thought we were hot shit or they wouldn't be so set on making sure we were all dead," Trag grumbled. "That's Jack's theory, and I'd be willing to bet she's right."

"Suit yourself," Lerotan said, leaning back in his chair. "But I can do things with a woman that you can't, and you don't see anyone trying to crash asteroids into *my* planet, do you?"

Trag knew it was true but hated to admit it. Dark-skinned and handsome with a long, black braid that hung over one shoulder, Lerotan looked human, except for the tail, and the rune tattooed on his left temple only added to his allure with women. Trag hadn't seen a woman turn him down yet; in fact, they tended to line up for the chance to be part of a threesome or get double-fucked when he used his tail on them. Trag had had the misfortune of walking in on him once; the tuft of his tail had opened at the point, enabling the erectile tissue inside to protrude, looking for all the world like a spare cock. He had almost as much control of it as Trag had with his own penis—which was considerable. Trag was good—and it was a given that no woman had ever complained—but he certainly couldn't do two of them at the same time.

Still, he couldn't let Lerotan think he was better at pleasing one woman than he was. It was a matter of pride. "I know you've essentially got two tools, but can your fluids trigger orgasms?"

Lerotan took a sip of his drink and smiled. "I like to think it's my own efforts that make women scream for more, rather than drugging them with some kind of orgasmic cock syrup."

"Yeah, well, somebody else must have felt that way too, but trust me, it wasn't a woman!" *And especially not Kyra.* Trag pushed himself away from the table and lunged to his feet. "We're coming up on the space station."

"Well, be careful," Lerotan warned. "I don't want the paint scratched."

Trag rolled his eyes and headed off to the helm, not bothering to reply.

Orleon Station was about the size of a small moon but was shaped like a crystal with points in every direction, its growth seemingly haphazard as new sections were added on. Once the pride of the sector, it had become seedier with age, and those of Lerotan's ilk frequented the dingier bars seeking the illegal goods that had been banned from the station in the beginning but were now the more common merchandise.

It was rumored that the new commander was attempting to clean up some of the corruption, but Lerotan had made the comment that it was probably too late for that. Trag avoided arguing with Lerotan about what he sold, but also knew from having met Jack that it was possible to amass a small fortune by dealing in legal commodities. Unfortunately, while Jack had a knack for knowing what would sell on every planet she visited, from medical supplies to exotic cuisine, Lerotan just knew a good weapon when he saw one.

The first hail from the station brought Lerotan to the communications console to respond. "Captain: Lerotan Kanotay. Ship: *The Equalizer*. Cargo: weapons of all kinds for all kinds of buyers." He said this last with the same smirk as always, and Trag suspected he derived some sort of pleasure from putting it that way. No, Lerotan would never give up the arms game—at least not until someone killed him.

"Permission granted to dock on level ten, section thirty," the reedy-voiced Kitnock said. "Follow the beacon."

Trag stared at the viewscreen wondering how anything that looked like a collection of twigs could possibly need a mouth that big in order to feed itself, but he was distracted when a red light began pulsing at one of the points of the crystal. Aiming the ship toward it, he was momentarily startled by a soft jolt on the controls. "Looks like someone installed a damn tractor beam since we were here last," he growled in disgust. "You can't blame me for scratched paint this time."

"Lucky you," Lerotan said. "Guess I'll have to find something else to blame you for."

"Like what?" Trag demanded.

Lerotan cocked his head to one side and pursed his lips as though trying to remember. Then his eyes widened in surprise. "Do you know, I've never had the slightest bit of trouble with you? Never had to bust you out of jail, patch you up after a fight, or pay off a woman you got too rough with."

"No shit," Trag grumbled. "If I'm so wonderful, then why the hell don't you pay me more?"

"I suppose I should," Lerotan said amiably. "Doesn't mean I will, but—"

"Just forget it, Leroy. You pay me plenty."

"No, I don't."

"Yeah, but I get to see the galaxy."

Lerotan laughed. "Now that you mention it, I'm probably paying you too much—and don't call me Leroy."

Trag leaned back in his chair and scowled up at his boss, but his expression brightened as the ship slid into the airlock with a loud screech. "There goes the paint. *Leroy*."

Lerotan shrugged and tried to hide his displeasure, but the twitching of his leonine tail gave him away.

Trag tried to focus his mind on shutting down the engines, but Kyra's memory was still there to tease him. Smiling at him. Laughing at one of his jokes. Rolling her eyes at what a poor musician he was. He was fairly certain no one suspected—certainly not any of his shipmates, who were as rough a band of mercenaries as you might find anywhere in the galaxy—but he was beginning to tire of the charade. He was tired of going into spaceport bars and feigning interest in the women who frequented such places. Tired of going through the motions when one of them smelled good enough to give him an erection. Sometimes he fucked them just because he could, but it wasn't what he was looking for, mainly because what he wanted apparently didn't exist—a woman who could make him forget Kyra.

FUGITIVE

BY CHERYL BROOKS

"Really sexy. Sizzling kind of sexy...makes you want to melt in the process." —*Bitten by Books*

A mysterious stranger in danger...

Zetithian warrior Manx, a member of a race hunted to near extinction because of their sexual powers, has done all he can to avoid extermination. But when an uncommon woman enters his jungle lair, the animal inside of him demands he risk it all to have her.

The last thing Drusilla expected to find on vacation was a gorgeous man hiding in the jungle. But what is he running from? And why does she feel so mesmerized that she'll stop at nothing to be near him? Hypnotically attracted, their intense pleasure in each other could destroy them both.

PRAISE FOR THE CAT STAR CHRONICLES:

"Wow. The romantic chemistry is as close to perfect as you'll find." —*BookFetish.org*

"Fabulous off world adventures... Hold on ladies, hot Zetithians are on their way." —*Night Owl Romance*

"Insanely creative... I enjoy this author's voice immensely." —*The Ginger Kids Den of Iniquity*

"I think purring will be on my request list from now on." — *Romance Reader at Heart*

978-1-4022-2940-4 • $6.99 U.S. / $8.99 CAN / £3.99 UK

OUTCAST

BY CHERYL BROOKS

Sold into slavery in a harem, Lynx is a favorite because his feline gene gives him remarkable sexual powers. But after ten years, Lynx is exhausted and is thrown out of the harem without a penny. Then he meets Bonnie, who's determined not to let such a beautiful and sensual young man go to waste…

"Leaves the reader eager for the next story featuring these captivating aliens." —*Romantic Times*

"One of the sweetest love stories…one of the hottest heroes ever conceived and…one of the most exciting and adventurous quests that I have ever had the pleasure of reading." —*Single Titles*

"One of the most sensually imaginative books that I've ever read… A magical story of hope, love and devotion" —*Yankee Romance Reviews*

978-1-4022-1896-5 • $6.99 U.S. / $7.99 CAN

ROGUE

BY CHERYL BROOKS

Tychar crawled toward me on his hands and knees like a tiger stalking his prey. "I, for one, am glad you came," he purred. "And I promise you, Kyra, you will never want to leave Darconia."

"Cheryl Brooks knows how to keep the heat on and the reader turning pages!"

—Sydney Croft, author of *Seduced by the Storm*

PRAISE FOR THE CAT STAR CHRONICLES:

"Wow. Just…wow. The romantic chemistry is as close to perfect as you'll find." —*BookFetish.org*

"Will make you purr with delight. Cheryl Brooks has a great talent as a storyteller." —*Cheryl's Book Nook*

978-1-4022-1762-3 • $7.99 U.S. / $9.99 CAN

WARRIOR

BY CHERYL BROOKS

*"He came to me in the dead of winter,
his body burning with fever."*

EVEN NEAR DEATH, HIS SENSUALITY IS AMAZING…

Leo arrives on Tisana's doorstep a beaten slave from a near extinct race with feline genes. As soon as Leo recovers his strength, he'll use his extraordinary sexual talents to bewitch Tisana and make a bolt for freedom…

PRAISE FOR THE CAT STAR CHRONICLES:

"A compelling tale of danger, intrigue, and sizzling romance!"

—Candace Havens, author of *Charmed & Deadly*

"Hot enough to start a fire. Add in a thrilling new world and my reading experience was complete."

—*Romance Junkies*

978-1-4022-1440-0 • $6.99 U.S. / $7.99 CAN

SLAVE

BY CHERYL BROOKS

◇◇

"I found him in the slave market on Orpheseus Prime, and even on such a god-forsaken planet as that one, their treatment of him seemed extreme."

◇◇

Cat may be the last of a species whose sexual talents were the envy of the galaxy. Even filthy, chained, and beaten, his feline gene gives him a special aura.

Jacinth is on a rescue mission… and she needs a man she can trust with her life.

PRAISE FOR CHERYL BROOKS'S *SLAVE*:

"A sexy adventure with a hero you can't resist!"

—Candace Havens, author of *Charmed & Deadly*

"Fascinating world customs, a bit of mystery, and the relationship between the hero and heroine make this a very sensual romance."

—*Romantic Times*

978-1-4022-1192-8 • $7.99 U.S. / $9.99 CAN / 4.99 UK